Advance Praise for City of Angles:

"*City of Angles* is an uplifting look at a side of Los Angeles too little seen in fiction. Like John Fante, Loving turns a compassionate and comic eye on the downtrodden and elevates them in his assured debut."

—Ivy Pochoda, author of *These Women, Visitation Street, Wonder Valley,* and *The Art of Disappearing*

"In his sterling debut, William Loving unpacks the story of a man who loses everything after a deadly fire and then pinballs through Los Angeles' sad, though somehow ennobling, underbelly. Entertaining and finely crafted, spotlighting the marginalized like the Book of Job as envisioned by Nathaniel West, *City of Angels* reminds us that when we disdain the needy, we ir spellbinding, original work."

—Chip Jacobs, author of *Arroyo*

D1124808

"Homer Virgil Innes (rhymes with Guinness), searches the hills, valleys, rivers and beaches of greater Los Angeles for his runaway son and a place to call home in this clear-eyed reimagining of *The Aeneid*. Loving spares Innes no tribulation as he creatively finds ways to survive homelessness, deprivation and loss. But hope and love fill these pages, a modern epic set under the pitiless Southern California skies."

—Don Cummings, author of *Bent But Not Broken*

"William Loving's *City of Angles* is a big-hearted book, full of memorable characters, crackling scenes, and superbly evoked settings, its well-wrought prose sprinkled with tears and spiced with laughs along the way. An unforgettable debut."

—Charles Harper Webb, author of *Sidebend World*

City of Angles

CITY

OF

ANGLES

WILLIAM LOVING

 Heliotrope Books

New York

Cover photograph by William Loving
Cover design and typesetting by Heliotrope Books

For Rhonda

"The gates of Hell are open night and day
Smooth the descent, and easy is the way
But to return, and view the cheerful skies
In this task and mighty labor lies."

—Virgil, *The Aeneid*

Book I

THE CASA GRANDE TOWERED OVER OLD TOWN

Pasadena for more than a century. Once a hotel, its bizarre architectural style was labeled Victorian-Turkish-Moorish Revival. Multiple towers, turrets, and dark red domes topped her seven stories. Dozens of small wrought-iron balconies and red awnings protruded from her tan stucco skin. Covered porches and outdoor decks wrapped around her base. Like a reproachful great aunt, the ancient hulk cast a disapproving gaze across her poor relations scattered along the streets below. Those storefronts, office buildings, and bungalows still had many of their original Art Deco and Craftsman shells, but were now festooned with the garish graphics of modern commerce. Sandwich shops. Nail salons. Thai restaurants. Coffee bars. Sports bars. Chain stores. The Casa Grande stood apart, proud in her old age, wearing her elaborate façade like a Victorian dress buttoned up to the neck over corseted waist.

She was built in 1898 during Pasadena's early years as a resort town when wealthy Midwesterners and Easterners escaped winter by means of the Santa Fe Railroad, drawn to the palm trees, mountain views, and citrus orchards. She was once a member of an elite sisterhood of grand hotels, now mostly passed away. The Raymond, foreclosed and torn down in 1934. The Maryland, now just a section of it standing as an apartment block, almost forgotten behind City Hall. The Vista del Arroyo, bankrupted in the Great Depression, now a federal courthouse; still there—but a stranger. And the Huntington, demolished and rebuilt in the 1990s, now called the Langham, a handsome replica but not the same. The Casa Grande stood alone as one of the five still in her original state and was now a co-op apartment building

Her one-hundred-and-seven residents formed an eclectic menagerie of artists, musicians, elderly long-timers, singles, and young families, all in various stages of shabby gentility or bohemian squalor. Some had lived there for decades, jealously guarding the Casa Grande's ambiance and traditions.

A tall iron fence, overtaken by an eight-foot high hedge, demarcated her sedate world from the modern cacophonies of Green Street, Raymond Avenue, and Pasadena Central Park. Behind the barrier a vast lawn spread under the shade of a few palms and one enormous fig tree. Clusters of camellia bushes surrounded a handful of lichen-blackened concrete benches. To enter through the gate was to enter an Impressionist painting, frozen in time. Tea was served daily on the front veranda. People played croquet on the lawn. They wore wide-brimmed Panamas or floppy sun hats in bright pastels, as if they knew they were elements in a tableau and dressed for the part.

On a warm Halloween morning, Homer V. Innes of Apartment 2A approached the gate with a sack of beignets in one hand and a newspaper rolled under an arm. At first he didn't detect the noxious stench that cut through the lingering aroma of burning forest. His mind was elsewhere, on the coincidence of Southern California bursting into flames as the last of his dreams went up in smoke. At the iron security gate of the Casa Grande, he spied a figure huddled on the ground. A man of uncertain age. Thirty? Fifty? Wrapped in a ratty blue tarp, he looked up and stood unsteadily, maybe drunk or stoned, and gave Innes a gap-toothed smile. He reeked of urine and vomit.

"How about it, buddy?" the man said. He sounded like something was stuck in his throat. "Got some change you can spare?"

Innes stopped and shifted the sack to his other hand, unsure if he should pull out his keys and hurry through the gate or help the poor guy. He was used to Pasadena's army of panhandlers and usually avoided them by giving wide berth. They reminded him of things he wished not to be reminded of.

That morning he had taken his usual circuitous route to the bakery, crossing the street twice to avoid the gauntlet of cardboard signs and outstretched palms. He traversed Green Street to bypass the hacking bag lady he called Typhoid Sherry, who from her seated station on the sidewalk hurled insults and occasionally saliva at passersby, then jumped Fair Oaks Avenue to evade the emaciated old man on rollerblades he called Baryshnikov for his pink tutu, who was shaking a coffee can full of coins in people's faces outside the bridal shop.

No way to elude this one. About six feet tall, the man was thin, with matted hair under a grimy knit watch cap bleached by the sun to slate gray. Deep lines etched his leathery face. A scraggly beard covered his neck. Bare feet, nearly black with calloused grime.

"Only need a buck or two," the man slurred. "So's I can catch a bus to Eagle Rock." He had positioned himself in front of the gate, blocking the way.

Innes tightened his grip on the sack. Anxiety bloomed deep within. "You got a name?" Innes asked, unsure what else to say.

"You can call me Willie. So, how 'bout it?"

"No, I don't got a buck or two." He reached into his Levi's pocket for his keys. It was the truth, not a dime on him. "What I got is some advice: Get a job."

"Oh fuck, a lecture." The man's rheumy eyes rolled skyward. "I want that, I could go to the mission."

"Me, I lost my job. A few years ago," Innes said. "Did I give up and beg in the street? No, I did not."

Willie stepped closer, obviously unimpressed. "So, what's it gonna be?" he said, head back, arms out sideways, palms up, as if seeking an answer from heaven.

Innes slid past him and inched closer to the gate. A young couple with a pair of toddlers in a tandem stroller approached on the sidewalk. Innes tried to make eye contact, hoping to be rescued. Too late. They got one look at Willie and turned back toward Central Park.

"Not today, okay?" Innes said, regretting how callous he must have sounded, like some sanctimonious country club asshole.

Willie scissored his arms down, slapped palms on thighs, and gazed longingly at the sack of pastries. "Whatcha got in the bag?" he asked. "Can I have some?"

For a moment Innes considered giving him a beignet, then remembered he had promised them to Annie, a half-dozen, and she would count them. "I would, but my wife would go all Lorena Bobbitt on me," he said. Willie stared at him blankly. "Nobody gets between her and her beignets and lives to tell about it."

"How 'bout that newspaper?" Willie said, eyeing the Sunday *Los Angeles Times* folded under Innes's armpit.

Irrationally attached to the comforting smell and feel of ink on newsprint, Innes clenched his armpit tight on the paper. Still, he hadn't paid for it. He'd excavated it from the bakery's recycle bin and had already paged through it. Annie wouldn't want it; she, like their teen-age son Caleb, read the news on a phone. "Sure, I'm done with it," he said and offered the paper.

"How 'bout I take those," said Willie. He lunged at Innes and snatched the bag of beignets from his other hand.

"Hey! Not cool!"

Innes dropped the newspaper and grabbed at the sack. Willie stretched his arm back and held the sack high, out of reach. He pushed Innes away, scooped up his tarp, and backpedaled toward the park. Innes grabbed the man's filthy army surplus jacket by the collar and yanked him back. Willie tried to twist away, but Innes bearhugged him and found himself enveloped in the nebula of the man's foul beery breath. The two men grappled like dancing bears, Willie laughing while holding the sack aloft, Innes reaching for it. Instead he got a fistful of blue tarp and yanked it from Willie's shoulders.

"Get off!" Willie yelled and grabbed a corner of the tarp.

The plastic-coated sheet stretched taut between them. They faced each other in a brief standoff. Willie grinned menacingly. Innes suddenly saw himself, as if from above, frozen in an improv comedy tableau, and burst out laughing. Willie responded with a throaty cackle, in on the joke. The frayed corner in his grip tore away and he stumbled and fell back with a groan on the sidewalk. He dropped the sack of beignets. Innes swooped in and snatched the bag, then dug out his keys, opened the gate, slipped inside, and clanged it shut. Willie struggled to his feet and gathered himself, wrapped his tarp around his shoulder, and looked at Innes, the creepy grin replaced by a look of supplicant regret.

"I'm sorry, man. I'm hungry. So hungry."

"That's no excuse." Innes heard his voice quaver. He could see now that the man was more pathetic than threatening. The odor of stale beer, cigarette smoke, urine, and vomit lingered in Innes's own clothes. He glanced at the Sunday *Times* strewn across the sidewalk. "You can have the paper." He turned to walk away to end this confrontation without further eroding his—or Willie's—dignity.

"Okay then. Have a nice day," Willie said.

Innes turned back toward the gate. They faced each other through the bars, a few feet apart. He looked into Willie's bloodshot eyes and saw traces of exhaustion, hope, and terror. He had seen those eyes before, the eyes of another Pasadena derelict. Twelve years on, he was still haunted by them, which he had seen devolve from steely determination to grief to fury to despair and finally to vacant stare.

Willie blinked and broke the spell. Innes pulled a beignet from the sack and offered it through the bars, as if to an animal at the zoo. The man snatched it and stuffed it into his mouth in one bite. Bits of dough and powdered sugar and saliva dribbled down his chin, his eyes bright with triumph.

"Thamps fuh the donut," he chew-mumbled, and turned toward the park, dragging his ragged tarp behind him like the long train of a wedding dress.

Innes had spent the early part of that morning alone in Pasadena Central Park, taking the long way back to his apartment from the French bakery. He'd gazed at the towering Mexican fan palms tilted toward the sun, wandered past the playground and the dark piles of the homeless encampments, and watched children, already in their Halloween costumes, cavort on monkey bars while old men rolled bocce balls. He settled on an empty park bench under a palm with his sack of beignets and newspaper. The beignets, doused with powdered sugar, had been Annie's comfort food ever since their long-ago honeymoon in the French Quarter of New Orleans.

When he'd left the apartment, Annie was cross legged on the bedroom floor, tears striping her cheeks, surrounded by U.S. Postal Service boxes filled with bubble wrap waiting to be packed for shipment to eBay buyers. Stacked on the bed were vintage Fiestaware teacups and saucers rescued from yard sales along with various tchotchkes. Innes made a mental note to count the pills in Annie's vial of Zoloft to confirm she was still taking them. Meantime, the healing powers of beignets would have to suffice.

He wiped beads of sweat from his brow. Hot for late October, eighty degrees by ten o'clock. The park's grass was mostly brown from five years of heat and drought. Above the San Gabriel mountains to the north, smoke from a distant fire rose high into the sky like a cumulonimbus. The brush fire had burned for days, the wind carrying its smoke and ash all the way down to Pasadena, coating the city like a light dusting of snow. 2015 was shaping up to be the worst wildfire season in memory, leaving thousands of acres of barren, scorched hillsides and canyons.

His thoughts turned to the job interview, his first in months, on Monday morning. Public relations, the thing he'd sworn he would never stoop to. He would have to fake his enthusiasm, something he'd grown rather good at. He promised himself he would shave this time. And wear socks. Maybe a haircut, even.

Innes looked up at the dead palm fronds, brown and gray, dangling precariously from the tree's crown seventy feet above. He had a neurotic fear of getting whacked on the head by one of them. They were nasty-looking things with sharp, frayed edges. After windstorms in Southern California, fallen fronds dangled from telephone wires and piled up in the streets like carcasses of desiccated, beached sea creatures. They gave him the creeps. He loitered on the park bench for a while, lost in thought, as if waiting for the palm frond with his name on it to impale him on the scalp.

The approach of Chief Running Deer signaled it was time to leave. The Chief was a familiar sight around town. His mane of white hair and Santa Claus beard nearly obscured his sunburned face under a crumpled straw cowboy hat. Despite his *nom de la rue*, he was Native American only in his mind, as much an Indian as Clint Eastwood. Along with his overstuffed shopping cart he toted a slate-gray sandwich board with his message in hand-written chalk: "I Chief Running Deer am a political prisoner because I blew the whistle on George Soros the CIA and the Human Genome Project." At the bottom were Instagram and GoFundMe addresses. Innes had once asked him about the sign, and twenty minutes later finally extricated himself from a mind-bending trip down the rabbit hole.

When he got home after his wrestling match with Willie, his father-in-law George was gone, leaving only the blanket and pillow and the deepening dent in the sofa cushions. Innes settled his forty-five-year-old bones into the sagging sofa and ran his hands through his swept-back hair, parted in the middle so the locks covered his receding hairline. He cupped his hand around his narrow jaw, feeling for the extent of his three-day stubble, and wondered whether he really needed to shave before the job interview. His thumb lingered over the cleft in his chin, a distinctive feature women had told him was adorable since he was a little boy. Sometimes recently, too, although with less frequency.

Also adorable, they told him, was his name. He had lugged his handle, Homer Virgil Innes, through life like stone tablets draped around his neck, constant reminders of his failure to live up to his parents' hopes for him to be a great writer. He preferred to answer to his initials H.V. Or better yet, just Innes. "Rhymes with Guinness, like the beer," he liked to say. His mother, a college professor of classics and literature, and his father, a failed novelist and unhappy public relations man, saddled their only child with the names of ancient Greek and Roman epic poets. The names mocked him as he toiled in obscurity as a suburban newspaperman. In his eighteen years at the *Star-News*, he had risen from general assignment reporter to assistant arts editor, and no further. In retrospect, he traced the demise of his career to a decision he'd made years before, after he'd become a father, to limit his hours in the office, to seek "work-life balance," as they say in HR. He vowed not be the distant, absent father like his own. His reward for this commitment to family was to be sidetracked into low-profile jobs, then jettisoned in the Great Recession. In the four years since he lost his job, tossed to the curb like a pile of broken furniture, he had wallowed in a stew of impotence, resentment, and rage at the betrayal of his credo that loyalty and good works would be rewarded. Now it was every man for himself and God against all.

Between the two of them, Innes and Annie pulled in scarcely enough to keep up the payments on their co-op loan and health insurance and put food on the table for themselves and eighteen-year-old Caleb. They had saved a decent pile of money when times were good, but the pile was perilously close to bottom. A series of odd jobs and gig economy hustles barely kept them afloat. It was a losing battle. Their car was too crummy to drive for Uber. Freelance writing was the only thing close to a regular paycheck.

When they were young, their elders referred to their generation as the Slackers. They'd worked hard to disprove that stereotype, and yet, some twenty years later, here they were, unemployed, alienated, and cynical.

Lately, Innes had been filling the hours volunteering at the Humane Society's animal shelter, but he couldn't bear to continue, having formed attachments to too many stray dogs only to see them euthanized; with each loss a little piece of him died inside. He would have adopted every single one himself if not for Annie's allergy to pet fur.

He found Annie asleep on their old bird's-eye maple bed, her collectibles on the floor among the boxes. He put the sack of pastries in the tiny kitchen's buzzing old Kenmore fridge.

Innes returned from a Casa Grande co-op board meeting to find Annie in the kitchen in her pink chenille bathrobe. She had piled her boxes on the counter in neat stacks and attached mailing labels. He paused a moment to admire her graceful neck and upturned nose framed by frizzy light brown hair parted in the middle. The insouciant way she stood, pelvis tilted forward, torso gently curved, making a slender S—still girlish at forty-four. She had been an eBay seller since she lost her antiques and collectibles shop when her rent doubled. That storefront was now a Mexican-Korean-Brazilian fusion café called Mexkobra.

Annie turned toward her husband and smiled. Telltale traces of powdered sugar dusted her lips.

"I see you found the beignets," Innes said.

"There was one missing," she said and wiped her mouth with her sleeve.

"I gave … I got hungry."

"You owe me one. So, where have you been?"

"The co-op board, remember?" he said. "Have you seen Vanessa? She didn't show."

"She was just here," she said, and picked up a small, flat box. "She woke me and helped pack my boxes. We got to talking."

Innes was mildly annoyed at Vanessa Alfonso for skipping the board meeting, but he knew she was a good friend to Annie and was grateful for that. "You're in good spirits," he said. "Feeling better?"

"Vanessa helped." She put down the box and turned to face him. "Was June Heron there?"

"Of course. She's the chair. No June, no meeting."

Annie's gaze bore into him like a drill bit. "You know how I feel about June. I don't like the way she flirts with you."

Innes braced himself for the conversation he'd grown weary of. "June flirts with everybody. But I have to deal with her on board stuff. I can't totally avoid her."

"For God's sake, she put her hands down your pants last year." She peeled a label off its backing and pressed it onto a small square box with a slap of her palm.

"She did not put her hands down my pants, she only grabbed my crotch. She was drunk. And she apologized."

"Stop defending her."

He wrapped his arms around Annie and kissed the top of her head. She hugged him for a second, then pushed away and sat down at the kitchen's tiny yellow dinette, which was wedged between the end of the Formica counter and the small window that overlooked the parking lot. He pulled up the other chair, the one with the duct-taped crack in the vinyl seat, and sat facing her.

"You know how much I love you, right?" he said.

"Our sex life is not exactly triple-x rated these days," she said.

"Ouch."

"I'm not blaming you. I know that's my fault."

"How you can resist my animal magnetism is a mystery to me."

She stared at him, blank expression.

"That was a joke. I'm about as magnetic as Urkel."

More blank stare.

"You know, Urkel from 'Family Matters' …" His voice trailed off. The joke was bombing. "I used to make you laugh."

"You also used to call me Dreamboat Annie, remember?"

"Yes, but—"

"Don't worry, you're still sexy, mister blue eyes, mister chin cleft. A real chick magnet. Just ask June." She made the I'm-watching-you gesture with forked fingers pointing from her eyes to his.

The squeak of a hinge and bang of a slammed door signaled

Caleb was up, most likely headed for the fridge. A well-worn trail crossed the faux Persian rug between Caleb's room and the kitchen, like a deer path in the woods. In only black boxers and his ubiquitous Pestilent Vapors T-shirt, he marched into the kitchen past his parents without a word, yanked open the door of the old Kenmore, and stared inside for several seconds before closing it too hard. Glass jars of condiments in the door rattled and clinked inside.

"I need twenty bucks," he announced.

"What for?" Innes asked.

"To do stuff. If I had a job—"

"We've already gone over this, Cal," said Innes. "Last time you had a job, you almost flunked out of school."

"Last time you had a job, George Bush was president."

"Cal!" Annie protested.

"Untrue," said Innes. "My life of leisure falls entirely within the current administration. Thanks, Obama."

"Good, Dad. Blame the Black guy." Caleb sidestepped to the kitchen counter with his back to his parents and stared at his Samsung, texting with someone. His surly silence filled the tiny kitchen like smoke from a burning fry pan. Innes and Annie gazed at his back, at each other, then looked away.

Caleb reminded Innes of the old Alice Cooper song, "I'm Eighteen." His own father had sung it to him on his eighteenth birthday, embarrassingly in front of all his friends. If Caleb were a song, that would be it. The brain of a baby with the heart of an old man, or something like that. He couldn't remember all the words, but recalled what it was like to be eighteen, sort of. It helped take the edge off his frustration with his son and stoked the embers of affection for his only child. There was nothing unusual about the boy's surliness; he was at the age when teens turn contemptuous of their parents. It began at about age twelve, when Caleb began to morph from Dad's little buddy into a secretive, withdrawn adolescent who spent most of his time behind his closed bedroom door. Innes thought his unemployment would at least provide more time with his son, but Caleb withdrew even more after his father lost his job, as if in judgment.

Innes rose from the dinette to give his son a pat on the back, muss his hair, like he used to. Caleb shrank from his touch and continued to tap with his thumbs. Innes withdrew his hand and ran his fingers casually through his own hair. He stood inches from his son's back, but a chasm yawned between them. Caleb was sailing toward the horizon of adulthood, leaving Innes behind, stranded on a desert island. He stood silently, awkwardly, while Caleb tapped and Annie wrote on a mailing label with a squeaking Sharpie.

George soon joined them and bantered with Caleb about band gigs, hot girls, and the sweet burn of a swallow of Jack Daniels, which Innes suspected the old man had plied his grandson with on the sly.

"Daa-aad," Annie said, in a tone straddling reproach and amusement.

"Nice," said Innes. "Encouraging the kid to drink whiskey at eighteen."

"C'mon, Dad, you drank in high school, too," said Caleb.

"I can't stop you, but you better not drink when you drive my car," Innes said, his voice rising.

"Like I'd ever want to be seen in your dadmobile," Caleb said.

"I'll remember that next time you ask to use it," Innes said.

The conversation escalated into a clatter of raised voices, everyone talking over each other, until Caleb brought it to a close with a slam of his bedroom door. George withdrew to the sofa. Angry amplified thumps from a bass guitar vibrated through the walls from Caleb's room.

Innes paced the floor of the bedroom, fussing with the buttons on the vest of his 1920's vintage outfit assembled from thrift stores. He was dressed as Nick Carraway for the Casa Grande's annual Halloween party, this year with *The Great Gatsby* theme. Annie was supposed to go as Jordan Baker, but had changed her mind at the last minute. She pulled on her favorite top, the off-white peasant blouse with the yellow flowers, over a tan leather miniskirt and yellow ballet slippers. He loved that outfit, the hippie-chic look he'd fallen in love with so long ago.

"I don't get it. You were all for it this afternoon," he said. "You have everything you need to be Jordan. I even found my old golf clubs for you."

"I know, sorry, but I don't like those parties." She attached a pair of gold hoop earrings to her lobes. "Anyway, I got a better offer."

"Who are you going with?"

"I told you. The ladies from my book group. We're seeing *Young Frankenstein* at The Playhouse. Special Halloween showing."

He sat on the end of the bed and admired the way her thighs strained against the leather of her tight skirt as she moved about the room. Her brisk motions exuded confidence and purpose he hadn't seen for a while. It filled him with longing for better times. He sidled up behind her, gently placed his hands on her hips, and nuzzled her neck.

"Wanna get naked?"

"I'm already late," she said. She turned and gave him a peck on the cheek.

"Want me to come with you?" he said.

"You're not invited, honey. Girls' night out," she said and slipped out of his grasp.

For a brief moment, he wondered again if there was something going on with Annie, something he wasn't sure he wanted to know. Her loss of interest in sex, her increasing absences, ostensibly to hang with her book group ladies or bargain hunt for things to sell on eBay, sometimes engendered thoughts he'd rather not have, and he pushed them out of his mind.

He was glad to see Annie her old self again, happy and looking forward to something, even if it didn't include him. And without her at the party he could cut loose, no one to nag him about too many beers. Maybe chat up Vanessa Alfonso, muster the courage to dance with her. Innes allowed himself the indulgence of fantasies about Vanessa. And pure fantasy it was. She was out of his league, fifteen years younger, lovely, intelligent. Not to mention married—although separated. Anyway, he would never cheat on Annie. Not even with Vanessa. *Especially* not with Vanessa, Annie's best friend, her "little sister."

He kissed Annie on the back of her neck and headed downstairs to the party. He paused on the landing overlooking the lobby to take in the sea of bobbing top hats, straw boaters, and cloches from the Gatsby era. The Halloween party was Vanessa's idea. All funds left over after expenses went to the Casa Grande's constantly depleted fund for maintenance and repairs, without which the co-op faced the prospect of fines, or worse—loss of control of the historic building. A long line of developers waited eagerly in the shadows for the chance to swoop in and convert the Casa Grande to luxury condos.

From his perch on the landing, Innes spied June Heron and another woman at the front door greeting guests as a matched pair of Daisy Buchanans. They both brandished long black cigarette holders and wore identical white flapper outfits with fringed short dresses, feather boas, and rhinestone-studded white cloches. He had to admit the look flattered June, like she was born to be a flapper. Petite and slim, she wore her black hair, streaked with a few strands of gray, in a crisp bob, with a long swoop of locks angled dramatically across the right side of her forehead, nearly obscuring one eye. Her piercing laugh soared above the din all the way across the room.

June was a sort of godmother to the Casa Grande. She'd lived there for all her forty-two years in one of the two penthouse units with her widowed mother Millie. Her late father, a real estate investor, had left his wife and daughter with a portfolio of rental properties around Los Angeles, which allowed them to live in grand style. Never married, she dedicated herself to her ailing mother, as well as to the Casa Grande. Her knowledge of the ins and outs of Pasadena ordinances proved an asset in her role as board chair for the ancient edifice, which had become a fragile icon occasionally in need of special dispensation from city bureaucrats.

In the rounded end of the great room, bathed in an orange glow from a dozen candlelit jack-o-lanterns arranged on the floor, Sam and Tammy Templeton of Apartment 5B cooked up a smoking-hot rhythm with their makeshift jazz band. Sam, in a vintage tuxedo and top hat, slapped his upright bass. Tammy, rocking a ruby red flapper dress with a bejeweled headband that set off her black hair and mocha skin, belted out "Hard-Hearted Hannah the Vamp of Savannah." The Templetons' son, Eric, down from Oakland, strummed rhythm on his electric Gibson.

Innes found Vanessa by the great room's enormous fireplace, swaying to the music in a vintage floor-length, aquamarine, bias-cut gown, with a pink camellia tucked over one ear. A resident of Apartment 1A, she was tall and slender, with shiny raven hair pulled back in a tight bun and dark, intelligent eyes that often betrayed worry or fatigue. A Frida Kahlo-like unibrow feathered a thick line across the shelf above her eyes. When she squinted or expressed disapproval, the fine hairs above the bridge of her nose stood up as if to take notice.

Vanessa was deep in conversation with a flapper, one of several Daisy Buchanans in the house. Innes walked over and gave her a hug. She kissed him on the cheek.

"You look fantastic," he said.

"Thank you, daahling," Vanessa said, attempting a Tallulah Bankhead drawl and spinning around so Innes could take it all in. He took it all in.

"What about me, daahling?" said Daisy Buchanan. She hiked the hem of her dress to expose her knees.

Innes stepped back and looked her over. Cute legs in strappy heels and opaque white hose. He was about to say something suggestive when his eyes met hers, familiar hazels under the cloche and blonde bob. Pancake makeup obscured the distinctive freckles. "Terry. I should have known," he said with a forced laugh. "Well done, as always."

Every detail perfect, right down to the faux feminine voice. In a building of artists and eccentrics, Terry Delacroix was the Casa Grande's quintessential nonconformist. Five days a week, he put on a seersucker suit and went to work at his mother's art gallery in San Marino. When he came home to his apartment, the other penthouse unit next to June's, off came the suits and on went the dresses. Terry vamped around the halls and grounds of the building at night in a vintage gown, heels, and jewelry. He favored glamorous Hollywood looks from the 1930s and '40s and had an extensive wardrobe that was the envy of the women of the Casa Grande. The men mostly tolerated him. To some, a crossdresser in the building gave the place a *soupçon* of bohemian street cred.

"I think she looks absolutely perfect," Vanessa said and gave Terry a kiss on the cheek, devaluing the kiss she'd given Innes, which had raced his heart like a shot of espresso.

"She?" said Innes. "I never know whether to call you he or she, Terry."

"I don't care. Really," said Terry, dropping from alto to tenor. He looked away toward the band. "Excuse me, I need another drink."

Vanessa glared at Innes. "You're embarrassing yourself," she said. The center of her eyebrow squished together and formed a hairy quilted box.

To Innes, Terry was a spoiled rich kid who liked to play dress up, like a little girl trying on mommy's clothes, while he soldiered on in his role as main family breadwinner. He was about to say so but thought better of it. It was not a role he'd particularly excelled at.

"Look, there's Junie," he said. "She's got some poor schmuck cornered. He'll be lucky to get out with his dignity intact."

"Beer makes you mean, did you know that?" said Vanessa.

"I haven't even had one yet. Stone cold sober. For now, anyway. Did you know she grabbed my crotch at last year's party?"

"Yes, so you've told me. You got over it, didn't you?"

"She's wanted to get me into the sack for years. It's embarrassing."

Vanessa placed her hands on her hips and tilted her head, like a schoolteacher about to scold a recalcitrant child. "I know she can be inappropriate. But she's harmless. She's single, and she's free to do whatever she wants. Why is that so threatening to you?" She turned and walked away toward the band, shimmying to "Black Bottom Blues." She turned and glanced at him for a second, long enough to catch him admiring her backside.

Innes stood there alone, as if on a stool in the corner under a dunce cap, the perfect asshole. He didn't know why he'd stuck his foot in his mouth again. June he could do without, but he didn't really dislike Terry; he even envied his ability to slip into an alter-ego. Innes sometimes wished he could slip into an alter ego, take an occasional vacation from his life. Truth was, he knew exactly why he acted like an ass. The grievances bottled up inside at times escaped like noxious gas. He vowed to be better.

He hadn't had a drink yet and felt like the party was ruined. He considered going back upstairs, but then a massive pair of arms wrapped him from behind in a bear hug and lifted him off the ground.

"Innes, my man," said a deep baritone voice as he was gently let down, like a doll placed carefully on a shelf.

He turned around and straightened his blazer. "Geez, Clif. I wish you wouldn't do that."

"Sharin' the love, my man."

Clifton Tompkins Jr.'s six-foot, six-inch, three-hundred-pound frame loomed over the party like a nightclub bouncer at a velvet rope. Clif, a dentist who lived in Apartment 4C with his wife Beverly and ten-year-old daughter Latasha, was on the co-op board with Innes and one of his best friends.

"Where's your drink?" said Innes. "Can I get you one?"

"You know I don't drink, Innes."

"Where's the family tonight?"

"Bev and Tash at her mother's house. The wife and I didn't care for all the drinking and carrying on at last year's party. Didn't think it was a good environment for the girl."

"But you're here."

"Duty, my man, duty. Got to show the flag at these things." He fingered the enormous ring on his right hand, a memento of the Super Bowl from his brief Pittsburgh Steelers career.

"Not in costume, though."

"Consider me a chaperone."

Innes glanced past Clif's hulking figure at the cash bar across the room. His mouth was dry, and after the verbal spanking from Vanessa, he wanted a drink. In line at the bar was one of those absurd horse costumes, designed for two people inside, one in front, one in back. But there was only one person, in front, and the ass end hung limply, dragging on the floor.

"Check that out," said Innes. "Is there a horse in *Gatsby*? I don't remember."

"Never read it, to tell you the truth," said Clif.

"Weird costume for a party like this. Anyway, where's the guy in back?"

By the time Innes got to the bar, the horse was gone. He ordered a bottle of Beck's and scanned the room for Vanessa, hoping for a chance to get back on her good side. There she was, in her aqua dress, right in front of the band, dancing with the recently married gay couple Seong Song and Michael Roberts of Apartment 6D. It was not exactly a 1920s dance, more like '70s disco, bumping their hips and butts against each other.

For the next hour-and-a-half, he wandered the rooms, chatted with Casa Grande friends, emptied and refilled his aging despot of a bladder, watched the band, tried to work up the courage to dance with Vanessa. After one last beer, Innes checked his watch. Five minutes to twelve, time to call it a night. As he started toward the staircase, the front end of the horse appeared, heading toward the main floor bathroom with its head still on. The open back of the faded gray costume dangled to the floor. The horse's ass was nowhere in sight. With an audible belch, Innes wobbled up the stairs.

When he returned to the apartment, the old man was snoring on the sofa, fully clothed as usual. Caleb's bedroom door was open; he wasn't home from his band gig. Annie, back from the movie already, was asleep. Innes peeled off his vintage suit and laid it carefully over the back of the oak rocking chair in the corner and climbed into bed in his underwear. He lay on his back and stared at the ceiling, which was spinning. He closed his eyes and was out in minutes.

The bird was still chirping in his ear. Poo-tee-weet, poo-tee-weet. Innes sat up in bed and looked around the darkened room. He blinked twice and shook his head to clear his mind of the remnants of a strange dream. It took a few seconds to get his bearings and realize there was no bird. The chirping was the sound of a smoke alarm. Several smoke alarms, in fact, in staggered three-part harmony. Beep. Toot. Squee. Beep. Toot. Squee. He stumbled out of bed and checked the clock radio on the nightstand. Almost two. Annie was still asleep. He grabbed his Ombre cowboy bathrobe from the closet door hook and wandered into the living room to investigate. His father-in-law was still snoring on the couch. No sign of Caleb; he checked his phone and saw a text from his son: Going to afterparty home tomorrow.

Innes entered the narrow hallway outside his apartment. More smoke alarms chimed in from their array along the hall ceiling. A string quartet of chirps swelled into a symphony. Doors opened, and enrobed shapes came into the dimly lit carpeted corridor.

"What's going on?"

"Another false alarm?"

"Maybe somebody's cooking. Set off the smoke detectors."

"Sounds like alarms all over the building."

Innes smelled the smoke before he saw it. "It's probably nothing," he shouted above the murmuring and chirping. "But let's do the fire drill, just to be safe." He was second-floor safety coordinator and needed to clear his boozy head and take charge. "You know how it goes. Don't use the elevator. Walk down the stairs. Everybody assemble on the front lawn in five minutes."

He went back into the apartment to wake Annie. As he passed through the living room, he put a hand on his father-in-law's shoulder and shook him. "Wake up, George. Fire drill."

The old man's eyes opened, startled, confused. "What?"

"Fire drill. Get up." Innes moved to the bedroom.

Annie sat up in bed. "What's going on? What time is it?"

"I don't know if there's really a fire, but I smelled smoke and heard alarms. Come on."

Annie threw on her pink chenille robe and stepped into her fuzzy slippers. Innes returned to the living room to make sure George was up. He wasn't. He'd rolled over and buried his head under his pillow.

"C'mon, old man. Get up."

"Leave me be," he said. He lifted the pillow from his head. "I'm on to your tricks. You'll not toss me into the street."

"Nobody will toss you out. You can come back in when it's all clear."

"I'm not stupid, you know. Got locked out of the YMCA once with the old fire drill scam."

"No you didn't, they evicted you for peeing out the window. Now move it. Can't you hear the alarms?"

George turtled under the pillow.

"Annie, come get your old man off the couch." She didn't respond. Innes returned to the bedroom and found her stuffing clothes and items from her dresser into a pillowcase. "What are you doing? It's probably nothing," he said.

"I only need a few things. Just in case."

"Don't...."

A thunderous boom from deep in the bowels of the Casa Grande stopped Innes in mid-sentence. The floor shuddered under their feet. Perfume bottles on Annie's maple dresser clinked and rattled and fell over. Like a five on the Richter scale.

Innes dashed out of the apartment into the hallway and passed a clutch of people moving toward the main staircase. The building's central fire alarm system clanged and echoed through the corridors, drowning out the chirping smoke alarms. The heat from the stairwell hit him in the face before he reached the landing. Thick gray smoke billowed up from below. Clif Tompkins descended the stairs two at a time from the upper floors, a towering sight in the orange hard hat and reflective yellow vest of the building safety coordinator. "Fire drill. Everybody out," he bellowed.

"What was that sound?" said Innes.

"An explosion, in the basement, I think. Get your floor out to the front lawn. Use the side exits to the fire escapes." Clif charged back up the staircase.

Innes sprinted back toward his apartment, shouting at everyone to use the fire escapes. He passed an antique fire hose mounted on the wall, flat as a tapeworm, wrapped uselessly around its tarnished brass reel, disconnected from the water supply years ago when the fire code was updated. He wondered how long it would take the Pasadena Fire Department to arrive.

Annie was in the living room with a stuffed pillowcase over her shoulder, arguing with her father. The pillowcase now looked like a good idea.

"Get him out of here," he yelled to Annie. "Side exit."

In the bedroom, he yanked the case off his pillow, stuffed it with the books on his nightstand and the clock radio, and swept the contents of the top of his dresser into it. He pulled out the top drawer, dumped its contents into the sack, and went back to the living room in search of his wallet, keys, and phone.

Annie and her father wrestled on the sofa. He was a small man, but wiry and ornery. Innes grabbed George to yank him off the sofa. The old man jerked his arm away. "Get your hands off me, pig. I know my rights."

Innes put his pillowcase down and used both hands to grasp George under the arms, lift him off the sofa, and drape him over his shoulder like a sack of onions, his legs kicking.

"Put me down, you fascist!" George struggled, but Innes was too strong for him.

"Shut up, Dad. Shut. Up." Annie was near hysterics. She grabbed the pillowcases, and the three of them entered the smoke-filled hallway, Innes with his burden cussing and kicking on his shoulder. A mob fought to get through the exit at the end of the hall to the fire escape, like lemmings hellbent for the cliff's edge.

"Stay calm," Innes shouted above the din of panicked voices and clanging alarm. "One at a time." He turned toward the other end of the hall and made a snap decision. "Follow me," he told Annie. They headed to the main staircase, which was filled with billowing smoke but no sign of flames. Annie was coughing. His eyes watered. "Let's make a run for it," he said. "Hold your breath until we get outside."

They descended the stairs into the searing heat. With one free hand Innes kept a grip on Annie's arm and with the other clutched the cursing leprechaun on his shoulder who was pounding him on the back with his fists. Through the billow of smoke in the lobby he glimpsed the back of Vanessa Alfonso in her crimson kimono running from her ground-floor apartment toward a side exit. He moved forward toward where the front door should be. The faint glow of the streetlights on Raymond Avenue came into view like a beacon. He led Annie toward the light, through the open door, across the front veranda, and down the steps into the cool night air. They ran several yards out into the lawn, stopped, and fell to the ground.

Sirens pierced the air. Firefighters in long yellow overcoats poured onto the lawn, pulling hoses that looked like fat snakes in the grass. Innes looked up at the Casa Grande. Smoke poured out of open windows on multiple floors. The grounds filled with people streaming out the front and side doors. Some carried household objects and pets. Most still in their bedclothes, only a few fully dressed. The widow Mrs. Dignam scurried past with a potted sansavieria clutched in one arm, the cloth-covered cage of her two parakeets, Orpheus and Eurydice, in the other. Another figure passed. Terry Delacroix in a floral bathrobe, leading June Heron by the hand with her mother riding on his back.

"We should move out to the street," said Annie.

They slipped between the fire trucks, stood across the street under the canopy of a row of storefronts, and stared at the conflagration in stunned silence. Tongues of flame lashed out of lower floor windows where the glass had shattered from the heat.

A blue TV news van pulled up at the corner, its satellite antenna a rising periscope. A man and a woman jumped out and unloaded equipment. Innes recognized the TV reporter, Gloria something, well known around Los Angeles as the Master of Disaster, the Mistress of Distress. Earthquakes. Floods. Accidents. Murders. Fires. She was always the first one on the scene, as if she had a police scanner implanted in her brain.

Innes put his arms around Annie and pulled her close. She stood on tiptoes and craned her neck, scanning the crowd as if searching for someone.

"Cal texted me, he's safe," he said, and kissed her on the cheek. "We got out. We're all safe."

"I hope so," she said weakly, then fell silent. She stared at the rising column of smoke lit up by searchlights in the night sky.

Innes fell silent, too, along with the swollen crowd, the only sounds the whooshing of hoses, the shouting of firefighters, and the sirens of approaching trucks. Everything happened so fast, it didn't seem real. A fog of dread expanded from the pit of his stomach to his fingers and toes as he absorbed the full weight of it all. He didn't think things could get any worse after he lost his job, struggled with unemployment and rejection as his worth as a human being shrank with each passing year. Now this. Their home. Nearly all their irreplaceable belongings. His book collection. Annie's piano. Caleb's guitars. Their photo albums. Gone. He exhaled deeply and allowed himself a moment of gratitude that his family was safe. He looked up again at the column of smoke pouring out of newly formed holes in the Casa Grande's roof. Only a few hours earlier he had been drinking the night away at a Halloween party, oblivious to the disaster waiting in his path.

Innes turned toward George in time to see him wander off toward the TV crew, like a moth to a porch light. He let go of Annie's hand and chased him, but the Master of Disaster had the old man in her sights and swooped in with her cameraman. She grabbed George by the shoulder and turned him to face the camera. "Can you tell me what happened?" she said.

"I'm George A. McQuillen. Let me tell you about my useless fucking son-in-law, the world-famous writer," he said as if on cue when the cameraman lit him up.

Innes stepped between them.

"What are you doing?" she said. "What's he talking about?"

"Never mind," Innes said and pulled George away. "He's not right in the head. Trust me. You don't want this guy on camera." As if to prove the point, George unleashed a torrent of profanity.

"How about you?" she said and swiveled her head as if scanning for competitors' news vans. "I need somebody. Right now."

"Go find Clif Tompkins. Or June Heron. They run the place."

"How do you spell that?" she called after him, but he had already moved away, pulling George back toward Annie. "Thanks, asshole," said the Master of Disaster.

Annie dashed across the street toward the Casa Grande gate. "Annie! What the hell...?" Innes yelled.

She turned and shouted something indistinct, her face scrunched with worry. He thought she said, "Wait for me...," as she disappeared between a hook-and-ladder and a pumper truck.

"Stay here," he said to George and took off across the street after her. George followed him. "I said stay there!" Innes yelled at him.

"No way. We gotta get Annie."

Innes called out to a firefighter, "Stop that guy! He's trying to go back in!"

The firefighter grabbed George in a bear hug and lifted him off the ground, legs kicking. Innes slipped past them through the gate. Annie approached the main entrance, which now spewed black smoke like a tire fire. He sprinted past several firefighters who yelled at him to stop, and ran into the lobby after her. Covering his mouth, he groped for the staircase handrail, found it, burned his hand, recoiled, and blindly ran up the stairs. At the landing he was met by an imposing figure in a yellow overcoat and a black helmet with clear faceguard.

"Where the hell are you going? Get out!" he boomed from behind the mask.

Another firefighter appeared behind him in the smoke. "Wrong way, buddy."

Innes shouted, "My wife. She ran back in here. Second floor. Follow me."

"No you don't, pal," said the yellow giant. "Check this floor, Larry," he shouted.

Innes tried to rush past, but the big man stepped in front of him. Before he realized what was happening, he was hoisted in the air and flopped over the fireman's shoulder like a rescued cat. He kicked and screamed. "Put me down, I have to find Annie."

Carried down the stairs into the heat and smoke, Innes gagged and choked on the toxic fumes of a building burning down. His throat and eyes burned. Then he was out in the cool night air again and dropped onto the wet grass. "Get this guy out of here," the fire-fighter said to one of his fellows. He bent over Innes and he said, "Don't worry, we'll find her," and ran back into the inferno.

A police officer escorted him to the street. Her strong grip pinched his bicep.

"My wife…," he said.

"If she's in there, they'll get her out," the officer said. "Stay back and let them do their job." He struggled against her as he coughed and sniffled, eyes stinging. She tightened her grip. "Listen," she said, and turned to face him. Six inches shorter, she had to look up at him. "Are you listening? We're setting up a staging area in the park. We'll move everybody over there. I suggest you head over right now."

She let him go on the sidewalk and stood guard at the gate. Innes glanced across Raymond looking for George. He crossed the street and wandered through the crowd. No sign of him or the pillowcases. He walked toward Central Park to rendezvous with Annie.

Hoses at full blast now, firefighters directed the streams into the broken windows of the top floors. All seven floors were fully en-gulfed. Smoke and flames lit up the night sky. Innes thought of those grainy old newsreels of the Hindenburg dirigible aflame over Lake-hurst, New Jersey. The afterimage of Annie running back into that hellscape burned into his retinas. "Annie. What the fuck." He wasn't sure if he said it aloud or merely thought it. He shivered, despite the hot breath of the raging fire.

A crowd had gathered in the park. Vehicles flashing red and blue lights lined the streets. Emergency medical technicians erected a white tent next to the playground. Several stretchers lined up in a row. He wandered among the crowd, seeking a glimpse of Annie's pink bathrobe.

The first figure he recognized was Tammy Templeton, in an orange dashiki, knelt next to a stretcher, wailing and moaning, her hands buried deep in her Afro. Two EMTs spoke calmly to her. A figure was covered on the stretcher. Another stretcher was next to it, with a blanket over the outline of a body. Tammy saw Innes, got up and ran to him. She wrapped her arms around him and nearly knocked him over. She let out a piercing howl and dissolved into quaking sobs.

"Sammy. Eric. Sammy. Eric. Oh, God, no. Oh, God, no." She fell to the ground and hugged her knees to her chest.

Innes dropped next to her. Both Templeton men, her husband and son. They were among the Innes's oldest friends in Pasadena. "Oh no, Tammy. I am so sorry." He covered her with his body, shielding her from gawkers, unsure what else to do or say. He hugged her tight for several moments, kissed her gently on her cheek, and whispered in her ear, "Stay here. I've got to find Annie."

"Yes, go," she said and somehow managed a smile for him. She resumed her fetal position, quivering. Innes gestured to the EMTs to see to her.

Seong Song walked by, dazed and smeared with soot, in only boxer shorts and flip flops. Innes called to him. "Steven," he said, using the anglicized first name Song preferred. "Where's Michael?"

Steven stopped, stared at him, and mumbled, "I don't know. I don't know. He was with me. Then he wasn't."

"Have you seen Annie? She's in her pink bathrobe."

Steven shook his head and stared at the flames as if trying to understand what he was seeing. Innes touched his shoulder, then moved on. He roamed the park for several more minutes, searching the faces for Annie, calling her name until he grew hoarse. His throat tightened as panic and fear overtook him. After a complete lap around the perimeter of the park, he approached a tent where EMTs gathered around a stretcher. June Heron was with them. Their eyes met. She looked away, spoke to the EMTs, and pointed at Innes. One of them walked toward him with a grave look on his face.

"Mr. Innes? I'm sorry. We need you to make an identification."

He couldn't move. "Oh no. No way. No fucking way," he heard someone say.

June approached and hugged him, burying her face in his chest. She led him by the hand to the tent.

"No. I can't," the voice said.

Then there he was, standing over the stretcher. The blanket pulled away. Innes dropped to his knees, unable to look. Then he looked. Annie's face, pointed toward the ceiling of the tent, crushed him. Her skin was alarmingly red, as if severely sunburned, almost purple in some spots. Eyes and nostrils blackened with soot. Her mouth hung slightly open, as if she were about to say something. He waited for the words. Silent, she looked peaceful in her pink robe. He stroked her hair. She felt warm.

"Sir?" asked the EMT.

"Yes. It's my wife," he heard himself croak.

June knelt beside him. "God, Innes, I am so sorry."

"I don't understand," he said.

"Smoke inhalation, sir," said the EMT. His name tag said James. "The firemen carried her out, but she was already unconscious. We couldn't save her."

Innes's head began to spin, and he fell over sideways, retching, his face pushed into the wet grass. June was talking softly to him when he passed out.

When he woke, he was still face down on the wet turf. The grass, recently mown, was pungent in his nostrils and evoked memories of childhood yardwork and football practice. June was stroking his hair and whispering to him. He couldn't make out her words. His first thought was whether Annie had eaten all the beignets. Then he remembered where he was. He sat up and looked around. Annie and the stretcher were gone. A bad dream? Vanessa was there, in her crimson kimono, eyes red, nose running. George sat on the grass with the two pillowcases next to him. Clif was there, too, in his hard hat and yellow vest. Innes twisted around to face the Casa Grande. The trucks, the water plumes, the billows of smoke—still there, all too real. The image of Annie running into the fire was replaced by a vision of her scorched face staring blankly at the roof of the tent, as if seeking the stars.

Nausea swept over him. He fought the urge to vomit and put his hand on the grass where Annie had been. "Where is she?" he said. "Where'd she go?"

Clif knelt next to him and put a hand on his shoulder. "They took her to the coroner. The others, too. Sam and Eric Templeton. Michael Roberts. Janet Boyle, the old lady on the fifth floor. Everyone else accounted for, far as I can tell."

"Why is she at the coroner?" Innes heard himself say. His voice had a distant, surreal quality, like listening in on someone else's phone call.

"They said they need to get official cause of deaths," said Clif. "It's a possible crime scene. They think it was arson. It started in the basement."

"Could have been a vagabond asleep down there," said June, "or somebody from the party passed out drunk with a cigarette."

"Why didn't you wake me?" Innes said.

"We thought it best you didn't see them take her away," said Clif.

"I want to see Annie," said Innes, his voice a near-whisper.

"We can go in the morning," said Clif. "We have to talk about where you want to take her body. Arrangements and all."

Innes stood up, shaky on his feet. Clif steadied him with one massive hand on his arm. Vanessa came over and hugged him, sobbing, and repeating Annie's name softly in his ear. June joined them, then Clif, in a group hug.

"Where's Terry?" Innes heard himself say.

"He's with my mom," said June. "He took her to the Langham to get a room for the night. I'm headed there now. Want to come?"

Innes shook his head. "I have to find Cal." He looked over at George, who stared at the ground, his lips moving, no sound. "Old man. Seen Cal?"

George struggled to his feet and glared at Innes. "Why are you alive and she's dead? Why are you here and she's not?" Spittle collected on his lips.

"Calm down, old man. We need to find Cal."

"You stupid fuck-up. I could've found her. I could've saved her. But no. You had to rat me out and be the big hero. Some goddamn hero you are." George was yelling now. "I saw the whole thing. You let her slip away. Then you run after her, big hero. And then you come out slung over a fireman's shoulder like a baby, no Annie. So where's Annie? Where's Annie?" He hocked and spit in Innes' face.

Innes wiped the spit, stunned by the old man's accusation. "Don't you dare blame me, you old bastard," he said. He stepped forward and pushed him with both hands. The old man tumbled backwards and landed hard on the ground.

Clif wrapped his arms around Innes. "Have some respect for the dead. Both of you," he said. "Coupla children."

June and Vanessa helped George up. He stared lasers at Innes and stumbled out of the tent.

Clif released Innes. "Do you have someplace to go?"

"I don't know... I don't know." A place to sleep was the last thing on his mind.

"I'm going to my mom's in Alhambra," said Vanessa. She sniffled and wiped tears from her cheeks. "Want to come? There's room."

"Thanks, but I need to find Cal. We've got to be together. We're still a family." He said it, but he wasn't sure he believed it. A family, without Annie?

"Suit yourself," said Clif. "Me, I've got to join Bev and Tash at the in-laws."

"You sure you won't come?" said June.

Innes shook his head and looked away, avoiding the pity in everyone's eyes.

Vanessa touched his shoulder. "Call me," she mouthed silently, put her thumb and pinky to her ear and lips, attempted a smile, and failed. She, June, and Clif departed, heads down.

Innes reached into his pocket for his cellphone. Nothing there. "I lost my phone," he called after her.

"We'll meet you here in the morning," Vanessa called back to him. "We can go with you ... to fetch Annie." Her voice cracked into a squeak when she said the name.

"She wanted to be cremated," he said softly to no one in particular.

Innes collected the pillowcases and sat in the damp grass under an ancient live oak, trembling uncontrollably but grateful for the chance to be alone and collect his thoughts. He lowered his head onto his knees, pulled himself into a tight ball, and tried to squeeze away the grief. When he closed his eyes, images of their twenty-five years together played on the backs of his eyelids like a slide show. The first moment he saw her, in the Philosophy 101 lecture hall, when her gummy ingenuous smile melted his too-cool-for-school facade. The day they brought newborn Caleb home from the hospital, ecstatic and terrified at the same time. The day her antique store closed and she carried out the last few boxes of collectibles, she'd curled up in his arms on the sofa and cried. They say when you're about to die your whole life passes before your eyes. Horrible as he felt, Innes was surely not about to die. So why the slide show? It occurred to him he was about to experience a death of another kind. The thought made him wish for the real thing.

When George returned, Caleb was with him, red with rage, tears streaming down his face. Smeared black eyeliner streaked his cheeks. His usual get-up: black Pestilent Vapors T-shirt with his band's smoke logo, ripped black jeans, and laced-up Doc Martens.

"Where is she?" Caleb screamed through his tears.

Innes pulled himself to his feet. "Cal... Cal... she's..."

"Dead. I know. She's dead. Pops told me. Where is she?"

"They took her to the coroner. We can see her in the morning."

"Why did you let them take her?" He bent over, hands on his knees, and gasped for breath between sobs. George watched in silence.

Innes stepped forward to give his son a hug. He gently put his hand on the boy's back. "Cal..."

"Don't touch me," said Cal. He stepped back. "Why did you let her die? Why didn't you save her?" His voice cracked.

Innes glanced over at George, who looked away, and back at Caleb. "I went in after her... I couldn't find her... It was all smoke and fire in there..."

"Don't make excuses." Cal's face contorted into a mask of fury. "You fucked it up like you fuck everything up and now she's dead."

"Your mother ran into the building because she thought you were in there." He blurted it out, not sure why, too late to take it back. Maybe it was true, maybe it wasn't. The words hung in the air like smog.

Caleb stared at his father with a look of shocked disbelief. "Bull-shit." He cocked an arm and let fly with a right cross that connected square on Innes's jaw. The force of the blow jerked his head side-ways, and he fell to the soft ground with a *thwomp* of middle-aged bones and creaky joints. When he opened his eyes, the tiny leaves of the oak above, dark green and brown, danced in the breeze amid the smoky haze. Innes struggled to his feet and spat blood. Massaging his jaw, he looked across the park in time to see Caleb in a dead run toward Old Town. "Cal!" he yelled. He was drowned out by the commotion across the street, the firefighters' voices on megaphones, the sirens of more trucks and emergency vehicles arriving, the roar of smoke and fire still billowing out of the top floors. The crowd in the park swelled, herded by police and firefighters who set up yellow tape and barked instructions to stay back. Some of the onlookers swayed drunkenly, loudly offering commentary. Others, horrified, stared upward with mouths agape.

"Rubbernecking vampires!" he screamed at them. Innes wanted to plunge into the crowd with fists flying. Instead he ran out of the park after Caleb. He crossed the street, stepped over fire hoses, and jogged north into the heart of Old Town. Crowds streamed toward the fire. Innes pushed against them going the opposite way. "Cal!" he shouted. "Cal." His cries were lost in the noise and commotion. Out of breath, he stood at the corner of Colorado and Fair Oaks and sur-veyed the intersection looking for Cal, for any black-clad young man. Dozens fit the description, along with an equal number of black-clad young women in high heels and short skirts, arms entwined, laughing, shrieking, and swerving toward the apocalyptic late show. Innes wandered up and down Colorado, passed the boutiques, bars, and restaurants, long closed now. Small groups of young revelers clustered on the sidewalk. They pointed at his bloody mouth and laughed and taunted the demented figure in a cowboy bathrobe.

"Rough night, old man?"

"Dude, I hope your old lady didn't do that."

No sign of Caleb. He gave up the chase. The boy would come to his senses by morning. They would go together to the coroner to see Annie. He walked back toward the park.

The Casa Grande still spewed smoke through collapsed sections of roof, but the flames had died down under the torrents of water. George was under the same oak tree, holding the pillowcases, as he watched the geysers rain down on the hissing cauldron.

"I lost him in the crowd," Innes said. "I guess I'm losing everybody tonight."

George turned and looked him in the eye. "I'm sorry what I said. I shouldna said those things. It wasn't your fault. It just happened is all."

Innes put his arm around his scrawny shoulder. "I'm sorry, too. I should have saved her."

"My girl. She was all I got."

"No. You got me, old man. You got Cal. We're still a family." It was as if he kept repeating it, it would be true.

They stood there for a long while, gazing across the street at the roaring disaster their lives had become, contemplating what they had lost.

George said: "What do we do now?"

After a sleepless night in the park with George, under a tree like the homeless regulars, Innes rose in the morning with a stiff neck, his clothes damp with dew. What was he doing there? He couldn't recall the last time he'd spent the night outdoors, without even a tent over him. Childhood? His mind was clouded by something dark, shapeless. He couldn't remember why, until he did. The smell of smoke lingered in the morning air. He replayed the scenes from the night before, over and over, until he closed his eyes to make it stop. It didn't stop.

He had to pee. A row of blue Porta-Potties lined the edge of the park like soldiers at attention. Homeless men and women clustered outside, awaiting their turns. Inside, the toilet smelled horrible, but he was grateful for it. When he returned, George was up and about, subdued but functional, as if it were completely normal to sleep outside after losing your daughter and home in a fire. On closer inspection, he was almost catatonic, unresponsive to Innes's attempts at conversation.

In the afternoon, they retrieved Innes's black 1997 Honda Civic hatchback from the Casa Grande parking lot, wet and smelling of smoke but otherwise undamaged, and checked in to the Sage motel, a pale-green-colored cinderblock relic of the 1960s on East Colorado Boulevard, where the George knew the night manager, "an old girlfriend."

Over the next few days, in the cracks between hours of despair, Innes sometimes forgot Annie was gone, as if his mind could not hold such a thought. A favorite song from their college days, "Nothing Compares 2 U," the Sinead O'Connor cover of Prince, wafted into the street from a boutique, and he immediately thought to tell Annie he'd heard it and would play it for her on Spotify. Then he remembered, and never wanted to hear that song again.

There was another song he hoped never to hear. He would have to find some way to avoid it, else he would simply implode, collapse into a black hole of grief. He fought against the words, but they forced their way into his mental playlist. Oh Annie, Dreamboat Annie, little ship of dreams.

He remembered Annie said she wanted to die in the Casa Grande. She hadn't meant it literally—she meant she never wanted to move, to live anywhere else. The subject had arisen frequently in recent months. Innes suggested they might not be able to keep up the payments on their co-op loan, and it might make sense to sell and move somewhere cheaper.

Annie was adamant. "I'm leaving feet first."

Those words tormented him as he tried to picture her exit from the burning building. Was it feet first? He obsessed about Annie's final moments. Was her death quick? Did she suffer? Why did she run back into the building? What was she looking for? Would he have found her if he had taken a different path through the smoke and flames? Would George have found her if he'd let him help? What if George was right? What if he'd been selfish by stopping George from helping, trying to be the hero, and Annie's death was his fault? The thought metastasized in his brain like a tumor.

The two firefighters he'd met on the staircase later told him they eventually found her not on the second floor but in the first-floor hallway, unconscious. They surmised she had become lost or confused in the smoke and went down the wrong hall. The carried her out across the rear parking lot and over to Central Park, left her in the care of emergency personnel, and returned to the building to search for more people. That was the last they saw of her; it was all they could tell him.

This loss was incomprehensible. One black moment of memory and reflection would be taken over by another, a dark cloud obscured by one darker still. He wondered what it would be like to jump off the Colorado Street Bridge, how it would feel the moment his skull slammed into the concrete bed of the Arroyo Seco, far below the ancient span known as Suicide Bridge. Would it be over in a millisecond? Would he feel anything?

He had lost his wallet and keys in the fire, along with his iPhone and MacBook. No cash, no ATM card, no IDs. It was as if he had ceased to exist. Everything from his life with Annie was gone, except for the few items stuffed into two pillowcases, which he hadn't inventoried yet, aside from the jeans and sweatshirt he pulled out after he'd tossed his smoke-fouled robe. With the spare set of keys in a magnetic box attached to the undercarriage of the old Honda, at least they were mobile.

It wasn't until Tuesday morning he remembered the job interview scheduled for the day before. He considered walking to the agency's office to apologize and reschedule. Surely they'd understand. But what was the point? Groveling for a job in PR was too awful to contemplate. He was in no shape to talk to anybody.

On Tuesday afternoon, he went to the Wells Fargo branch in Old Town and cleaned out the checking account and the rest of their meager savings despite no ID or debit card. The teller and branch manager remembered him, offered genuine condolences, and offered to issue a new debit card. Innes didn't see much point to it. No money coming in. No home, no phone, no computer, no income. He left the bank with three thousand dollars in his pocket, all the money he had in the world. Within a few days the stash would be reduced by half after he payed the bill to cremate Annie's body.

June and Terry offered to take up a collection for him, but Innes politely declined. There would be no collection. They would have given him the money out of their own pockets. Things were bad enough without feeling like a charity case. He was reminded of a book he'd read long ago, George Orwell's *Down and Out in Paris and London*, in which the author wrote the memorable line: "a man receiving charity practically always hates his benefactor." He had enough things to hate.

There was also the matter of insurance. Innes had worried it was a mistake when they canceled their life insurance policies to save money when things got tight. He was so right. A homeowners' policy for up to two hundred thousand dollars was Innes's main hope for solvency. But an insurance company adjuster warned there might be a delay in paying claims because of the possibility of arson. He told Innes to keep an eye on his mail for more forms to sign and return. His mail, along with everyone else's who had been made homeless by the fire, would be held for him at the main downtown Post Office. Another thing he would have to deal with.

Innes decided to scatter Annie's ashes on the grounds of the Casa Grande after a memorial service in Central Park to honor her wish never to leave her beloved home, even in death. He wasn't sure it was a good idea, or if it even made any sense, but the notion of good ideas and good sense seemed vague and amorphous as they sloshed around in a stew of confusion and grief.

The service took place on a Wednesday, three days after the fire, under the shade of a live oak next to the playground. June and Vanessa attended to the arrangements, as Innes was unable to do much beyond the most basic level of daily functioning. Clif, a deacon at the Christian Life Center congregation in Altadena, presided and said some gracious words about Annie's gentle loveliness, which Innes was grateful to hear, but then only made him feel worse.

June was there, along with Vanessa, Terry, the two firefighters, and Annie's book group friends. George muttered quietly to himself, his back to the ceremony, as he stared at the smoke-blackened, roofless hulk of the building. Tammy Templeton was there, too, despite having to arrange the unfathomable double funeral and burial of her husband and son the next day. She stood next to Steven Song, her arm around him, Steven still nearly catatonic, a pair united in grief. Steven's husband Michael would also be cremated, with his ashes to be scattered in his favorite spot: the Japanese garden at the Huntington.

Caleb didn't show for his mother's memorial. Unsure whether to be furious or despondent, Innes settled for both, a mixture of emotions with which he'd grown familiar.

He waited until dark to scatter Annie's ashes at the Casa Grande. Was it even legal? It probably wasn't a good idea to lurk about the grounds, as it was still a crime scene marked off with yellow police tape around the perimeter of the border hedge. As the November sun sank behind the Linda Vista Hills, leaving Old Town in near darkness, Innes drove to the Casa Grande from the motel, parked on Raymond, and crossed the street with a cardboard box containing a plastic bag filled with the remains of his wife of nineteen years. In the fading twilight, the old tower loomed like ancient ruin, no lights anywhere inside the grounds, the charred exterior barely visible in the faint glow of the streetlamps and neon signs across the way.

For years, Innes had wondered how long this antique pile of memories would survive Southern California's relentless drive for redevelopment. Now he had his answer. The Casa Grande was a total loss, along with the contents of all fifty-two apartments. No floors were spared. The mayor was quoted in the *Star-News* that the remains of the building would have to be torn down—a tragedy, not only for the people who had lived and died there, but for all of tradition-loving Pasadena, which had lost one of its most beloved architectural icons.

Innes walked around to the side of the grounds to avoid the well-lit and possibly monitored front entrance. He opened the side gate with his spare key, ducked under the police tape, and closed the gate quietly behind him. In the dim light the grounds appeared undamaged from the fire. The grass was still wet from the torrents of water spent to extinguish the flames. He wandered across the front yard, his shoes squishing in the muddy turf. Inside the front gate, next to the four-leaf-clover-shaped koi pond, stood a venerable

Canary Island date palm, its massive trunk armored with flattened diamond-shaped scales. Annie's favorite tree. He pulled out the bag and scattered her ashes in the grass around the base of the palm. There was no breeze, and the coarse gray dust fell softly onto the wet grass. He stood there for a moment, trying to make out the pale film the ashes left on the lawn. He realized he hadn't cried since she'd gone, instead he'd stumbled around for days in a catatonic state, going through the motions of a widower attending to arrangements. It was time. He knelt in the grass, put his hands on his thighs, and let it come.

Nothing. No tears, only a melancholy emptiness. He remained still for several minutes, soaking the knees of his pants, shivering, looking down at the gray film on the grass and up at the crown of the palm tree. He imagined her face projected on the undersides of the feathery fronds illuminated by the streetlights.

He stood and turned toward the ghost of a building. Why had she run in? Who or what was she looking for? All he'd heard her say was "Wait for me..." before her words disappeared with her behind a fire truck. His mind wandered from the afterimage of Annie vanishing into the smoke and focused on the imagined sight of a shadowy figure in the basement with a gas can and a lighter. The insurance company investigators said it looked like arson. The fire department was not so sure. They said there was no evidence of fuel—"accelerant," they called it— although the speed at which the fire spread suggested it may have had help. The explosion in the basement was attributed to a gas leak ignited by the fire, but it was unclear whether the leak was accidental or deliberate. The investigators said if someone set it, they left few traces. If it was a professional job, that suggested something more sinister, like a real estate developer tired of waiting for a choice property to come on the market. June adhered to the sleeping-drunk-in-the-basement theory, but Innes wasn't sure he bought it.

Innes let himself out through the side gate. He ducked under the yellow tape, closed the metal latch gently, and took one last look at the charred remains of the Casa Grande.

"Looking for something?" said a *basso profundo* voice from directly behind him.

Startled, he turned to face the blinding beam of a flashlight in his face. He squinted and looked away until the beam was lowered. A policeman, tall and broad shouldered, was silhouetted against the lights of the park. A squad car was on the street, engine running. The driver's side door opened, and another figure climbed out. "What have we here?" the figure said.

"I'm hoping he'll tell us," said the first one. "How about it, pal? What brings you out on a fine night like this, wandering around a crime scene?"

"I... I... lived here. My... my wife... died... in the fire."

"I'm sorry," said cop number one. "What's your name?" His face was barely visible in the near darkness, but his white teeth gleamed.

"Innes. Homer Virgil Innes. Rhymes with Guinness."

"Are you getting this, Tony?" asked the first cop.

"Yeah. HomerVirgilInnesRhymesWithGuinness," said the cop named Tony as he wrote in a notepad. "That's got to be legit. Nobody would make up a name like that."

"See if his story checks out." The other cop moved back toward the squad car. "Can I see some ID?" the first cop asked.

"I... I... lost my wallet in the fire." Innes read the name tag on the policeman's crisp white shirt. Luis Sandoval.

"What were you doing in there?" said Sandoval. "You know this is a crime scene, right? You know what yellow tape is for, right?"

"I was... I..."

"What's in the box?" said Sandoval. He pointed his flashlight at the object tucked under Innes' arm.

"It was my wife's ashes. I spread them on the lawn in there. It was her wish." Innes lifted the lid to show the empty plastic bag.

"That's definitely a no-no. But as you've already done it, we'll let it go," said Sandoval. "Again, I'm sorry for your loss. But given that this is a possible crime scene, and you're not supposed to be here, we need to ask you some questions. You mind coming with us?"

"Am I under arrest?"

"No, just questions is all. You want to call a lawyer?"

Innes thought about phoning the co-op board's attorney, but he didn't want to pay him out of his dwindling funds. Anyway, nothing to hide.

The cop named Tony called out from beside the squad car. "Yup, he checks out. Innes, wife Annie Innes, DOA at the scene." The words pierced Innes's ears like an ice pick. He looked away to hide his pain.

"Again, so sorry," said Sandoval.

The three of them climbed into the squad car, Innes seated in the back like a perp. He spent about an hour at the Pasadena Police headquarters recounting his version of the events leading up to and including that night. An investigator working the night shift, a stone-faced detective named Darius Jackson, took notes. Jackson thanked him for his cooperation, and Officer Sandoval gave him a lift back to his car.

It occurred to Innes he could use a drink. A foamy pint of Guinness called to him from his favorite hangout, Lucky's Irish Pub, a couple blocks away. He could almost taste the creamy stout and hear the chummy murmurings from the barstools.

Another image entered his mind: his father, drowning his grief in tequila after his mother died.

He recalled that night. The panicked drive from his dorm in Riverside to Pasadena. Traffic jammed on the 210 Freeway. Dark, raining, the usual gridlock. Echoing in his mind was her weak, confused voice when she'd called him, before falling silent. The empty space that had emanated from the receiver tormented him as he accelerated, changed lanes, braked, skidded, looked for an opening. He punched the accelerator, tapped the brakes again. Trucks hemmed him in. Near miss. Horns honked. Red brake lights reflected in wet pavement. Arriving, too late, the ambulance already at the house. Strapped to a gurney, her face obscured by an oxygen mask. No sign of Dad. Where was he? They wheeled her out the front door. He held her hand. Still warm. The paramedic's face told him she was too far gone. A stroke, or aneurysm. By the time they arrived at Huntington Memorial, it was over.

A quarter-century gone, and his mother's grip on him never loosened. In so many ways, he was Faith Innes's son. He'd inherited her love of culture, high and low; his encyclopedic knowledge of movies, literature, art, and music he owed to her. It pained him to know she never approved of his choice of journalism as a career. She had hoped for something more academic or literary from her only child.

After she died, Innes and his father, never close, slowly drifted apart, separated by a wall of blame over the events of that rainy night. Dennis Innes circled the drain for another ten years. It had not ended well. Innes vowed he would never end up like that.

He got in the car and returned to the motel.

Innes and George stayed another week at the Sage. They ventured out each day on foot or in the Honda to search Pasadena and environs for Caleb. The two men settled into a tense alliance, united by the shared pain of loss and their love of a teenage boy. Innes had always been envious of the *bonhomie* between his son and father-in-law. He knew Caleb viewed him as a loser, a drone expelled from the beehive, buzzing around aimlessly, as opposed to George, a Kerouacian hero of the gritty streets, a relic of some romantic 1960s past of Caleb's imagination. To Innes, his father-in-law was a foul-mouthed bag lady in trousers, a constant source of vexation who never failed to remind him he was a failure and not good enough for his daughter. A one-time suit salesman, short-order cook, and restorer of junked cars, George was a permanent member of what he called "the leisure class." At Annie's insistence, he had a key to their apartment and showed up from time to time to make himself at home on the living room sofa, often reeking of whiskey, cigarettes, marijuana, or all three. Annie forbade smoking in the house, but it hardly mattered, the place stank like a bar as soon as he arrived. He was nearly always decked out in his signature ensemble: taupe gabardine high-waisted trousers held up over his pot belly with rainbow striped suspenders; partially buttoned black vest over a dingy, white, button-down shirt. Perched atop his shaggy, snowy hair was a red, yellow, green, and black knitted tam-o-shanter, which made him look like a Scotsman from Jamaica. He'd assembled the outfit years before when he was the unofficial grand marshal of the Doo-Dah Parade, the counter-culture parody of Pasadena's most cherished tradition, and had never taken it off. Innes was loath to admit it, but knew deep down that despite, or perhaps because of, the old man's irascible disregard for convention, he really loved the old coot.

Their initial forays proved fruitless. Caleb had vanished. With no phone, Innes relied on Vanessa and June to try to reach his son with calls and texts. They said he didn't respond, and his mailbox was full. Innes found himself almost envious of his son and wished he could vanish as well.

At Blair High School, they were told Caleb had not been on campus since the fire. The guidance counselor they spoke with, a thin lady named Margaret who looked and acted close to retirement, told them runaway teens usually returned within a few days, a week at the most, in her experience.

"What if they don't?" said Innes.

She leaned back in her chair, took off her glasses, and polished them. "Then it becomes problematic," she said. "Once they're gone for more than a few weeks, they often don't come back. It usually means they've found a new life they like better. Or it means something worse."

Innes did not want to ask what she meant by that. But he could guess.

"Now that Caleb is eighteen, a legal adult, your options may be limited," she said as she showed them out of her windowless office.

Two weeks of motel living spared Innes and George from more nights sleeping in parks, but it was a scant fig leaf over the reality of their homelessness. Forced together in close quarters, without Annie to mediate, they bickered constantly. As the days dragged on, and Caleb had not returned, Innes's focus to avoid losing his mind was to keep calm and carry on while trying not to dwell on the image of Annie's face.

Their mounting motel bill threatened to drain the last of their cash. Innes returned to the friendly folks at Wells Fargo and asked about a personal loan to tide him over until the insurance paid off. They said they'd like to help, but with no income and no assets, save the homeowner's policy, uncertain under the cloud of arson, he had little chance of approval. They suggested he try one of the disaster relief charities, like the Red Cross, but Innes, clinging to his last shreds of pride, was unwilling to go there. He would have to find a job at some point, when the money ran out, some kind of job—exactly what, he wasn't sure. Anyway, a job would take time away from the search for his son. First things first.

They decided on a new plan: Hit the road in the Honda, sleeping in the car if necessary, and drive the length of LA County if that's what it took to find Caleb.

Book II

"ARE YOU GONNA TAKE THE 134?"

Innes gripped the steering wheel, bracing for another verbal assault. "No, I am not *'gonna take'* the 134, old man. You know how I am about the freeways."

"I know you're a pussy in a tin box," said George.

"How about I let you out right here by the side of the road?" said Innes. "There's a dumpster over there with your name on it."

"Fine by me."

They drove west on Colorado Boulevard in the black Civic, headed for Highland Park in possession of a list of Caleb's friends from his various rock bands and their home addresses provided by another Blair High School parent. They were down to the last name on the list. They climbed the gentle grade past the Norton Simon Museum and the Elks lodge toward Orange Grove Boulevard, where the Tournament of Roses floats make the big right turn on New Year's Day under the TV cameras mounted high on scaffold towers. November now, the steel and wood temporary grandstands soon would rise on both sides of the street as the city began its annual dress-up ritual. They stopped at the light at Orange Grove. Innes gazed across the intersection at the gaping maw of the on-ramp to the Ventura Freeway. On the left was the welcoming path to the gentle curves and lovely vistas of the Colorado Street Bridge. The light turned green.

"Here's your chance, pussy," George said as Innes pulled into the intersection. "Get on the damn freeway. Cal's out there somewhere. We got no time to waste."

Innes ignored him and bore left onto Colorado.

The LA freeways to Innes were not so much a highway system as a living organism, a tentacled beast that could trap you in its grasp forever. It was a phobia, like the palm fronds. He traced it to an incident he'd had as a teenager. A freshly minted driver, celebrating his independence in a red 1975 Volkswagen Beetle convertible his parents had bought for him, he motored with the top down on a sizzling summer day, an INXS cassette blasting from the custom Bose speakers, headed for Venice Beach to meet friends, and, he hoped, girls. He should have taken the Santa Monica Freeway to Lincoln Boulevard to Venice Boulevard, but instead made a fateful rookie decision to take the 101 to the San Diego Freeway, the dreaded 405. By the time he realized his mistake, it was too late. He was already on the interchange, no going back. The ramp disgorged him slowly onto the freeway, where six lanes of traffic stood frozen in the hazy sun. He was soon trapped in a slow-moving river of steel, rubber, plastic, and glass, horns honking, inching forward, bumpers nearly touching, diesel-belching semis, cars of every make and model, white delivery vans, pick-ups jacked high on big wheels, motorcycles darting between lanes like pilot fish among whales. Stuck behind a big rig, his main scenery was a pair of black mud flaps decorated with chrome silhouettes of kneeling women. He was somewhere between the Sherman Oaks Galleria and the Sepulveda exit, on the edge of two o'clock, when the panic began to take hold. An orange Caltrans sign crept into view: the exit was closed for maintenance, his last escape route cut off. Rivulets of sweat ran down his back. His heart raced under his tank top. When the traffic stopped again and his VW sat frozen in the river of steel, he made a rash decision: abandon ship. He maneuvered the Beetle over to the shoulder and parked, put the black cloth top up, locked the doors, and walked away. Drivers honked, which sounded to him like hoots of derision. Beep-beep. Wimp gave up. Honk-honk. Go back to Pasadena, punk. He walked across the ramp and along Sepulveda until he found a pay phone at a Chevron station and called his mother to come get him, his humiliation complete.

"You should see a headshrinker," said George, breaking the silence.

"What? Did you say something?"

They neared the end of the Colorado Street Bridge. Innes admired its sweeping curve and the way its antique streetlamps formed parallel totems in a gentle arc. He congratulated himself for the wisdom to not jump from it to his death. They continued on, headed for points unknown.

"I said you have a mental problem. With freeways. This will take us all day on these streets."

"Freeways are not necessarily faster," said Innes. "We could hit a jam and be stuck out there for hours." He turned on the car radio tuned to an AM news and talk station. "See for yourself. It's about time for the traffic report."

The radio squawked to life with the tinny, breathless sound of AM newscasters. "...with traffic on the ones. How's it looking, Cee Cee?"

"Charlie, we've got an awful mess on the southbound 5 at Burbank Boulevard. Major SigAlert, with three left lanes closed due to an accident. There's an overturned semi involved. Could be an hour or so till things get moving again. Meanwhile, the westbound 134 in Toluca Lake is backed up to Glendale. Reports of a load of mattresses spilled into the center lane. CHP is on the way, but it could be a while..."

Innes snapped off the radio. No comment required. He switched the radio over to the CD player which soon filled the tiny car's interior with the machine-gun crossfire of Miles Davis and John Coltrane in the song called "Four." He hoped for a few moments of silence from the old man. No such luck.

"You suffer from a retarded worldview."

"Retarded worldview? Really?" said Innes. He reluctantly turned down the volume. "Where do you get this stuff?"

"What you need is a good whipping. Do you some good."

"And who's gonna do that? You?" Innes felt an urge to knock that stupid tam-o-shanter off his wrinkled head.

"You'll feel the sting of my lash on your scrawny backside," said George, pantomiming the crack of a whip with his right hand.

"Do you make this shit up, or are you quoting from somewhere? I can never tell."

Annie had found her father's theatrical pronouncements hilarious and somehow profound. Innes suspected the old man merely repeated memorized phrases he'd heard or read somewhere, like a deranged mynah bird. George spent hours among the stacks and the study carrels in the beamed high-ceilinged rooms of the Pasadena Central Library as if aiming to read every book there. All those words simmered and bubbled in his muddled mind until expelled in random torrents of blather.

"Which way you going, Magellan?" said George.

"Eagle Rock Boulevard," said Innes.

"No, take Avenue 64 to York Boulevard. More direct. Or better yet, Figueroa."

"It is not more direct. There's always construction on York and Fig."

"Fucking Wrong-Way Corrigan."

"Okay, Mr. Mapquest, we'll try your way."

Innes hung a right onto Avenue 64 and they proceeded south through the leafy affluence of the San Rafael neighborhood. The road curved past sycamores, magnolias, live oaks, and hedges of white oleander and pink bougainvillea, before a long winding descent into the flatlands of Highland Park in Los Angeles proper. The road narrowed, and the big old homes of West Pasadena gave way to tiny arts-and-crafts and Spanish bungalows with bars on the windows and doors.

George prattled on, but Innes had stopped listening. Something about Fortune's Wheel, Boethius, and the Consolation of Philosophy. At York Boulevard, he made another right and entered a world jarringly unlike the one they had left. The streetscape featured tall, garish signs for dollar stores, gas stations, and supermarkets with unfamiliar names like Big A and El Super, and block after block of painted storefronts, a rainbow of dark blues, bright pinks, deep reds, screaming yellows, and matte blacks. They housed chop shops behind tall steel bars, hair and nail salons, *lavanderias, panaderias, carnicerias, pupuserias*, and *iglesias* squeezed next to drive-in liquor stands announcing *cerveza fria*. Ficus trees shaded sidewalks torn up by overgrown roots. Mixed in with the old Latino *mercados* along York were the unmistakable signs of creeping hipsterdom: coffee bars, sidewalk cafes, retro boutiques and antique shops, bike shops, tattoo parlors, and vape vendors with sardonic names like Vapist, Inkster, and Lustluxe. Here and there he spied a bearded Millennial in a fedora on a skateboard and a pink-haired young woman with handcuffs for earrings riding a neon-hued bicycle. They shared bike lanes and sidewalks with sunbaked old men in white cowboy hats and faded denim pedaling ancient Schwinns.

"Are you listening to me?" said George.

"What? … Yes, I'm listening. Wheel of Fortune, right?"

"I ain't talking about no game show, idiot. I'm talkin' about Fortune's Wheel. We're on it."

The old man launched into a monologue about the ancient

view of life as a wheel in which everyone on top would someday be brought low and everyone at the bottom would someday rise. He seemed to be making a point about their current situation, but Innes was in no mood for philosophizing right now. His mind wandered. Many years earlier, he remembered as he gazed at the store façades, he had been here on a distant afternoon when his father took him to buy ice. Then the vision of Caleb's back as he vanished into the crowd forced its way into his consciousness again, as it had so many times since that night.

Paused at the light at Avenue 51, Innes glanced at the paper on his lap, and turned right on the red. The road climbed into the hills between Highland Park and Eagle Rock. After a few more turns they found themselves on top of a rise in front of an imposing three-story Victorian perched high above the street. Innes rolled down the car window and craned his neck to take it in. It wanted paint. At street level, a ten-foot high wall of small boulders embedded in concrete gave the place the look of a fortress. Bars on the windows added to the effect. A flight of crumbling steps switch-backed up to the door.

"Where the hell *are* we?" said George, his soliloquy interrupted. "Who lives here?"

"Paco Murias, supposedly, according to this." Innes exited the car and headed toward the steps.

"I'm stayin' right here," said George, eying the staircase.

Innes was out of breath when he reached the front door. His thighs ached from the climb and his pants stuck to his sweaty skin. Under the relentless sun, beads of sweat trickled into his eyes. The barred gate on the front door stood wide open. No bell or knocker in sight, he rapped on the sun-bleached wood door. Some strain of hip-hop music drifted from inside. After a minute, the door opened a crack, and a teenage girl with black hair pulled into a top bun peeked her head through and rested her chin on the outstretched security chain.

"What do you want?"

"I'm looking for Paco. My son Cal is a friend of his. I hope Paco can tell me if he's seen him."

She unchained and opened the door and evaluated him as only teenage girls can do to middle-aged men. She wore a black sweatshirt with UCLA in blue block letters. "Paco's not here," she said. "I know Cal. Haven't seen him though."

He handed her an index card with June's and Vanessa's cell numbers. "If you or Paco see him, would you give him a message? Have him call one of these numbers and let us know where he is?"

"Why don't you call him yourself?" she said.

"He doesn't answer calls or texts, and his mailbox is full."

"Sounds like he don't wanna be found." She took the card and closed the door.

As the Civic pulled away from the curb, an older woman ran after them waving her arms. Innes pulled over and lowered the passenger side window.

"*Señor, señor,*" she said, out of breath, bending over to peer in. The sight of the old man and his Jamaican tam-o-shanter startled her for a moment. She was heavy set, about Innes's age. "You Cal's papa?"

He nodded.

"My daughter. She lied. Cal was here."

"When?" he asked, braced by this news.

"*La semana pasada* ... last week?"

"Last week? Do you know where he went?"

"Where?" she repeated.

"*¿Donde?*" the old man said.

"Oh. Cal *y* Paco, they go to Maria's *casa*. House."

"Maria?"

"Maria de la Rosa."

"*¿Donde?*" Innes repeated his newly acquired Spanish vocabulary.

"*Se llama* ... Elysian Valley. *No sé donde esta.*"

"Maybe she means Elysian Park," George said.

"No Elysian Park," she said. "Elysian Valley." Vye-yay, she pronounced it.

"*¿Qué calle?*" George said.

"*No se.* Wait ... Nawks. It is Nawks. I think."

"She says she lives on Nawks Street."

"Grab the Thomas Guide," Innes said. They thanked her, and she called into the open window, "Tell Paco ... call his Mama." With the map book on his lap, George stuck his hand out and gave her a thumbs-up.

In the Thomas Guide, Elysian Valley, a.k.a. Frogtown, appeared as a narrow strip of land wedged between the 5 Freeway and the LA River. West of the freeway, right down to the edge of the pavement, a wall of steep brown hills encloses Elysian Park, Solano Canyon, and Chavez Ravine. Fortifying the river barrier on the east side are the railroad tracks and the commercial-industrial corridor of San Fernando Road, which sealed the neighborhood in a concrete prison. With a single main street through its heart, crossed by short perpendicular streets dead ending at the river, Frogtown on a map resembled the bones of a filleted fish. Innes drove slowly through the neighborhood as George pored over the map, looking for a cross street named Nawks. In the shadow of the hills and within the roar of the freeway, Frogtown was an island of little one-story stucco bungalows from the 1920s to the 1950s. Short fences of painted metal or chain link marked off tiny front yards dotted with ironic lawn ornaments and unironic holy statues. A cluster of boys in green and orange soccer jerseys kicked a miniature ball around in the street.

"Knox. She means Knox. K-N-O-X," said the old man. "It's about ten blocks ahead."

They did a slow loop and stopped where Knox dead-ends at the river. Innes gazed across the wooded expanse of the riverbed. Dark clouds collected to the north above the Verdugo Mountains in Glendale and the San Gabriels in Altadena. The setting sun illuminated the purple-pink mountains and silver-blue clouds like a Maxfield Parrish. They parked at the end of the street by the chain link fence separating the river and bike path from the houses.

"Now what?" said Innes.

"We wait," said the old man. He settled into the frayed gray upholstery. "See if anybody comes or goes."

"I'm getting out." Innes wandered over to the fence and looked down at the river. Unlike the all-concrete stretches of the LA River well known from countless filmed car chases, this section had a muddy soft bottom between its banks that supported a verdant isle of shrubbery and young trees. Not much water to speak of, only a trickle from lawn-sprinkler and car-wash runoff collected by thousands of storm drains, barely enough to keep it green until the next rainy season, if and when another should come.

The sun dropped behind the chaparral wall of Elysian Park. A breeze took the edge off the day's heat, clouds pushed in from the north, and the light began to fail. They decided to spend the night.

"Sleeping in the car. We're real homeless bastards now," said George.

"How long have you known Spanish?" said Innes as he balled his sweatshirt into a pillow.

"Had me a Mexican girlfriend once. Esmeralda." The old man smiled as her name hung in the air like an old song remembered. He leaned his head against the door and closed his eyes, still smiling.

Raindrops, the first to fall on LA in nearly a year, splashed the Civic's windshield around ten o'clock. By midnight, they became a roaring torrent, banging the car's sheet metal roof like a snare drum, waking Innes and George with a start, before lulling them back to sleep with its rhythmic cadence.

When they woke shortly after dawn, the rain was still thrashing its drum solo on the car's roof. The windows had steamed up from their night breathing. Innes lowered the driver's side glass a few inches. Knox Street was flooded, the water at least six inches deep at the curbs as it sloshed over onto the sidewalk. Autumn leaves, palm fronds, and branches that had fallen during the night clogged the storm drains. Soon the floodwaters would overrun the curbs and pour directly into the river.

Innes had not seen a deluge like it in at least five years. The rain would be welcome after such an extended drought. But he remembered what happened the last time the winter rains returned to Southern California. They arrived not as an orderly rescue mission or a bucket brigade of relief, but as an unruly mob of drenching Pacific Ocean storms. Curtains of wind-driven rain soaked the parched mountains, spawning rivers of floodwaters that cascaded into the valleys and canyons and filled city streets to knee deep. Los Angeles County's latticework of concrete flood control channels, near bone-dry most of the year, filled with angry torrents that swept away anything unlucky enough to be in their path. Steep hillsides, denuded by wildfires during drought years, collapsed into walls of mud and rock, wiping out entire neighborhoods. Such winter rains emerge from *El Nino*, a particular Pacific Ocean weather pattern, although to call such a calamity The Boy seemed to Innes a cruel misnomer. The *El Nino* winters, though rare, were especially cruel to the thousands of homeless in LA County. In those years, the warm dry climate that makes Southern California so hospitable for transients turns hostile, making life on the streets a constant battle to stay dry, or to dry out, under any kind of shelter, from freeway overpasses to open crawlspaces.

It occurred to Innes they'd picked a bad time to take to the road. From the Civic's trunk he fetched an umbrella, practically unused for years. He splashed through the ankle-deep water, crouched under its faded canopy, and walked toward the river. What he saw when he reached the fence and looked down into the riverbed shocked him. A deep surge of brown water rushed southward between the banks, bending trees, dragging uprooted bushes. The angry currents rocked and bucked like intertwined ropes. On the other side sat a row of emergency vehicles, red lights flashing. Rescue workers surveyed the swamped island in the middle. A helicopter descended through the wind and rain toward the trees. A beer cooler with a blue-and-yellow Corona logo floated by, dipping and spinning in the whitecaps kicked up by the rotor. Patches of blue, green, and orange fabric moved past. White plastic or bare metal poles protruded at odd angles, twisted and broken. Ruined tents.

A line of people emerged from upstream. They balanced on the slanted embankment as they walked arm in arm. He scanned their faces for signs of Cal. Not seeing his son, he called out, "Paco Murias? Maria de la Rosa?"

A young woman in a yellow poncho pointed back in the direction they had come. "Maria's back there," she said, and moved on.

Innes walked along the bank, balancing under the umbrella to avoid tumbling into the river. After a hundred yards of this tight-rope act, he came upon a young woman in a clear plastic poncho on the other side of the fence. She appeared to be searching the wooded riverbed. Behind her, a pair of men in big rubber boots and raincoats next to a fire truck prepared ropes and a small inflatable raft.

Innes found a gap in the fence and sidled up to her. "Are you Maria?" he said.

She nodded and stared into the river, expressionless.

"Have you seen Caleb Innes and Paco Murias? I'm Cal's dad."

She looked at him, pained and alarmed. Through her tears she said the three of them were together last night, under the trees in the riverbed, drinking beer and smoking weed. When it rained, she went home. The two boys said they would stay and finish their beers, spend the night if it didn't rain too much. When she awoke this morning and saw it was pouring, she went out to find them. What she found instead was this monster river. They had wanted to hang out in Griffith Park today. She buried her face in her arms.

Innes gently lay a hand on her shoulder and stood in stunned silence. He couldn't believe it. Possibly he had looked right at Caleb, hidden in the trees, the day before. His mind dialed up a new scene, of Caleb swept down river, strong arms and legs flailing helplessly against the powerful current as he called to his father to save him. The panic he'd felt the night of the fire returned. He blinked, trying to cut away from the movie in his head.

The search and rescue crew told them two bodies had been pulled from the river so far, but no teenage boys, far as they knew, just an old couple, a man and woman, passed out or too drunk to get out of the way. Innes and Maria waited around until the chopper and the crews departed after they determined there was no one there to be found. He walked her to her house, gave her a card with Vanessa's and June's numbers, and asked her to call if Caleb showed.

"You won't believe this," Innes said when he got back in the Civic. "Goddammit! Cal was right here last night. He may have spent the night down there in the riverbed. We gotta hope to God he wasn't in there when the flood came." Innes pounded the steering wheel again and again and again and rested his forehead on it. "Fuck. Fuck. Fuckety. Fuck. Fuck."

"Where to now, genius?" said George.

From Innes's perch on the observation deck of the Griffith Observatory, the Los Angeles Basin stretched to the east, south and west, from the San Gabriel Mountains to the humpback Palos Verdes Peninsula to the Pacific Ocean at Santa Monica, fifty miles from end to end. The morning after the rain, as the sun returned, the air was clear of smog, the San Gabriels dusted with fresh snow, and a silvery strip of the Pacific shimmered in the distance. He traced the north-south boulevards of the city, Vermont, Normandie, Western, as they parallaxed southward for thirty-five miles, straight as rifle shots, all the way to the harbor. Small planes and helicopters silently glided by, looking like toys as they passed the glass towers of downtown. Clusters of more office towers formed replicant downtowns from Hollywood to Mid-Wilshire to Century City, creating a vertiginous lack of center. A soft murmur of traffic and city life rose from the basin floor, faint and pleasant from the heights of the Observatory. It reminded him of the comforting sound of a loved one in sleep. Annie.

Up close, Los Angeles often looked gritty, garish, and disorienting, an endless graffiti-covered, polyglot grid of double-decker mini-malls, nail salons, muffler shops, taco stands, burger joints, food trucks, billboards. Exhaust from cars and buses in traffic jams fouling the air under the constant drone of helicopters overhead. From his distant vantage, it all faded into the background of the city's setting of mountains and hills, valleys and canyons, sandy coastline and bile-green sea stretching to the western horizon. Los Angeles lay before him, forbidding and enticing at the same time. Somewhere out there in that immense expanse, he hoped, was his son.

"Annie would know how to find him," he said to the city. "She would just know."

The alternative was unthinkable. The movie played again in his mind's eye: Caleb struggling against the current as the river swept him downstream, his eyes locked on Innes, arms waving, until he disappeared into a dark tunnel. Innes failing to save him, as he failed to save Annie.

George napped in the back seat. They had spent several hours driving around Griffith Park's thousands of rugged acres in a futile search for Caleb. They checked out the golf course snack bar, the

Greek Theater, the Los Angeles Zoo, the Travel Town train museum. The last two induced memories of Caleb as a little boy, marveling at the wild animals and antique engines. Twice Innes had parked, left George in the car, and walked a couple miles up and down muddy trails, eyes and ears peeled not only for Caleb but for rattlesnakes and mountain lions. Recently spotted in the vicinity was the puma known as P-22, a celebrity due to its many appearances on wilderness webcams, often with bloody fangs deep in the neck of an unlucky deer.

Innes returned to the car from the Observatory after pausing to inspect the monument to James Dean and an iconic scene from *Rebel Without a Cause*. They drove back down to the golf course snack bar in search of a pay phone to call June and Vanessa. They found one by the men's room door, a neglected graffiti-covered relic, but operational. A call to Vanessa went into voicemail. Innes left a long message summing up the events of the last twenty-four hours before a beep cut him off in mid-sentence.

On the second call, June picked up after the first ring. She sounded thrilled to hear from him. "The hell you been, boy?" He was about to tell her, but she talked over him. "I got a message for you. From some girl named Maria. She said she heard from some boy, Pedro or something."

"Paco. Paco, right?"

"That's right. Paco. He said Cal's in Burbank. Said he was headed there last night."

Innes felt as if a bird of prey perched on his head had finally flown away. "Burbank? Thank God," he said. "I was worried he'd drowned in the river." Innes palmed the receiver and turned to George. "Cal's okay!" He was about to tell June about the river, but she was still going.

"She left a name of another kid. Said Caleb may be headed to his house. Hold on. I wrote it down... Daniel. Daniel Deukmejian." She spelled it. "She said he lives somewhere on Magnolia."

"OK, thanks. Magnolia," he repeated. "What's up with the arson investigation? Any suspects?"

"No, I don't think so."

"If I ever find out who did it, I'll wring his fucking neck myself."

"Don't be stupid," she said. "Let the police do their job. Someday, you may have to accept there will be no resolution. Maybe it goes unsolved. Maybe it was an accident."

Innes was in no mood to accept anything. He changed the subject again. "What's going on with everybody? Vanessa, Clif, Tammy, Steven?"

"Vanessa's at her mom's. Not sure about Tammy and Steven. Haven't seen them since … Annie's memorial. Clif and Bev are at her mom's in Altadena. Terry's at his mom's in San Marino."

"Thank heaven for moms," said Innes, remembering he had none, his and Annie's both long gone.

"We're all worried about you, Innes. You seem … unwell … since the fire. George, too."

"We're fine. Just keep me posted on how everyone's doing. Once we find Caleb, we can all get back together somewhere and start fresh."

After a pregnant silence, June said, "So, where are you staying meantime?"

"Nowhere right now. The old man and I slept in the car last night."

"Oh, Innes. That's terrible."

"Not so bad. The old man didn't snore, or at least I didn't hear him, the rain was so loud." A long-forgotten nursery rhyme presented itself: It's raining, it's pouring, the old man is snoring.

"Listen," said June, after another brief silence, "I own a building in Burbank. There's a vacant apartment there, if you need a place to stay. No charge, stay long as you like, or until I get another tenant."

A free place to stay, out of the rain. It made sense, especially if the search for Caleb had shifted to Burbank. But he hated the idea of owing a debt to June. He'd seen her perform extravagant favors for people, then never let them forget it, sinking her talons into them like a bill collector. Once, he'd had to borrow five hundred dollars from her, too proud to tell Annie. June held it over him for months until he could pay it back. She even suggested unsubtly that he could "work it off."

"Where is it?" he stalled, trying to think of a good reason to decline the offer.

"Just off Buena Vista, not far from Magnolia."

"Let me check with the old man," he said, still stalling. To his disappointment, George said it was the best idea he'd heard yet. Innes was fresh out of reasons to say no. He picked up the dangling receiver. "Okay, June," he said. "We'll take you up on that."

"Good boy. Can you meet me there in an hour? I'll let you in and give you the key." She gave him the address and hung up.

The apartment building was one of those Southern California architectural oddities known as a Dingbat, a nondescript two-story box, pale yellow with kitschy 1950s-style designs embedded in the stucco, and room for two cars to park under an overhang supported by steel poles. By the time Innes and George found it, June was already there, in the covered driveway next to her big black Escalade. They parked next to her. The little Civic, with its eroded sections of paint marked off by chalky white outlines like sweat stains on a black T-shirt, was dwarfed by her shiny land yacht. June hugged Innes and planted a kiss on his stubbly cheek. He could smell her perfume. Lilac, or something. She grabbed his hand and led him up the metal staircase to the second-floor unit, like she already owned him.

The empty apartment bore a faint odor of cigarette smoke and needed fresh paint. Cheap plastic mini blinds with bent or missing slats covered the living room windows. The chocolate-brown carpet was pocked with dents from the weight of tenants' furniture, years of compressed dander and dust pounded into gray circles and squares. June gave him a quick tour of the galley kitchen, small bathroom, and single bedroom.

"It's not a luxury unit by any means, but it will keep you warm and dry for a while," she said, and handed him the key.

He wanted to say, "You're not fooling anyone, June. You're a slumlord." Instead he said, "We'll only be here a couple days. Either we find Cal here, or he's moved on to another part of town."

"I brought you a few things," she said. "Two sleeping bags. Some pillows. A sack of groceries. In my car."

"You don't have to feed us. We're not destitute. I can pay you a couple days' rent."

"Don't be stupid. Let me do this for you. Save your money."

After they unloaded her car, she gave him another kiss on the cheek and one of her patented deep looks into the eyes. He recognized this gaze, her Jedi mind trick. "Innes. Look at me," she said. "You don't have to be out here on the streets looking for Cal. You should stay with us. Mom and I have moved into one of our buildings on Orange Grove. It's nice, three bedrooms. You can use it as a base until you find him."

Innes almost accepted. It would be so easy.

"I hate to see you out here on the streets," she continued. "It's not good for your boyish good looks." Her smile gave him the creeps. He remembered that booze-soaked night at the previous year's Halloween Party when she grabbed his crotch and gave him a squeeze.

"Thanks June," he said. He looked away from her, unwilling to meet her eyes. "We're fine. Really. And I need to get away from Pasadena for a while. Too many bad memories."

"Suit yourself," she said, and pushed him away. She did her head-snap thing, a gesture to flip a lock of hair out of her eye when she was annoyed or nonplussed. "The offer stands. You know how to reach me." She climbed into the Escalade and slammed the door. The tires squealed as she backed into the street.

George waited until June left before he got out of the car and climbed the stairs to the apartment, hauling the pillowcases with him. "Smells like a goddamn fart in here," he announced. He plopped down on the floor, rolled over onto his stomach, and within minutes was snoring.

Innes examined the paper sack of groceries. Toiletries. Cups of ramen noodles. Boxes of mac-n-cheese. Like a care package for a kid at summer camp. Or worse, a food shelf donation. The smell of pity wafted out of the bag. At the bottom was one more item: a pre-paid cellphone, still in its plastic packaging. "Smart girl," he conceded.

He stared at Annie's pillowcase for a moment. He wasn't ready to open it, hadn't summoned the courage to look inside. He would have to touch her things, smell her scent on her clothes. Too much. Too soon.

Instead, he emptied his own pillowcase onto the floor and sorted through the items. Two changes of clothes: Cargo shorts, faded jeans, a UC-Riverside hoodie, and a Dodgers T-shirt. A dusty clock radio, analog not digital, but still functional. Two dog-eared paperbacks from his nightstand: *Slouching Toward Bethlehem* and *Play It as It Lays*. His old Seiko watch with the round dial and flexible metal band showed half-past six. On the floor amid the pile was a picture frame, face down. He paused a moment, not sure he could bear to look at it, and left it there. Done in from several miles of hiking the hilly trails of Griffith Park, Innes dragged a sleeping bag and pillow into the bedroom, out of range of the snoring, and was asleep in minutes.

In the morning, he woke to the sight of George in the bedroom doorway. "Did you move the car?" George said.

"What?" said Innes as he sat up in his sleeping bag.

"Where did you park the car?"

"Right where we left it. Out in front."

"Well it sure as hell ain't there now."

Innes rubbed the sleep out of his eyes, climbed out of the sleeping bag, and hurried down the staircase in the chilly dawn air. There, in the tuck-under parking spaces, was a big concrete patch of nothing. Grease stains. Tire skid marks. No Civic.

"Fuuuuuck," was all he could think of to say.

"Exactly. We're fucked," said George.

"Who the hell would steal a Honda Civic?" Innes said.

"Did you lock it?" said George.

"Of course I locked it. I always lock it."

"Maybe it got towed."

"It's parked on private property. With permission of the owner." Innes' voice rose with irritation.

"Or the repo man took it."

"Are you nuts? That car was paid off fifteen years ago."

George stared at an oil stain on the concrete pad. Innes walked into the street and looked this way and that, thinking he'd moved it out there and forgot. Nada. When he returned, George hadn't moved a muscle, still staring at the patch of oil. The stain was shaped like the state of Maine.

"Are you okay, old man?" Innes asked. No response. OK, no help from him. Innes assessed the situation. First thing, call June. Then the police. It might be awkward with the cops. No permanent residence, no driver's license or ID of any kind, no title to the car. He hoped a call to the DMV would confirm his ownership.

"Well," he said after a long pause. "At least we brought all our things in from the car last night. We still got our stuff."

That snapped the old man out of his examination of the state of Maine. He looked up at Innes. "It's worse than you think," he said.

"What do you mean? Worse how?"

"Our money was in the car."

"What?" Innes wasn't sure he'd heard right.

"Our money. Or most of it. I put it in the glovebox and locked it, for safe keeping."

"You … did … what?"

"It's in the glovebox."

"In the glovebox? What the hell were you thinking?"

"It seemed like a good idea. At the time. We couldn't lose it if it was locked up."

"That's just perfect. How much?"

"A grand. An even thousand. I counted it out and wrapped it up real nice in a rubber band."

"Are you kidding me?" Innes glared at him. "I entrusted you with our money—my money—because you said you're used to carrying cash and know how to protect it. And I fucking believed you."

"We still got some, right?" said George. "How much you got on you?"

"About a hundred, in my pants pocket upstairs," said Innes, shaking his head in disbelief. "You?"

"Couple hundred."

"Great. We have a grand total of three hundred bucks between us. And no car."

Innes felt the urge to puke and went upstairs, leaving the old man with the oil patch. He knelt and grasped the cool rim of the toilet bowl and stared into its calm whiteness. He couldn't call forth the cleansing projectile, only a few dry retches. The tranquility of the porcelain soothed him. He picked himself up off the bathroom floor and went into the living room to collect his thoughts, make a plan. Start with ditching the old man and continue the search for Caleb alone.

He would have to figure out a way to earn some money. Would they take him back at Starbucks? Unlikely, given the way abrupt way he'd left. The Henry Miller line he'd scribbled on the chalkboard seemed funny at the time: "No money, no resources, no hope, I'm the happiest man alive." Pure hubris. Now it just seemed pathetic. With no car, no decent clothes, his options were limited. The thought of begging for a low-wage job nauseated him. He would have to think of something. Later. First things first.

Innes grabbed the prepaid cellphone, ripped off the plastic packaging, and read the instructions. He'd never used one before. To him, "burners" were an exotic tool of drug dealers, terrorists, and others out to avoid detection. Once he figured it out, he called June. She didn't sound upset by his news and said she would be right over. He detected an "I told you so" tone.

"Don't talk to the police until I get there," she said. "I'm the property owner. I should be there."

He delayed a few minutes before calling the police to give June a head start and waited for them outside. It was futile, he knew, but he called Caleb anyway, and got no answer. Mailbox full. George was nowhere to be seen.

The two officers who arrived were polite but appeared bored by the whole thing. They indicated car theft was epidemic in Burbank, everywhere in LA.

"Who would want to steal an old Civic?" asked Innes.

"Civics are a hot item, especially hatchbacks," said one officer. "It's probably in a chop shop right now, turning into a lowrider."

"A Mexican Maserati," the other cop said with a smirk.

Their bored nonchalance shifted to suspicion when they asked Innes for ID and he had none. When tried to explain about the fire and his losses, they peppered him with questions about where he lived and if he really had a car to steal. One cop ran his name through the computer to check for warrants or a record. Passing cars slowed as drivers gawked at the spectacle of two cops questioning a lone, poorly dressed, unshaven man. Innes had done the very thing himself, slowing down to glimpse a confused or angry man on a curb, hands cuffed behind him. He wondered if that was next. For the first time in his life, he felt like a true outcast, a person worthy of the pity, suspicion, and contempt in the drivers' eyes as they rolled by.

June arrived and vouched for his identity and residence, which the officers verified on their computer, along with a 1997 Honda Civic registered to one Homer Virgil Innes. They asked more questions, filled out a report, and left Innes with the impression he had less than zero chance of ever seeing the Civic again, and there was less than zero chance the Burbank PD would make it a priority, given he was a homeless loser with no ID.

After they left, June leaned against the Escalade's grille and gave Innes another one of her long, meaningful stares. "I'm really sorry," she said. "Nothing like this has ever happened at one of my properties. And this is not a bad neighborhood."

He nodded, avoiding her eyes.

"But, sorry, I've got more bad news for you."

"Of course you do," he said.

"I got new tenants for the apartment. They want to move in this weekend. I have to get the painters in here tomorrow. I'm afraid you and George will have to move out in the morning. I'm sorry."

Innes let out a snort and was about to say something caustic, but realized it was just as well. He had doubts about this whole June-to-the-rescue bit. "Fine," he said. He stared at the state of Maine.

"I feel terrible about this," she said. "Why don't you let me make it up to you? Come stay with me."

Same answer. Same response. Door slammed. Tires squealed.

Innes went upstairs to do what he could put off no longer. He stared at Annie's pillowcase on the floor for a minute and knelt beside it. Before looking inside, he spotted the overturned picture frame on the floor among his pile of things. He held it in his hand for a moment, then turned it over. There it was. His eyes went right to it. That face. The upturned little nose. The guileless smile that displayed her upper gums. In her arms Annie held baby Caleb. Twenty-eight-year-old Innes had his arm around her, smiling, proud Daddy, no gray hair. The black-and-white family portrait was taken in the late '90s at Descanso Gardens.

He remembered the day Caleb was born—a long delivery, nearly twenty hours, without much sleep for either of them, Innes awed by Annie's stamina and tolerance for pain. When Caleb finally arrived, the nurses cleaned him up, swaddled him in the standard hospital-issue baby blanket, and handed him to an exhausted, sweaty Annie. Then it was his turn. He took the bundle in his arms. A tiny pink monkey. They say newborns can't see much, but Innes was sure Caleb looked him right in the eye and regarded him with wonder and amazement. Innes returned the favor. At that moment, he knew his life would never again be about himself. The center of gravity had shifted, and he was holding it in his arms.

Until then, Innes had thought of himself as hot stuff, a rising star of journalism. From intern at the *Riverside Press-Enterprise* in college to staff writer at the *Pasadena Star-News*. Next stop, *Los Angeles Times*. In time, he would learn he wasn't such hot stuff. There was a scene he played over and over in his mind. Seated in an ergonomic chair in a glassed-in office called "the fishbowl," he faced the managing editor of the *Star-News*, who from his ergonomic chair across the desk explained how Innes's nearly twenty years at the paper were much appreciated "especially when you won us a prize for the museum scandal but times are tough there's a recession we have to make cuts the pressure's on from upstairs there are no easy choices I hate to do this so sorry we have to let you go you can pick up your severance materials at HR on your way out after you clear out your desk sorry-Ihaveameetingtogotonow." Innes sat there speechless, torn between the need to leave the office and end this nightmare as quickly as possible and the urge to grab the sharp diamond-shaped Plexiglas trophy for Best Local News Coverage and jam it deep into the man's condescending face. To his everlasting relief, he chose the former.

A drop of water beaded on the glass of the picture frame and obscured Annie's face. And another. He snorted, wiped his eyes with the back of his hand, then grabbed a T-shirt from his pile on the floor and swept the drops from the picture. He put the picture down and reached for Annie's pillowcase, grabbing the first thing off the top, something soft. Smooth, lacy fabric. A camisole. He closed his eyes and held it to his face and drew a deep breath through his nostrils. That smell. Her scent exploded across his cortex like tear gas. Twenty-five years of memories flooded his mind's eye: co-ed Annie, bride Annie, pregnant Annie, shopkeeper Annie. The way their bodies fit perfectly when they spooned. Her laugh, her lovemaking, her tears. He hated himself for ever doubting her. He let out a primal howl of sorrow and sobbed into the fragrant silky fabric. After several moments, he put the camisole down and picked up the picture, hugged it to his chest, rolled over, closed his eyes, and descended into the abyss.

When he woke, the photo was still clutched in his hands and George was standing over him. The old man dropped to the floor next to him, picked up the camisole and examined it. Innes sat up and looked at his watch. He'd been out, and the old man gone, for hours.

"This was hers?" George said.

Innes nodded. The two were silent for a long while. Eventually, Innes turned the pillowcase on its side and pulled out more items, making neat piles on the carpet. A long skirt in a multicolored exotic print. The tan leather miniskirt. The yellow ballet slippers. More underwear—two white cotton bras and three candy-striped panties. A lilac scoop-neck T-shirt. Pale peach cropped cardigan sweater. Beige tights. Two pairs of socks rolled up in neat little balls. He pictured Annie in all of them, had seen them on her a hundred times. It was as if she had been in the room and then vanished with a poof, her clothes falling to the floor.

George clutched the camisole and swayed to and fro like a trauma victim.

There was more in the pillowcase. Innes pulled out a pair of jade earrings he had given her on an anniversary. A pair of antique plastic bracelets, one dark yellow, one moss green. Bakelite, she called them. A small framed picture of Caleb, a school photo taken at age twelve. Short hair and boyish smile, far from the shaggy, scowling adolescent he had become. Innes was grateful to have it, a freeze frame from a time in his life he cherished, before he'd lost his job. From the bottom, Innes fished out a small, tan, leather-bound notebook, held closed by a tiny brass lock. Her diary.

No way, he thought. Not anytime soon. Maybe not ever.

He stared at the pile, trying to make sense of it. Why did she choose these things, and not others? Was it a hasty grab for whatever was handy, or did she carefully select things that were precious? And what was missing? What wasn't here that should be? What did she run back into the damned building for?

George emerged from his stupor and stood up. "I'm sorry about the money," he said. "I screwed up, I know."

Innes's irritation had faded, subsumed into sorrow and self pity. "You didn't know the Civic would get stolen."

"Anyway, I got us some new wheels."

"What, you stole us a car?"

"Not exactly. Wanna see it? It's in the driveway."

Innes followed him out the door and down the stairs. "What next, old man?" he said.

There it was, parked right where the Civic had been. Innes had to blink a few times. Was this a joke? He looked at the old man, searching for signs of mischief. Poker face. Innes circled the thing, inspecting. It looked brand new. Clean, shiny, sporty. Bright red, gray trim, smooth rounded edges. Four wheels. Roomy inside. On its side was a medallion, its marque of distinction: the familiar white-and-red concentric circles logo of Target stores.

"A shopping cart? That's our new wheels?"

"Not just any shopping cart," George said. "This is a goddamn Target shopping cart. Top of the line. All plastic. Boosted it myself." He beamed with pride.

"What the hell are we supposed to do with this?"

"We put our stuff in it, dummy, so we don't have to carry it while we look for Cal."

Innes paused, and spoke slowly, as if to a toddler. "I ... am ... not ... going ... to push ... a fuckingshoppingcartaround!" He dashed up the stairs to put as much distance as possible between him and ... that. He stuffed his and Annie's things back into the pillowcases. A banging clanging scraping cursing cacophony echoed from outside, and when he went to the door he saw George struggling to haul the deluxe, top-of-the-line, all-plastic Target shopping cart up the stairs.

"What the hell are you doing?" Innes shouted.

"If we leave it outside, it's gonna get stolen, or hadn't you noticed?"

"Fine. Bring it inside." He met him halfway and helped haul it into the living room. "But tomorrow, we leave it. June's tenants can have it."

"No way. Not after what I went through to get this."

"Where did you get it?"

"Where d'ya think? Target. The one by the freeway."

Innes tried to picture the old man pushing a stolen shopping cart about thirty blocks under the warm autumn sun. "Why didn't you swipe one from Costco?" he said. "The one on Burbank Boulevard. That's closer."

"Because, genius, Costco carts suck. They're way too big and they weigh a ton. Try to push one of those tanks through sidewalks and traffic. These Target carts are state of the art. Plastic, light, and strong. Perfect size."

Innes had no idea there was a science to this. "So you just walked off with one of Target's shopping carts? I thought they had those anti-theft thingies on them."

"They do. You gotta remove 'em. Nothin' to it. Just takes a hammer and a screwdriver."

"A hammer and screwdriver? Where did you get those?"

"Bought 'em at Target. Where the hell you think I got 'em?"

The conversation gave Innes a headache. "Wait. Let me get this straight. You bought tools at Target to use them to steal one of their shopping carts?"

"You catch on quick."

Innes regarded him with amazement. "Too much. You are too much."

"They won't miss one lousy cart," said George. "They got millions of 'em. And I spent some money there." He pulled a red-and-white plastic Target sack from the basket. "Got us some garbage bags, plastic ponchos, bungee cords, a tarp, flashlight, scissors, duct tape, wire cutters."

The old man sounded so earnest, like an Eagle Scout. Now was the time to tell him. "Look, old man, I think it's time we go our separate ways. We might find Cal faster if we split up."

George stared at him, mouth agape. "Split up? Split up?" He cackled. "Boy, you wouldn't last two days out there without me."

"What makes you so damn street smart?"

"Where you think I've lived the last two years? Ever since they kicked me out of the Y?"

"I thought you crashed with all your girlfriends, when you weren't on our couch. That's what you told Annie."

"I was. Sometimes. But I tend to wear out my welcome with the ladies pretty quick."

"I can't imagine why."

"Anyway, I been outside plenty. I know my way around. That's why I carry this." He reached into an inside pocket of his jacket and brandished a nine-inch hunting knife. "Street life is not for pussies."

"You didn't have to sleep in the streets. Why didn't you move in with us?" Innes asked, trying not to stare at the terrifying blade.

"Yeah, like you wanted that," George said with an eye roll and put the knife away. "Anyway, I like the street. There's freedom out there. Nobody to nag you. After a while, sleeping inside in a room feels like a cage. I got friends out there, too. We got each other's back. Usually."

Innes didn't know the first thing about living on the street. Definitely wouldn't have thought of the shopping cart caper or all those Boy Scout supplies. He decided to sleep on it and see how things looked in the fresh light of a new day.

In the morning, they availed themselves of the shower in June's apartment then hauled the cart down the stairs and loaded it with their gear: sleeping bags rolled up with their bedding in a garbage bag on the lower shelf; pillowcases in the basket along with their other things in the Target sack; the tarp partially unfolded, ready for deployment, as it looked ominously like more rain. Innes gathered their remaining cash and hid it inside the back of his clock radio. They headed south toward Magnolia. George pushed the cart. Innes walked a healthy distance behind to avoid the humiliation of being seen with a shopping cart but also unwilling to let the old man out of his sight.

Book III

THEY FOUND A DRY SPOT UNDER THE 134 FREE-
way across from Walt Disney Studios and squeezed themselves and
the shopping cart through a gap cut into the rusty chain link fence
surrounding a Caltrans truck depot. George took out his sleeping
bag and prepared to settle in for the night.

They had spent the last few days—Innes had lost track of them—
pushing the cart up and down Magnolia Boulevard and through the
side streets of Burbank in the intermittent rain, vainly searching for
signs of Caleb. They went as far west as Hollywood Way, where that
morning George led them to the parking lot behind a Cuban bakery.

"Best goddamn pastries in LA," he said as he stood on tiptoes and
lifted a heavy steel lid.

Innes screwed up his face in disgust. "I am not eating out of a
dumpster."

"Suit yourself. ... Sweet! Check out these babies." George pulled
out a white cardboard box filled with a dozen round pastries, center
dollops of cream cheese topped with yellow fruit filling. Peaches. They
glistened as the light rain put a fresh sheen on them. Innes grabbed one
and took a bite. Still moist. He stuffed the whole thing in his mouth and
nearly choked on it, bits of peach and cream cheese dribbled down his
chin. He didn't realize how hungry he was. Trying to conserve cash,
they hadn't eaten since yesterday. All thoughts were pushed aside by
the question of where to find the next meal. He thought again of Orwell, who had said poverty "annihilates the future," focusing the mind
on the present moment, the next meal, eliminating the ability to plan
rationally for the future. He understood that now.

They stood in the drizzle next to the reeking dumpster and
chewed in silence. Homeless for weeks now, carless for days, Innes
began to feel like he was in quicksand, torso still above the surface
but for how long? They had been sleeping in parks, trying to stay dry.
They took turns guarding the cart while the other sought out a bathroom, an increasingly urgent need. Though he was only forty-five,
Innes peed like an old man: frequently and unsatisfyingly. He had
read somewhere that groups of women living in close quarters over
time tended to see their menstrual cycles synchronize. He wondered
if he and his father-in-law were synchronizing their bladders.

The last shave he'd had at June's apartment was now a memory, lost under an itchy fuzz. He could smell his own stench, and his whole body itched. Tiny red welts appeared on his lower legs, like an acne breakout. Fleas? Lice? Bedbugs? The thought of walking into a coffee shop or bar to ask for a menial job—don't even think about a white-collar job—made him laugh out loud. Still, he would have to do something.

"What so damn funny, idiot?" George said and put the box of pastries under the tarp, out of the rain.

They continued south toward the freeway. In a small neglected park with rotted wood benches and rusted play equipment, they came across a cluster of vagabonds milling about in the drizzle. Some had carts, some only backpacks, all with plastic ponchos or garbage bags with holes cut for their arms and heads. George knew some of them and picked up a tip on a place under the freeway where they could dry off and spend the night.

After the old man climbed into his sleeping bag, Innes pulled out the cellphone and called Caleb again. Same result. Then Vanessa. "Pick up, dammit," he said as if she could hear him across the ether. Voicemail again. He left her a short message with his burner number and pleaded with her to call back, with or without news of his son. He sounded pathetic, but was beyond caring, and switched off the phone and tossed it back in the cart.

He exited through the cut fence and headed west on Riverside Drive in search of a hot meal and food to bring back for George. He had fourteen bucks on him. The rest of their stash, down to a couple hundred dollars, remained hidden inside the clock radio. The rain eased to a soft mist as he walked several blocks past the massive Warner Brothers lot into Toluca Lake, where Riverside merged with Alameda in a tangle of curved streets. There loomed the welcoming sign of Bob's Big Boy. It was nearly dark, and the sign's multi-colored neon tubes flickered against the purple sky.

Innes spied an empty booth by the windows and settled onto a padded bench seat with a red vinyl banquette. His clothes still damp, face in need of a shave, he hoped he was nevertheless presentable, not obviously a homeless moocher. He snatched a plastic-coated menu from the metal bracket on the table and perused the offerings. The nearest waitress was at the far end of the counter, chatting up a fat short-order cook in a white paper hat and apron splattered with grease stains. Innes noticed how the waitress filled out her tight uniform dress. Her curves strained against the fabric like a thoroughbred at the starting gate and her red underwear showed through the thin white material. He realized he was staring and looked away. He didn't believe in heaven and the afterlife but still sometimes imagined Annie was watching him.

As he studied the menu, out of the corner of his eye he saw the waitress approaching. She stood over him with a notepad and pencil in her hands. Probably in her mid-thirties, dark hair streaked with bright red dye, pulled back in a bun. Her name tag said Cheryl.

"So, honey, are you gonna order something, or are you gonna stare at my ass all night?" She smiled.

Innes felt his face flush and gaped at her for a full beat. "Sorry," he said, exhaling. "Was I that obvious?"

"It's okay, honey. I'm used to it," she said and leaned closer, as if to give him a better view of the reasons she was used to it. "Just try to be more subtle, ya know? It's creepy to be ogled like that." She stood up straight and said in a brisk waitress voice, "So, what'll it be?"

For a second he felt transported into the diner scene in *Five Easy Pieces*.

You want me to hold the chicken?

I want you to hold it between your knees.

"Coffee, black, for now," he said instead.

Cheryl came back with his coffee and took his order for a grilled cheese on sourdough, plus an onion bagel schmear to go for the old man. She ripped a sheet from her pad and left it on his placemat, next to the photo of a tall stack of pancakes smothered in melted butter and syrup. He picked it up after she walked away. It said, in tiny neat handwriting: I get off in 20 minutes—wait for me?

He read it twice. Three times. Was this a joke? He looked around to see if anyone was watching to see how he'd react. Nope. Was she only flirting with him in hopes of a nice tip?

When she returned with his grilled cheese, she stood there for a second, her eyebrows raised in expectation.

"Oh... yeah," he said, her note still in his hand. "I'm game. And I'll take the check, whenever you're ready."

"No worries. You're covered," she said in a whisper.

He waited for her behind Bob's. The rain had stopped. Reflections from the neon sign danced in the parking lot puddles. Innes remembered it once was a drive-in. The covered row of parking spaces for curb service was still there, but anyone who expected a waitress on roller skates would have a long wait.

With no idea what the hell he was getting into, he thought about old George back there under the freeway, and hoped the old man was guarding the shopping cart, not wandering off. He should skip this little charade and go back. She's not coming. What would she want with such a loser?

Cheryl emerged from the back door, changed out of her waitress outfit into skinny black jeans, a tight black T-shirt with a white LA logo on her chest, and flip flops. He forgot about old George.

"There's a place across the street," she said. "I'll buy you a drink."

They found an open table in the rear of a dark bar, once a dreary spot for sots but showing signs of creeping hipsterdom. A list of handcrafted cocktails filled a chalkboard.

"Sriracha martini?" he read aloud. "Is that a thing?"

"Where you live?" she said, ignoring his question.

"I'm from Pasadena. But the truth is … I'm sort of between homes right now. Between jobs, too. Mister In-between."

"Yeah, I thought you seemed lost."

"Is that why you picked up my tab?"

"It was only twenty bucks."

"I'll pay you back."

"Please don't. Spoils my good karma," she said. "Pay it forward, do somebody else a good turn."

A pierced and tattooed waitress in black leather with neon green spiky hair placed their drinks on the table and sashayed back to the bar without a word.

"You never told me your name," Cheryl said. She took a sip of her mojito.

"Innes."

"First name?"

"Homer," he said. "Homer Innes. Rhymes with Guinness."

"Homer?" she said with a hoot. "Like Homer Simpson?"

"No, like Homer the Greek poet. My mother's idea. Don't ask."

"Cruel woman. Don't you have a middle name?"

"Virgil."

She let out a soft whistle. "Okay then, let's stick with Innes."

He drained his icy mug of Sam Adams in three gulps. She took another sip of her drink and regarded him with furrowed brow. "How long have you been homeless?"

He set his mug on the table with a bang and launched into his tale of tears. When he finished with the part about leaving the old man with the shopping cart under the freeway, she sat in silence for a moment.

"How much money you got left?" she said.

"Couple hundred. This keeps up, I'll have to panhandle out there with the rest of the drunks and junkies and mental cases. I swore to myself I would never be one of those losers by the side of the road with a cardboard sign. I won't do it. I'll find some other way to get money."

She took another sip of mojito. "How would you like to earn some real money?" she said. "Tomorrow. A hundred bucks, cash."

That got his attention. "Depends," he said. "What would I have to do for it?"

"Just be yourself," Cheryl said. She reached across the table and squeezed his hand. A charm offensive. "How would you like to be in a movie?"

"Now you're messing with me," he said. "Making fun of the homeless guy."

"No, I'm serious. This waitress gig is just a side hustle. My real job is documentary films. I'm—we're—making a film about the home-less crisis in LA. All you have to do is come to our studio, sit in a chair, and be interviewed about your life and how you ended up on the streets, et cetera." She no longer spoke like a waitress in a diner.

"Why me? Some random guy who just wandered into your restaurant?"

"I like your look, Homer. Liked it right away."

"Innes."

"Innes. Sorry. You're a good-looking man. More presentable than a lot of the folks we're interviewing. We feel like if all our subjects are scruffy, sick, or high, et cetera, it will be too easy for audiences to dismiss them and not care about the crisis. Which is what most people do anyway. We want to change that. Maybe people will see themselves in you."

"Who's we?"

"We call ourselves Angels in Paradise, an all-women, feminist filmmaking collective." She grabbed her purse from under the table and handed him a pink business card. It said Angels in Paradise.com in red embossed letters, set above a pair of what looked like angel wings. In small print below it said: In Cinema Veritas.

He stared at it for several moments. "I like the wings. Nice touch," was all he could think of to say.

"It's part of our brand," she said. "So." She paused and smiled. "Is you in, or is you ain't? I can pick you up at Bob's in the morning, say ten."

She was entirely serious.

"I don't know," he stalled. He had a vision of a theater full of people pitying his sorry face up on a big screen. Or worse, a million households watching him on Netflix.

"A hundred bucks, remember?" she prompted.

"There's the old man. I left him back there--"

"He'll be fine," she assured him. "It'll only take a few hours, then I'll give you a lift back to your ... bridge or whatever."

He stalled, considering his options. One, he could stay under a dismal freeway overpass with the daft old man, or two, earn a hundred bucks cash-money. He stared at the pressed tin ceiling of the bar. I need the money, Annie, he said silently. Then we'll find Cal. I promise.

"Okay," he told Cheryl. "I'm in."

The Angels in Paradise "studio" would never be confused with the storied motion picture factories nearby—Warner Brothers and Disney in Burbank, Universal up the hill, Paramount over in Hollywood, or Sony in Culver City. The studio Innes and Cheryl pulled up to was a nondescript 1960s tract house in Van Nuys, a one-story stucco box set on a half-dead lawn on a street of nearly identical non-descript tract houses on half-dead lawns. Only the colors of the exteriors varied, a pallid palette of whites, off-whites, eggshells, beiges, ecrus, and tans. The rain had stopped, but it was still overcast, which heightened the drabness of the San Fernando Valley neighborhood.

Cheryl nosed her little red Fiat 500 into the driveway and through to a dirt parking lot in back. A two-car garage with the door open exposed a space jammed with lighting equipment, microphones, metal stands, furniture, racks hung with clothes.

"The prop room," said Cheryl as they climbed out of the car.

Inside, a nearly naked young woman stood at a kitchen counter mixing a drink with tomato juice and Smirnoff. Innes didn't want to stare, but he couldn't avert his eyes. She wore only a silver thong and matching spike heels. Head shaved, body festooned with tattoos, piercings glinted all over her face and through her navel and nipples. A pair of white feathered wings, about three feet across, attached to her upper back with straps around her shoulders.

Innes blinked. She was still there.

"Hey, Syl," said Cheryl.

The woman turned and smiled, rolled her eyes, and stuck out her studded tongue. She looked about twenty. Her skin was pale, her eyes puffy.

"Rough night last night?" said Cheryl.

"Just taking the edge off, Cher. So I don't puke," said Syl. She took a sip of her drink, added a squirt of Tabasco, and stirred.

"This is my friend Innes, from Pasadena," said Cheryl. "This is Sylvan, one of our angels, obviously."

"Hey, Pasadena," said Syl.

"Wait here," Cheryl told him. "I've got to find Lee An and see what's what. When we're starting, et cetera. She's the boss." She left them alone in the kitchen.

Syl slammed the glass down on the counter and let rip an impressive multi-note burp. Innes nodded to her, not sure what to say to a belching naked tattooed winged bald chick drinking a Bloody Mary at ten-thirty in the morning. She staggered out of the kitchen, weaving precariously on her five-inch stilettos. Innes wondered what kind of documentary she was in.

After a minute, Cheryl returned. "Umm, change of plans," she said, looking a bit sheepish. Or was it wolfish? "Lee An says we're not ready to start yet."

Innes wasn't sure whether to be relieved or disappointed. He could use the hundred bucks, but also hadn't come to terms with seeing himself forever captured on film as a pathetic homeless loser.

"But good news," she said. "We can still use you today. The hundred bucks offer stands. You in?"

"Sure, I guess. What do I have to do?"

"Only what you were thinking about when you ogled me at the diner yesterday."

He felt his face flush again. And he wasn't sure he'd heard right. "You mean sex? With you?" he said. He half expected her to burst out laughing in his face.

"No, not me," she said with a swallowed giggle. "Somebody younger and prettier, and ... in front of a camera." The raised eyebrows again.

He stared at her, not comprehending. It took a moment, but the idea slowly took shape in his mind. "You want me to ... be in a porno?"

"Please. Adult video." Was she kidding? She wasn't kidding. "As it happens, we need an older guy for a vid we're making right now."

"I thought you made documentaries."

"We do. But we also make erotica. High-quality erotica that doesn't degrade women. It's how we raise the money to make our documentaries. So ... game?" She tilted her head and smiled enticingly.

He found himself considering her indecent proposal. Had he fallen this far, were things this desperate, that he would debase himself for money?

Anger rumbled up from within. "This is like a bait-and-switch, right? There never was any documentary about the homeless."

"Scout's honor," she said, holding up her hand. "You can still be in the doc. Maybe tomorrow, next week. But since you're here now, and I promised you a hundred bucks..."

He looked at the ceiling and closed his eyes, conjuring Annie's face staring down at him from wherever. She made the I'm-watching-you gesture. A hundred bucks, Annie, he reminded her.

"Look, if you don't want to do it, no worries," said Cheryl. "But I can't give you a ride back to Burbank right now, sorry. I've got work to do. You can either wait till the end of the day when I'm free. Or walk back."

He was trapped. She'd brought him here, miles from George and all their things. The sky had shed its morning haze, and it was already hot and humid out. He couldn't face the long walk back through the asphalt jungle of the Valley. Was there a bus to Toluca? For days, he'd reconciled himself to finding work, dreading the unavoidable. And here was a job, dropped into his lap, bizarre as it was. Screw it, he thought, just do it.

"Okay," he said.

Cheryl led him to an office with stacks of metal file cabinets and an old wooden desk in the corner. The walls were covered in B-movie posters and blow-ups of 1950s pulp fiction paperback covers with scantily clad women brandishing guns or whips. Seated behind the desk was a tiny Asian woman dressed in black, forty, maybe fifty, her gray-streaked hair pulled back into a bun. Through black cat's-eye glasses she studied a stack of papers propped on her knee.

"This is the guy," said Cheryl.

The woman lifted her gaze and examined Innes for a few seconds. "What's your name?"

Innes cleared his throat to answer but Cheryl jumped in. "I think we should call him Pasadena. Oh, by the way, this is Lee An. She runs the place."

"Pleasure," said Innes.

"That's the general idea," said Lee An. She looked at Cheryl. "Nice-looking man. Experienced?" She spoke to Cheryl as if he weren't there.

"Nope. But I think he's got potential."

"Well, Pasadena, welcome to Angels in Paradise," said Lee An, smiling for the first time. "Show me what you got."

After an awkward pause, Cheryl said, "She wants you to take your clothes off."

"Are you serious?" he said. A strong brew of humiliation and dread percolated.

Lee An smiled again. "This is adult video, Pasadena. We make movies about naked people. I need to see."

Innes sighed, and slowly peeled. When he was done, Lee An said, "Nice. Very nice."

He felt like an animal in a zoo, or an anatomy class specimen. "Can I get dressed now?" he said.

"If you want," said Lee An. "Better you stay naked so you get comfortable."

He compromised and pulled on his boxer shorts.

Lee An turned to Cheryl and said, "Make him take shower first."

"What am I supposed to do?" he asked Cheryl after his shower.

"Very simple. You play a college professor. One of your pretty young students comes to your office to plead for a passing grade. You can guess what happens next."

"We trade sex for a grade?"

"Bingo."

"Porn that 'doesn't degrade women'?" He made finger quotes.

"We usually have a twist ending, where the girl comes out on top, so to speak." She said it quickly and automatically, like a script she'd often used. "As soon as your co-star arrives, we'll go over the scene. You'll like her. Candy Barr's her name. She's cute."

"Candy Barr? And I thought my name was funny."

"So, anyway, Candy will go down on you. Then you do her on the desk."

"I see," he said. He pictured the scene in his mind. It was ludicrous. How would he manage to perform with all these women gawking at him?

Another vision popped into his head: the time he walked in on Caleb in his room watching porn on his laptop. His son, fifteen at the time, slammed shut the lid of the computer and yelled at his father to get out. Innes, startled by the sight of his son gaping at a screen full of asses and elbows, retreated in shame and shut the door. He never mentioned it, not to Caleb and certainly not to Annie. His own mother had caught him with *Hustler* magazine at about the same age, *in flagrante delicto*, and the shame of it burned in him still. A common rite of passage for adolescent boys, the lurid moment of lost innocence, but one he never acknowledged, not even with his own son. It occurred to him Caleb probably still watched porn. What if he saw his own father *in flagrante*? He was mortified by the mere thought of it.

"Will my face be on the screen?"

"Not if you don't want to. We can shoot it POV. The camera operator stands right behind you and shoots over your shoulder, so the whole thing is like from your eyes. Guys like that. They can pretend it's them while they jerk off."

"Too much information," Innes said. He tried to stay focused on the hundred bucks.

The kitchen door opened and in walked a young woman, about the same age as Syl. Her short spiky hair was bleached a brassy shade of blonde. She wore a black Che Guevara T-shirt, white Cal State Northridge gym shorts, and flip flops.

"Candy," said Cheryl, with forced enthusiasm. "Meet the professor. We call him Pasadena."

"Hey," Candy said. She moved to the refrigerator and put an insulated lunch bag inside, like a worker punching in for her shift.

Cheryl took Innes out to the garage to find suitable clothes for a college professor. They found him a pair of jeans, a beige polo shirt and a tweed sport coat with suede elbow patches. When they returned, the set was crowded with women setting up lights and diffusers and reflectors, arranging furniture. The room fairly hummed with metallic scraping and clinking. One held a big black video camera on her shoulder. Innes counted enough piercings and tattoos to fill an NBA locker room.

Candy walked in like she owned the place. "Let's do this. I've got a class at three." She still hadn't made eye contact with him.

Cheryl had Innes practice his lines with her. He was still wondering whether he should go through with it when Candy walked into the room and began talking. The lines came out of his mouth as if spoken by someone else. Before long his were pants off and a video camera peered over his shoulder, pointed down at Candy. She performed her part with practiced efficiency. It felt more like a medical procedure than a sex act, a visit to the urologist turned weird. There was nothing arousing about it. In fact, it was all quite ridiculous. Sex now seemed to him a primitive ritual of the animal kingdom. He felt like the subject of a wildlife documentary, as if Cheryl had been on the up-and-up after all, and this was a documentary of sorts. The thought made him giggle, to the annoyance of everyone on set. The absurdity of the situation didn't do wonders for his performance, either. They had to stop a couple of times and re-start. Candy exuded impatience and contempt, but gamely soldiered on, skillfully bringing him and his anatomy back into focus. After several false starts, Cheryl declared the scene acceptable.

"OK, everybody break for lunch," she announced.

Innes pulled up his pants, entered to the kitchen, and plopped on a broken-down couch. Candy came in a few moments later and extracted a bottle of Arrowhead water from the mini fridge. She was back in her flip-flops, gym shorts, and T-shirt. It was the first time he'd gotten a good look at her. He'd mostly seen the top of her head, studying her spiky blond do and inventorying her many ring and stud piercings—nose, tongue, nipples, up and down both ears. Under all the spikiness, piercings, tats, and blasé posture was a quick wit, an intelligence in her eyes that signaled everything was a joke and only she was in on it.

"I said, do you want one?" she said too loud as if he were hard of hearing.

He nodded and she tossed a plastic bottle across the room, which he fumbled and had to pick up off the floor.

"Nice catch, gramps," she said. She sat next to him on the sway-backed couch.

"Gramps?" he said. "I'm not that old."

"Whatever. You're old to me." She smiled at him. "Pasadena's not your real name, right? What should I call you?"

"Innes. Rhymes with Guinness, like the beer," he said.

She took another swig of water.

"I suppose Candy's not your real name?" he said.

"Ya think?" She leaned toward him and crossed her eyes.

"But Candy Barr? Seriously?"

"Don't knock it. It's a great *nom de porn*." She batted her eyelashes melodramatically.

They fell into an awkward silence, sipping their waters. She slapped her tongue stud against her front teeth, which made an irritating click.

"So, how'd I do?" he asked, and immediately regretted how needy he sounded.

"You did fine," she said and patted him condescendingly on the knee. "It's not exactly Shakespeare we're doing, amiright? Once you got over your nerves, you followed the script and you stayed hard. That's all that matters."

"That's all I gotta do, huh?"

"When a dude loses his hard-on, the whole production stops. So don't lose it. Guys have techniques. Take a pill if you have to." She took another swig of water. As if anticipating his next question, she said preemptively, "I'm not gonna do this forever, you know. I'm only doing it to pay for school. Ima be a writer. This is good money. And there's nothing wrong with it."

"How much money, if you don't mind me asking? Can't be much. I'm only getting a hundred."

"A lot more than that."

"That's not fair, is it?"

"Life's not fair. Look, this is how it works. Just about everybody who watches porn is a dude. And dudes want to see naked girls. So I'm the main attraction. You're just a prop."

Innes contemplated his lowly place in the porniverse. Candy took another swig of water and examined her nails, long and squared off at the tips, painted red and decorated with what looked like peace signs.

"You know, I'm a writer," he said, then checked himself. "Sort of. Was a writer--"

She cut him off. "You know, I don't want to know any of that stuff. The less I know about you the better. You're just a dick with an old man attached. Play your part, take your money, and go."

One of the crew showed up with a box of sandwiches. Innes grabbed a roast beef on wheat. Candy took her lunch bag outside. Innes was unwrapping his when Syl came in. She had covered up with a lavender floor-length strapless cotton dress. Still had the wings on and sported a silver Cleopatra-style wig. With both hands on the counter, she leaned over and emitted another thunderous belch, followed by a sustained flatulent backfire that would have delighted any nine-year-old boy.

"I feel like shit," Syl said to the cupboards.

"You should eat something," said Innes.

She turned quickly, as if just noticing him. "Scuse me," she said with a pained smile. "My stomach probably couldn't handle any solid food right now."

"You can try my sandwich if you want. I haven't touched it."

She walked over unsteadily and hovered. She emitted essence of armpit and flatulence. "What is it?" she asked.

"Roast beef on wheat."

"Oh, Jesus Christ," she said, and put her hand to her mouth. Too late. With another belch she projectile vomited all over him, soaking his lap and sandwich with a thick spray of pink liquid and chunks of what looked like partially digested tacos.

"Oh, Jesus," he concurred.

"Oh my God, I am so sorry," she said. She wiped her mouth with her hand. "Too many cosmos last night. And the taco truck was definitely a mistake." She belched again. Innes flinched. "Excuse me, I got to go puke some more," she said. "There's a shower in the bathroom where you can clean up."

The sandwich was a total loss. Innes hoped there was another one somewhere in the house. After he showered for a second time, he walked into Lee An's office with a towel around his waist. Cheryl and Lee An were conferring over the desk.

"I'm ready for my close-up," he said.

"Are you okay?" said Cheryl. "I'm so sorry. Syl is totally mortified, so embarrassed. We sent her home."

"We can send clothes out while we finish," said Lee An. "You won't need them for next scene anyway." The women barely concealed their amusement behind facades of helpful concern.

Candy came in and Lee An ushered them all back to the set. "You wear condom for this part," Lee An told him. "You not in STD database."

The afternoon went more smoothly than the morning, although it remained an out-of-body experience. He tried to keep his focus by studying the enormous, multicolored, Phoenix-rising-from-ashes tattoo that covered most of Candy's back. He performed his role more than adequately in the opinion of all present, except Candy, who left without saying a word when Cheryl called it a wrap.

"Is she pissed off at me?" Innes said.

"I don't think she likes you," said Cheryl. "But she's a pro. She compartmentalizes. We all do."

"So, when do I get paid?"

"Ah. Yes," Cheryl said. "I think we better go talk to Lee An."

Peering over the top of her glasses, Lee An explained they wanted to add another scene but would have to tape it tomorrow, as Candy had left for the day.

"So... can I get paid for today?" he asked.

"Sorry, we only pay after we wrap. You get paid tomorrow. Two-hundred, not one hundred."

"Okay. But why not half now and half tomorrow?" An extra hundred sounded good, but he wasn't sure he wanted to endure another day of humiliation for it.

"Policy. We burned before. We tape one day, then dude not show up next day."

"How about the documentary? Can I still be in that?"

"Maybe next week," she said, and reached for some scripts on her desk, dismissing him.

"I can spot you a few bucks till tomorrow," said Cheryl. "C'mon, I'll give you a lift back to Burbank."

In the car, Innes pressed Cheryl for more details on the porn business. "Don't the neighbors complain about that house? With all those young women coming and going?"

Cheryl snorted. "Umm, no. I'd guess about half the houses on the block are used to make pornos. This is the Valley, after all." She turned right onto Lankershim and aimed her Fiat south toward Toluca.

"Do you always use guys off the street like me? Don't you have professional porn actors?"

"We try to avoid them as much as possible," she said as she navigated the stop-and-go traffic. "We have enough problems with the girl divas. Anyway, it's cheaper."

"How much cheaper? I mean, how much money do you save by using me?"

"Not much. So, how did you like your first day as a porn star?" she said, deflecting his question.

"It was weird. I kind of felt like a meat sack."

"We're all meat sacks, Innes," she said.

He let that sink in, the cynical and undeniable truth. "Tell me straight, Cheryl. There's no documentary, right? You lied to get me to do porn."

She didn't answer right away, waiting until she rolled to a stop at the next light, then turned toward him and lowered her sunglasses. "Would you have said yes if I'd asked you to do porn yesterday at the bar?"

"I don't know. Probably not."

"Right. And after tomorrow, you'll be two-hundred dollars richer. So it's all good, see?"

Cheryl pulled over by the Caltrans depot and offered him a twenty-dollar bill, which he gladly accepted. "Pay me back tomorrow," she said. "I'll pick you up at Bob's again, around ten?"

Innes pulled open the gap in the chain link fence and slipped inside as Cheryl drove off. He looked around. No shopping cart. No sleeping bag. No George. He scanned the deserted depot under the roar of the traffic above and spotted a flash of red—the Target cart, pushed out of sight behind one of the massive pillars that held up the freeway overpass. Both sleeping bags still there, rolled up on the bottom rack. He pulled back the tarp and rifled through the bags and pillowcases. The knife, tools, duct tape, clothes, still there. Missing were the box of pastries, half of their food, and the cellphone. The cash stashed in the clock radio was reduced by half—only a hundred dollars left.

"Bastard," he said aloud to no one. "How did he know?"

When he'd left George to meet Cheryl in the morning, the old man was still snoring in his sleeping bag. He'd been especially ornery and argumentative the night before, but nothing out of the ordinary.

Innes tucked the five twenties in his sock along with the bill Cheryl had given him, unsure what to do next. Had George simply stepped away for a minute? Should he wait for him? Leaving the cart unguarded was careless and stupid. Everything Innes owned was in that cart, every last link to Annie and Caleb.

He was starving and needed to get a bite somewhere but didn't want to leave his things unguarded, so he grabbed the cart, pushed open the gap in the fence, and headed west on Riverside. Soon he passed the glass towers and movie studios of Burbank, where four-story-tall hanging banners of TV lady cops and sit-com families stared down on him with pity. At Bob's Big Boy he parked the cart in the rear behind a dumpster. When he returned with a turkey club sandwich in a brown bag and a couple of ice-cold water bottles, a scruffy Black man was pawing through his things, holding the tarp back like an opened refrigerator door. Innes was reminded of videos on the TV news of bears ransacking suburban garage freezers.

"That's mine, buddy," Innes said. He hoped he sounded the right note, firm, but not too provocative, unsure of the proper form of address among vagabonds. He remembered George's knife and wondered if he would need it.

The man looked up. He was short and fat. Early sixties. Ratty backpack, faded denim overalls, black Oakland Raiders hat, and rubber flip-flops. "Shouldna left it here, Susie," the man growled. "This my dumpster." He replaced the tarp and backed away. Then he lifted his right hand and pointed the hunting knife at Innes.

This is where I die, Innes thought. He saw an image of his filthy body fished out of a dumpster behind a diner, a knife protruding obscenely from his belly.

Then the man turned the knife around and offered the handle to Innes. A friendly gesture, but he was scowling, not smiling. "Keep this on your own damn self at all times," he said. "Never leave it where somebody else can get it. Damn fool. Don't you know nothin'?"

Hands shaking, Innes took the knife and stuffed it clumsily in his pants pocket. "Thanks," he said. "I'll remember that."

"You'd best," the man said. His tone became friendlier, the scowl eased into an almost smile. "Got sumpin' you can share, Susie?" he said, gazing hopefully at Innes's paper bag.

"The name's Innes." He wasn't sure how to respond to 'Susie.' "I got a turkey sandwich." He held up the sack. "Want half?"

"Fuck yeah, I'm starvin'. Was gonna see what's for supper in there," the man said, gesturing toward the big blue dumpster.

His name was Jefferson. Innes wasn't clear if it was his first name or last, but given his own preferred handle, he didn't inquire. They sat on the ground with their backs to the wall of the diner and shared the sandwich. Jefferson said he was in the Army in the last years of Vietnam but never shipped out and separated early with an unspecified medical discharge. "Been on the streets mostly ever since," he said. "I don't consider myself homeless. I prefer to say 'houseless.' I don't got a house, but I got a home—wherever I lay my head. People who are homeless don't belong anywhere. I belong everywhere."

Innes asked him if he'd ever had a job, a so-called normal life.

"Wasn't for me. I need my freedom. Going to work, buying stuff, paying bills, it's all a damn hamster wheel."

After a while Jefferson reached into the back pocket of his overalls and pulled out a pint of Old Crow. The bottle was nearly full. Innes felt a rush of anticipation and realized he hadn't tied one on since ... since ... Halloween. At least three weeks. Odd that he hadn't tried to drink away the pain, the way his father had done. Would have been so easy.

Jefferson handed the bottle to Innes, who hesitated, not sure he wanted to share a bottle with a vagabond.

"Go ahead, I ain't got cooties," the man said.

Screw it, thought Innes, the alcohol will kill any germs. He took a long slug. It burned, and he coughed like a rookie.

"Don't chug it all. Save me some," said Jefferson. He took back the pint and continued his monologue on the hard knock life. They passed the bottle until it was gone. Innes felt the familiar warm glow. Well lubricated, he shared his own story. When he got to the part about Caleb running away, Jefferson advised him to head for Hollywood. "That's where all the runaway kids end up. They got a whole community there—teens and young folks. They like to be together, I guess. For some of 'em, it's the best place for hustling."

"Hustling?"

"You know, selling sex."

Alarm bells clanged in Innes's head. He remembered what the Blair High guidance counselor had warned him about runaway teens, and he stood up, ready to proceed directly to Hollywood.

Jefferson thanked him for the sandwich; Innes thanked him for the booze. He pushed his cart toward the sidewalk, then paused. Should he go back to the Caltrans depot first and wait for George? And meet Cheryl in the morning? Two-hundred dollars awaited him—supposedly—in Lee An's office. What kind of sick shit did they have in store for him tomorrow? Would they really pay him, or just play him for a sucker? The whole thing smelled fishy the more he thought about it, like they recruited homeless guys to take advantage of the poor losers. His head was spinning. He struggled to think straight.

"Fuck 'em all," he said.

Book IV

DESPITE THE CITY'S BEST EFFORTS AT URBAN renewal, Hollywood Boulevard had lost none of its signature strangeness. In the chill of the November morning—a weekday, Innes surmised by the rush hour traffic—the sidewalks thronged with tourists and gawkers. The passersby, mostly young people smoking cigarettes and carrying beverages, ignored him, as if he were a street performer overshadowed by the edgier weirdness all around. Navigating his shopping cart through the crowds was an effort, but he managed, and was grateful for George's wisdom in cart selection and wondered where the hell the old man had wandered off to.

He made his way west, still limping and palms bloody from a fall he'd taken that morning on a steep hillside road in Beechwood Canyon during the long trek down from the Lake Hollywood Reservoir where he'd spent the night. He had slept on the cold concrete path atop the ancient Mulholland Dam, high above the surface of the reservoir, with a view through the scrawny eucalyptus trees of the towers of downtown Hollywood far below and the vast grid of lights of the LA Basin. The name Mulholland conjured the complicated history of Los Angeles, the water wars, and the movie *Chinatown*. He went to sleep with visions of Roman Polanski slicing Jack Nicholson's nostril with a stiletto. The back of his shirt was still damp from the large cup of soda flung at him from a passing white convertible BMW full of teenagers, one of whom had hollered, "Get a fucking job!"

He pushed past the phantasmagoria of Hollywood storefronts. New glass office buildings and loft apartment towers squeezed in among dingy, incongruously ornate storefronts from the 1920s with dive bars, tattoo parlors, costume shops, lingerie shops, wig shops, strip clubs, sex-toy boutiques, T-shirt kiosks, and countless tourist traps hawking Hollywood gewgaws. A whole street dedicated to fantasy and dress-up of a particularly sexual nature. The costume shops displayed fetish-wear outfits, most with fishnet stockings. The wig shop windows blared racks of wild hairdos in fluorescent colors. It was like year-round Halloween, Las Vegas style.

By the time he'd passed the Playmates sex shop, the Déjà Vu strip club, the Wax Museum, and Ripley's, he was creeped out—an odd reaction, he realized, for someone who had recently performed on a porn movie set in Van Nuys. Empty liquor bottles, beer cans, plastic soda bottles, and fast-food wrappers littered the sidewalks. Vagabonds staked out sections of sidewalk in front of doorways, belongings spread out before them like property boundaries. Most stared at him, an arriviste. He imagined they were gazing enviously at his state-of-the-art Target cart.

At the corner of Hollywood and Highland, he craned his neck to take in the side of an office tower covered by a vertical billboard with a kneeling naked woman viewed from behind, her long blonde hair covering most of her tanned back, her bare butt cheeks enormous, dominating the street below like an erotic totem. He was reminded of the gigantic video screens that adorned buildings in the movie *Blade Runner*, one of the film's futuristic visions that had actually come true thirty-three years later. No flying cars, though. No constant rain. Innes stared at the fifty-foot woman, unable to look away. He couldn't tell what it was advertising. A resort? A casino? Everywhere he looked, the female buttocks were fetishized with near-religious fervor, like those ancient goddess and fertility artifacts with exaggerated breasts and butts. Not only fetishized—commoditized. Special underwear and blue jeans were advertised on bus stop shelters and the backs of benches, promising to lift women's sagging cabooses into perky teenage wonders. He'd read some women even had butt implants installed, like custom automotive accessories. More than once, Annie had caught him ogling and never failed to lecture him about objectifying women. He averted his eyes from the billboard. Pasadena always struck him as a hip and happening place, but Hollywood Boulevard made him feel like a wide-eyed rube from Iowa.

He crossed Highland and fought his way through the throngs. Scattered among the crowds were young women, some alone, some in small clusters, in tiny miniskirts that barely covered their rears, skimpy halter tops, and knee-high black or white boots. They smoked cigarettes and looked bored while also seeking eye contact with passersby. A few glanced at Innes, then looked away. He was beneath the gaze even of streetwalkers. Stuck behind a crowd blocking the sidewalk, he attempted to hold eye contact with a hooker who stood atop the Walk of Fame Star of Erik Estrada, hoping to elicit a minimal level of acknowledgment. She held his gaze and smiled. After a few seconds, he realized he was staring into the dark brown eyes of a boy, a teenager, dressed as a girl. Innes experienced the same vertigo as when Terry fooled him at the Halloween party. He moved on, then stopped, turned back to the boy, and said, "If you were a teenage runaway in Hollywood, where would you go?"

The boy looked Asian or Latino. Filipino? He was dressed in a Hello Kitty outfit—short red-and-white polka-dot schoolgirl dress, red bows in his black bob, knee-high white socks, and black patent leather shoes. He smelled like strawberry soda. "Try the LGBT Youth Center," he said. "It's down Highland a few blocks."

"My son's not gay."

"Are you sure?" the boy said with a wry smile. "Then try Covenant House. It's on Western, by the freeway. Or Hollywood Homeless Youth Program, on Sunset."

Innes had more questions, but Hello Kitty waved at someone down the block and scurried away.

By midafternoon, a Pacific Ocean fog had descended upon Hollywood like a damp towel, dense and low as in San Francisco, not the typical LA haze that dimmed the sun and turned the sky milky white. Innes pushed his cart east along the boulevard through the rolling mist, unsure where to go next to find Caleb. He had lost track of time and was unsure how long he'd wandered the streets of Hollywood. Two days? Three? They all blended together, identical in their pointlessness, each alley or doorway sleeping berth the same as the last. Once, he'd pissed his pants when he couldn't find a place to go soon enough. He wondered how bad he stank now and thought of Willie and his Pig Pen cloud of reek. The only day he could pin to the fading calendar in his mind was yesterday, Thanksgiving, which he discerned only when he joined a line for free food at a homeless shelter and was served turkey, cranberry sauce, and mashed potatoes. When the cheerful young lady volunteer, waving a ladle like a cheerleader's baton, asked him what he was thankful for, he only stared at her.

His visits to the LGBT Youth Center and Hollywood Homeless Youth Services turned up nothing. The framed photo of Caleb at age twelve, they said, was next to useless, given Innes' description of the boy's appearance at age eighteen. At HHYS, they offered to make photocopies of the picture anyway and suggested he post them around Hollywood along with all the other flyers for missing teens. He took a dozen copies and a roll of tape, wrote the two cellphone numbers on the flyers, and taped them on walls and lampposts up and down the boulevard. After that, he was out of ideas. There was still Covenant House. Then what? This whole enterprise of searching for Caleb seemed like a fool's errand.

In front of a McDonald's, he spied a payphone and thought to call Vanessa to see if she had any news. Working pay phones were rare, but not unheard of. Upon closer inspection, this one was disgusting, like someone had puked on it. The ground beneath was dark and greasy and smelled like a bus station bathroom.

The call to Vanessa went into voicemail. Her recorded voice brought him a cheerful sorrow. She was the person he longed to talk to above all others. With Annie gone, Cal and George on the lam, and June—he'd had enough of June for a while—Vanessa in his mind had become a guardian angel, hovering somewhere nearby but out of sight, as if in a set of those wings from Angels in Paradise. He left her another message—leaving out certain parts—that the old man had gone missing and he hoped she had news of Cal. He hung up and stared at the payphone for a long while, and then made a second call.

As usual, June picked up right away. She said she was surprised to hear his voice from an unknown number. "What happened to the phone I got you?"

He filled her in on George's disappearance and cellphone heist. She probed him for details on his whereabouts of the last few days. He told her the truth, mostly, about the shopping cart and sleeping under the freeway and Bob's Big Boy and Jefferson and Lake Hollywood but omitted the side trip to Van Nuys.

"You think this Jefferson character has any clue where Caleb is?" June said. "Why did you leave Burbank?"

"Do I need to remind you?"

"I'm sorry about that, Innes. Couldn't be helped. But you could have come and stayed with me."

Weary of that conversation, he changed the subject and inquired about the rest of the Casa Grande gang. Vanessa. Tammy. Steven. Clif. Terry. As the days passed, he began to miss them terribly. He'd begun to fantasize a reunion, all of them starting a new life together somewhere clean, dry, and safe. June said Clif and his family had found an apartment in Altadena. Vanessa had gone AWOL. Tammy had also gone missing, and Steven had hit the road to find her. Innes listened in silence, his heart aching.

"Any mail for me?" he asked, hoping for news from the insurance company. He had arranged to have his mail forwarded to June. Nothing, she said, only junk.

There was a long pause before June spoke again. "There's no gentle way to say this, and if there was, I wouldn't know how. So I'll just say it. You have got to get on with your life. Annie is not coming back. Hear me? She's not coming back. And it's nobody's fault."

Innes stared at the greasy sidewalk, trying to control his anger. "I know damn well Annie's not coming back. What the hell kind of a thing is that to say? I am reminded of the fact every goddamn moment. My life now is about finding Cal."

"Speaking of Caleb," she said, "I have news."

"What? Why didn't you say so?"

"I wasn't sure how to tell you. That girl, Maria? She left me a voicemail. Said she talked to Paco, and he had a message for you—Caleb says stop looking for him. He's not coming back."

"Sounds like bullshit."

"Why would she lie?"

"I don't know, but I don't buy it."

"There's more," said June. "She said Caleb is leaving California, somewhere you'll never find him."

Innes contemplated this news and felt himself sink back into the abyss. Would Cal really disappear, go out of his life forever? Where would he go? The only place imaginable was Tempe, Arizona, home of Annie's Aunt Sylvia, a bilious old woman who in her brief encounters with Innes barely concealed her loathing for him and her brother-in-law George. After Annie's mother died, ten years back, long after divorcing her gadabout husband, Sylvia had tried to convince Annie to ditch her "loser" husband and father and come with Caleb to live with her in Arizona. When Annie declined, her aunt cut off all contact, except for her reliably punctual birthday cards and cash for Caleb. She hadn't bothered to come to Pasadena for Annie's memorial, claiming she was too ill to travel. Would Caleb go to the miserable old bat?

"I'm not giving up," Innes said. He looked down at his grimy Topsiders, pristine compared to the filth beneath them. "I refuse to believe he never wants to see me again."

"Let it go," said June. "Caleb is eighteen years old, an adult, old enough to get a job. He can fend for himself. And your father-in-law—he's lived on his own for years. It's what he wants. Leave him be." Her voice descended into a feline growl. "Come home with me, baby. Let me take care of you. It's cold and wet out there. It's warm and dry at my place. We can search for Caleb together."

Innes considered her offer, then remembered she would expect something in return, possibly his very soul.

She broke a long silence. "Someday you'll appreciate me and all I do for you. Meantime, at least let me help you today. How about I come to Hollywood and meet you? I can bring you another phone and lend you some money."

"I don't need your money, June," he lied.

"I can't stand the thought of you begging in the streets."

"I am not begging in the streets."

"What will you do for money? For food?"

"I don't know yet," he said. For a moment he regretted that he'd walked out on two-hundred bucks at Lee An's. His wad was down to about sixty dollars. "I'll think of something."

"You should try day labor," she said. "You know, where guys stand around in a parking lot until somebody offers an odd job? In fact, there might be one across the street from the Pantages. I was there last month to see *Annie*. Oh ... Sorry. I mean the musical." He pretended he didn't hear. "Anyway, you know where that is?" she said.

The Pantages Theater was a few blocks down the boulevard. Innes said he'd think about it and promised to check in with her in a day or two. He left his cart by the side door of the McDonald's and slipped inside to wash his hands. The bathrooms had security-coded locks and signs that said customers only. No bums allowed.

He resumed his trek along the boulevard until the vertical 1930 marquee of the Pantages came into view, looming in the mist as if in a film noir. Adding to the mood was the art-deco and neon façade of the Frolic Room, untouched since the 1940s. Across the street was a parking lot, fenced off with chain link, marked for a future construction site. Inside a group of men was clustered at the corner. Innes crossed at the light and entered the lot through a driveway opening. The men eyed him and his cart and muttered among themselves in Spanish. Innes nodded, friendly-like, but stood off to the side to see how this day labor thing worked. Four o'clock now. It would be dark soon. He wondered who would hire laborers at this hour. Were these guys selling their labor, or something else?

A vehicle pulled into the lot and drove around the perimeter, as if looking for something. It blended into the mist, only its headlights visible from the far end. Around again it came and slowly rolled toward the clutch of young men and stopped. A big silver SUV. The driver lowered the window. A woman's voice said "*¿Ingles? ¿Ingles?*" They mumbled and shook their heads. The SUV moved toward Innes and stopped alongside his cart. The driver's door opened and out stepped a tall, dark-haired woman, dressed in black designer clothes and dripping with gold jewelry.

"*¿Ingles?*" she said. "You speak English?"

"Yes, ma'am," he said, embarrassed how deferential he sounded.

"Do you want to work? I've got a job for you."

"Yes, ma'am," he repeated, unable to think of anything else to say.

She walked around the SUV to get a better look at him, like a shopper perusing the deli case. "You look fit," she said smiling, a hint of approval in her voice. "I need some heavy pieces of lumber moved. I'll pay you fifty bucks."

"I can do that."

"Great, hop in," she said and opened the passenger door.

Innes hesitated and looked at his cart. "There's this. I don't want to leave it here."

"I take it you're homeless?"

"Yes, ma'am." He was shrinking with each word.

She considered that for a moment. "Alright. I think it will fit in the back. Come on around." She opened the hatch. A Mercedes G550, one of those tall boxy SUVs with a spare tire mounted on the back. A hundred-thousand dollars' worth of sheet metal, at least. The California license plate said QUEENSH. She helped him empty the cart and load his things, and they hoisted the cart inside.

"Thank you, ma'am," he said after sliding into the gray leather passenger seat, unable to stop calling her ma'am even though she was clearly younger than he.

"Please, call me Sherri," she said as she pulled out of the lot onto the boulevard.

He glanced at her, trying not to be too obvious. She looked about the same age as Cheryl, mid-to-late thirties. Long black hair pulled into a loose ponytail and tied with an Hermes scarf. Cascading layers of gold dangled around her neck and clinked on her wrists as she turned the wheel. She looked familiar. He cleared his throat and managed to say something other than yes ma'am. "Are you on TV or something?"

"No," she said. "But I get that a lot."

"You look like someone. Aren't you … what's her name? The one with the reality show?"

"God, no. Don't even say her name. I despise that woman. People say I look like her and it makes me ill."

He dropped it. "Where are we going?"

"Beverly. It's just a few minutes. So, what's your name?"

"I go by Innes. Rhymes with Guinness, like the beer."

Interview over, she turned the radio on. NPR, All Things Considered. She maneuvered over to Sunset Boulevard and soon they were in Beverly Hills, indicated by the sharp shift from the crowded streets of West Hollywood to the wide boulevards and tall hedges hiding gated compounds. They passed the Beverly Hills Hotel and went right on Benedict Canyon Drive. Sherri turned right again into a tangle of curved streets, then left, then right, then right again, not slowing around the bends, tires squealing, the top-heavy SUV leaning dangerously in a dizzying piece of Grand Prix driving as if to disorient him so he wouldn't remember the way should he ever try to return. She slowed as they came to a high wall covered in the tiny green leaves of climbing fig vines. Sherri tapped a remote unit on the visor, a black steel gate slid open, and they drove through.

Innes glimpsed a metal panel with a phone receiver and a keypad near the gate and a security camera atop the wall. "Like a fortress," he said.

"I have an art collection," she said. "Can't be too careful. This is LA, after all."

The cobblestone driveway ended at a circular drive that wrapped around a small fountain to an imposing front doorway between manicured Cypress trees. French chateau? Tuscan villa? Something vaguely Mediterranean. She pulled around the left side of the manse and into an empty bay of a five-car garage in back. A high wall encircled the grounds. Sherri climbed out of the Mercedes and led Innes through a back door into an alley. Against the wall was a pair of pallets that supported a stack of eight-foot-long two-by-fours.

"This is it," she said. "I need you to carry these boards into the garage and stack them neatly on the floor. The contractor left them here this morning with nothing to cover them. It's supposed to rain tonight, and I don't want this wood to get wet."

"Don't you have a tarp?" he said. He needed the fifty bucks but wasn't keen on this much heavy lifting.

"I don't want to leave these out in the alley where someone can steal them. I want them locked in my garage."

"You don't have anyone here who can help with this?" he asked. He sized up the stack, estimating the total weight. Half a ton at least.

"I have a gardener, but he's not back till next week. I have a cook, she's on vacation back home in Thailand. My house cleaner comes every other week, but she wouldn't be much help here. So, are you up for this, or not? It will be dark soon, and you might want to get to it before the rain comes."

He nodded. She left him alone in the alley with the wood pile. The individual two-by-fours weren't heavy, about ten pounds each, but there were at least a hundred of them, and after an hour and a half of hauling and stacking, Innes was sweaty, hands raw and sore. Sherri came to check on him as he placed the last piece.

"Fabulous. Thank you so much," she said. "Come inside and I'll get you some cash."

The kitchen was the size of Innes and Annie's living room and dining area combined and gleamed with black commercial-grade appliances and granite counters. Stained cabinets, probably maple. Dark red tile floor. A Bose radio on the counter tuned to the same station she had on in the car.

"Do you need me to drop you off in Hollywood?" Sherri said. She paused while reaching for her purse and looked him over. "Are you alright? You look pale."

"I ... I need to sit down for a minute. Is that okay?"

"Of course." She pointed to a row of barstools lined up at a counter. "Let me get you a glass of water."

The radio emitted a report on the controversy over an *avant-garde* public art installation in Santa Monica. Innes was familiar with it; he'd written an article about it for the LA Weekly. It was a twelve-foot tall pink metallic sculpture meant to look like giant balloon art of something obviously phallic.

"That's thing's a monstrosity," he said after a long swallow of cold water. "I still can't believe they approved it."

"I know, right?" she said with a derisive cackle. "Whenever I drive by, I want to put a giant condom on it."

"The two red balls at the base are a particularly graphic touch."

She smiled at him for a moment, as if seeing him for the first time. They chatted for several more minutes and mocked the pretensions of the art world. He wondered if she'd forgotten about the fifty bucks she owed him.

"Know what?" she said. "Instead of letting you go like this, how about I make you dinner first?"

Absolutely, he thought. "You don't have to do that," he said.

"I know, but I want to. I could use the company. I can drop you off later, if that's okay?"

He didn't need much persuading.

"Would you mind cleaning up first?" she said. "No offense, but you're kind of grubby. There's a bathroom with a shower through there."

A shower sounded good. A shave, too. He hadn't got cleaned up since Sylvan puked on him, and he was rather ripe. When he emerged from the shower, his clothes were gone, a fresh set on the toilet lid. They looked expensive. Black gabardine pleated trousers and a dark gray golf shirt with a circular country club logo on the right breast, black slippers. They fit well enough, the pants snug, the slippers too large.

It was all a bit weird. He thought of Cheryl and wondered if this woman also had some perverse proposition up her sleeve, but decided to roll with it. Fifty bucks and a free meal. Maybe more.

In the kitchen, Sherri pulled dinner plates from a cabinet. She whistled. "Look at you. You clean up real nice." She set a table in a dining room dominated by heavy cream-colored draperies and a crystal chandelier: white tablecloth, lit candles, a bottle of red wine, and two goblets. The dinner was excellent, a Mediterranean baked chicken dish with dates and couscous, his first decent meal since ... before the fire. They killed the whole bottle of Tempranillo, and she uncorked another. Tongues loosened, they swapped stories.

Sherri's full name was Scheherazade Rafsanjani. She came to America from Iran as a child, married at eighteen to a restaurateur twelve years her senior named Ronnie Rafsanjani, also Iranian, who she said was killed by a hit-and-run driver in 2010 while he walked across Sunset Boulevard at night. No kids.

"It was basically an arranged marriage," she said. "My parents never got out of Iran—they're both dead—so I was raised here by relatives. They couldn't wait to marry me off. When I met Ronnie, he had two restaurants—Olive & Fig—in downtown and Beverly Hills. Ten years later, we owned twelve. Restaurants, bars, clubs. We were about to get into the hotel business when he died."

"What happened?"

"Nobody knows. His body was found crushed in the middle of the road, run over. It was late, after midnight, and no one saw it. I still don't know for sure why he was out so late, but I have some ideas. He'd been cheating on me for years."

Innes took another sip of wine and processed her story. "Are these his clothes I'm wearing?"

"Does that bother you?" she asked. "They're basically brand new. There's a closet full of his stuff I never got around to donating."

He wasn't sure how he felt about that. "I noticed your license plate said Queen S-H. Is that you?"

"Queen Sherri. Ronnie's nickname for me. Not necessarily a term of endearment. But I owned it."

After dinner, she led him to a couch in the living room and placed a third bottle of wine—an Oregon Pinot Noir—on the mahogany coffee table. The room was more sumptuous than the dining room. Tall windows covered with heavy draperies and crescent valances, framed oil paintings hung and illuminated as in a museum, vases and urns on display tables. The collection was incoherent for Innes's taste, Modern mixed in with Classical, neo-Classical, Renaissance, and pre-Raphaelite, as if curated by someone with more money than discrimination.

Soon came the sound of drops pelting the windows, and the taps became a thrash of wind-driven rain. After some prompting from Sherri, Innes launched into his tale of unspeakable sorrow, the whole saga of him and Annie and Caleb and George. He even told her about Angels in Paradise—his inhibitions melted away after the second bottle of wine—a tale Sherri found fascinating and hilarious.

When he was done, she reached for his hand and said, "I've got another job for you, tomorrow, if you want to earn another fifty bucks. Anyway, I'm too drunk to drive you back. Stay." She leaned into him and rested her head on his shoulder. Her hair smelled like jasmine.

The morning sun streamed through a narrow gap in the curtains, painting a stripe across the Persian rugs and shiny taupe sheets. They lay in her bed in each other's arms. Sherri's head rested on his chest. She played with the hairs on one of his nipples, twisting them around her long nails. Innes, still damp with sweat, stared at the ceiling. For the third night in a row, they had barely slept. They had scarcely left the bedroom, except for more wine, coffee, and occasional meals.

Innes wasn't sure how or why he had transitioned from live-in handyman to live-in lover. It happened slowly at first, then suddenly. One day he'd been perched precariously on a painter's ladder scooping clumps of wet leaves from her second-story gutters, and the next he was hauling heavy boxes full of old clothes, magazines, and newspapers up from the basement and into the garage. Two days became three, then four. She had promised him fifty dollars a day to stay in one of her guest rooms and work as long as he liked—or until her checklist of deferred household chores ran out. If he stayed a week, he could leave with at least three hundred dollars, more than enough to make up for what he'd foregone at Lee An's, enough to get a foothold on the long climb out of despair. Get a cheap used bicycle and a backpack for his things. Move up in class from a shopping-cart-pushing vagabond. Get a job, even if minimum wage. He'd cleaned himself up at Sherri's and might be presentable enough. Much as it pained him to admit it, June had tossed him a lifeline with the day labor idea.

Sherri had joined him in some of his tasks and they eased into a cozy camaraderie. Their bodies bumped and rubbed as they sweated and groaned through heavy lifting chores, moving furniture and art in pointless circuits around the house. Over time she drew him out of his self-pitying shell and built a growing sense of intimacy. After one evening of wine-binging, he woke in the morning next to her in her bed, hungover but with images of an all-night bacchanalia still fresh in his mind. A Rubicon had been crossed. The passage had pushed the last weeks out of his mind and filled it instead with the feel of Sherri's skin, the taste of her mouth, the smell of her hair, the sound of her voice. It was not antiseptic porn sex, as with Candy; it was something the likes of which Innes had not experienced since he and Annie were young, before their sex life had settled into a comfortable routine, with decreasing frequency. He felt twenty-five again.

They had hours-long conversations about art and culture and politics and history. She was well read, a wealthy woman of leisure with the time and means to improve her mind. She described herself as "feminist-agnostic-libertarian," with a live-and-let-live attitude, a distrust of ideologies and authorities—especially patriarchal ones— and a businesswoman's resentment of government and taxes. When he asked if she had any qualms about inviting a stranger into her house, she said she kept a loaded gun handy and knew how to use it.

As Sherri played with his chest hairs, Innes glanced over at one of the enormous wall hangings in her bedroom. "Tell me about your tapestries," he said. He pointed to one that depicted a man in a warrior's tunic, a plumed helmet on his head, and a blue cape streaming behind, looking off in the distance. A woman with two infants on her lap sat beneath him on a low bench, beseeching him with an arm outstretched.

"That's Jason and Medea," said Sherri, without looking up.

"Medea was that crazy lady from Greek tragedy, right? What goes on there?"

"Jason is telling Medea he's dumping her for a younger woman, even though Medea saved his life and bore him two sons," said Sherri, turning to face him. "That would make any woman crazy, don't you think?"

"How'd that work out?" he asked.

"Let's just say he came to regret his decision," she said and lowered her head back to his chest.

"Okay, now that one," said Innes. He pointed to another tapestry based on a neo-Classical painting. A naked man emerged from some bushes, holding a branch to cover his genitals, looking humbled. A young woman in a long gown of royal blue, bare shoulders, looked down at him skeptically.

"You must know this one, being named Homer and all," said Sherri. "Odysseus and Nausicaä."

"Odysseus, of course. But Nausica...who?"

"Naw-SICK-ah-ah," she pronounced slowly.

"Naw-SICK-ah-ah," he repeated. "What's this one about?"

"Odysseus washed up on the shore of her island, naked and alone. She took him in, clothed him, and brought him to the palace to meet her parents, the king and queen. They treated him like a prince. She fell in love with him. They wanted him to stay."

"Let me guess. He didn't."

"Exactamente. Ran off like a cad."

"I think I see a pattern here," said Innes. He looked at Sherri and smiled. She lifted her head to meet his gaze. She wasn't smiling.

"You catch on quick," she said.

"Did he also regret his decision?"

"No, the bastard got away with it. They gave him a ship to sail home to Ithaca."

"Wait, was she one of the Phaeacians?" said Innes. "I know that story."

He considered telling her about his one piece of published fiction, written while still in college, in an obscure online journal that specialized in literary fan fic. He had submitted a short story called "Phaeacians," pitched as the "missing chapter" from James Joyce's novel *Ulysses*. In it he imagined the adulterous tryst between Molly Bloom and Blazes Boylan, supposedly consummated while Leopold Bloom made his rounds through Dublin. The act itself is only indirectly depicted by Joyce, but it hangs over Bloom throughout the novel like a storm cloud. Innes had always thought it a glaring omission. In his version, the tryst came out quite unlike Bloom's fevered fantasy about his cuckolding or Molly's gauzy reminiscence: Boylan couldn't perform, which elicited a pages-long torrent of stream-of-consciousness invective from Molly. It ended with an enraged and humiliated Boylan giving her a spanking. Innes wrote the whole thing in dactylic hexameter. ("YOU'RE no man, YOU'RE just like MY old man, GELded man, UNpleasing Boylan.") It sounded like bad hip-hop when recited aloud. Annie, his college sweetheart at the time, said it was weird, but she was proud of him when it was published. Truth was, he'd written it only to impress his mother. She died before he heard from her. So often in his dreams he imagined that reading it was what killed her—it was so godawfully pretentious that her head exploded. He never wrote another piece of fiction.

He decided not to bring it up.

"I get the picture," he said. "Men who ran off like shitheels. Are you trying to tell me something?"

"They're a reminder to myself what cads you all are."

"Lovely," said Innes. "Me too?"

"I hope not," she said, and leaned over and kissed him. "Better not."

"You know," he said as he looked over at Odysseus and Nausicaä, "as I recall, Odysseus spent most of *The Odyssey* trying to escape from possessive females. Like Calypso, right? And who was the other one? Circo? Circus?"

"Circe," said Sherry, correcting him. "SIR-see."

"So," said Innes, "apparently, I am Odysseus, brought in from the cruel sea. Who are you—Calypso or Circe?"

"Be careful what you wish for," she said with an enigmatic smile.

"Both had magical powers. Calypso held Odysseus prisoner for seven years, her love slave. Circe turned most of his crew into pigs."

"Are you saying you would turn me into a pig?"

"Wouldn't be much of a stretch," she said. "Men act like pigs. That was the point of the Circe story."

"And would you keep me prisoner for seven years, like Calypso?" he said.

"You're not a prisoner, baby. You can leave anytime. But I'll make you want to stay. Seven years. Even longer."

She rolled on top of him and positioned herself to demonstrate how.

They went on like that for days. Eat. Talk. Screw. Sleep. Repeat. Between cycles of seduction and release, Innes was haunted by guilt. His wife gone less than a month, his son and his father-in-law roaming the streets. But what if Annie *had* been cheating on him? Didn't he deserve his own dalliance? And maybe June was right: The old man was happier left alone, and Caleb was old enough to make his own way. He pushed thoughts of them aside, for a while at least, convincing himself he deserved a break, he had it coming. The events of the last weeks—the horrific loss of his wife and home, his abandonment by the only family he had left, his rapid spiral into poverty and homelessness—hardened his conviction that the world was Hobbesian in its randomness and cruelty. Every man for himself and God against all, indeed.

In their three weeks together, not once did Innes and Sherri depart her walled compound. As the household chore list dwindled to occasional maintenance, it was clear to Innes he'd been given a new chore list. She owed him about a thousand dollars now. Enough to start fresh? How much was enough? A thousand? Two thousand? And what exactly was he being paid for now? He knew the answer but preferred not to dwell on it. It wasn't just an adventure, he told himself, it was a job.

One evening, in bed, Innes's thoughts turned to Caleb, as they had so often over the last weeks. He tried to picture where his son was and what he was doing and whether he would ever see him again. Sherri at first had been sympathetic and assured him they would be reunited one day. She would help find him. But she gradually began to take Caleb's side and suggested it was time for Innes to let an eigh-teen-year-old young man find his own way.

"You're thinking about him again, aren't you," she said, scooch-ing over and putting her arm around him. "I can tell when you go to that dark place."

"I still can't accept that he doesn't want to see me."

"He'll see you when he's ready," she said. "He'll come find you. Chasing after him when he's asked you not to will only drive him farther away, don't you see?"

He saw her point. Still, he felt the eyes of Annie on him, under that arched brow of hers. One day, Annie, he told her. One day. I promise.

In time, Innes turned restless—a prisoner of luxury—and suggest-ed they go out for dinner somewhere. Sherri accused him of whin-ing—"like a bitch."

"Why don't you ever want to go out?" he persisted.

"Because I don't have any friends in this town. They all hate me, and the feeling is mutual. They say horrible things about me, and Ronnie, and our business. It's envy, is what it is." She sat up in the bed and touched his arm, her voice softer. "Anyway, why would you want to go out, baby? I've got everything you need right here. All the food and conversation you want. All the wine you can drink. And all the sex you can handle. What more do you want?"

"I know, but it would be nice to get out sometime. A restaurant? A movie?"

"Not interested," she said icily. "I don't want those Beverly Hills bitches anywhere near you. They see a good-looking man on another woman's arm, they start their little games."

"Seriously?"

"You have no idea what goes on between women when it comes to competition for men and sex," she said. "Especially rich, bored women. That Real Housewives shit is no lie."

Innes processed that piece of insight into the female world, and for some reason thought of June.

Then Sherri said, with a sly smile, "Alright. I have an idea. We can go out. Tonight even. But under one condition. You have to be in disguise. I'm keeping you to myself. My little secret."

"Disguise? Like what, Groucho glasses? A fake nose?"

"No, a dress."

"A dress? Like, in drag?"

"Exactly," she said.

Innes pictured Terry Delacroix strutting around the Casa Grande like Joan Crawford. It looked like fun when he thought about it—a thought he found alarming. "Don't be absurd," he said. "I would look ridiculous. No one would be fooled."

"Wanna bet? I've got a walk-in closet full of dresses that would fit you. We're about the same height. Shoes too. And wigs. I can make you up real pretty. No one would know." She pinched his cheek and smiled seductively.

His intriguing vision of Terry was replaced by a rapid slideshow of Jack Lemmon and Tony Curtis in *Some Like It Hot*, Robin Williams in *Mrs. Doubtfire*, and John Travolta in *Hairspray*. Ridiculous-looking clowns, all.

"No way. I won't do it."

"That's the only way you're going out with me tonight." She lay back on her pillow and picked up a book, as if to end to the discussion.

"So, this is a command performance?" he said.

"They're all command performances, baby." The seductive smile was gone.

He was beginning to see why Ronnie called her Queen Sherri. "What's with you?" he said. "You boss me around like I'm your slave."

"Baby, you can leave anytime," she said. She climbed out of bed and stood with her arms crossed over her chest. "Pack up your shopping cart and go back out to the boulevard and panhandle. But I know you won't. You love me and you love this cushy life."

The L word again. The second time she'd invoked it. It was as if she repeated it often enough, it would be true. He ignored it again.

"So anyway, how about it?" she said. "You know you're dying to try it—go out in drag. I can see it in your eyes. They went all wide when I said it."

She had him there.

Sherri pulled the Mercedes up to a valet parking stand on Ventura Boulevard in front of a bar called The Proud Mary. It was raining again and the mist spray painted its shine on the cracked, faded asphalt. Innes sat frozen in the passenger seat, clutching a black purse, and stared at his feet in the beige pumps, his knees in black opaque hose sticking out of his beige dress hem. A short black cashmere cardigan sweater covered the dress's bare shoulders and felt warm and comforting on his skin. Thick auburn locks fell across his face, something to hide behind.

Sherri came around and opened the door. "Are you coming, honey?" She extended her hand. "Let me help you." He struggled to stand up in the heels while keeping his knees together, as Sherri had shown him, and stumbled, rolling an ankle. The valet attendant grabbed his other hand and steadied him. Sherri laughed and said, "She's not drunk, she's just new at this."

"Yes, ma'am, I can see that," the valet said grinning. He jumped into the Mercedes and drove off. No escape now. Sherri grabbed his arm and guided him inside. Walking in heels felt precarious, but he was getting the hang of it.

"Where the hell *are* we?" he asked.

"The best drag bar in LA. You'll love it."

"A drag bar? No way."

"Don't be a baby. The place will be full of men in drag. You'll be invisible."

Once inside, Innes felt inconspicuous, as Sherri had promised. The place was dark and loud and packed shoulder to shoulder with sweaty men and various versions of womanhood. They inched their way close to the stage and watched a drag performer named Rockola, dressed as a 1970s rock diva, belt out a version of "Hit Me with Your Best Shot."

Innes had to pee. He pictured himself in the men's room, in a dress and heels, surrounded by dudes. No fucking way. They went to the ladies' room together. Innes locked himself in a stall and stood facing the toilet for a moment, not sure how to proceed. How to pee in a dress without making a mess?

"Hike your dress up, pull your pants and hose down, and sit. It's not rocket science," Sherri called from her post at the sink, as if reading his mind. A chorus of feminine giggles rang out from the adjacent stalls. He sat, but couldn't pee, and waited to exit the stall until the women had left.

"These Spanx are crushing my balls," he complained as he tugged at his underwear and examined his painted face in the mirror.

"That's the idea," she said.

Sherri ordered them drinks at the bar then left him alone with his pink cosmopolitan. Within minutes, a broad-shouldered man in a dark gray suit, about the same age as Innes, planted himself on a barstool and ordered a single-malt scotch, rocks. His head was huge, like a bowling ball, hair silver, face ruddy from too much sun or too much scotch or both. After a couple sips of his drink he turned to Innes and said, "So, are you on next?" He nodded toward the stage.

"God, no," said Innes. "I'm only here to watch." He took another pull on his cosmo.

"Pity. You'd kno-o-ock 'em dead," he slurred. The scotch was obviously not his first drink of the evening. Innes said nothing. He stared at the ridiculous pink liquor in his glass.

"I'm Dave," the man said, and stuck out his hand.

"Ynez," he said, extending his hand and volunteering the *nom de drag* Sherri had bestowed on him.

Dave vice-gripped him and held on. "You look spectac ... acular," he said. "How come I never seen you here before?" Innes pulled his hand back. Dave released him and casually put his hand on Innes's lower back.

"Knock it off. I'm not interested," said Innes. He reached back and pulled the man's hand off him.

"Oh c'mon, don't be coy. You're sittin' here alone, with a drink, wearin' a dress, in a gay bar. What am I s'posed to think?"

"I'm not alone. See this other drink? My girlfriend will be back in a minute." He scanned the room and wondered where she had gone.

Dave leaned in close and whispered in his ear, "My car is parked on a side street downa block. Why dontcha come back there and blow me."

"Fuck off, asshole," said Innes. He snatched his purse, slid off the stool, and stalked away, looking for Sherri. He spotted an open door at the back of the bar and stepped outside. It was raining steadily now. A cluster of men and women stood under umbrellas smoking cigarettes. No sign of Sherri. Innes turned to go back inside, but there, blocking the doorway, was Dave.

"C'mon in outta the rain. I'll buy you 'nother drink. The bartender took yers away," he said, steadying himself against the door jamb.

"I said fuck off," said Innes, raising his voice. The smokers stopped talking and turned toward him.

Dave stepped outside and grabbed Innes's hand. "I was jus' kiddin' what I said."

Innes jerked his hand away and looked around for a bouncer. A bar stool propped open the door, but no one was on it. The smokers looked away and wandered farther into the parking lot. Dave reached out and grabbed the neckline of his dress. Innes shoved him away. The dress tore. Dave stumbled backward, recovered, and threw a sloppy drunken punch that hit Innes square in the mouth. He reeled, stepped off the patio curb, and fell backward into a puddle. The hard landing and the shock of cold water on his back made him piss his pants. He tasted blood in his mouth. The punch had landed on the same spot where Caleb had hit him weeks ago. He scrambled to his feet. One of the heels on his pumps had snapped off, and he wobbled toward Dave in a blind fury and unloaded a haymaker on Dave's jaw with the pent-up force of weeks of pain, rage, and humiliation. The big man went down like a sack of cement. The smokers whooped and cheered.

Innes grasped his fist in his other hand and dropped to his knees. It felt like his knuckles were broken. "Thanks for the help," he called to the smokers. They turned away and sucked on their cigarettes, the little orange dots glowing in the night like fireflies.

An enormous bald bouncer emerged from the door. Dave had pulled himself up, holding his jaw, and pointed at Innes. "That crazy bitch attacked me. I got witnesses. I'm gonna press charges."

"He hit her first," one of the women smokers called from the parking lot.

As the bouncer stooped to help Innes to his feet, Sherri appeared in the doorway. "Oh my God, baby, what happened?" she said, bending over him.

"Asshole here knocked her down," said the bouncer as he nodded toward Dave.

"Sherri?" said Dave, looking stunned. "Is she with you?"

"Yes, idiot. She's with me."

"Oh shit. Sorry, Sherri. I did'n know."

"You better get out of here," the bouncer said. Dave slinked back into the bar, rubbing his jaw. "You're banned, asshole," the bouncer yelled at his back.

"God, look at you," Sherri said to Innes as he stood. "Look at my dress. Your mouth is bleeding."

He wiped his mouth and glanced at the blood on his hand. "You know that creep?" he said.

"Rudy? Unfortunately, yes. I thought he was banned. He's a sexual predator, has a thing for transvestites."

"Rudy? He told me his name was Dave."

They were silent in the car all the way back over the hills. Innes marinated in his urine-soaked undies and an acid broth of anger and embarrassment, massaging his right hand. Sherri's only comment was, "You smell like pee. Did you wet yourself or something?"

When they got home, Innes went straight upstairs, through the bedroom into Sherri's dressing room, chucked the broken-heel pumps into the corner, peeled off the damp underwear and pantyhose, sat on the stool at the vanity table, and stared at himself in the mirror. The dress was ripped at the neckline, wet and splattered with grime and a few drops of blood. The wig was askew on his head, chestnut tresses falling into his face. He yanked it off and tossed it on the table. At the start of the evening he thought he looked pretty good, not bad, can't complain. Now he looked ridiculous, like a circus clown, lipstick smeared, lower lip cut and swollen, mascara and eyeshadow smudged. He reached for a towel and rubbed off the mask, quite sure, much to his relief, that he was not cut out for crossdressing. Fun to do once, as a lark, but way too much work. He reassessed his opinion of Terry, who obviously put in serious effort every evening to look absolutely fabulous. It was clear now why Terry never went out in public in drag, instead stayed within the safe confines of the Casa Grande. He put down the towel and looked at himself again. An abused Barbie doll. If Caleb could see him now, he'd never get him back.

He heard Sherri's footsteps in the bedroom. "So, I take it you owned The Proud Mary?" he called out.

"Not only did I own it, I created it," she said from the bedroom. "It was a dreary gay bar ten years ago, before I turned it into the number one venue in LA for drag performers."

"Why do you get off on men in drag?" he said.

He turned to see her in the doorway, leaning casually against the frame, regarding him with patient amusement. "All women love drag," she said. "We like to see men try to be us. Sometimes it's funny. Sometimes it's sweet. But it's always fun. Gender is socially constructed, after all. It's a performance. Drag has satirized that for centuries."

Innes continued to stare at his performance in the vanity mirror. "Fun, huh? Except when you get hit on by creeps."

"Sucks, doesn't it?" she said. "Women have to put up with that shit all the time. Anyway, feminizing tends to have a civilizing effect on men. Walking a mile in our shoes—literally—makes them more empathetic toward women."

"Like *Tootsie*," he said. He hoped he looked better in drag than Dustin Hoffman.

"Exactly. Like *Tootsie*. It tells me something about a man if he's willing to put on a dress and heels to see the world from my perspective."

Innes felt like he'd taken a mid-term exam. Did he pass? "Help me out of this dress," he said.

Sherri unzipped him and pulled off the ruined dress and gazed at him for several seconds. "Come to bed now," she said. "Tonight was quite a turn on. For me at least."

In bed, Sherri was ravenous, even by her sybaritic standards. Innes lay there exhausted, staring at the ceiling, while Sherri read a

Simone de Beauvoir book and hummed some opera aria to herself. His mind wandered to a question he'd meant to ask but was reluctant to bring up. He wondered about her Guatemalan house cleaner Juanita, her status and relationship with Sherri.

"Is Juanita illegal?" he said.

"Illegal? Why do you care?" She put her book down.

"How about your gardener? Your cook?" He hadn't really met them but had caught glimpses and heard them occasionally going about their business. Sherri kept them at a distance.

"Look, my attitude is don't ask don't tell. It's good policy. You should try it." She smiled and reached for a nail file and went to work on her manicure.

"Do you pay minimum wage, social security?"

"I pay what I pay. They're happy. It's all good. What's with the questions?" She put down the file and faced him. She was not smiling.

"I just wonder if you might be exploiting them."

"How dare you." She raised her voice. "Don't lecture me about immigrants. I'm an immigrant. I had to be sneaked into this country as a child, through Canada. The only reason I got to stay was I had relatives with pull who sponsored me. Most people who want to come here don't have that advantage."

"You think illegal immigration is okay?"

"Our immigration system is racist." She sat up and leaned in close. "You wouldn't see anybody protest immigrants if they were all white Canadians. What people don't like is immigrants with dark skin or foreign names. Like me."

Sucked into the vortex of another debate with Sherri, he swam against the current. "So, it's okay for people to break the law because the law is racist?" he said.

"Yes! Read Thoreau on civil disobedience. Read Gandhi, Martin Luther King. The system is broken. It doesn't serve people who want to come here and contribute. It doesn't serve our country's needs. It doesn't serve businesses who need workers."

"Businesses like yours?"

"Yes, like mine. Do you see native-born Americans lining up for jobs washing dishes, changing dirty hotel sheets, picking strawberries in the hot sun? No, you don't. I know. I've tried to fill kitchen jobs.

The idea that Mexicans are stealing jobs from Americans is a joke. Immigrants come here to do the work no one else will do for minimum wage. Our economy would collapse if all the undocumented were deported."

An odor of righteous indignation filled the room.

"But what about the rule of law?" he said, grasping for a handhold. "Do immigration laws mean nothing?" For once, he was on the conservative side of an argument with her. He wasn't sure he even believed what he was saying, he just felt the need to oppose her, to start an argument.

"Don't talk to me about the rule of law," she said, brow knitted. "Have you ever driven over the legal alcohol limit? Over the speed limit? Ever talked or texted on your cell phone while driving? Ever fudged a deduction on your tax return? Of course you have. Everybody has. So don't talk to me about the rule of law. People cry 'rule of law' only when it serves their interests."

"But it's not only that laws are broken, it's the consequences, right?" he said, still scrambling for footing.

"And the consequences are? What, exactly?" she said. "Strawberries get picked? Sheets get changed? Poor people get a leg up? Our national gene pool gets refreshed by the world's seekers and strivers and risk takers?"

Exhausted by her verbal blitzkrieg, he rolled over and turned out the light, his usual strategy when losing an argument with Sherri.

Innes sat up, confused, heart pounding, alone in bed. The digital clock blinked seven. He'd had one of his increasingly frequent and disturbing dreams and woke in the middle of it, the details still fresh in his mind.

He was on one of those Hollywood tour buses as it inched forward in a traffic jam. Standing room only in the lower level, bodies jammed together in the aisle, slammed against each other as the bus lurched, people sweating, smelling foul, losing patience. Innes stood in the aisle and held onto an overhead handrail, trying to see out the windows. He was stark naked while everyone else was clothed, but nobody seemed to notice. The bus came to a stop in front of the Chinese Theater. A crowd packed the sidewalk in front where the movie stars made their handprints in the wet cement. They all stared at something in their midst. The driver opened the door and said over a loudspeaker, "Chinese Theater, everybody out." As he was about to descend the steps, a woman in front of him pulled off her wraparound skirt and handed it to him. He wrapped himself in it. The passengers pushed toward the exit and squeezed him out into the mob, toward the eye of the storm where a lone figure lay on the ground. A police officer knelt over the figure. He turned the body over. It was George. The policeman took off his hat and placed it over the old man's face and stood up. "He's dead. Everybody move along." Innes tried to get closer but was pulled away by the shifting mass of bodies. The unruly crowd carried him farther down the block onto a red carpet in front of the Dolby Theater. There posed a trio of young women in miniskirts, halter tops, and knee-high boots. People hurled insults and spat at them. "Whores!" they yelled. Innes moved toward them. One looked like Candy Barr, the other like Syl, without the wings. The third was ... Caleb. Tarted up with pink lipstick and a silver wig. A transvestite prostitute. Innes reached out to him, but Caleb smacked him across the face with his purse, and the three hookers ran off into the crowd.

The slap in the face woke him up.

The dreams became weirder each night. In another, he was in a dark, seedy bar at the rear of a Mexican restaurant. Faded paper bunting in the red, green, and white of the Mexican flag hung from the suspended shelves over the bar. Dusty margarita goblets and beer glasses dangled upside down from rows of wooden dowels. A small TV over the bar aired a *fútbol* match narrated in Spanish. The lone bartender in a black vest and white T-shirt watched the match, ignoring the few customers on a hot summer afternoon. A lazy overhead fan rotated ineffectually. Seated at a small table in the corner was an old man, bent over, forehead on the backs of his hands. Next to his head was a half-empty bottle of Jose Cuervo—or was it half full?—and a shot glass. Innes sat in the other chair. The old man looked up. Innes asked why he hadn't come to see his little baby boy, the sole grandchild. "God, look at you. You're a mess," Innes said. "Do not take the Lord's name in vain," the man thundered like a fire-and-brimstone preacher. Innes told him to stop blaming the whole world for his wife's death, he had a grandson to live for. "Foulness! Foulness!" the man shouted. The bartender turned from the TV for a moment, then turned back. "Fuck you, old man. Drink yourself to death," were Innes' last words to his father. He left the bar with the demented ravings of Dennis Innes ringing in his ears.

It was a variation of a recurring dream he'd had for years, a bizarre amalgam of real and imagined events, distorted the way dreams are, salted with made-up or remembered dialogue from who knows where. It was as if something, or someone, were sending him a message. What that message was, he wasn't sure. Still, it was clear what he had to do.

Christmas Eve would be the fifth anniversary of Ronnie Rafsanjani's untimely demise. In the morning, Sherri told Innes the story of their last night together. The cook was off for the holidays, like now, and Sherri had made them Christmas Eve dinner—rack of lamb. They drank two bottles of a 2004 Syrah from the cellar and went to bed around midnight. When Sherri woke around two, Ronnie was gone. She was wandering the house calling his name when the front gate intercom buzzed. The police, bearers of bad news.

Innes thought it strange that Sherri wanted to make another Christmas Eve feast on the anniversary of becoming a widow. He raised the question as she assembled ingredients in the kitchen.

"Don't you see, baby?" she said. "It's the perfect time to put my old life behind and start a new one. You've brought me out of my five-year funk."

Innes nodded, but he wasn't listening. He was thinking about his decision. It tore him up. Despite her mercurial mood swings, he was enraptured, a captive of her beauty, intelligence, and passion. She had provided an escape from the horrors of the autumn, a safe harbor. It was hard to imagine leaving this luxurious and lusty adventure to go back on the streets, push a shopping cart, and search for an old man and a son who didn't want to be found. Sherri had restored his self-respect, from vagabond to Beverly Hills stud. Or was it Beverly Hills gigolo? Truth was, he was little more than that. Her control of him was inescapable. Maybe he *was* under a Calypso spell.

He had wrestled with the conflict for days, and finally decided after his strange dreams to resume the search for Caleb and George and reunite with his Casa Grande people, build a new life with them, before it was too late. He wondered about Vanessa and Clif and Tammy and Steven and Terry, even June, and what they were up to, how they were coping. He'd thought several times about calling them to check in, but didn't, out of shame. Walking out on Sherri would likely forfeit the nearly fifteen-hundred bucks he'd "earned" in the last month, but he was haunted by visions of the people he had abandoned. Christmas Eve dinner would be his valediction.

Innes wore one of Ronnie's tuxedos. Sherri insisted. He felt festive and ridiculous at the same time. Sherri wore a wine-red, floor-length designer gown with a plunging neckline that showcased her cleavage and a plunging back that showcased her other cleavage. She filled the rooms and hallways with white votive candles in glass holders and turned the lights low. They cooked a turkey breast in a big applewood smoker on the patio.

After dinner, as they opened a second bottle of Pinot Gris from the cellar, Sherri presented him with a small, gift-wrapped box. He protested, and confessed that he didn't get her anything.

"You're my Christmas present," she assured him. "Go ahead, open it."

Innes peeled off the white ribbon and the green-and-red-striped wrapping, exposing a jewel box. He feared she'd done something extravagant, like a diamond-encrusted Rolex. He pried open the hinged lid. Inside was a single house key, attached with a piece of twine to a plain leather fob embossed with the initials HVI. He looked up at her, unsure what to say.

"I know it doesn't look like much," she said. "But it means a lot to me, and I hope, to you."

"What *does* it mean, exactly?"

"It means *mi casa es su casa*. I want you to stay. Live with me."

Innes felt like he'd swallowed a brick. About to spring the bad news on her, and here she was offering the key to her house, to her life. This was far, far worse than a mere Rolex, so freighted with obligation. He grasped for words. None came. He looked down at his left hand. The wedding ring Annie had slipped onto his finger almost twenty years gone was still there.

Sherri's eyes followed his. "I know you still wear your wedding ring," she said. "You'll always love her. I know that. But you can love us both. Love Annie's memory, and love me in the here and now."

He stared at the key in the box, then closed the lid with a sharp snap. "I don't know, Sherri. It's just …," he said, stalling, unsure what to say.

"Of course. I'm sorry. I shouldn't have sprung it on you like this. This is a big change in our relationship. We should have talked about it first. Anyway, they key is yours. Do with it what you will."

He put the box on the table. Sherri stood up. "Come to bed. You can give me my Christmas present there." She tilted her head and smiled suggestively.

"You go ahead," he said. "I'll clear the table. I'll be up in a few."

Sherri glided toward the stairs, humming something from Puccini—"Musetta's Waltz?"—and left Innes alone at the table.

What now? He would never be able to tell her face to face. Her overpowering personality would melt him like chocolate left in the sun. He stood for a while over the stacked dishes in the sink and watched the yellow turkey grease congeal on the white china plates. In the end, he knew what he had to do. Run out on her, like Jason and Odysseus. Go to bed and pleasure her to sleep, then slip away under cover of darkness. There was no other way.

In bed they went at it for about an hour. Sherri insisted he make love to her with the tuxedo on until she passed out from the wine. Innes lay next to her on his back, fully dressed, wide awake, staring at the ceiling, taut as a guitar string. Sherri's tapestries loomed over him accusingly. Shitheel, they said.

When she started to snore, he slipped out of the bed and slinked down the stairs. He considered a change of attire but was afraid to wake her and figured he could ditch the tux for his own clothes in the shopping cart at the first opportunity. Time to move fast: Disarm the security system, slip out the back Jack, collect the Target cart in the garage, exit through the rear door into the alley, and disappear into the night.

The motion detectors triggered the lights as he descended the stairs into the center hallway and skulked through the living room toward the rear door. He thought he heard a footfall and stopped to listen. Silence. His heart thumped, a nagging metronome. He reached the alarm keypad and punched in the code. The box emitted a chirp.

"What are you doing?"

He turned, startled, to see Sherri appear in the light at the far end of the living room, hair hanging in her face, her expression a twisted mask of confusion and nascent accusation. She was in her beige negligee, her nakedness visible under the gauzy fabric. In her right hand she gripped a big black revolver, pointed at Innes's chest. It looked like a cannon in her delicate fingers. Innes was reminded of the lurid posters in Lee An's office of scantily clad women brandishing guns and whips, and almost laughed out loud. Except this was no campy dime novel.

"I … I need something from my cart," he lied, but only partly.

"It couldn't wait till morning?" she said.

"I couldn't sleep. I need to get a book. What's with the gun, Sherri?"

She looked at the revolver and lowered it to her side. "People who mess with my security system in the middle of the night must be criminals," she said, her voice flat, unemotional. "Are you a criminal?"

"No, Sherri. I'm no criminal." Only a thief in the night.

"You're sneaking away, aren't you?" Her voice rose an octave and cracked into a squeak.

"No," he lied again.

She stepped toward him and pointed the gun at his chest. "I know how to use this."

He believed her and reached for the knob, pulled the door open, and dashed outside. He crossed the patio and headed straight for the garage, expecting to hear the blast of gunfire and feel the hot poker of a bullet in his back. An image entered his mind: William Holden floating face down in a pool with a bullet in him, from the opening scene of *Sunset Boulevard*. Sherri was nutty as Norma Desmond.

He looked over his shoulder. No sign of her, no gunfire. Was she letting him go? When he reached the garage, the motion detector lights blinked on, and there, right where he'd stashed his cart, was nothing. Back to the yard, lit by floodlights. Sherri was outside on the patio, still brandishing the pistol. The Target cart was next to her. She aimed the gun at him. He ran toward the side yard wall. She fired. An ear-splitting blast pierced the air and echoed off the house and across the grounds. He felt nothing and turned to see if another volley was coming. She was pointing the gun in the air. A warning shot. He grabbed the top edge of the wall and hauled himself up, one leg over, one leg back, and hesitated.

"Bastard!" she shrieked. "You're a shit like all of them."

All of *whom?* he wondered. "I can't stay here," he said. "I have to find my son."

"You goddamn coward. You couldn't tell me? You have to slink away in the night?"

"Okay, I'm a coward. I admit it."

The confession seemed to calm her, and her voice lowered. "Come down off that wall, baby. You don't mean it. Please. I'm offering you all of this."

"Don't you get it? I need my son, not … this," he swept his arm across the yard.

She raised her free hand, which held something small. "I knew it might come to this. So I took your cart." Her voice had shifted from shrieking to pleading to ice. "You. Will. Not. Humiliate me." She flicked her thumb and a flame popped up from a cigarette lighter. "I know what's in here. I looked. Her picture. Her clothes. Her diary. I poured lighter fluid on everything. Come back now, or … I'll do it. I will."

Innes froze. Would she? She had just pointed a gun at him and fired a round into the air. She would do it. He had to decide. Now. Was he ready to leave behind the last traces of his life with Annie? Could he stay with this madwoman?

It was not a hard decision. "I'm sorry, Sherri." He lifted his leg over the wall.

She dropped the lighter onto the cart. An orange flame roared high into the air, obscuring her face.

Innes lowered himself into the narrow passage between Sherri's wall and the neighbor's hedge. He jogged toward the street with only a general idea of the direction back to Sunset, trying to remember the sequence of squealing turns Sherri had made weeks before. A few lefts and rights brought him to a corner bordered by oleander hedges, their knife-like leaves and white blossoms aglow in the moonlight. It occurred to him this is where Ronnie Rafsanjani had been exactly five years before, in the wee hours of Christmas Day, when his crushed body was found in the middle of Sunset. What if it was Sherri who killed Ronnie? What if she came after *him* tonight in her big SUV? Fortuitous to be dressed in black, all the better to hide in the darkness. And if she caught him and ran him down? A beautiful corpse he would make. He giggled aloud and realized how drunk and scared he was.

Somehow, she had anticipated his escape plan, and knew exactly how to destroy him—torch the last of his memories. But she was wrong about one thing. Inside his tuxedo jacket was a square bulge in the pocket. Annie's diary was all he had left in the world now, aside from a dead man's tails, the watch on his wrist and, in the other jacket pocket, the nine-inch hunting knife.

He turned right, jogged a few more blocks, and there it was, Sunset Boulevard, quiet and dimly lit in the misty night air by the streetlamps, the tree trunks wrapped in corkscrewed strands of tiny white Christmas lights. He turned toward the east, eyes peeled for places to duck into the shadows, and began his lonely trek back to Hollywood.

Book V

THE MORNING SUN PEEKED OVER THE MOUNTAINS
as he arrived at the corner of Sunset and Vine. Innes had walked for
hours. He'd stopped to pee in a woodsy patch behind a yellow railroad dining car on Sunset and slept for a few fitful hours in an alley
behind a dumpster, like the bums in *My Man Godfrey*, shielded from
the street, a dirty rag for a pillow, skittering, squeaking rats for companions. The trek from Beverly Hills through West Hollywood had
taken him past low-end bars and strip clubs and high-end boutiques
and specialty services, including a laser airbrush tanning parlor and
a temp agency that advertised nannies, housekeepers, butlers, maids,
tutors, and couples. Couples? A falafel joint on Sunset was closed,
but someone had left the flat screen TV on behind the counter, tuned
to a local news channel running the all-night highlights feed. Innes
rested his forehead against the cool glass of the window and watched
the images flicker past. ABC-7 looped aerial video of a naked man
dancing atop a Metro bus near King's Road in WeHo. Innes wondered if the Master of Disaster was on the scene.

Christmas morning and Hollywood was practically deserted, save
for a few souls stirring from under their tarps or shuffling around,
commencing the day's search for their next drink and the cash to pay
for it. Innes was no better than any of them now, equally homeless,
penniless. He fingered the satin lapels on his tuxedo jacket. "Best-
dressed goddamn bum in Hollywood," he announced to a lump under a grimy Spider Man child's blanket. His belly was full, but by the
end of the day he'd be hungry again and had no money. He walked
up Vine and east on Hollywood Boulevard. None of his signs taped
up weeks ago were still there, all replaced by fresh searches for fresh
runaways.

In front of the Museum of Death, a trio of young streetwalkers
displayed their wares. Look what Santa brought. One of the hookers
acknowledged the season with a red-and-white felt Santa hat atop
her spiky blonde hair, which blended fetchingly with her red lipstick, white boots and purse, red hot pants, and short white cardigan
sweater open over a red bra. Innes stopped, remembering his dream
about Caleb and the hookers at the Chinese Theater, and wondered
if these girls knew any runaway boys from Pasadena.

"Morning, girls," he said.

"Nice monkey suit, gramps," said Santa's elf. The other two, one Black, one Asian, snickered.

"Musta been some party," said the tall one from under a medicine-ball sized Afro.

Innes pondered the meaning of celebrating the birth of Baby Jesus by peddling blowjobs on Nativity morn. "You don't get customers on Christmas morning, do you?" he said.

"You'd be amazed," said the other girl, who looked about fourteen.

"Beats a new pair o' socks," said the one with the Afro.

Innes was about to ask if they knew anyone named Caleb, when his gaze locked on the elf. The term "gramps" snapped a memory into focus. He looked at her closely.

"You lookin' for a date?" she said and held open her sweater to better display her Christmas gifts.

"Candy? Is that you?"

The shock of recognition in her eyes confirmed it was. "Professor? What was your name again? Guinness?"

"Innes," he corrected her.

"You know this dude?" said the other girl.

"Him and me made a porno together, didn't we Professor?" Candy said with a conspiratorial wink.

He looked down at his black oxfords, trying not to remember.

"Except you ran out on us before we finished. They used our little scene anyway. It's on the site if you want to see it. Get this," she said to the other girls, "he was a college prof and I was his student. We did it in his quote-unquote office."

They rolled their eyes at the cliché.

"You back for 'nother go-round?" said the tall one.

"You want to do me again, this time you gotta pay," said Candy.

Innes recalled the conversation he'd had with her at Angels in Paradise. He'd thought about her more than once, and hoped she would someday finish school, like she said. Finding her walking the streets on Christmas was too damn depressing. "Are you really a college girl working your way through school, or was that bullshit?"

"Fuck you. Yes, I am in school. And yes, I turn tricks sometimes for extra money. So keep your judgy opinions to yourself."

"Do you have a pimp?"

"None of your business," she said with the same contempt she'd shown him on the broken-down couch in Van Nuys.

"You're out here on the streets on your own?" he said.

"I got my posse here, Sharone and Tina." Candy put her arms around the girls and pulled them into a three-way hug. "And Lee An helps us out."

"Lee An?" he said.

"She owns a place in Hollyweird she lets us use."

"So Lee An's your pimp."

"I got no pimp," she said and turned her back on him dismissively. "She's just a friend who helps us out."

"That's quite an empire Lee An's got," he said.

"Don't knock it." She turned back to him. "Lee An says women should be able to do what they want and help each other do it."

That sounded like something Lee An would say. He had to admire the woman's unabashed entrepreneurship. She reminded him of Sherri, a successful, fiercely independent immigrant. Cheryl had confided that Lee An had got her start in "the business" as a professional dominatrix while in grad school at Cal Poly, with a steady clientele of tenured senior faculty. In retrospect, his encounters with Lee An and Sherri both seemed like sadomasochistic farce, staged for their amusement.

His thoughts turned from Lee An and Sherri and back to the entrepreneurs before him. "Do you girls think this is safe?" he said. "Don't you worry about the cops? STDs? Dangerous creeps?"

"Thanks, Daddy, but we know what time it is," said Sharone. She pulled a switchblade out of her purse, snapped out the gleaming business end, snapped it back, and returned it to her purse, all in less than three seconds. The flash of the blade startled Innes into momentary silence.

"So, Guinness, we gonna do it or not?" Candy said.

He almost mentioned he'd dreamt of her as a hooker in Hollywood, a startling bit of prescience, but thought better of it. "Sorry, girls, I don't have a cent on me."

"Bullshit. You're in a tux, dude. You look rich to me," said Tina. She ran her index finger along his lapel.

"This tux is the only thing I own. And I had to steal it. I got no money, no food, no nothin'."

"You could always do what we do for money," said Candy.

"Very funny," he said.

"Nobody would pay his sorry ass," said Sharone.

"Well, Guinness. I guess you're gonna have to beg, like all the other bums out here," said Candy. "You too good for that?"

"No, but I've never done it."

"Nothin' to it," she said. "Make yourself a sign and find a nice corner with a traffic light and you're in business."

"Make sure there ain't no one else on that corner if you don't want a blade in your belly," said Sharone.

"How do I make a sign?" he said.

"You were never in kindergarten?" Candy said. "You only need some cardboard and a marker." She reached into her purse and pulled out a fat felt tip. "Here, this is my contribution to Guinness Enterprises."

He added it to the trove in his pockets. "Where do I get cardboard? I don't have any money."

The girls regarded him with looks of pity and contempt. "You go behind one of these stores and grab an empty box out of a dumpster," Candy said slowly, as if speaking to a child. "Tear off a side of the box, and presto, you got a sign."

"I dunno about the tux," said Tina. "People will think you don't need money. Rich dude having a laugh."

"People might think it's funny," said Candy. "A hobo with a sense of humor. Just might work."

Innes was about to walk away, then remembered why he'd wanted to talk to them in the first place. "I'm looking for my runaway son, Caleb, from Pasadena. Ever heard of him?"

Blank stares.

"I think he might be in Hollywood," he continued. "Any ideas where teenage runaways would hang out?"

"Try the shelters," said Tina.

"Tried that."

"Doesn't he have a cellphone?" asked Candy.

"He doesn't return calls or answer texts."

"Sounds like he don't wanna be found," said Sharone.

Innes wandered into Barnsdall Art Park on the eastern edge of Hollywood, almost in Los Feliz, and found a secluded spot under a tree to take a leak. He had finally made it to Covenant House, a month late. No one there recalled a boy who matched Caleb's description, but then again, they saw dozens like that. They seemed reluctant to help a sketchy-looking adult in a sketchy-looking tuxedo, searching for a child who likely didn't want to be found.

After he took a leak, oblivious to the disgust of passersby, he sat under another tree, pulled out the marker Candy gave him, and stared at the rectangle of brown cardboard, admiring the crisp edges where he had torn it free from the box. What to write? Keep it simple. HOMELESS. PLEASE HELP, he wrote. He embellished the lettering with curly serifs. A beggar in a tux should have a classy sign. He ambled over to the corner of Hollywood and Vermont, turned to face the traffic, and held up the sign. The first car honked at him. The next one produced a middle finger salute from the passenger window. This went on for an hour, then two. Innes's stomach growled. He sweated under the hot sun, his tux fast becoming gamey and wrinkled.

A cluster of men and women in their twenties walked by and found him and his tux fascinating. They surrounded him, full of questions. Was this performance art? Part of the art park? They took turns posing for selfies with him, individual and group shots. They gave him ten dollars, enough for a cheeseburger and a Coke at the walk-up burger stand on Vermont. As he finished the last bite, perched on a stool at the counter, he had a brainstorm. He pulled out the marker and cardboard and wrote on the back SELFIES WITH CLASSY BUM ONE DOLLAR and went back to his corner. Within an hour, he'd made another four dollars.

Late in the afternoon, a woman in a black leather jacket riding a pink scooter with a matching helmet rolled toward his corner. As she slowed for the red light, their eyes met. She stopped by the curb and studied him, and he her. It took a couple of seconds to register.

"Oh, God," he said under his breath. Nowhere to hide.

"Innes?" she said.

He nodded to Vanessa Alfonso. She pulled the scooter onto the sidewalk, dismounted, and hung her helmet on a handlebar. Her long black hair was in a single braid that reached halfway down her back.

"*Dios mío*, Innes. What are you doing here? Where have you been?" She grabbed the sign out of his hand, flung it to the ground, and stepped back to look him over. "I don't know where to start," she said. "That tux. That beggar sign." Her brow was stitched in the center into the quilted box of disapproval.

Innes laughed, and wiped a tear from his cheek. "I know. Ridiculous, isn't it?"

"What happened? You dropped off the face of the earth. Nobody could reach you. I've been riding all over Hollywood for days looking for you."

Gratitude, regret, and shame overcame him. He'd needed so much to talk to her and felt abandoned. Yet all along she had been searching for him, while he was… Too painful to think about. "I called you and left messages," he said. "You never called back."

"I was out of the country for a while. And then you were impossible to reach."

"Anyway, I still haven't found Cal," he said. "And the old man wandered off. I found a place to live for a while. It was weird. I thought about calling to check in, but I was, I don't know, ashamed."

"Ashamed?"

"Yeah, ashamed. I was living with a woman. In Beverly Hills, if you can believe it. She sort of took me in. And I stopped looking for Cal. That's what I'm most ashamed of." He stared at the sidewalk, unable to look her in the eye.

"Beverly Hills?" Her brown eyes looked like big copper coins. "I was cruising the homeless encampments of Hollywood, and you were shacked up in Beverly Hills?"

Innes couldn't tell if she was furious or amused. If she slapped him hard across the face, he wouldn't blame her, and almost hoped for it.

She stared at him for a moment, arms akimbo, the way she had done at the Halloween party, which seemed so long ago. "I am such a fool," she said. "I searched for you out of loyalty to Annie's memory. What the absolute fuck? *¡Pendejo!*"

"It's a long, strange story," he said. He looked past her at the traffic zooming by. "I'll tell you about it sometime."

"Anyway. I've got news for you," she said, softening her tone. "I know where George is. It's not good. He's down in Skid Row. He's in poor health. And mentally, I think, he's losing it. I've tried to help him, but he acts like he doesn't want to be helped."

"Damn." Innes gazed up at the sky. Should have gone back for him. "Can you take me to him?" he said.

"Hop on. Two can fit on this thing. Sorry, I don't have an extra helmet."

The scooter, a battered old Vespa, looked old enough to be the one Audrey Hepburn terrorized Italian pedestrians with in *Roman Holiday*. He hoped Vanessa drove it better than that. He reluctantly climbed on and wrapped his arms around her waist. She maneuvered the antique machine into traffic and continued on Hollywood Boulevard toward Sunset. The scooter rattled like an old lawn mower and smelled like burning oil. Innes felt ridiculous on the back of a pink Vespa in a tuxedo, clinging to a woman in a pink helmet, her braid flapping in his face as if in reproach. They rumbled and smoked down Sunset until they looped around to Glendale Boulevard and passed Aimee Semple McPherson's Angelus Temple and the palm-tree-lined lake of Echo Park. At a red light, a vagabond wandered between the stopped cars, holding an old black landline telephone with the cord dangling, and shouted profanities at drivers inside their cars talking on their cellphones. Hanging from his neck was a homemade sign: STILL HUMAN.

They entered downtown and continued through Little Tokyo to San Pedro Street, where Vanessa turned right and into a world that made Innes gasp aloud. Both sides of San Pedro were lined with a massive tent city. The side streets, too. Tents of all colors and sizes, ragged, torn, dirty, covered with blue tarps, jammed together cheek by jowl, a few draped with strands of blinking Christmas lights, somehow plugged into some unseen power source. Wedged between them and spilling into the streets were lawn chairs and makeshift stools, stacks of boxes, old bicycles, shopping carts, hand carts, stuffed trash bags, sleeping bags, old television sets with no tubes used as liquor cabinets, empty bottles and cans, and discarded Christmas trees—some still halfway decorated with sad looking tinsel and broken ornaments. Herds of thin and mangy dogs and cats explored enormous piles of stinking garbage. And everywhere—in chairs, on sidewalks, gathered at corners, in the middle of the street holding beverages, pushing shopping carts piled high with scavenged recyclables—were hundreds of the shabbiest, most vacant looking people Innes had ever seen. It was a city within a city, at least twenty square blocks. He couldn't see the edges of it. A place Innes had heard of but never seen. Hundreds, maybe thousands, of invisible people, the cast-offs, the opt-outs, the disposables. It looked like the Syrian refugee camps he'd seen on the TV news, except this was America. The terrible vastness of it stunned him into silence as Vanessa maneuvered the Vespa through a slalom course of bodies weaving in the street. On the grimy side of an old brick building someone had written in spray paint: Abandon Hope.

Vanessa pulled over in front of the Rescue Gospel Mission on 6th Street and locked the scooter to a signpost with a heavy chain sheathed in black plastic. Innes stood by the curb and gawked at the endless street carnival. "I had no idea," he said.

"Nobody does," said Vanessa. "That's why we have such a problem."

"How big is it? Skid Row."

"About fifty square blocks ... and growing."

"My God. How many people?"

"Hard to say. Four, five thousand." She sounded weary of the conversation, as if she'd had it too many times.

Innes noticed several children, some merely toddlers, wandering in and out of the encampments, a few with new toys most likely from holiday charity drives. "Children, too? How many?"

"Couple hundred. Breaks your heart, doesn't it?"

"Who are all these people? Where do they come from?"

"Everybody's got their own story. A lot of them are mentally ill, and there are no institutions or group homes to take them. Everybody knows that story. A lot are addicts—drugs or alcohol or both. Some are here by choice. Dropouts, disillusioned with quote-unquote normal society. Some are disabled veterans, some are runaway teens from violent homes. About one-third are women, and there aren't enough beds in the women's shelters. Some just fell into poverty and homelessness due to things beyond their control, like job loss or illness or bankruptcy, or getting evicted when their landlord decided to do condos, and ended up here."

People in the street were staring at him, as if *he* were the freak show.

"Where is he, in there?" Innes said, gesturing toward the mission.

"No, George is in a tent I got for him out here on the street. But I can't get him to stay put, he keeps wandering off, and some other guy tries to claim squatter's rights."

"Sounds like the old man," he said as he followed her down the street. "So, what's your role in all this, Nessa?"

"I'm a volunteer with a non-profit agency that contracts with the county."

"Volunteer? What are you living on? Same old?" They walked west in the middle of the street, the sidewalks impassable, the blended odors of urine and rotting garbage inescapable.

"Same old. Hostessing at La Casita. Temping," she said. "The usual gamut for people with useless art history degrees. The emergency cash from insurance helped, but that's gone now."

"What emergency cash?" he said. He stopped.

"From my homeowner's," she said. She turned to face him and walked backwards. "A thousand bucks to tide me over until my claim is approved. Didn't you get that?"

"What? No. From your insurance? I didn't get anything like that."

"Maybe your policy doesn't include it. Didn't you get any mail from them?"

"No, June gets all my mail. She would have said something, right?"
"Ask her."

Innes made a mental note to do just that next time he talked to June, as unpleasant a prospect as it was.

He hustled to catch up with Vanessa. "Where are you living now, still with your mother?" he asked. He wondered if she would offer him a place to stay.

"It's complicated," she said. "I'll explain later."

So much for that idea.

As if reading his mind, Vanessa said, "I don't understand why you didn't stay with June when she offered, instead of bumming around the streets and shacking up in Beverly Hills. George would have been better off, don't you think?"

"You know why. There's always strings attached with June. Anyway, we did stay at one of her places, for one night. Then our car and most of our money got stolen, and she kicked us out the next day to make room for new tenants."

Vanessa had no response to that. "This should be him right here," she said. They stopped in front of a new-looking red-and-white backpacking tent squeezed between two others on the sidewalk in front of a rusty chain-link fence. It was small, roomy enough for two people to lie down but not stand up. They peered inside: empty, aside from a single sleeping bag and a brown paper sack. Vanessa crawled in while Innes gazed up and down the street, still trying to comprehend the horrific enormity of it all.

"How long has he been here?" he said.

"Couple weeks," she said as she backed out and sat on the curb. "He refuses all services, won't even use the free shower truck. Won't seek medical care. Food. Counseling. Detox. Anyway, it's a bureaucratic nightmare. Like, I tried to get him mental health services? Get this. They told us if he was seeking mental health services, he can't be mentally ill. Because seeking help is a rational act."

"That's ... Catch-22!" he said.

"No, they said Catch-22 is already taken. They call it Catch-23."

He let out a whistle and said, "That's some catch, that Catch-23."

"It's the best there is," she said without missing a beat.

Innes smiled at her wit. She wasn't smiling. "What about temporary housing?" he asked.

"That's Catch-24," she said. "They told him they wouldn't provide emergency housing unless he proved he was homeless. And to prove he was homeless, he had to ... wait for it ... show proof of residence."

"Proof? Like what, a utility bill? For a patch of sidewalk?" he said, incredulous. He was about to ask more questions when a voice behind him said, "That's my tent."

Innes turned to see his father-in-law, looking confused and annoyed. He wanted to hug him, but his appearance and demeanor cautioned him to hold back. George was in the same outfit, but it was filthy. His white hair was longer and more unkempt under his Jamaican tam-o-shanter, his eyes bloodshot. A dark spot around his fly formed a corona of dust and grime.

"Old man. It's me," said Innes.

"Stay out of my tent," George rasped.

Vanessa stood up. "I was just checking to see if you were home," she said. "Do you need anything, George?"

"I need you to leave me alone."

The old man sat on the curb, crossed his legs, and pulled out a pint of Jack Daniels. He took a long swig and stared at an indeterminate spot across the street. Innes sat next to him and put an arm on his shoulder. George didn't offer to share the pint. Vanessa stood over them like a playground monitor.

"I'm sorry I ditched you," Innes said. He was consumed by regret. He realized how much he'd missed the endearingly infuriating old man. "But when I came back, you were gone. I didn't know where you'd run off to. So I left. I should have stayed and looked for you."

George continued to stare across the street. He was silent for several moments then took another swallow. Innes waited to see if he would speak.

"I am in a dark wood of error," the old man said.

"Same old George," Innes said, looking up at Vanessa. "He's quoting from something, I think. He does that."

"That's from Dante," she said. "*The Divine Comedy.*"

"Maybe he's the one who spray painted 'Abandon Hope' back there?" Innes suggested, half joking.

He heard whistles and catcalls from across the street and noticed he was the object of staring and pointing. He stood, fingered the satin lapels of his tux, and felt utterly ridiculous. Vanessa noticed it, too.

"I've got to get you some proper clothes," she said. "Why don't you hang out here with George. I'll be back." She stuck her hand in his pants pocket and shoved something in. "Get some food for you two," she said. "There's a convenience store down the street. Food, not liquor." She glared at George and walked back toward her scooter.

Innes sat and extended his hand to the old man, who after a few seconds handed over the pint. They sat in silence for several minutes, passing the bottle back and forth. When George finally spoke, he said, "I got food in the tent. Energy bars. The mission's got food, too. We don't need no money for dinner. Why donchta take that twenty she gave you and get us another one of these." He held up the pint, empty now.

"What twenty?" Innes dodged.

"I saw her stick it in yer pocket, like she does to me alla time."

Innes complied. If he was to spend the night sharing a tent with the old man in this hell on earth, might as well be shitfaced. As they drained the second bottle, Innes tried to get him to talk, but George fell back into silence, staring across the street. When he came out of his trance long enough to inquire after the shopping cart and its contents, Innes lied and said it was stolen.

"What about Cal?" George asked.

"Don't know. Haven't found him yet."

"You're a useless idiot," said George.

He couldn't argue with that.

Shortly after sunset, Vanessa returned with an extra sleeping bag for Innes and a change of clothes—powder blue UCLA sweatpants and sweatshirt, Army camo pants with cargo pockets, clean socks, running shoes, all used and frayed, but clean. And a three-pack of men's boxers, still in its wrapper.

"Salvation Army," she said. "Why don't you change in the tent and give me the tux. I'll donate it." She climbed aboard her Vespa. "I'll be back tomorrow. We'll start looking for Caleb again." She stared at him for a moment, as if to drive home her disappointment in him.

"You still want to help me?" he said.

"I'm helping George," she said. "Make yourself useful if you want." She buckled her chinstrap and rode off.

❖

In the morning, Innes woke stiff and sore from sleeping on the cold sidewalk, the tent floor and flimsy sleeping bag offering little comfort. His head ached from a whiskey hangover. The old man was still asleep. With six bucks in his pocket, he climbed out of the tent in search of breakfast. Halfway down the block, a section of newspaper drifted along the sidewalk like a runaway ghost and wrapped around the base of a lamppost. He picked it up. The Metro section of the LA *Daily News*. In the lower left-hand corner, a headline caught his eye: "1 Dead in Beverly Hills Mansion Fire." Innes folded the page in quarters to better see the article. The headline gave him a sinking feeling. As his eyes fell to the words, the sinking feeling plunged into a pit of nausea.

Daily News staff writer

A Beverly Hills woman died in a Christmas Eve fire that destroyed a historic mansion in the Benedict Canyon Drive section of the city. Fire investigators said the cause of the blaze appeared to be accidental.

The victim was identified as Scheherazade Rafsanjani, 38, the occupant of the house and a former owner and operator of several well-known restaurants in the Los Angeles area along with her late husband Ron Rafsanjani, who was killed by a hit-and-run driver on Christmas Eve 2010. Neighbors said the woman lived alone and had become reclusive since her husband died.

Innes looked away from the paper. His hands were shaking. This can't be happening, he thought. He continued reading.

One neighbor reported hearing a sound like gunfire sometime after midnight. A Beverly Hills police spokeswoman said a .357 magnum revolver that belonged to Rafsanjani was recovered from the rear patio, with one round missing from the chamber. Tests showed the gun had been fired recently. The spokeswoman said no slug was recovered at the scene, and the coroner's office said the badly burned body of Rafsanjani showed no signs of a bullet wound.

A police source, who spoke on condition of anonymity, said investigators were seeking clues indicating the possibility of a robbery and murder, with arson used to cover it up. However, fire investigators said it appeared Rafsanjani might have set the fire herself in a possible barbecuing accident. A smoker-type grill was found on the patio, where the blaze apparently started, with a large can of lighter fluid and a cigarette lighter. Several empty wine bottles were recovered from the kitchen area, which suggested possible inebriation, an investigator said. Police said there was evidence suggesting one or more guests might have been present, but neighbors reported seeing no one else at the house for months aside from a gardener and house cleaner. Police were seeking those workers for questioning.

Rafsanjani's body was found inside a back door, wrapped in the scorched remains of a set of draperies the woman apparently had pulled down and wrapped around herself to smother flames, the investigator said. She was surrounded by several glass candle holders that had fallen to the floor.

The source said investigators were also interested in what appeared to be a badly burned plastic shopping cart found on the patio. The cart had melted into a charred lump with the remains of what appeared to be clothing, bedding and tools, but there was little identifiable, the source said.

(Continued on Page 2B)

Innes fumbled with the broadsheet pages flapping in the breeze as he struggled with trembling hands to open the section to page 2.

Mansion Fire (Continued from Page 1B)
Rafsanjani, known as Sherri to her few friends and relatives, sold her restaurants in 2011 and dedicated herself to her art collection. Destroyed in the fire were numerous paintings and other art objects worth an estimated $5 mil-

lion, said a Beverly Hills gallery owner who knew Rafsan-jani. More art objects, valued at $3 million according to the gallery owner, were stored in a fireproof basement locker and survived the blaze. Investigators said they saw no evidence of missing artwork, such as blank spaces on walls, and discounted the robbery theory.

Rafsanjani was born Scheherazade Mahmoud in Tunisia to Lebanese parents who had migrated there from Beirut, and then to Iran in the 1970s, according to a relative who asked not to be identified. After the Iranian revolution, she was sent to live with relatives in Los Angeles. Her parents were convicted as spies and executed in Tehran during the Iran-Iraq War, the relative said.

Innes couldn't process the words. They seemed to rearrange themselves on the page like some kind of code. He read it again. And a third time. Another fire. Another woman dead. Another woman he had failed. He crumpled the paper and tossed it aside, then knelt and vomited on the sidewalk. Lingering on all fours for several minutes, staring at the mess, he tried to augur some meaning from its splattered pattern. People walking by said nothing, the sight of a wino puking on the sidewalk not a noteworthy event.

His mind replayed the last image he'd had of Sherri—the cigarette lighter snapping open, the cold steel of her voice, the orange flames leaping up, obscuring her from his view as he slid down the other side of the wall, running away like a thief in the night. If he'd stayed, Sherri would be alive now. He let that sink in for a long while.

Innes lay awake alone in the tent. George had wandered off again. As he dwelled on yet another horrible fiery death, it occurred to him that the Beverly Hills police might somehow link him to the fire. His shopping cart was still there, burned up but maybe holding some recognizable items. He'd lived there for weeks, surely Sherri's workers had seen him, although he hadn't interacted with any of them. And what about the security cameras? The newspaper article didn't mention any surveillance video, so there was that anyway. He pushed it out of his mind. He was invisible now, they'd never find him in Skid Row.

He crawled out of the tent and wandered down the street again, still trembling from the hangover, toward the convenience store for the breakfast he'd never got. Another street person walked toward him. The Black man looked familiar, shirtless in his overalls and Raiders cap.

"Jefferson?" Innes called out. It was him, no question. These happenstance meetings were freaky. First running into Candy on the street. Then Vanessa. Now Jefferson. Like the strange dreams, it was as if some unseen entity were manipulating events in an attempt to guide him toward some mysterious end.

The man stopped and regarded him warily. "Who the fuck are you?"

"It's me, Innes. Remember? We shared a pint behind Bob's Big Boy in Toluca."

Jefferson stared at him and screwed up his face. "Naw, I don' remember you."

"Old Crow, right?"

"Yeah, that's how I roll. Howdja know?"

"I just told you. We shared a pint at Bob's."

"Mine or yours?"

"Yours. I shared my turkey sandwich with you. Turkey and Old Crow. Two birds made for each other."

"I don' remember no turkey sandwich. But if you drank my pint, Susie, you owe me one."

"The name's Innes, remember? I've only got a few bucks. And I need breakfast."

"I got some money. C'mon, we'll go Dutch."

Innes hesitated. His stomach was empty, he would need food soon. But the images of Sherri and the flaming shopping cart played in his mind like a bad horror movie and would not cease. Could he drink them into submission?

They went in on a pint of Old Crow, and Jefferson led Innes a few blocks away. They passed a mock Los Angeles neighborhood insignia painted on a wall—Skid Row City Limit, Pop.: Too Many—

then alit on a shaded bench in San Julian Park. A patch of leafy green behind a tall iron fence, the park was a living room of sorts for Skid Row, Jefferson told him. The locals slept on the mostly dead grass, played cards or chess at cafe tables, shared bottles and food, sold drugs, swapped supplies and stories. The park also included a popular attraction: a free-standing public toilet on the sidewalk outside the fence, a big green enclosed kiosk, about the size of three phone booths lashed together, the preferred alternative for those who avoided the vermin-infested bathrooms in the rescue missions. Innes gratefully availed himself of the facility and made a mental note to keep its location in mind at all times.

By noon, the bottle was gone, Innes was drunk, and the images of Sherri and flames had receded. "Let's go for a walk," said Jefferson. "I'll give you the nickel tour of hobohemia."

They weaved through the streets together, a couple of inebriates. Jefferson slurringly narrated the dismal hundred-year history of Skid Row, street by street, corner by corner, mission by mission, storefront by storefront, vagabond by vagabond. He called them "vagabones."

"Why are so many people talkin' to themselves out loud?" Innes said.

"They crazy, that's why. Live down here long enough, you'll turn crazy, too."

"That is not gonna happen."

Shortly after noon, Jefferson plopped down on a bench and passed out, leaving Innes somewhere several blocks from the old man's tent. He continued his tour of Skid Row alone and spent the rest of the day meandering like a tipsy teenager through a carnival midway, a stranger in a strange land, trying to forget his latest nightmare. Many of those huddled on sidewalks or in doorways had dogs or cats with them and seemed genuinely attached to their pets, as if they were their only true friends. Or perhaps their main defenses against Skid Row's legendarily enormous rats. Innes thought of the sad, lonely dogs he'd tended to at the animal shelter and wondered if they could have been offered as companions to the homeless, instead of ...

On one block, Millennial urban pioneers on skateboards took turns doing ollies over the stumps of a legless Iraq war veteran perched on a wheeled platform who laughed and swiped at them with his hands as they zoomed by. Innes stooped over bodies passed out in the street to see if they were still breathing. Should he try to do something? Help them? No, he decided, leave them alone. That's what everyone down here wants: to be left alone.

The things they carried in their shopping carts and backpacks and trash bags slung over their shoulders were largely determined by necessity. Among the necessities, far as Innes could tell, were extra shoes and socks, tents, sleeping bags, shopping bags, tarps, ponchos, water jugs, coolers, liquor bottles empty and full, carpet remnants, pillows, blankets, towels, American flags, Mexican flags, Christmas ornaments, sheets of cardboard, markers, pens, pencils, flashlights, batteries, extra trash bags, clotheslines, stuffed animals, plastic buckets, cellphones, propane stoves, tongs, teakettles, coffee cans, screwdrivers, hammers, pliers, duct tape, dope, pipes, rolling papers, syringes, rubber hoses, spoons, forks, sewing kits, bandages, aspirin, tampons, sunscreen, bug spray, talcum powder, toothbrushes, lipsticks, cigarettes, lighters, decks of cards, poker chips, books, magazines, newspapers, Bibles, Korans, old photos, can openers, bottle openers, pet food, pet toys, paper towels, toilet paper, discarded food and other detritus excavated from dumpsters, cans and bottles and pieces of found or stolen scrap metal for redeeming, various odds and ends collected to be someday sold or swapped, Swiss Army knives, hunting knives, switchblades, slingshots, brass knuckles, blackjacks, hatchets, and occasionally, loaded pistols.

Cats rode. Dogs walked.

They carried all they could, and then some, including the invisible but not weightless burden of the daily struggle for survival. The accumulated weight of these necessities sometimes reached into the hundreds of pounds. Jefferson told him about a man called Gene Gene the Gaming Machine, a gray-haired Vietnam vet named O'Brien, who weighed about three hundred pounds by himself, and was hauling at least two hundred pounds—three overcoats and a stuffed backpack, a shopping cart plus a handcart toting a bungee-corded stack of mini-fridge, Xbox, laptop and boom box all wrapped in gold foil—when he dropped dead from a heart attack in the middle of San Julian Street, landing with a dull thud under the weight of his burden, followed by the crash and clatter of his stacked machines.

"Boom. Down. Just like that," Jefferson said. "Like he was dead before he hit the ground."

The queen of carriage was Jane the Train, an old woman known for her caravan of eleven shopping carts she pushed and pulled and bullied through the streets of Skid Row. Attached with twisted wires made from old coat hangers and plastic zip ties, the carts moved as one, like a steel snake, each piled high with her decades of street life accumulations. No one knew how she managed the strength to move it; she couldn't have weighed more than ninety-five pounds in her faded house dress, gold San Francisco 49ers warmup jacket, and black high-top Chucks. When Innes tried to help her, she drove him off with a geyser of profanity. She spent each day wagon-training her freight inch by inch, foot by foot, block by block. Cops sometimes had to stop traffic at intersections while she rumbled past, her carts' bockety wheels protesting like braying donkeys.

Innes marveled at the ingenuity the vagabones and their creative mechanisms of transportation. They concocted elaborate vehicles out of bicycles and child trailers and wagons, sometimes hooking all three together like a triple semi.

The undisputed king of wheels was a man known as Chopper, whose gob-smacking dream machine resembled one of those Transformers toys, all sharp metallic edges and angles, pipes and wheels, rubber and enamel paint. It was once a simple shopping cart. The shiny metal basket remained at its core but was surrounded by years of bolted-on embellishments—the rear end of a go-cart in back with the front wheels and frame chopped off and attached to the bow of the basket, sections of sheet metal pried loose from old appliances forming the sides, mounted by fiberglass fins taken from large model airplanes, and the metal-pipe superstructure of a dune buggy above, topped by an eight-foot long helicopter tail rotor. It looked like it might fly. Chopper pedaled it around from his seat in the cockpit with blinking Christmas lights connected to an old car battery. The sight of him in his rig, with his dreadlocks streaming out from under his sticker-covered crash helmet, never failed to entice passersby to pose for selfies with him and his machine, for which he cheerfully extracted donations. His was the kind of makeshift entrepreneurship Innes witnessed daily in the streets of Skid Row and it filled him with wonder and admiration.

Presiding over this empire of squalor was a man known as The Pope of Skid Row. His name was Jamal, and he advertised himself as "the first Muslim Pope" when Vanessa introduced them on the corner of 6th and Main where he was handing out Kirkwood water bottles from an ice-filled cooler. A former hip-hop artist from Inglewood, he broke into the business in the early nineties at the same time as N.W.A. and Snoop Dog, but quickly flamed out and ended up in prison for a string of armed robberies of ampm stores.

"He got religion in Lancaster," Vanessa told Innes on their way to meet him. "He's lived here almost twenty years. This is his life's work now, looking after the homeless, calls it his 'atonement.' You want to learn the ropes here? You want help finding Caleb? You need to meet Jamal."

The man was an imposing figure in a white caftan with a gray goatee and shaved head under a white kufi. He looked at Innes with an arched eyebrow and said, "'Sup." He didn't offer his hand, only a closed fist, which Innes bumped self-consciously.

"I don't think he likes me," Innes said to Vanessa as they continued down the street after their brief conversation.

"You'll have to prove yourself to him. He's seen too many well-intentioned White folks from the 'burbs come down here like slumming tourists and never come back."

"I notice he called these folks 'undomiciled'," he said. "Is that the latest acceptable term? Is 'homeless' no longer PC?"

" 'Homeless' works for me," she said. "I also like 'urban camper' or 'free-range human.' Don't be judgmental, like 'bum' or 'tramp' or 'hobo' or 'beggar' or 'wino' or 'derelict.' "

"Or 'dumpster diver'," he offered.

"Most of them don't give a damn what you call them."

After a few days of urban camping, Innes had grown dependent on Vanessa and George for sustenance. George had a preternatural talent for locating and hoarding food. Innes preferred not to ask where it came from. The patina of cleanliness he had acquired at Sherri's had faded, replaced by itchy skin and greasy stubble. The little red welts on his ankles had reappeared. He stank, and he knew it. It was as if the constant stench from the mountain ranges of garbage rising in the streets had seeped into his pores. Several cases of typhus had been reported. *Typhus,* he marveled, as if this were the nineteenth century.

When the shower truck parked on 6th, Innes ran to get in line, grateful for the chance to wash off the stink of the street. He also needed to pee again, and a shower was preferable to an open storm drain. As he waited, a passing car emitted a familiar tune from the open window. He couldn't hear the words, but the melody stuck in his mind, and he was humming it when his turn came to enter the enclosed shower stall. The words came back to him as he stood naked under the hot stream, and he found himself crying, his tears washing into the drain. It was "The Circle Game," the old Joni Mitchell song about the passage of time as a little boy grows to adulthood. Painted ponies, a carousel of time, et cetera. It was one of his mother's favorite songs. He hadn't understood the significance of the words she had sung to him until he was grown with a child of his own. The song never failed to make him tear up. He'd heard it several times over the years as Caleb had moved from infancy to adolescence, growing farther from his reach with each birthday. He shook with sobs. The pain and longing extended not only to his son, but to all he had lost, and still hoped to recover. He wondered again where Tammy and Steven and Clif were, and if he would ever see them again or instead vanish into the vagabone army.

He dressed, exited the shower truck, and went in search of whiskey.

Innes was sleeping off another bender in the tent when Vanessa shook him awake. "Get up," she said as she squatted next to him. "The police are coming through on a sweep to force everybody off this street. Today, I think."

"What?" he said, not sure he heard right. "Can they do that?"

"It's complicated. There's a law says people can sleep in the streets while LA has a housing shortage. But developers are pressuring the city to clear some of the streets close to their fancy new buildings."

Through the open flap of the tent he could see a giant yellow crane that loomed over the neighborhood with an HVAC unit dangling from a long cable, like a stork delivering the future.

"We have to figure out where to move everyone," she said. "All the other streets down here are packed, there's no room, unless we go outside of Skid Row. Thousands of people already have. The freeway overpasses and underpasses are lined with tent cities. Some end up in the flood channels and riverbeds."

"This is so wrong," said Innes. "I just got settled here, back with the old man. I need a place to regroup and plan the next move for finding Cal. I'm not leaving."

"You won't have a choice. I've seen LAPD do sweeps before. If you don't move voluntarily, they will physically lift you off the sidewalk and into police vans and deposit you at one of the missions and let them sort you out."

"That's obscene."

"Welcome to my world," said Vanessa.

Innes said nothing, dumbfounded by the callous injustice of it all.

"I brought you some things," she said. She opened a paper sack and dumped its contents on his sleeping bag. Another cellphone. More energy bars, water bottles. "I've got to go warn people about the sweep," she said and left the tent.

When George returned, he was more confused and disheveled than ever. He smelled terrible, like a dumpster at a fish market. Innes hoped Vanessa would help get the old man cleaned up inside the mission. Innes dreaded the half-dozen missions in Skid Row, as if entering one would somehow absorb him permanently into the faceless masses. The last time he saw his father alive was at the Union Street Mission in Pasadena, one of the most depressing experiences of his life. A few weeks later, the mission director called to tell him his father was found dead in the alley from alcohol poisoning.

George sat with his legs crossed and stared bleary-eyed at his knees. His torso weaved slightly side to side as he hummed and quoted random bits of dialogue. Innes asked the right question and George emerged from his fog.

"What did you do with our cellphone?"

"Threw it away," George said. "Damn things rot your brain."

"You never told me how you got here from Burbank."

"I got a ride, from that lady friend of yours. The bossy one."

"June?"

"Yeah, that one."

"Jesus H. Christ. Where did she find you?"

"In a park somewhere. She said she'd buy me lunch. She asked about you. I said hell if I know."

"Then she drove you down here?"

"Dropped me at the mission. Took me inside and left me there. But I didn't stay. Place gave me the creeps. Bunch o' hobos."

"Why did you take off like that? Why didn't you wait for me under the freeway?"

"You said you wanted to split up. So I split." Done talking, he belched for punctuation, rolled over onto his sleeping bag, and within minutes began to snore.

Innes sat with his legs crossed as fumes of self-loathing wafted over him. He had abandoned the old man, as he had done to his own father. And Sherri. Was there no end to his faithlessness? Maybe it was karmic justice that his own son appeared to be doing the same to him now.

He stepped out of the tent to stretch his legs as Vanessa pulled up at the curb on her Vespa. "It's true," she said as she pulled off her pink helmet. "The police are coming through here—today. We need to warn everybody and tell them to gather their things. Will you help me?"

"No. This is bullshit. What if we all resist? You know—lock arms. Block the street."

Vanessa stared at him. "You're not serious."

"I am. Annie and I went to an Occupy demonstration at LA City Hall a few years back. People sat in rows and locked arms. The cops couldn't break them apart. They gave up and watched."

"So, you want to Occupy Skid Row?" Vanessa said, her voice

drenched with incredulity.

"Absolutely."

"You're crazy. Jamal has tried to organize these people for years. Can't be done." She turned her back to him, as if putting an emphatic end to the conversation.

"What's the harm in trying?" he persisted. "Worse thing they can do is force us to leave. Why make it easy for them? How much time do we have till they get here?"

"I'm not sure," she said, consulting her phone. "Might be only an hour."

"That gives us enough time to work the street and tell everybody to hang together. I'll take this side, you take the other."

Vanessa looked at him for a few seconds and smiled. "You mean it, don't you? You really want to do something."

"Hell yes."

"Okay," she said slowly, still skeptical. "But we need to check with Jamal. Let me talk to him first. Don't do anything stupid."

Innes had a flash of inspiration: the image of the Master of Disaster and her cameraman at the Casa Grande fire. "We've got to tell the media," he said. "Get them down here to witness this travesty."

Her eyes widened and the skepticism drained from her face. "I've got numbers for reporters in my phone."

"It's perfect," he said. "Homeless people rousted a few days after Christmas. It's a slow week for news. They won't be able to resist."

Vanessa returned a few minutes later with Jamal, who eyed Innes with wary regard. "What's this occupy shit?" he said.

Innes explained his idea of mimicking the Occupy Wall Street protests. After conferring privately with Vanessa, Jamal said, "This sweep is illegal. And they know it. Fuck 'em. Let's try it." He poked Innes in the chest with his index finger. "Anybody gets hurt, it's on you, White boy."

The three of them canvassed the street, stopping everyone they met, leaning into tents, shaking awake those asleep or passed out, telling them what was coming down and what to do. Most told them to fuck off, but several said, hell yeah, they'd join. After an hour, Jamal, Innes, and Vanessa had persuaded nearly half the people on the block to line up on the curbs. George woke up and persuaded Vanessa to give him money for food, which he spent instead on three for-ty-ounce bottles of Colt 45 to pass along the street for liquid courage.

The first squad car appeared at 3:31 p.m., driving slowly down the middle of the street, lights flashing, no siren. A moment later another appeared at the other end of the block and parked broadside, blocking traffic. From the first car's loudspeaker came a mechanical burp followed by the announcement that everyone had one hour to pack up their belongings and leave the block.

More of the street's residents emerged from their tents and sat on the curb. The first "fuck you" was announced at 3:42, as a TV news van arrived and parked a block away. Channel 7 of course. Innes recognized the *Times* columnist Gustavo Sanchez, renowned for siding with the underdog, interviewing Jamal.

The first empty beer bottle shattered against the driver's side door of the lead police car at 3:53. Four police cars stopped in mid-street, and blue-clad officers emerged. One more TV news van entered the block, then another.

Innes and Vanessa strode up and down the block yelling instructions to lock arms. Another empty beer bottle exploded on the pavement a few yards from an officer. More police cars arrived. Two officers on horseback appeared. Innes and Vanessa exchanged worried looks. Throwing bottles at the police was not part of the plan.

Jamal ran up and down the street. "No, no, no. Don't throw shit," he shouted. "This is a peaceful demonstration."

A police officer on horseback, a Black man with massive biceps, clip-clopped toward Innes. "Who are you?" he called from his mount. "Where's Jamal?"

The horse's enormous chestnut head bobbed and swayed, yellow teeth bared inches from Innes's face. He nearly wet himself.

Jamal appeared by his side. "This shit is illegal," he said, glaring at the policeman defiantly, unfazed by the horse's jaws. "You know that, Lester. There's supposed to be a moratorium."

"I'm sorry, Jamal. I have my orders," said the policeman. "We're not moving these folks off the streets, only this street."

"You're supposed to give twenty-four hours' notice," said Jamal.

"We posted flyers yesterday," Lester said. "I can't help it if your people tore them down."

The officer rode away toward a mob that had spilled into the street. More mounted police entered the block, dismounted, and descended on those seated on the curbs, applying gentle persuasion. A third empty beer bottle landed with a crash on the windshield of a cruiser. Three officers converged on the man who threw it and tried to lift him off the sidewalk. His mates latched onto him, hooking their arms and legs around his limbs until the officers and the resisters formed a trembling, swaying tower of human appendages. The pile of humanity shuddered, and tumbled into the street, protesters landing on top of the men and women in blue. A half dozen more police ran over to pull them apart. Camera crews moved in for a closer shot.

The time for gentle persuasion ended with the third bottle. Police grabbed for the curb sitters and pulled them up.

For some reason, Innes chanted "Attica! Attica! Attica!" A few protesters joined in, but most, including Vanessa and Jamal, only stared at him in confusion. He stopped, feeling foolish. "You know. *Dog Day Afternoon?* Al Pacino?" he said. They shook their heads and looked at him like he was unhinged. He resumed the chant. The revelers showed no sign they knew what it meant, but they liked the sound of it. A few chimed in, then more; soon dozens shouted in unison. Vanessa joined in the chant, laughing the words. The TV crews converged on them. George went to the curb to sit down.

After a few minutes, Innes stopped chanting. People were hollering, laughing, and partying, but it wasn't funny anymore. Dismounted horses, reins held by officers on foot, reared and struggled and whinnied. A cop spun around in crazy circles and flailed blindly at a woman perched on his back, her legs wrapped around his torso and hands covering his eyes. The batons came out. Demonstrators fought back and threw objects from their tents at police. The sounds of shattering glass punctuated the shouting and swearing. Jamal frantically shouted at police and demonstrators, trying to de-escalate. Too late. It was now a riot.

Innes looked for Vanessa and the old man. Vanessa was arguing with Lester as another cop grabbed George under the armpits and heaved him up off the sidewalk. He staggered, still drunk probably, and fell forward, hitting his head on the flared metal base of a streetlamp with a sickening thwop, like a ripe watermelon dropped on a tile floor.

"Oh no, George!" Innes yelled and ran to him, followed by Vanessa and Lester.

The old man rolled off the curb onto his back in the street and stared up at the sky, his Jamaican tam in a puddle in the gutter. They knelt over him.

"He's still breathing," said Vanessa.

A crowd gathered. Lester told them to back off and radioed for an ambulance.

Innes knelt over the old man and studied his blank expression, reminded of Annie's gaping stare into space so many nights ago. He tried not to think about what had just happened or who had the brilliant idea to organize a homeless uprising that had turned into a riot and left his father-in-law in the gutter like a sack of garbage.

The crowd dispersed; the chants stopped. People drifted back to their tents to collect their belongings.

When the ambulance arrived, Vanessa told the EMTs George was still breathing but hadn't moved since he fell. They strapped him to a gurney and loaded him into the back. Innes and Vanessa climbed in and rode with him to Good Shepherd Hospital. Innes held the old man's inert hand. Vanessa put her arm around Innes's shoulder. At the hospital George was wheeled into the ER and Innes and Vanessa were ushered into a family waiting room. A cheerful young woman with the hospital staff asked if they'd like coffee.

At 10:56 p.m., George Aloysius McQuillen, age seventy, suffering from "acute intracranial hemorrhage from blunt force trauma," was pronounced dead.

Book VI

INNES BURIED HIS FACE IN VANESSA'S NECK. They shared a loveseat in the fluorescent-bathed waiting area outside the ER. It was mid-morning, and Innes had spent the night there, sleeping on a cracked vinyl couch. Vanessa had returned after accompanying George's body to the coroner and looking into burial arrangements. Innes couldn't move from the couch, much less deal with anything. He had barely begun to process the horrible, fiery death of Sherri when he was forced to witness the random, pointless, brutal end of his father-in-law's life.

"You're right," he said. He lifted his head and looked her in the eye. "It was random, pointless, and brutal."

"What did you say?" Vanessa said.

"His death was random, pointless, and brutal. Like you said."

"I didn't say that. But I suppose it's true."

"It's my fault. I killed him. My stupid Occupy idea. He's dead because of me."

"Stop it. It was an accident. It's nobody's fault."

"I dreamt of George, dead in the street, surrounded by a mob, a cop standing over him. Couple weeks ago. How do you explain that?"

"Weird. But a coincidence," she said.

"Jamal was right. I should mind my own goddamn business. Everybody I care about ends up dead because of me. My mother. My father. Annie. Sherri. Now George." He felt the need to ask forgiveness from someone, but from whom?

"Sherri? Who's Sherri?" Vanessa said.

That story would have to wait. "Never mind," he said.

She had brought him a newspaper, a sack of donuts, and a plastic bottle of orange juice. "I know it's no consolation," she said as she handed him a donut, "and it won't bring George back, but our little homeless rebellion did some good."

"What do you mean? It was a complete disaster, like everything else in my life."

"It was all over the TV news. Gustavo Sanchez has a great column on it today." She offered him the *Times*, but he looked away. "Look," she said. She cradled his jaw in her hand and turned his face toward her. "I've had mixed feelings about helping you. I don't understand your choices. Maybe I hold you to too high a standard, in Annie's memory. Sure, you've fucked up sometimes. We all have. But I admire your passion."

More families filed into the visitor room, looking tired or desperate, talking softly in Spanish, Korean, Vietnamese, Tagalog. Innes turned away, chewed the donut and sipped juice. Vanessa was still talking but he wasn't listening.

"Did you know it was June who brought him down here, to Skid Row?" he interrupted.

"Yes, of course, that's how I found out he was here. She told me. What does it matter?"

"How is it she happened to find him?"

Vanessa paused for a moment. "She was following him. Both of you, ever since you left Pasadena, until you disappeared."

"Following us? Like a spy?"

"She was worried about you. We all were. She reported your whereabouts to me and Clif and Terry every day."

It was heartening to know they hadn't forgotten him, but he bristled at the implied conspiracy. "Like I was a runaway child? Why?"

"Because you were so stubborn. You wouldn't accept help from anyone. And we thought you seemed unhinged. After Annie. You know."

He knew. He was. More than she imagined.

"Why didn't you answer when I called, or call back?" he said.

"I was in Mexico for a week, I told you."

"With Juan?"

"I don't want to talk about it."

Juan Alfonso was her absent husband. A tax accountant, he had been splitting his time between Pasadena and his hometown in the mountains of Oaxaca, ostensibly to look in on his aging mother and the family's small organic coffee plantation. His time in Mexico had been increasing in recent years, leaving Vanessa to fend for herself for months at a time. Innes hadn't seen Juan for a long while, maybe a couple of years. He was never quite sure what was going on in that relationship or why she never went to see her husband in Mexico. He'd pressed Annie for details, but she was protective of Vanessa's privacy and advised him to mind his own business.

He changed the subject. "What happened to Jamal?"

"He's at the lock-up, bailing folks out of jail."

"Jail? Shit. Is he pissed at me?"

"Yes. But he blames himself, too, for going along with it. He called you 'Crazy White Boy.' I'm not sure he meant it in a bad way, though. I think he secretly admires the way you put yourself out there, on the street, instead of in some soup kitchen."

Vanessa got up to leave. "I need to go and retrieve your things. Wait for me, okay? It's not a good idea for you to show up at the police station right now."

"I'm not staying here another minute."

"Why don't you hang out at the mission till I get back."

"I hate those places."

"Only for an hour. You don't have to sing or pray, if that's what you're worried about. You don't have to ask for a meal, either. I can get you something later."

As much as he dreaded the rescue missions, he did not relish wandering the streets. "What? What was that?" he said.

"I said I can get you something to eat later."

"No, I mean after that. Something about relish?"

"Nothing. That's all. Come on. I'll drop you off."

The main hall of the Rescue Gospel Mission was relatively cheerful, well-lit, and clean, with bright blue, freshly painted walls. Twenty long communal dining tables lined with plastic folding chairs filled the space. On the walls hung framed posters with Bible verses superimposed on photos of natural wonders—mountains, lakes, seashores. A handful of people scattered around the tables.

Innes sat by himself and scanned the room, studying faces, trying to suss out the life stories etched into those leathery visages. Then a powerful set of arms wrapped him from behind and a baritone voice said, "Innes. My man."

The arms released him, and Innes turned to see the smiling face of Clifton Tompkins, Jr. He stood and wrapped his own spindly arms around the man's vast torso and hugged hard as his waning strength allowed.

"Whoa there, Innes, you'll bust a rib," said Clif.

Innes released him and stepped back. "God, am I glad to see you, Clif."

The big man beamed. "I'm sure God had a hand in bringing you here."

"No, that was Vanessa," Innes corrected.

"Ah yes, the angel of mercy. I've seen the Lord's work in Vanessa." Clif put a gentle hand on his shoulder.

Innes sat. "What are you doing here, Clif?"

"I'm a volunteer. Couple days a month, when I can get away from the office."

"Does Vanessa know you're here?"

"Yes, of course. I asked her to bring you. We've all been worried about you, Innes. Vanessa, June, Terry. Bev and me. Bev sends her love."

"Love right back at her. Tasha, too. How is everybody?"

"We're doing fine, fine. I'll fill you in later. Let's talk about you."

"Me? How about this: I hate shelters. My father died in one of these places."

"I understand. But I'm glad you came." Clif sat down and turned to face him. The flimsy chair squeaked under his mass. "I am so sorry about George. Terrible, just terrible. And so soon after you lost your lovely Annie." He reached out and again laid a hand on Innes' shoulder. "You've borne a burden of sorrow no man should have to endure."

Innes stared at his knees, grateful for Clif's sympathy, but unsure he wanted to wallow in his burden of sorrow at the moment.

"But I'm here to tell you all is not lost," Clif said. "You must not lose hope. Nessa tells me you're drinking heavily, hanging around with some of these lost souls down here like you're one of them. You are not one of them."

"Sure about that?" Innes responded. He wasn't sure himself.

"You have friends, people who love you." Clif gave his shoulder a gentle squeeze. "I know it's a temptation to drink it all into submission. I am asking you as your friend, Innes, do not go down that road."

"What's the point? Everything I touch turns to shit. Everyone I love dies."

"I know, you feel like you've fallen into a bottomless pit. I'm telling you there is a way out. But you can't do this alone. You need to open your heart to the Lord and let him show you the way."

Sensing a sermon coming, Innes looked away. "Vanessa said I wouldn't have to sing or pray in here."

"Nobody's asking you to sing or pray. Just hear me out. I know you're not a churchgoer, Innes. God doesn't care about that. He offers hope to anyone who will listen."

Any chance God ever had with Innes had evaporated the day his mother died, and he was in no mood for reconciliation now.

"What evaporated?" Innes asked.

"What?" answered Clif with a momentary look of confusion and concern.

"Never mind."

"Anyway," Clif continued. "Do you know the story of Job? God visited all kinds of misery on Job, though he was a good man, a rich man, a faithful man. Satan challenged God, said Job would turn away from God if he fell out of favor and suffered. But he didn't. He endured one torment after another and never lost faith."

"Sounds kind of sadistic."

"Not at all. God restored all His blessings to Job. Happy ending. The point is, if you keep the faith, stay hopeful that everything will work out in the end, you can endure anything, no matter how horrible. Did Job give up and drink himself into a stupor? No, he did not."

Innes contemplated Clif's words and glanced across the room. More people trickled in and filled the empty chairs—old women, teens in hoodies, young families with small children. "I know enough about the Bible to know the God in there is a cruel, vengeful God, always raining misery down on people who displease him. That's not a God I want to know."

"God has a plan for humanity, and we can't always understand his ways."

"Are telling me all the pointless suffering and agony in the world is part of God's plan? Centuries of war and slaughter and inhumanity?"

"That's not God's work. That's Satan's work."

"So why doesn't God stop it? Isn't he supposed to be omnipotent, more powerful than the devil?" Innes felt the itch for an argument building within. Rage seeking an escape vent. He realized he was channeling Sherri and her witheringly pointed contentiousness, tinged with his lingering guilt and grief over her demise, and that of George.

"God allows men to have the free will to choose good or evil. Many choose evil. Man is weak, fallen, sinful."

"Then how do you explain natural disasters, like earthquakes and tsunamis that kill thousands?" he said, voice rising in indignation. "That's not people choosing to do evil. That's God choosing to do evil."

"It only looks evil to us because we don't know God's plan. You would understand if you opened your heart, read the Bible. It all makes sense if you let it."

Innes said nothing and looked away. Clif stared at him for a moment, then studied his canvas high-tops. "I guess I'm not so good at this," he said. "I didn't go to divinity school, I'm no theologian. I'm just an old jock, a dentist. But it all makes sense to me. It gives me purpose. It fills me with hope and love."

"I'm happy for you, Clif, I am. Sometimes I'm envious of religious people. They seem happier. I'd like to be happier. But I can't make myself happy by believing in fairy tales."

Clif furrowed his brow. "You are a proud man, Innes. Fatally proud. You choose to turn your back on a loving, merciful God out of sheer pride."

"A loving God?" Innes rose, looking down at Clif. "Where was your loving God when my mother was cut down in the prime of her life by some stupid random blood clot? Where was He when my father drank himself into an early grave over the senseless death of his one true love? Where was He when some bastard torched my home and killed my wife? Where was He when a frail old man who never hurt a fly was slammed against a light post cracking his skull open only because he was in the wrong place at the wrong time? Huh? Where the hell was He? Can you answer me that?"

He was shouting now and trembling with rage. Everyone in the room was staring at him. The look on Clif's face filled him with regret. "I'm sorry. I shouldn't yell at you."

"You're in pain. I understand." Clif rose to leave and put his hand on his shoulder. "I'll always be your friend. Don't forget that." He walked toward the rear of the hall.

Innes sat alone, filled with regret at his knack for alienating the people who care about him. The long tables were now crowded with street people. The place depressed him. He wondered where Vanessa was, and got up to wait for her outside.

Innes's mind reeled. What if they all were right about God and he was wrong? Why couldn't he see what they see, feel what they feel? A surge of doubt cascaded across his mind and leaked into his soul, if he had such a thing. The powerful sense of loss that had eased during his verbal jousting with Clif returned. He had an urge to lie down, go to sleep, and never wake up.

Instead, he exited to the street. It was drizzling again. He walked down 6th toward San Julian with no idea where to go next. The death of George and the angry exchange with Clif had exiled him to the far-off land of Catatonia. He felt like one of those lost souls he'd seen in the middle of San Pedro Street.

"I'm not lost. I know where I am," he said. He stopped and looked around to see if someone was behind him. Seeing no one, he kept moving and again wondered where Vanessa was. The rain was not unpleasant, but the dark clouds moving in from the north looked ominous.

"Why is there a weather report inside my head? Hello?"

He looked around again. Still no one. His attention turned to the thing Clif had inserted into his consciousness: the thing called God.

"Are you there?" he said aloud. "Am I Job? Why don't you show yourself?"

Silence.

God had never played much of a role in Innes's life. Yet there was an undeniable possibility God was real and talking to him now. What would a supreme being possibly want with such a wretched soul? Clif's words echoed in his mind. Mercy. Hope. Love. Maybe, if the voice continued, he should listen.

Later in the afternoon, as he strolled aimlessly along 7th Street, he spotted the familiar overalls and black ball cap of Jefferson. The man had a brown paper sack in one hand. Innes jogged ahead to catch up with him, hoping for a pint to share. "My man," he said.

"Oh, it's you. You shadowin' me, Susie?" said Jefferson.

"Got anything to drink?" said Innes, walking with him stride for stride. He had resigned himself to the fact that it was easier to answer to "Susie" than talk him out of it.

"We'll see. I'm on my way to get some sump'n. Wanna come?" Jefferson turned into an alley and led Innes halfway down the block to a dumpster at the rear door of a Taco Hell. "They always got good stuff in here," he said as he opened the lid and peered inside.

No longer a dumpster virgin, Innes suppressed his natural revulsion. All he'd eaten was a couple donuts, and his stomach was growling.

"My stomach is not growling."

"Susie say what?" said Jefferson as he retrieved a white Taco Hell sack. They continued down the alley and perched on a stoop under an awning out of the drizzle. The bag contained several burritos in thin foil. Innes unwrapped one and took a bite. Rice and beans mostly. But warm and chewy. Spicy, too.

Jefferson pulled out a pint, and the two men resumed the fine dining and drinking conversation they had started back at Bob's Big Boy in Toluca.

"Do you ever hear voices?" said Innes. "Like, in your head?"

"Naw. But I know plenty o' people around here what do. Some of 'em talk back to 'em, too." Jefferson twirled his index finger around his ear.

"I think I'm hearing them," Innes said. "It's like somebody's narrating what I'm doing, as I do it. Like just now. I heard somebody describe me eating this burrito."

"Not a good sign, Susie. Don't start talkin' back to 'em or everybody think you crazy. You don't want that. The crazies get picked on down here."

"It started yesterday, or the day before. I thought it was someone nearby talking. I looked around and didn't see anybody. But I definitely heard it. Not talking to me, exactly, more like talking about me."

Jefferson regarded him with a look of concern, shrugged, and took a long pull on the pint.

"Do you believe in God?" Innes asked.

Jefferson looked at him, contemptuous, and waved a hand around. "Look at this world we live in," he said. "What you think?"

They polished off the bag of burritos and passed the pint until it was empty. Jefferson curled up against the door and closed his eyes. Innes sat with his legs crossed, stomach full, and head buzzing. He leaned against the wall and waited to pass out in a drunken haze and, he hoped, to silence the voice.

He was awakened by rainfall on his face and a sharp gas pain and turbulence in his gut, slumped sideways on the cold, wet concrete. He sat up and checked his watch. He'd been out over an hour. The soft mist had turned into a steady downpour and beat a staccato rhythm on the aluminum awning above. He had the urge to puke but belched instead. It didn't help. A rumbling in his lower intestines warned him he'd better find a toilet, and fast.

"Goddamn dumpster burritos." Nudging Jefferson, he said, "I think I'm gonna be sick."

"Don't puke on me," said Jefferson without moving from his fetal position.

"No, I gotta take a shit. Real bad. I don't think I can make it to the toilet at the park."

"Do what everybody else does," said Jefferson. "Crap in the sewer. There's one over there."

Innes was repelled by the idea of defecating in public. The sewer grate was exposed from both ends of the alley. He had to do something. Now. Two gray plastic trash bins on wheels stood by the rear door of another business a few yards away. He pulled himself up, waddled across the alley with clenched sphincter muscle, and rolled the two bins over to the sewer grate, positioning one on each side to grant himself a modicum of privacy. They smelled like rotting fish guts marinating in dumpster juice. He might have to puke after all.

Lowering his sweatpants and jockey shorts, he squatted over the grate and leaned back with his hands behind him on the curb to keep his shoes out of harm's way. He closed his eyes and released his sphincter. Diarrhea exploded out of him, splashing on the metal grid, splattering his shoes and sweatpants. The wind-driven rain turned torrential, pelting his face. He opened his eyes in time to see the ghostly shape of a projectile descend on him from the heavens, followed by a blow to his forehead and the sting of ripped flesh just above one eye. A long brown palm frond lay in the gutter beside him. He pushed himself onto his knees. A trickle of blood leaked into his left eye. Was he dreaming? A million-to-one shot, getting hit by one of those things. Yet here it was, the frond with his name on it, arrived at last. Where did it come from? He looked around for a palm tree, saw none, and remained on his knees, unsure if his guts were done exploding. The smell from the grate reached his nostrils and mixed with the trash bin odor into a toxic perfume. He leaned over and puked into the street. Drops of blood joined the splatter and were swept away by the rushing water. He remained on all fours for several moments and contemplated his place in the universe.

"This is my goddamn place in the universe," he said to no one in particular.

"I am not talking to '*no one in particular*,' I am talking to you," he said.

Now he was shouting, as if arguing with himself.

"I *am* arguing with myself. Or whoever the hell you are." What if God really was talking to him as he wallowed in his own puke and shit? Was this hell?

"You talkin' to me?" Jefferson shouted from across the alley, through the din of the downpour.

"No, I'm talking to God, can't you see?"

Jefferson pulled himself up off the stoop and scrambled over to Innes. He wrinkled his nose. "Oh, that's nasty, Susie."

Innes stood up, pants at his knees, ankle deep in water.

"Hey, you're bleedin'," Jefferson said. "Better wash your pants and shoes in the rainwater. Better wash the shirt, too."

Innes peeled off his wet clothes and shoes, got on his hands and knees in the floodwaters, naked as the day he was born, and sloshed his things around in the gray current like an old-time washerwoman at the bank of a river.

"Very funny," he said. "Washerwoman."

"Say what?" said Jefferson.

"The voice. Just said I'm a washerwoman."

"Worried about you, Susie."

Innes sat on the grate and let the cold gray water cleanse him like a rustic bidet. The absurdity of his situation mingled with the weeks of lingering grief from fatal calamity after fatal calamity until his body shuddered with giggles and erupted into peals of roaring laughter.

"I'm not laughing, asshole," he sobbed.

His laughter dissolved into cries of misery. He rolled over onto his side and clutched his knees to his chest and let the filthy alley rainwater wash over him.

"Just. Shut. Up. Please," he beseeched.

"Oh, Susie," said Jefferson. "We better get you inside."

He jogged through the drizzle and pulled his shirt over his head in a vain attempt to stay dry. The end of the arcade came into view. He quickened his pace, hoping to reach shelter before the darkening skies opened. The knee-high wild grasses brushed his trousers, covering them with burrs and feathery seeds. From a distance came the rumble of thunder, strange to hear in these parts. The rain came heavy. He broke into a sprint only a few yards from the end of the arcade. As he was about to duck under the marble roof, down came the torrents that had threatened all day, soaking him in seconds. Then he was in shelter as the downpour outside pounded the pebbly gardens and stone fountains and walkways, the fat drops bouncing like ball bearings. The nearby trees disappeared behind a gray-white curtain. He held his arms out scarecrow-like to assess his drenchedness. Water dripped off him onto the terrazzo floor. His green T-shirt and blue jeans had turned black, and his running shoes squished water out their porous skins as he moved. At the far end of the arcade, a figure appeared in a stone archway, directly beneath a keystone. A young man, waving at him. "Dad. Over here," he called. It was Caleb. Innes jogged toward him, happy to be home and out of the rain. Another figure appeared behind Caleb, a woman. Annie. Caleb! Annie! The two waved from the archway but remained fifty yards distant. He looked down at his feet. The tiles moved beneath him. He broke from a run into a gliding stride like a long jumper approaching the sand pit, pushing off hard with one leg, lifting the other high into the air, gliding, almost flying, and repeating with the other leg, pushing, striding, gliding. The sensation made him silly with joy. Still he gained no ground on the waving pair. The woman called to him. "Innes," she said. "That tux. That sign." Stopped in mid stride, he focused on her. It wasn't Annie. It was Vanessa.

Innes woke on a cot under a thick blanket, naked but warm and dry, and stared at the ceiling, trying to get his bearings. A small room. A gooseneck lamp on a desk in the corner provided pale light. He had awakened from yet another dream. The chill returned to his bones. But he was home. With Caleb. And. And... "Vanessa?" he said aloud.

"Right here," she said.

He turned his head. Vanessa leaned forward in a big stuffed chair. She looked disheveled, no makeup, her hair loose around her shoulders. "How do you feel?" she said. She rose and sat on the end of the cot by his feet.

"I just had the freakiest dream," he said. "More like a nightmare. I was a bum in Skid Row, hearing voices like a crazy person, and puking in the gutter."

"Oh, dear," she said.

"Yeah, messed up, amiright?"

She nodded and looked away.

"Where's Cal?" he said.

She moved closer and lay a hand across his forehead. "I think the fever has broken. You were very sick. We wanted to take you to the hospital, but the doctor said you should rest here for a while to see if you stabilized."

"Sick? I was out in the rain for only a few minutes."

"You slept for a while. I think it helped." Vanessa returned to the chair.

"Where am I?" he said. "A hotel?"

She leaned forward, her eyes on his. "Innes, listen to me. Wherever you think you are. Or were. That was your dream."

He stared at her, unsure where she was going with this.

"The Skid Row part?" she continued. "That's real. That's where you are right now. At the Rescue Gospel Mission."

He groaned and rolled over, facing away from her. "Skid Row is a nightmare from which I am trying to awake," he mumbled to himself, recalling a line he'd read somewhere. Proust?

"Your friend Jefferson brought you in. He carried you in his arms. You were barefoot, in soaked sweatpants, blood all over your face, crying, making no sense. We thought you were having a breakdown. We called a doctor, who patched up your face and gave you something to help you sleep."

"What was I saying?" he said. He felt the bandage on his forehead.

"You said you were hearing voices and we should make it stop."

The whole dismal scene reassembled in his memory. He remembered the voices. "So it's true. I am crazy," he said to the wall.

"No, not crazy. You were distraught. Over George," she said. "After everything that's happened, it's no wonder."

George. Somehow, he'd forgotten. The horror of the last few days presented itself in full Technicolor. "What about George? Where is he?"

"Don't worry. I've taken care of it," she said.

"Shouldn't we have a funeral?"

"I said it's taken care of. Right now, you need to worry about your own self."

"He's my father-in-law. I should do something for him. After all--"

She cut him off mid-sentence. "The best thing you can do for him is pull yourself together and find Caleb. That's what George would want. Leave the rest to me."

Vanessa was firm, in control. Like June. He wasn't sure how he felt about that.

"Shouldn't we sue the police department, or somebody?" he said. "Wrongful death?"

Vanessa shook her head. "I asked June about that. She said it would be hard to find a lawyer to take the case. Juries are not likely to sympathize with a seventy-year-old homeless alcoholic who rioted against the police. The city would be unlikely to offer a settlement."

Innes wanted to argue the point, object to such a crass view of a human life, but he let it drop. He could see the cold logic in it.

"I brought you some fresh clothes." She pointed to a plastic bag on the floor. "I got the tent and sleeping bags, too. And your things. Some of them anyway. The cellphone was gone. There was a big knife, right? I got that. And Annie's diary."

He hoped she wouldn't press him about the diary. He could barely stand to acknowledge its existence, much less open it.

"Where *were* you?" he said, remembering she'd left him at the mission.

"I'm sorry," she said. "I ran into some people who needed help. I knew Clif would be there for you."

"Yeah, he was there, alright. He tried to bring me to Jesus."

"Sorry. How'd that go?"

"I'm still a heathen. Headed straight for hell. And whaddaya know, here I am. Where's Clif now?"

"He went back to Pasadena, after staying up with you all night. Anyway, how do you feel now?"

"I could eat something." He recalled that the last time he'd seen the man who stayed up with him all night he was screaming at him like a lunatic.

At the Penny Café on Main he ordered a BLT and wolfed it down, almost choking, shocked at how famished he was.

"Our little uprising has got momentum," she said between sips of black coffee. "The police tried to clear another block this morning, on 7th, and the homeless fought back. The TV crews showed up again, and this time the police withdrew. Jamal talked them into backing down."

"Well, that's good. I guess."

She reached across the table and squeezed his hand. He squeezed back, then let go, not wanting such a moment to linger past its sell-by date.

"I don't know how long this can last," she said. "The media will lose interest at some point. We have to figure out a way to make this resistance permanent, to change the whole conversation about the homeless and their rights, their human rights."

"You're really into this, aren't you?" he said.

"Yes, I am," she said. "For the first time in a long time, I feel like there is something to be done. These people should be organized into a movement, like the hotel workers, ten, fifteen years ago. That's always been Jamal's dream."

"A homeless people's union," he said. "Wouldn't that be something."

"Of course, Jamal still thinks you're loco. A White boy dilettante from the suburbs. And you are. But you've won a tiny bit of respect down here with your stupid antics."

Innes wasn't sure whether to be flattered or insulted. He chose both.

"There's one more thing you can do," she said. "We're not the only people from the Casa Grande in Skid Row. Tammy Templeton and Steven Song, too. They're sharing a tent over on 7th."

"Tammy and Steven? Sharing a tent?" He hadn't thought about them in days, and missed them now, terribly.

"Losing their families at the same time brought them together. Tammy went mad with grief. We thought she was suicidal. Steven's the one who found her down here. He pulled her back from the edge."

"What a pair. An Asian gay guy and a Black woman. Amazing what odd couples come out of tragedy."

"I'm not sure they're a couple, exactly. More like soulmates. Anyway, they're in trouble and need your help."

"Absolutely," he said. "What can I do?"

"This morning, Tammy hit a cop in the back of the head with a cinder block. Knocked him cold. The cop had Steven in a chokehold. Tammy went into a rage. Didn't know her own strength. Surprised everybody, including herself."

"I know exactly how she felt," he said.

"She and Steven ran off and hid in an empty tent. The cops gave up the chase, but they have a description out on them. The cop she hit is in the hospital with a concussion."

Innes pictured George McQuillen on the gurney at the hospital. "Karma's a witch," he said.

"I need to get them out of Skid Row, out of LAPD territory," she said. "I've arranged a temporary place for them in Santa Monica. They need to go, first thing in the morning. I can't take them. Can you? You can use my truck. It's parked here on Main, next block."

"Why can't you take them?"

"I have personal business to attend to in the morning."

"Why not tonight?"

"The place I found can't take them till tomorrow."

"Okay," he said. He liked the idea of helping Vanessa for once. "What's the plan?"

"You can sleep in my truck tonight. There are extra sleeping bags in the back. I'll take my scooter and meet you back here with Steven and Tammy in the morning, around seven. Okay?" She paid the tab, handed him her keys and left him to finish his BLT.

When he exited the café, it was dark. He paused on the sidewalk and gazed skyward. It had begun to rain again. He watched sleepily as the drops, silver and fat, fell heavily on the sidewalk. The time had come for him to resume his journey westward. The forecasts were right: *El Niño* rain was general all over the Southland. It was falling on every part of the flat central basin, on the treeless hills, on the LA River and, farther westward, loudly falling into the dark mutinous Pacific waves. It was falling, too, upon every part of the lonely yard where Annie Innes's ashes lay. It darkened the ruined roof of the Casa Grande, it filled the empty koi pond, it weighed on the sagging fronds of the palm trees. His soul swooned as he heard the rain falling faintly through the universe and faintly falling, like the descent of their last end, upon all the living and the dead.

"Now you're doing it," Innes said. "Just like the old man."

Innes spoke aloud to himself again, invoking the memory of George McQuillen, comparing his confused state to that of his dead father-in-law.

"No, I'm not. I'm talking to you, Mr. Voice in My Head. You're quoting literary shit. Henry James, right? You're not God, are you? You're just some pretentious asshole."

Book VII

THE SOUND OF KNUCKLES ON A WINDOW jolted Innes from a deep sleep. He sat up, expecting to be entering or exiting another strange dream, but this time it was no dream: He was zippered into a sleeping bag in the back of Vanessa's mud-splattered Ford Explorer. Peering through the rear window was Vanessa, flanked by Tammy Templeton and Steven Song. Innes clambered out of the bag and pushed open the rear hatch.

Steven hugged him as he stepped out. "We thought we'd lost you, Innes."

Tammy wrapped him in her arms and buried her face in the side of his neck. A trickle of tears ran down into his shirt.

"Easy, Tammy. You'll bust a rib," he said.

She broke the clinch and kissed him on the cheek. The despondency in her eyes the last time he saw her was still there, but she managed a hopeful smile. Her hair was in neat cornrows and she wore a simple patterned dashiki. Dignified and well put together, as always, despite the circumstances.

"I've been crazy worried about you," she said.

"You look good, Tammy." She did, compared to the last time, at the double funeral for Sam and Eric, a scene he hoped to never witness again. The Templetons' friends filled the AME church in Altadena. Tammy, dressed in black, sat motionless in the pew, staring at her knees. The music and the wailing were too much for Innes, and he went outside to be alone with his own grief. Afterwards, he and Tammy had cried in each other's arms.

Steven's mop of black hair appeared unwashed. A faded Manchester United jersey hung over his belly and he gripped an overstuffed dirty backpack. Not up to his usual sartorial standard. If Michael were in a grave, he'd be rolling in it right now, Innes almost said.

Waves of regret washed over him for abandoning his Casa Grande friends. He despised himself for hiding out with Sherri for so long, forgetting who he was and who mattered to him. He pushed thoughts of Sherri out of his mind—likely would be pushing her out of his mind for the rest of his life.

"Look at us," Innes said. He wiped a tear from his cheek. "A few months ago, we were happy with our families in the Casa. Now we're in Skid Row. What a world."

They had fallen so far in so short a time. The thin veneer that separates civil society from the raw state of nature—nasty, brutish, and short—could dissolve so quickly, like tissue paper in the rain. He looked at his companions and smiled, and for the first time in many weeks felt part of something larger than himself.

"I hate to break up this sweet reunion, but we have to get you two out of town, right now," said Vanessa.

They loaded their things into the Explorer, stacking their backpacks on top of a pile of soft suitcases, which Innes assumed were Vanessa's. "Where are you going?" he asked her as Steven and Tammy arranged their gear.

"I have to get to the courthouse before it closes early for New Year's Eve. But I'll meet you guys in Santa Monica. Tammy and Steven have the address."

"What about Cal? I still have no idea where he is."

"We'll find him," she said. "Last time I talked to June, she suggested we look in Santa Monica, so this works out perfectly."

"June? How would she know?" he said, annoyed. The return of the puppet master.

"Not sure, just a hunch, I guess. We'll search all of LA if we have to."

"Whatchu mean 'we,' lady?"

"Of course, 'we,'" said Vanessa. "Did you think I would abandon you? You, Homer Virgil Innes, have got to accept help from people. Without the attitude. And a little more gratitude."

The full name treatment. Like his mother used when angry at him. Vanessa was right, of course, and it pleased him to see she thought of them all as a sort of family.

"I know you have this phobia about the freeways," Vanessa continued. "But you have to take the 10."

"Oh, man. Not the 10," he said. The mere thought of it made his skin tingle. "I can get them there just as fast on Wilshire. Or Pico."

"No, you can't take city streets. The LAPD put out a BOLO on these two. They're not likely to be cruising the freeways."

Tammy, listening in, said, "Please, Innes, take the freeway."

"Okay, okay," he conceded.

Vanessa walked back to her Vespa. Innes climbed into the driver's seat and buckled up, the old freeway neurosis rumbling within. Tammy jumped into the passenger seat. With Steven issuing directions from the back seat, they maneuvered to the Santa Monica Freeway, the main connector from downtown to the beach, the arterial route for untold thousands of daily commuters or sand-and-surf seekers. A fifteen-mile-long parking lot, in Innes' mind, possibly the only freeway he dreaded as much as the 405.

With light traffic on New Year's Eve morning, the merge from the on-ramp was relatively painless. The sun was out, the sky royal blue as it is only after a cleansing rain. As they sped west, Innes caught glimpses, between the passing eucalyptus trees, of the Hollywood sign and the Santa Monica Mountains to the north. The flat LA basin between the freeway and mountains was punctuated with hundreds of towering fan palms in tidy rows, their tall skinny trunks topped by globes of feathery fronds, like giant darts impaling the landscape. He was reminded what a stunning place LA could be, depending on the weather outside and, more important, the weather inside one's own head. For the first time in months, he felt a surge of optimism. A week in Skid Row was more than enough, and he was happy to put it behind him, given the mess he'd made of things.

Tammy slumped in the seat, leaning against the door so as not to be visible, and talked, animated, gesturing with her hands.

"How did you two end up together?" said Innes.

"He chased me, all the way downtown, like a stalker," Tammy said. She turned around to face Steven and smiled. He reached over and squeezed her shoulder.

"Michael and I didn't have many friends," said Steven. "Both our families disowned us after we got married. Especially mine, Korean religious fanatics. After the funeral, I couldn't stop thinking about Tammy."

"I was a mental case," Tammy said. "Checked myself into the loony bin. They kicked me out after a few days, said I wasn't crazy enough. I didn't have an address, so, those kindly folks from the hospital? They dumped my ass down in Skid Row. Do you believe that shit?"

"Outrageous, don't you think?" said Steven. "I traced her to the hospital. They wouldn't release any information. But a janitor told me to check downtown."

"So, you're sharing a tent? Sleeping together? Living in sin?" Innes teased.

"Sleeping together, yeah," said Steven.

"But no sinning. Nunh unh," said Tammy with a laugh.

"She won't let me into her pants," said Steven.

"How do you know? You never tried," she said. "For real, that's what I love about this gay boy. He don't bother me. And he keeps me safe out here on these mean streets. If people think we gettin' it on, so be it."

"She's right, you know," said Steven. "It's hell for women on the streets."

"True story," said Tammy. "One woman I know down there? She was asleep in her own tent when some a-hole sliced it open with a knife, like shuckin' a damn oyster. Climbed in and tried to rape her. She fought back and screamed her head off, wakin' the dead, until he ran away. She was lucky."

"Stop, Innes, stop!" yelled Steven.

Tammy screamed.

Innes snapped his head around and saw a wall of red brake lights across five lanes, twenty yards ahead. He slammed on the brakes. The Explorer skidded and swerved, straightened out, and came to a tire-screeching stop about five feet from the back of a semi.

Innes was shaking, heart pounding. The pit of his stomach turned to concrete. Panic sweat gushed out of his pores and trickled down this back.

"Damn, Innes, you trying to kill us?" said Tammy.

"Sorry. Sorry," he said. He gripped the steering wheel, whiting his knuckles, both feet still jammed on the brake pedal. "I hate the freeways. It's like *Mad Max* out here."

"Maybe I should drive," said Tammy.

"I'll be okay," said Innes. "You guys stay out of sight. Looks like we'll be crawling for a while."

Traffic inched ahead. Innes let off the brakes and crept forward. He checked the rear-view mirror. Traffic was backing up behind them, trapping him again in the river of steel. The wheel was slippery in his wet palms, the concrete in his stomach spread outward to his limbs. Innes told himself it would be okay and repeated it like a mantra. He hadn't heard the voice in his head since yesterday, and he was silent for a stretch, listening for it. Tammy and Steven, recovering from the near crash, began to talk again.

"What was that about insurance?" Innes said.

"I was saying I wish I'd had a life policy on Michael, crass as it sounds," Steven said.

"I know how you feel," said Innes. "How about you, Tammy? Do you still have the music store?"

"Naw, that's gone," she said. "We were barely making it as it was. After I sold off the inventory, there was only enough money left to pay our debts and the funeral and burial for Sammy and Eric. That's when I started losing my mind, spiraling down."

"What about property insurance? We all had that, right?" said Innes. "My agent said we can collect someday, but who knows when?"

"The greedy bastards," said Steven. "I bet they try to screw us out of our claims by calling it arson."

"It *was* arson," said Innes. The subject of insurance reminded him of a question that had been nagging him. "Hey, did you guys get any emergency cash from insurance? Like, to tide you over until your claim is paid?"

They hadn't and had heard nothing about it.

"I guess Nessa had one of them dee-luxe policies," he said.

After thirty-five minutes of stop-and-go driving, they exited the freeway. Steven issued directions to the Safe Harbor shelter in a relatively sketchy neighborhood, by Santa Monica standards, south of the freeway. Innes waited in the truck while Tammy and Steven went inside. They came back after about five minutes. Tammy was shouting obscenities.

"You believe this bullshit?" she said as she jumped into the passenger seat. "They gave away our beds to somebody else. Said they have no room for us. Bull! Shit! It's because I'm a Black woman with an Asian man. You saw how they looked at us. Goddamn Christian hypocrites."

"Oh, come on, Tammy," Steven said. "This is Santa Monica.

People here don't think like that."

"Easy for you to say. You ain't Black."

"So, anyway," Innes jumped in, "did Vanessa give you any back-up plans? We should call her. You guys got a cellphone?"

"I do," said Steven. He tapped out a call. "Voicemail," he said. He left her a message and said they would check in later.

"Now what?" said Innes. "Santa Monica is supposed to be home-less friendly. Especially at the Palisades. We've got tents, sleeping bags. Why don't we carve out a spot near the beach? The weather looks nice."

"If we have to be living in tents," said Steven, "Santa Monica has got to be an improvement over Skid Row."

Palisades Park was a narrow, ocean-front stretch of grass and palm trees extending north from the Santa Monica Pier, atop bluffs that overlooked the beach and Pacific Coast Highway. A popular spot for tourists to gaze at the ocean before taking the ramp down to the pier. Also, a popular spot for the homeless to collect in small groups or wander around by themselves, killing time or panhandling. Innes recalled from the last time he was there the juxtaposition of the glory and grime of Southern California: gaudy sunsets, palm trees swaying in the ocean breezes framed by the Santa Monica Moun-tains, the sparkling Pacific catching the sun's dappled magic—and bedraggled panhandlers mooching coins or loudly cursing no one in particular.

They parked the Explorer at a meter on Ocean Avenue and were greeted by a big sign that announced the park closed at midnight and overnight camping was prohibited. Also: no golfing.

"Are they kidding? No golfing?" said Innes. He surveyed the shab-by figures lying about. No Tiger Woods in sight.

"It would make a very long par five," said Steven. "Big sand trap and water hazard if you hook left."

"Like Pebble Beach on steroids," said Innes.

"What are you boys talking about?" said Tammy. "Where are we supposed to sleep if it says no camping?"

Steven called Vanessa again, got through this time, and she said she would meet up with them in a few hours, depending on traffic. The three emigres from Skid Row spent the afternoon at the tourist-jammed 3ʳᵈ Street Promenade, watching the street performers—musicians, acrobats, snake and exotic bird handlers—along with the roving mobs of young people getting an early start on New Year's Eve debauchery.

Shortly before dark, Vanessa arrived on her Vespa and found the others at the concrete fence atop the bluffs watching the remains of the sunset paint the sky and the ocean tangerine. Vanessa presented Innes with a used backpack for his meager belongings. She opened another small pack and produced a block of cheddar, a baguette, and two bottles of cheap champagne surrounded by Zip-Lock bags of ice.

"Let's hang out here until midnight, then crack these babies open," she said. "We can sleep in the truck."

They ate the bread and cheese and watched the whitecaps roll ashore in the dark, lit by a silvery wedge of moon. Steven used his cellphone to count down the seconds till midnight. They popped the champagne, whooped and hollered, exchanged hugs, and passed the bottles around until they were empty. Innes tipped the last one upside down to suck out the last drops. Vanessa yanked the bottle from his hand and tossed it on the grass, threw her arms around his neck and planted a long, bubbly-tasting kiss on his mouth. Innes reached out to hug her back, but she pulled away laughing and said, "I'm sorry. I must be drunk."

He was drunk, too. But not sorry.

The morning light filled the truck's interior. Vanessa slept, slumped sideways in the driver's seat, her head on his shoulder. He smelled her hair, pulled tight across her head into a top bun. Vanilla, with a hint of orange. Inhaling the moment, he absorbed the fact they had spent the night together, however chastely, and were sort of cuddling. You're okay with this, right, Annie? he thought. He wanted to kiss the top of her head, but chickened out, unsure how she might react and if he was ready to find out.

She had drooled on him and left a dark trail on his shirt. It wasn't quite the romantic dream he'd imagined, but it would do. After a while, he nudged her awake. She smiled and covered her mouth.

"My breath must be vile," she said.

"Happy New Year," he said.

"Did I kiss you last night?" she said, then stretched and yawned.

"Yes, you did. Made my week."

"Don't let it go to your head."

Too late.

They left Tammy and Steven asleep in the back of the Explorer and set out in the blooming dawn in search of caffeine. They found a coffee shop, then walked across the grassy, palm-tree lined Palisades Park, passing dozens of shapes huddled under blankets on park benches or on the damp ground.

"I thought they didn't allow sleeping here," Innes said.

"I guess they've given up enforcing it," she said.

They stopped at the concrete fence atop the bluffs, balanced their paper coffee cups on the square posts, leaned their elbows on the top rail, and took in the wide beach far below and the infinite expanse of ocean. Pacific Coast Highway was empty of cars. The sun crept higher behind them, and slowly the black carpet of the sea turned gray-green. The white foam of the breakers grew brighter as they lapped on the beach. The two figures alone at the wall were silent for several moments as they contemplated the vastness of the Pacific.

"It takes your breath away, doesn't it?" said Vanessa.

"Here's where we run out of continent," Innes said. "Things had better work here."

"Thank you, Joan Didion," she said with a smirk.

"Is there anything you haven't read?"

She smiled but said nothing. After a pause, she said, "I talked to June, by the way. She sends her love. Don't roll your eyes, that's annoying. Anyway, I asked her about any insurance money for you. She said there's been nothing."

He was disappointed to hear that, but not entirely. That would have meant something else to be grateful to June for. His feelings of gratitude flowed in another direction.

"I don't know how to thank you, Vanessa," he said, turning toward her. "If you hadn't found me in Hollywood, I don't know where

I'd be right now. In hell, probably. Yet here I am, in one of the most beautiful spots in the world. Last night I finally had a roof over my head. Sort of. A metal roof. In a car. But a roof." Quit babbling, he chastised himself.

Vanessa continued to stare at the surf.

"What I'm trying to say is, you are a goddamn saint, Vanessa, and I'll always be in your debt."

"What are friends for? I was glad to do it," she said. "It's what Annie would have wanted. Sometimes I feel like she's watching me, to see if I look out for her family, like this is a test to see how loyal a friend I was."

He was deflated to hear she was doing it for Annie rather than for him. But he pushed on with his speech. "It's not only me who will be forever in your debt," he said. "All those lost souls in Skid Row. You know what Clif called you? The angel of mercy--"

"I'm no angel, Innes," she interrupted. "Please don't set standards for me I can't possibly live up to." She addressed the comment to him, but it was like she was talking to the sea. She turned toward him. It was not the look of intimacy he had hoped for. "You don't know me," she said. "We're friends. But you don't really know me. I've done a lot of things I'm not proud of."

"You're an an angel compared to me, I'll bet." A series of embarrassing and painful scenes ran past his mind's eye.

"Is there something you want to tell me?" she said with the beginnings of a smile. "You sound like you want to make a confession."

The words gushed from his mouth with the force of a broken water main. "I've been a complete scumbag since the fire. I ditched the old man. I treated June like crap. A waitress I met in a diner put me in a porno. I was the boy toy of a rich widow in Beverly Hills. She dressed me up in her clothes and took me to a drag bar where I got in a fist fight in the parking lot. She killed herself when I left her, or maybe it was an accident, I don't know. I ate out of dumpsters. I started a riot in Skid Row that killed my father-in-law."

She stared at him in disbelief. "Oh my God, Innes." She giggled. "I'm sorry," she said. "I shouldn't laugh. But ... you were in a porno? You wore a dress in a drag bar? A fist fight?"

Innes tried to laugh but couldn't. He stood there feeling ridiculous.

Vanessa stifled her giggles. "I'm sorry," she said. "It's not funny, I know. You've been through hell. ... Wait. Who killed herself?"

He told her the whole sordid tale. When he finished, they were leaning on their elbows again, staring out to sea. "So. Now you know everything," he said. "Are you still glad you came to my rescue?"

"Listen to me." She turned toward him. "Nothing you have done was a deliberate attempt to hurt anyone. It's not your fault Sherri torched herself and her house. Sounds like she was totally cray cray. You were right to leave her. And it's not your fault about George. For the umpteenth time, it was an accident." Her face lit up with a wide grin. "But the dress, and the drag bar? I definitely want to hear more about that. I wish there was a picture."

"I actually looked pretty good, I thought, for a middle-aged dude. Good enough that some creep tried to pick me up at the Proud Mary."

"That was the fistfight?" she said.

"You should have seen me, in a ripped muddy dress, bloody lip, broken high heel, smeared makeup, cock-eyed wig. I looked like a sad clown."

"You see the irony here, right?" she said.

He nodded, and looked down at his grimy running shoes, avoiding her smile. No need to mention Terry Delacroix by name. Point taken.

They stared out to sea again. Innes was relieved she didn't think he was disgusting and creepy. Ever since she'd picked him up on her Vespa, he had allowed his romantic fantasies about her to bloom in his mind like a field of poppies. But he hesitated to act on them. After his misadventures with Angels in Paradise and Sherri, he felt dirty and unworthy of Vanessa's affection.

She spoke to the waves again. "The reason I spent the night with you guys in the truck is I'm homeless now, too. My mom kicked me out. I don't have enough money to get an apartment. I used all my insurance cash to pay her rent. That's why I haven't offered you a place to stay, if you were wondering."

He said nothing and contemplated the implied suggestion that she would have offered if she'd been able.

"I couch surfed with a girlfriend from La Casita for a while, but I hated her boyfriend, so I left. I've been sleeping in my car for a week. Don't you want to hear why my mother kicked me out?"

"Do I need to know this?"

"It's because I divorced Juan."

Divorced. The word lit up in his mind like neon in the desert at night. "What happened?" he asked, trying not to sound too pleased.

"He'd been cheating on me. For years. With a woman in his hometown. That's why I was in Mexico. I forced him to sign the divorce papers. I got it finalized at the courthouse yesterday."

"I'm sorry. That's awful."

"Not really. It's for the best."

He wholeheartedly agreed but didn't say so. "Why would your mother kick you out over that?"

"She's a devout Catholic and doesn't believe in divorce, that's why. And Juan is a family friend of her cousin back in Mexico. It was basically a sham marriage. He only married me so he could live in the U.S. legally. My mother put a lot of pressure on me. I was twenty-two, just out of college, no job prospects, living at home. She was eager to get me out of the house. I'd known Juan since I was a little girl. Used to see him on family trips back to Oaxaca. Always had a crush on him. I thought I loved him. But he didn't love me. He used me. So, you see, I'm basically an immigration pawn."

"Don't say that, Nessa. You were young. Taken advantage of."

"I was an accomplice to a scam," she said, lowering her voice to a near whisper. "Still think I'm an angel?"

"I don't know what to say, Nessa. You got used. You did what you had to do."

"There's more. The last straw was when I told my mom I'd had an abortion." She went silent for a few beats to let that sink in.

"Okay, you had an abortion," he said, unsure what would be an appropriate reply. "Like a million other women."

"You don't understand." Her voiced wavered. "In my mother's eyes, there is nothing in the world worse than that. She screamed at me, called me a baby killer, said I would burn in hell, said I was no longer her daughter. She threw a statue of the Virgin Mary at me. I ducked, and it shattered against the wall. It was lunacy. I gathered my things and left right there, on the spot."

"I'm sorry. When did all this happen? The abortion, I mean."

"Couple years ago. I went down to see him in Oaxaca, a surprise visit. He'd been down there for several weeks, and I'd just found out I was pregnant. I wanted to give him the good news in person." She paused, as if searching for the words. "You know what I found there? He had another family. A wife, Selena, and two small kids, girls. They weren't legally married apparently, but still, might as well have been. She had a house, everything. Paid for by him. He'd been sending remittances to his mother, he said. All that money was going to that *puta* Selena. I went straight back to Pasadena, humiliated. I was so angry and betrayed, I couldn't stand the thought of carrying his baby for nine months and giving birth."

A squawking white seagull flew overhead and barely missed them with its payload. Innes realized he didn't know Vanessa as well as he thought he did, not even close. He was torn between joy at the news she was a free woman and anger and sorrow that she'd been put through such humiliation.

"The worst part?" she continued. "The bastard fought me on the divorce. For two years. My mother, too. She took his side, said if I forgave him he'd leave Selena and come home to me. No fucking way. They were still together when I was there last month. *Puta.*"

"Must have been tough on you. Abortion. Divorce. Everything." It was lame. He was far out of his element.

"You have no idea. I was raised a good Catholic girl. I was taught divorce and abortion were mortal sins."

"They *are* mortal sins, lady." An old vagabond appeared as if from nowhere. "But you can pay me an indulgence. A get-out-of-hell free card." He smiled a toothless smile and held out a greasy palm. He was ancient and so covered with grime it was hard to tell the color of his clothes or where they ended and his skin started.

"Who are you, the Pope of Santa Monica?" Innes said, not unkindly.

"That's me," he said.

Vanessa reached into her jeans pocket and gave him a dollar bill.

"Bless you, my child," he said, making a sign of the cross, "in the name of Saint Monica, holy mother of Augustine. *Dominus vobiscum.*" He turned and shuffled away.

"*Et cum spiritu tuo,*" she called after him.

"You see the irony of two hobos like us giving money to a hobo?" Innes said.

"Shut up. Anyway, what was I saying? Oh, yeah. My abortion."

She hesitated, frowning, as if unsure this was a conversation she wanted to have. Innes wasn't sure himself and searched for an exit line.

"You don't have to persuade me," he said. "I'm pro-choice all the way."

"It's not so easy. Pro-choice. Pro-life. It's not just a political thing. It's your body, your own flesh and blood. Was it a girl? Sometimes I imagine her in my life. I give her names. Like Maria. Estella. Daniella." She turned toward Innes and wiped a tear from her cheek. After a brief silence, she said, "I miss my mom."

He was genuinely moved by her words. It was time to declare himself. "Look, Vanessa, you've only done what you had to do. I think you are a moral, honorable person. The way you stand up for people, for the underdog. That night at the Halloween party when you tore into me for dissing Terry and June? It stung, but you were absolutely right. And the way you give of yourself to people and causes who can never appreciate or repay what you do. You are a goddamn saint. And that … is why I … need you … I, umm … I mean, George and Annie are gone. Cal hates me. I feel like you're all I've got in this world. Yes, Terry and Steven, too. But it's you… I … I …"

You're blowing it moron, he told himself.

She stared at him for an excruciating full second or two, with delight and worry and terror in her eyes all at once, waiting for him to finish the sentence he could not. "Don't," she said. "Please." She hugged him and kissed him on the cheek—not on the mouth this time, he noticed. "You need a shave," she said. She turned away to face the Pacific and said no more. Her silence, building from seconds toward a minute, roared in his ears like echoes from a conch shell.

"Say something," he said.

"I think I know what you're trying to say," she said after a long pause. "But I don't think I can tell you what you want to hear."

"But you're feeling something?"

"Yes, of course." She turned to face him. "Why do you think I spent all those weeks searching for you, crazed with worry? Why did I cruise those awful alleys and homeless camps? Do you know how many times I had my ass pinched and heard vile things said to me by derelicts? But I kept looking for you. And all the time you were..." Her voice tailed off and she looked away.

Innes stared at his shoes, unable to look her in the eye.

After another silence, she said, barely audible above the squealing of the seagulls, "What matters is, I'm here with you now. And I'm staying."

Book VIII

STEVEN AND TAMMY STUDIED A SHEET OF PAPER.

"Do you believe this shit?" Tammy said. "Some a-hole left it on the windshield. Allow me to read from it. Safe Streets Santa Monica, it says on top. Quote: Homeless derelicts are taking over our beautiful seaside community. It's time to fight back. Exclamation point, underlined. The city council will hold a hearing January fourth on the proposed Safe Streets ordinance to clean up our communities. Come and show your support. Exclamation point. Let's send the bums back to LA where they belong. Exclamation point. Unquote."

"Lovely," said Innes.

"Let me see that," said Vanessa. "I know these people. Triple-S M they call themselves. I've had run-ins when I was helping people here. They wear these yellow buttons. They've said horrible things. Called me Mexican cunt, asked to see my ID. I tell them to fuck off."

"That doesn't sound like Santa Monica at all," said Steven. "I thought this was the Beautiful People's Republic."

"Every community has its haters," said Vanessa.

"Tell me about it," said Tammy.

Innes considered his three companions. A Black woman. A Latina woman. A gay Asian man. All targets of hate. Himself? Straight White guy. Never hated, far as he knew. Until now. Vagabone. Bum. Vermin.

"This Safe Streets proposal essentially bans homelessness," Vanessa said. "One of these days it might pass if people do nothing to stop it."

Her words snapped Innes out of his musings. "Are you thinking what I'm thinking?" he said, raising eyebrows at Vanessa. "January fourth. Santa Monica City Hall."

She stared at him searchingly, then came the look of realization, and the quilted box between the eyes, her eyebrow hairs at attention. "You're not serious," she said. "After what happened last time?"

"What are you talking about?" said Steven.

"A little civil disobedience," Innes said.

"You wanna start another riot?" said Tammy. "I'm already in trouble from the last one."

"It's only a public hearing," he said. "What could go wrong?"

"Somebody could get killed again, that's what," said Vanessa. "Have you already forgotten about George?"

Low blow, he thought, but didn't say it. "No, of course not," he said. "That makes me want to do this all the more. We started something back there in Skid Row. If we quit now, the old man died for nothing."

"I thought you learned your lesson about White guys from the 'burbs playing hero in Skid Row," said Vanessa.

She was right, of course. But still. He sensed the homeless population was near a critical mass, evolving toward a level of self-awareness from which revolutions are made, if only someone gave a push, anyone, no matter how insignificant.

"What are you proposing exactly?" said Steven.

"Only that we show up in force at City Hall. Let them know they are talking about human beings here, not a faceless mass. We can make signs. You know. Human rights. Dignity. What would Jesus do?"

"You don't believe in Jesus," said Vanessa.

"Correction. I don't believe in God," said Innes, remembering the voice that had vanished into the ether. "I *do* believe in Jesus, and I'm not averse to invoking His name, throwing it in the faces of sanctimonious hypocrites."

"Very pious, Innes," said Steven.

"Piety's got nothing to do with it."

"Okay, against my better judgment, I'm in," said Vanessa. "But no beer this time."

"Dang, y'all are no fun," said Tammy. "Count me in, though."

"January fourth is what, Monday?" Innes said. "That gives us all weekend to work the streets, get everyone together, make signs."

They agreed to start their efforts on Saturday morning, giving them the rest of New Year's Day to relax and get acclimated to their new surroundings. Steven and Tammy wandered off in search of coffee, leaving Innes and Vanessa with the truck.

"You never told me what happened with George," said Innes, breaking an awkward silence. "I have a right to know."

Vanessa opened the rear door and pulled out her yellow backpack. She unzipped it and extracted an oblong wooden box, about the size of a shoebox, and lifted the lid to expose a large plastic bag full of what looked like crushed gravel.

He recognized it immediately. "What the...? You had him cremated? Without asking me?"

"It's what he wanted."

"How do you know? He never told me that."

"That's because you never really listened to him. You only yelled at him."

She was right. No denying.

"I'm sorry," she said. "I shouldn't have said that. I know how terrible you must feel. But Annie knew he wanted to be cremated, as she wanted to be. She told me."

"Who paid for it?" he asked.

"An anonymous benefactor."

"Oh, c'mon, Nessa. Tell me."

She thought about it for a moment. "Okay. It was June."

He was annoyed, but not surprised. Once again, June had stepped in to help, and once again he felt like he owed her a favor. He snorted, but said nothing.

"Come on," said Vanessa. She put the box in her pack. "George wanted his ashes scattered in the Pacific Ocean."

They descended the ramp to the Santa Monica Pier. The deck was packed with New Year's celebrants, many obviously nursing hangovers. They passed two young women in hoodies and cutoffs vomiting over the railing into the water below. Clusters of out-of-towners in LA for the Rose Bowl football game later in the day, identifiable by their black-and-gold Iowa jerseys and regalia, snapped group selfies. Innes and Vanessa passed the the arcade, the amusement park, and the Harbor Authority at the end of the pier, and stood at the rail, gazing across the gray-green expanse toward Hawaii. A strong breeze tousled their hair, the smell of salt air and fish guts invaded their nostrils.

"Did you ever see *The Big Lebowski?*" Innes asked as Vanessa opened her backpack to retrieve the box.

"Of course," she said. "I love that movie."

"Remember the scene where The Dude and Walter try to scatter Donnie's ashes at the ocean?"

"Oh, no," she said. "The wind blew it back in their faces, didn't it?"

"Exactamente."

"What'll we do?"

"We could toss the whole bag in," he said. "But it might float and get picked up by somebody. Not good."

Vanessa looked around. "We should do it soon, before somebody comes."

He knelt and opened the box and unzipped the plastic bag. Reaching down below the deck as far as he could, he dumped the contents, and the ocean breeze blew them back under the pier into the breakers. Close enough. He handed the box back to Vanessa. She put it away and pulled something else from her backpack.

"I thought you might want this," she said and offered him the ratty kaleidoscope of yarn that was George's tam-o-shanter.

They stood together at the rail for a while and gazed out to sea as the gulls circled above them. Innes held the tam, stretching it with his fingers to make it look like there was still a snowy-haired head inside, and reflected on the weird, wondrous life of George McQuillen. Dumpster diver. Quoter of literature. Big hearted, ornery old cuss. Loyal sidekick. Bon vivant. Total wack job. Progenitor of Annie.

He would keep the tam.

They stood in silence for several minutes, listening to the waves slosh against the pier's pylons, until Vanessa spoke. "The reason I'm struggling with my feelings for you is … is … I loved Annie. I was in love with her. I'm having a hard time dealing with that."

A mental image of Vanessa and Annie in a naked embrace forced its way into his mind's eye. The two women he loved. Simultaneous pangs of jealousy and arousal bloomed within. "I knew you two were close friends. But I never imagined--"

"Not like that," she said, as if reading his thoughts. "It was more like sisterly love. The kind of love between female best friends that men can never understand."

"Oh," he said.

"I have feelings for you, Innes. I do. It's confusing. I'd always looked to Annie as a sort of big sister, the one I never had. That made you like a brother-in-law. One I've admired for a long time.

You know how it started? From the things Annie used to say about you. What a smart man and a loving husband and father, she said. She was devastated when you lost your job. She saw how it tore you up and made you bitter. And she felt like she could never love you enough to make up for it because she was depressed herself. All I could think of was the lying *pedazo de mierda* I was married to and wished I had married a man like you."

Innes tried to process that last line as they walked back along the pier, the words "married a man like you" reverberating in his mind like a coda.

Monday, January 4, started out sunny and warm, but by mid-afternoon a thick layer of clouds rolled in from the north, unfolding over the Santa Monica Mountains like a down-filled comforter. The prospect of rain was a potential snag in the plans to march on City Hall, but Innes and friends remained hopeful. They had spent two full days working the streets, shelters, and homeless encampments, pleasantly surprised at the response they received. Tammy proved especially effective at recruiting, possibly because nearly half the homeless population was African American. Vanessa, too, brought in large numbers of commitments to show up on Monday, given her Spanish fluency and her renown among the homeless community for her good works. Innes and Steven had less success, as obviously college-educated suburban guys lacking street cred despite their months of homelessness. Probably three-quarters of the people they approached told them where to stick their civil disobedience, but still, they figured by Sunday night they had verbal commitments from at about a hundred men and women—Black, White, and Latino, teens to seniors.

Vanessa gave her news media contacts a heads-up. Steven bought a couple dozen sheets of poster board and a box of markers. The foursome spent Sunday evening gathered around the hood of the Explorer under a streetlight making signs. WWJD? was a winner, they agreed.

"A hundred hobos," said Steven as they worked on the signs. "It'll be like herding cats."

"Oh ye of little faith," said Innes.

The City Council hearing was to start at seven o'clock, which gave them all day Monday to reconnect with their recruits. About half of them could not be located. The plan was to gather in front of City Hall around six, where the signs would be handed out and they would go over the ground rules—no throwing beer bottles—and the chants they were to shout. Tammy was in favor of "Hell no, we won't go," but the others thought it too confrontational. Innes's suggestion of "Attica" was quickly vetoed. "That's just weird," was Vanessa's verdict. They settled on Steven's idea: "Santa Monica, shame on you. Look at us, we live here, too."

By the time six rolled around, the sun was long gone, and a light drizzle formed halos around the streetlights. Innes counted four-dozen dark shapes huddled together in groups on the undulating lawn in front of the art deco City Hall building. Most had hoods or wore plastic ponchos. Some held tarps overhead. The few sycamores were mostly bare of leaves and offered little protection. Steven advised waiting to hand out the signs until right before the hearing started so they wouldn't get soggy.

By quarter-to-seven, cars were pulling up on Main to let out passengers who marched past the fountains toward the front entrance. Innes spied the familiar blue truck of Channel 7 and exchanged smiles and thumbs-up with Vanessa.

Just before seven, Steven handed out the signs and led the chanting. It sounded good. The crowd of arriving citizens grew larger, and a few, with round yellow buttons attached to their raincoats, hats, and purse straps, hurled insults and middle-finger salutes at the disheveled horde.

The Master of Disaster and her cameraman set up their lights in a spot halfway between the homeless crowd and the front door as the first Santa Monica police car pulled up on Main, roof lights flashing, at seven sharp. Then a second. Followed by a third. Several officers got out, fired up their black flashlights, and converged on the gathering. The drizzle thickened into fat drops.

"Who's in charge here?" said the tallest officer.

Innes stepped forward, but Vanessa held him back. "Let me handle this," she said. Steven followed her with an opened umbrella. "I am," she said. "Vanessa Rodriguez, LA Homeless Outreach Foundation."

She handed him a card from her purse. He examined it with his flashlight. "It says Vanessa Alfonso," he said.

"I just got divorced. I haven't got new cards yet."

"Divorced, you say?" He grinned and pointed the flashlight at her face. "This must be my lucky day."

"Is there a problem, officer?" she said.

"Do you have a permit for this demonstration?" he asked, no longer grinning.

"We don't need one. We have a right to assemble."

"In Santa Monica, you need a permit to demonstrate in a park," he shouted to be heard above the chants. "This is a park." He waved his arm at the grounds in front of City Hall. The rain fell heavily, and the officers looked annoyed at being out in this weather with this unsavory mob. "You'll have to disperse," the officer said. "You're creating a public nuisance. People have a right to attend this hearing, but your presence is intimidating them."

The Master of Disaster sidled up to them. "What's the story, Jake?"

"Oh, hi, Gloria," said the cop. "There's no story. These people were just leaving."

"Doesn't look that way to me," she said. "I'll just get a few interviews and be out of your way." She walked back toward her cameraman and lights. Vanessa followed.

Nearly a dozen officers had gathered. Their long black raincoats shone wet under the streetlights. They fanned out into the crowd, gently trying to break up the group, pulling signs out of people's hands. Somebody pushed back, and a scuffle broke out between a handful of demonstrators and two cops. The chants diminished, replaced by the sounds of raindrops pelting plastic and scuffling shoes on wet grass.

"No, no, don't fight," Innes yelled, but was drowned out by the swelling cacophony.

The skies opened up and released a drenching torrent. A few people rolled up their soggy placards into floppy sticks and swung them at the cops. The batons came out, police swung back, and panicked demonstrators ran in all directions. Innes looked for Vanessa. She was lit up with Gloria, who held an umbrella over their heads as they spoke to the camera. Innes ran toward her and made eye contact. Vanessa broke away from the interview. The Master of Disaster and her cameraman followed to get better shots of the melee. Two more TV news trucks pulled up.

Innes grabbed Vanessa by the hand and led her away from City Hall, through the curved paths of Tongva Park toward the Palisades. He scanned the chaos for Steven and Tammy, hoping they were headed for the truck as per the plan. As they entered Palisades Park, they came upon crowds of gawkers drawn to the commotion, oblivious to the downpour. A group of five teenage boys joked and passed a bottle around. Innes smelled the marijuana smoke from several yards away. He stopped and stared at them.

"Wait," he said to Vanessa.

She let go of his hand. "I'm getting soaked. I'll meet you at the truck," she shouted through the din, and jogged ahead.

Innes didn't want to lose sight of her, but something ineffable made him freeze in place. He scanned the faces of the five youths, partially hidden by hoodies drawn low over their foreheads, eyes barely visible. They stopped and glared at him.

"What're you lookin' at?" bellowed the tallest and most imposing one, slurring his words.

Innes considered asking them if they knew anyone named Caleb but doubted they would tell him if they did.

One of them hung back, looking away, and backpedaled toward the stone fence at the edge of the bluff. There was something about his build and body language. Innes walked past the others and continued toward the boy, who had turned quickly in the other direction.

"Where you goin'?" the tall one yelled.

"Screw 'im, let's go," said another, and the foursome ran toward City Hall.

Innes pursued the lone figure. "Cal?" he called out, straining to be heard above the shouting and people running and heavy rain pounding the ground. The boy, with a dark green backpack that looked familiar, took off in a dead run. It had to be him. Who else would run away after hearing that name called? Innes pursued. "Cal, slow down," he shouted again. About twenty yards behind, Innes was unable to gain any ground. After a block-and-a-half of sprinting as hard as his middle-aged legs could take him, Innes passed the Petanque Courts and the Camera Obscura building, and lost him. He slowed, scanned the path, but didn't see anyone. He moved toward the side of the Camera Obscura to search the public restrooms in back. As he turned the corner, he and the boy collided. Innes stumbled and grabbed hold of an arm. The hooded figure tried to twist away. Innes gripped with every ounce of his strength and pulled them closer together. The boy's hood fell back. Father and son, face to face. Caleb struggled to free himself. Innes thought he was about to lose him again and grabbed with his other arm and pulled him into an embrace.

"Oh God, Cal. Don't run. Please." Innes was crying.

Caleb continued to struggle, broke one arm free and swung a fist into Innes's ribs. Innes buckled from the pain and let go of his grip. He was sure Caleb would run away, but the boy kept swinging, both arms now, raining blows on Innes's arms and shoulders and the sides of his head. He was sobbing, too. Innes bent over, absorbing the blows. At long last he had found his son, and as the fists thumped against him it occurred to him it was going about as well as their last encounter. The blows stopped, and Caleb stood his father up. Innes flinched, expecting another roundhouse to the jaw. Instead, his son wrapped his arms around him, pressed his face against his shoulder and sobbed.

"You bastard. You bastard," he whispered, sniffling.

"My boy. My boy. I love you Cal," Innes said into his ear.

"Why did she have to die?" he squealed, sounding like the little boy he once was.

"I don't know Cal. I don't know."

"Why? Why? Why her?"

"Okay. Okay. I do know. Some asshole burned down our building and if I ever find him, I'm going to rip his heart out like he ripped ours."

"Yeah. Me too," said Caleb. He stepped back and said, "Why did you say she ran into the building looking for me?"

"I'm sorry. I was wrong," said Innes. "I don't know why she ran back in there. I was angry and confused, and you were blaming me. I lashed out. It was stupid. I'm sorry." Innes took a good long look at him. He was thinner in the face. Wispy beginnings of facial hair. That was new. "Why did you run away?" Innes said.

"I don't know. I was … I hated you and everybody and everything. I wanted to go somewhere and die."

Innes pulled him into another hug. "Don't leave me, son. Please. Don't run away again. I love you, Cal."

"Yeah. Me too."

It wasn't quite "I love you, too, Dad," but it would do. "Come with me," said Innes. "I'm sort of living out of a car right now. With some friends. People you know. Come on."

Caleb hesitated for a few seconds, as if at a crossroad, then walked with his father. The rain had stopped, leaving only the dripping run-off from the palm trees above.

"Where's Pops?" Caleb asked.

"Ahhh … I'll tell you later."

By the time Caleb and Innes reached the Explorer, the crowd fleeing the City Hall melee had vanished into the invisible under-world of alleys, shelters, and freeway underpasses. Vanessa, Tammy, and Steven sat in the truck with the windows open. Steven, vaping an e-cigarette, was the first to spot them. Caleb walked several paces behind his father, hiding his face under his sopping wet hoodie.

"What a disaster," said Steven as he exhaled a cloud of smoke into the evening mist. "Like I said, herding cats."

"Don't listen to Mr. Negative here," said Tammy from the back seat. "It was a good idea. The rain ruined everything. Maybe the Good Lord is saying it's time to drop this White Savior trip you're on, Innes. … What's so funny?"

"It wasn't a complete disaster," said Innes, failing to suppress a grin. "Look who I found."

Caleb sidled up to the truck and pulled his hood back.

"Oh my God. Caleb!" shrieked Vanessa. She jumped out to hug him.

"Hey, Ms. Alfonso," he said with a grin after pulling his face off her neck.

"Just Vanessa, please," she said, and hugged him again.

Steven and Tammy emerged, and the five of them huddled.

"Boy, you about made your Daddy crazy," said Tammy.

"I'm so glad you're okay," said Vanessa. "Where have you been?"

"All over," he said. "Hung out in Griffith Park for a while. Then Hollywood. Then here."

"I'm so sorry about your mother," said Steven. "We missed you at her memorial service." He narrowed his eyes at Caleb in gentle reproach.

Caleb said nothing and looked away.

"Everybody loved her," Steven said. "George, too."

"What about George?" Cal said, turning to Innes. "Where's Pops, Dad?"

The group fell silent. The swooshing of tires on wet pavement was the only sound for a few moments. Steven, Tammy, and Vanessa looked at Innes.

"I'm sorry, Cal," he said after a long pause. "Your grampa is dead, too."

"No way." Caleb backed away.

"It's true," said Innes.

"Are you kidding me?" Caleb jackknifed at the waist and slammed his forehead and palms on the hood of the Explorer, which produced a metallic boom.

"I wish I was," Innes said. "There was a ... disturbance. In downtown, where George was living. A policeman shoved him, and he hit his head. Cracked his skull open. Died at the hospital."

"A cop killed him?" Caleb snapped himself upright, his face screwed up into a scowl.

"Not intentionally," said Innes. "I was there. Vanessa, too. We saw the whole thing."

"It was a terrible, terrible accident," said Vanessa.

"This is fucked," said Caleb, choking back sobs. "Everything is fucked." He leaned on the hood and lay his head on his hands. In a muffled voice he asked, "Where is he buried?"

"He wanted to be cremated, like Mom," said Innes. "We scattered his ashes in the ocean."

"Where are Mom's ashes?"

"Where she wanted them. At home. The grounds outside the Casa."
Caleb considered that for a moment.

Vanessa broke the silence. "Where are you staying, Cal?"

"Here and there."

"You should stay with us," she said. "This is a big truck. We can fit five in here. It's only for a while, till we get some housing figured out."

"Why are you living in a truck?" said Caleb.

"I'm homeless, too," she said. "We all are, since the fire. That's why we have to stick together."

In the morning, Innes and Caleb woke before the others. Caleb spent the night squeezed into a sleeping bag next to Tammy in the back of the Explorer, with Steven on the other side of her. An assbackwards Oreo cookie, Tammy called it. Innes and Vanessa assumed their usual nighttime position, leaning against each other in the front seats.

Father and son slipped out of the truck quietly so as not to wake their companions. The morning was beautiful and chilly. The clouds had moved on and the rising sun was turning the fading night sky electric blue. Innes asked Caleb to walk with him along the Palisades. There was catching up to do.

"What happened to your cellphone?" Innes asked. "We tried calling and texting but got no response."

"I saw some of the texts. I couldn't talk to you. I blamed you for everything. I know that's wrong, but that's how I felt."

"Do you still have it?"

"No, I lost it in the LA River, in a rainstorm. I had to scramble out of there quick. I must have dropped it in the water."

Innes recalled that night. "I almost found you," he said. "Pops and I were looking for you in Frogtown, by the river. Paco's mom said you were headed there. We probably just missed you."

"I would have run away. I was still mad at you. About what you said. Anyway, I was basically a zombie … after Mom. I couldn't think straight. I couldn't think at all."

Innes knew the feeling, all too well. After a moment, he said, "Why did you leave a message for me that I should stop looking for you, that you were going away somewhere and never coming back?"

"I guess I wanted you to forget about me and leave me alone, get on with your life. So I could get on with mine."

"I would never forget about you."

Caleb said nothing. They reached an antique cannon that overlooked the beach from the top of the bluff, pointing out to sea. Innes leaned against the base. Caleb wandered toward the retaining wall.

"Why did you stop running last night?" said Innes. "If you'd kept going, I never would have caught up."

"I dunno. I guess I was done running. Anyway, once you knew I was here, I figured you'd find me eventually. Might as well get it over with."

"What did you do for money? How did you eat?"

"After the fire, I sold my bass and amp and some other stuff to Ronaldo for three hundred. I left them at his house after the gig on Halloween. They were my only things didn't get burned up."

"How much do you have left?"

"Thirty-five, forty bucks."

Innes wished he could give his son some money, like a good father, and regretted begrudging Caleb a mere twenty dollars the last time he saw him at home. "We're all broke," he said. "We'll need to figure some things out. Where to live. How to live. Now that I've found you, we can focus on that."

"I know a place we can go," said Caleb. "I'm not sure where it is exactly. Malibu. Or Pali. The hobos say there's a big abandoned mansion near the beach somewhere, and people live there, like squatters. They call it Shangri-La."

"Sounds like an urban legend," Innes said. "The big rock-candy mountain."

"Yeah, might be. But one of the dudes I'm hangin' with, Charlie, says it's real. He's seen an article about it in the newspaper. Says he knows where it is, too."

Innes reflected on the fiasco of the homeless march on Santa Monica City Hall. Was there any point in trying to organize such an amorphous mob of dropouts, inebriates, and lost souls? He should have heeded Jamal's and Vanessa's skepticism. Now that he'd found Caleb, his mission in life clarified.

"I want to meet this Charlie," he said. "See what he knows about Shangri-La."

They found Charlie abusing an antique pinball machine in an arcade on the Santa Monica Pier. He was tall and alarmingly thin, his long blond hair streaming down from under a backwards Pioneer Hybrid seed cap, shredded jeans hanging precariously on his bony hips. They watched him for a few minutes so as not to interrupt his game. He was good, had the scoreboard above the busty Lucky Lady artwork on the back glass up to a million points, and displayed the pinball expert's body language, rocking his torso and hips to and fro and side to side like a dancer as he worked the flipper buttons, arms loose, gently shaking the table without tilting it. The machine pinged and bonged and booped and crackled in a hypnotic musical rhythm. Innes didn't know anyone still knew how to play pinball. He walked outside the arcade to wait for them by Zoltar the mechanical fortune teller.

After Charlie grew bored, having racked up multiple free games, he and Caleb walked out into the sunny salt air of the pier. Caleb had briefed his father that Charlie was a runaway from South Dakota who'd come to Hollywood to pursue his dream of becoming an actor. He had an uncle in LA with reputed industry connections, although nothing had come of it for Charlie, who ended up on the streets of Hollywood, Santa Monica, and Venice. Caleb warned his father the boy might appear eccentric.

They made small talk until Innes cut to the chase. "So, Charlie. How do we get to this so-called Shangri-La?"

Charlie stood still for a moment and looked at the sky. He spread his arms to the side as if to preach the gospel and closed his eyes. "To get there, you follow PCH northwest out of Santa Monica. It's a good highway, or was when it was new, and narrow and curvy. You look up the highway and it's bendy and twisty for miles, comin' at you, with a double yellow line down the center, comin' at you bright and shiny against the faded gray-black of the asphalt."

He swung his arms together in parallel, pointing straight ahead, as if pantomiming the yellow stripes, and opened his eyes.

Innes looked at Caleb with a raised eyebrow and nodded his head toward Charlie. Caleb shrugged.

"The hot bright sun bakes the road so the heat dazzles up from the asphalt until only that yellow double line is clear, comin' at you with the whine of the tires," Charlie continued, his voice sliding into a Southern drawl. "And if you don't quit starin' at that line and don't take a few deep breaths and slap yourself hard on the back of the neck, you'll hypnotize yourself and you'll come to at the moment when the road curves away from you and you find yourself driftin' over to the left into the oncoming traffic, and you'll try to jerk her back to the right but you cain't 'cuz it's too late and you're about to hit a beer truck head on so you turn hard left to miss it and slam into the guardrail and flip over, and down you go, crashing and rolling until you land on the beach, upside down, in flames."

"What the hell are you talking about?" said Innes. "I just want directions to Shangri-La."

"I told you, Dad. He does this," said Caleb. "Like Pops."

"Hold on. I'm gettin' there," said Charlie, closing his eyes again as if summoning the muse. "Then a tanned beach bunny lyin' on a towel in the sun a mile away will look up through her Ray-Bans and see the little column of black smoke rising up against the violent, metallic, throbbing blue of the sky, and she'll say to her beach bunny girlfriend, 'OMG, another one's gone over the guardrail.' And the other girl will say, 'OMG' and the first girl will take off her Ray-Bans and the shiny black lenses will flash in the sun like a heliograph."

It sounded vaguely familiar to Innes, but he couldn't remember what it was from. "This is ridiculous. Who talks like that? Nobody," he said. "I get it, Charlie, you're an actor, reciting lines from a movie or something, right? *Wild at Heart* maybe? Very good." He mock clapped. "Can you please give us the damn directions now?"

"Almost there," said Charlie. He resumed the recitation. "But if you wake up in time and don't drift into the other lane you'll go whippin' on into the dazzle and the beer truck will pass you with a snatching sound as though God-Almighty had ripped a tin roof loose with his bare hands." Charlie lowered his arms and opened his eyes. "Then about a mile or two past Latigo Canyon Road? You make a left onto a dirt road with a metal arch over the entrance that says Alba Longa in big capital letters. And you're there."

"Finally," said Innes. "Alba Longa? I thought it was called Shangri-La."

"That's what the hobos call it," said Charlie. "Nobody can remember Alba Longa."

The strange case of the mysterious Mr. Li and his unfinished Malibu estate called Alba Longa was well known in the West Side beach communities, a subject of controversy and local news coverage for years, Innes learned during a trip to the public library. There was an article in the *Times*, but only one, a kind of journalistic malpractice Innes knew as a "drive by:" Reporter drops in, does one write-up on a local controversy, then disappears, never to be heard from again. He had been guilty of it himself more than once.

Little was known of Mr. Xing Li other than that he was supposedly a Chinese billionaire from Chengdu who made his fortune manufacturing children's clothes for Wal-Mart. He had acquired the narrow one-and-a-half-acre parcel on a bluff that overlooked the ocean some twelve years before. The land remained undeveloped for several years, and when permits were filed to begin construction of a massive, neo-Classical estate, little notice was taken, aside from the few gadflies who opposed everything new along Malibu's rarified coast and canyons. Construction was nearly complete when it halted in 2012, followed shortly by the news from China that Mr. Li had been arrested and charged with securities fraud and various other financial crimes against the People's Republic. It didn't sound too promising for Mr. Li.

The Malibu weekly newspaper article included an aerial photo of the property, which showed an ostentatious compound that resembled a Greek or Roman temple, with outbuildings, walled courtyards, and unfinished layouts for what appeared to be elaborate gardens and fountains. The property was under the control of an entity known as Pacific Rim Bank & Trust. The article said several neighbors raised concerns about rumors of homeless people breaking into the fenced-off construction site and squatting in the nearly completed buildings.

Once he read that line, Innes knew had to go there and see for himself. He wasn't sure why. The peculiar history of the place appealed to his reporter's curiosity, and the strange name Alba Longa intrigued him. What language was it? Spanish? Italian? There was something compelling about the place from the aerial photo, the layout of the grounds, the gardens and paths and fountains, the terra-cotta roofs, columned arcades, and porticos. It looked familiar. Then he remembered: His dream about coming out of the rain into the protection of a long columned arcade and running toward Caleb and Vanessa. He didn't believe in omens, but this was beyond coincidence. Two visions from a previous dream had come true: Candy a prostitute and George dead in the street. They say dreams are the mind's way of making sense of new experiences, organizing them into long-term memory, like a filing system. How could they file away experiences that hadn't happened yet? Never a superstitious sort, Innes decided he'd better keep heeding his dreams.

He broke from his reverie and Googled "Alba Longa." According to Wikipedia, it was Latin, the name of an ancient city in Italy, said to be a predecessor to Rome by the Roman historian Livy.

Innes headed back to the truck to share his discovery with the others and talk them into taking a trip up the coast.

Book IX

WHEN THE RAINS CAME AGAIN IN THE MIDDLE of the night, Caleb was the first to wake. He bolted upright in his sleeping bag to the roar of a downpour hammering the metal roof. Soon everyone was up. Innes checked his watch: just after two o'clock. He rolled down the passenger window a few inches. It was raining every bit as hard as that night in Frogtown. The storm continued through the night. Eventually, the constant roar lulled them back to sleep.

By morning, the sky was clear, and the sun peeked through the spaces between the high rises of downtown Santa Monica. The air still misty with humidity, the rain-soaked surfaces gleamed in the sunlight. Early rush-hour traffic rumbled past, tires splashing through flooded sections of the street where the storm drains had clogged. Tammy, Steven, and Caleb went to fetch coffee. Vanessa turned on the radio to an all-news station. The reports focused on the flood damage from the night's deluge. Mudslides were reported from La Crescenta to Pacific Palisades. Houses careened down hillsides, crushing everything in their paths, blocking roads. Parched by drought for five years, Southern California was drowning in the wettest *El Nino* season in decades.

Just before the commercial break, another reporter came on the air with news of a major hillside collapse above Pacific Coast Highway in Malibu, which wiped out a long stretch of the road. A house perched atop the hill slid down with the mud and rock, crashing onto the highway.

"What part of PCH?" Innes said. "Where exactly?"

"I didn't hear them say." Vanessa reached for the dial.

"Try KNX."

For the next several minutes they channel surfed, catching snippets of fresh reports. Multiple sections of PCH were closed by mudslides, the precise locations unclear. One slide was somewhere near the Pepperdine campus, another farther up the coast by Kanan Dume Road. Reports were sketchy.

When the others returned with a tray of coffee in blue paper cups with Greek lettering, Innes and Vanessa filled them in on the developing disaster on PCH.

"That's our road to Shangri-La," said Tammy. "I don't see how we get there now."

"There might still be a way in," said Innes. "From the north, one of the canyon roads."

They agreed to drive up PCH and see how far they got. At first, only Caleb was on board with Innes's vision quest. The other three came around after a day of debate and consideration of their alternatives, which were few and unpalatable. Altogether, they had nothing close to enough money to rent an apartment, much less pass a credit check, as they were homeless and, except for Vanessa, unemployed. June's offer of housing, apparently, extended only to Innes. They were sick of crowding into the Explorer, especially given Steven's snoring and Caleb's farting. No one wanted to stay in a vermin-infested shelter, especially Innes. The possibility of free lodging on the beach, even if temporary, was too good to pass up. Vanessa, the last holdout, yielded to the majority.

When they attempted to access the highway from Ocean Avenue, they were met at the bottom of the ramp by two California Highway Patrol cars blocking the road, lights flashing. The troopers told them the entire highway was closed from Santa Monica to Point Dume, probably would be for days. Once the road was cleared of debris, they said, the hillsides not yet collapsed would have to be secured. And if the rains keep up like this all winter, who knows?

"How about coming in from the north, say Malibu Canyon?" Innes asked. Also closed, he was told.

"So, we're basically screwed," said Caleb.

Vanessa maneuvered the truck around and gunned it back up the hill to Ocean Avenue. "So much for that idea," she said, sounding relieved. She was skeptical of the whole Alba Longa thing. She referred to it as El Dorado, the lost city of gold.

"I guess we'll have to get there by boat," said Steven.

"Great idea," said Innes. "Whose boat?"

"I was kidding," said Steven.

"Wait," said Caleb. "I know somebody's got a boat."

"It's a joke, Cal," said Innes. "We're not getting there by boat."

"Why not? This Alba Longa place is on the beach, right?"

"Not exactly," Innes said. "From the photo I saw, it looked like it was on top of a cliff. I didn't see any beach there."

"Who you know's got a boat?" said Tammy.

"My friend Charlie. My Dad's met him, right, Dad?"

"That wack job?" said Innes. "He doesn't have a boat."

"It's his uncle's. Keeps it at the marina. Charlie has the keys some-times. His uncle pays him to check on it when he's out of town. Keep it clean and stuff. Whatever you do with boats. Anyway, his uncle's down in Cabo now. And Charlie has the keys."

They all pondered this unexpected development.

Later that morning, as Caleb went off in search of Charlie, Innes returned to the library to look at the aerial photo of Alba Longa from the Malibu weekly. He zoomed the web browser in to enlarge the picture and saw what looked like a footpath rising on a diagonal across the steep face of the bluff, all the way to the top, from a nar-row sandy beach at the bottom.

"I can't believe we're doing this," said Steven. They motored south on Lincoln Boulevard toward Venice, the supposed current location of Charlie the indigent mariner, the five of them squeezed into the Explorer with all their backpacks, sleeping bags, and accoutrements of street living jammed into the rear compartment.

"Who knows if we can find this Charlie," Vanessa said as she ma-neuvered through heavy traffic. "And if he'd let a group of strangers on his uncle's boat for some crazy booze cruise."

"Booze cruise? We're not bringing alcohol," said Innes.

"Speak for yourself," said Tammy. She pulled a plastic pint bottle of Popov vodka out of her purse. "I don't know about y'all, but I ain't getting' on no boat sober." She giggled nervously. "Listen to me, college-educated woman talking like a country girl."

"You can take the girl out of Louisiana, but…" said Steven.

"Hush now," she said.

The farther south they went from Santa Monica through Dog-town into Venice, the grimier became the streetscape. An LAPD cruiser roared past northbound in the opposite lane, weaving through traffic, lights flashing, forcing Vanessa to pull over to the curb until it passed.

Tammy ducked in the backseat. "Don't stop," she squealed. "Keep moving please, Nessa."

"Calm down, sweetie, they're not looking for us," said Steven. He put an arm around her.

"I'm about to crack open this vodka right here and now," said Tammy.

Caleb, staring at the passing storefronts, said, "Turn right up here on California. Take it to Abbot Kinney, and over to Venice."

"You seem to know your way around here, Cal," said Innes. He recalled those long-ago days when he was about Caleb's age, coming to Venice with his Pasadena friends, drawn from their proper old town to the gritty glamour of Muscle Beach.

"Hung out here with Charlie a few times," Caleb said. "He does a street performer thing on the boardwalk."

Vanessa turned right on Venice Boulevard, took it all the way to the beach, and parked in the municipal lot at the end of the road. They walked north along the boardwalk, past the marijuana dispensaries and the storefronts hawking T-shirts, sunglasses, bikinis, and a multitude of ethnic fast-food eateries. The aromas of street tacos and Korean barbecue and Greek souvlaki skewers and Italian sausages blended into a heady brew. At the Muscle Beach temple to narcissism, inflated men in tiny shorts and bikinied female body builders bench pressed and grunted and screamed and flexed for the tourists.

They found Charlie on the boardwalk exactly where Caleb said they would: center stage for street performers, hip-hop dance teams, snake handlers, broken-glass walkers, jugglers. The crowds of onlookers were sparse, and Charlie was easy to find. He was doing a slow-motion *Tai Chi* thing and reciting lines from a book or movie in a vaguely Chinese accent, poised like a crouching tiger. Or maybe a hidden dragon. An audience of puzzled-looking Japanese tourists snapped photos of him and whispered among themselves. Steven snickered. Vanessa and Caleb watched politely. After a moment, Tammy broke in: "Boy, what *are* you doing?"

That broke whatever spell he was under. "Dude," he said to Caleb. He glanced over at Tammy. "Lady, you're harshing my mellow."

The tourists wandered away. One of them tossed a crumpled bill into the upside-down black fedora at Charlie's feet. "You're costing me money, man," he said as he watched his audience recede.

"Take a break, C-Man," said Caleb. "I got somethin' to throw atcha."

Charlie picked up his hat, stuffed the wad of bills and coins into his pocket, and walked toward the skate park with Caleb. The others wandered over to observe the sunbaked, half-naked, red-bearded old surfer with a giant yellow snake wrapped around his shoulders. The python was fat as a firehose. Another bearded guy glided past on rollerblades, an arresting sight in a white caftan and Sufi turban, with a beatific smile, playing an electric guitar plugged into an amp strapped on his back.

"Venice Beach," Innes said to Steven. "Don't ever change."

Caleb returned after a few minutes, leaving Charlie at the skate park. "He'll do it. He wants fifty bucks."

"Deal," said Vanessa.

Innes wondered where all her money came from, as a part-time restaurant hostess, and felt himself torn between gratitude and resentment for her largesse.

"But we have to do it now," said Caleb. "His uncle gets back from Cabo tomorrow, so we may not get another chance anytime soon."

With Charlie jammed into the rear of the truck, perched atop the sleeping bags, the six ventured out of the parking lot and headed south for Marina del Rey. The clouds grew darker as the day sagged deeper into the afternoon.

"Don't go back to Lincoln, please," said Tammy. "Too many police cars."

"You guys on the run from the cops?" said Charlie.

"I'll fill you in later," said Caleb.

"Cool," said Charlie. "Outlaws."

"Won't it be dark by the time we leave?" said Steven. "Can we do this at night?"

"No problemo," said Charlie. "We got lights and instruments. My uncle and me have taken *Sweet Pea* out at night lots of times. It's better to do this at night anyway, seeing as you're criminals on the lam and all."

Vanessa guided the Explorer past the tightly packed pink, yellow, and beige beach houses, all glass and balconies, while Charlie filled them in on the story of his uncle's boat. Uncle Ed was an investment broker who put together syndicates of dentists and the like to invest in movies but remained a Hollywood fringe player. The boat they would commandeer was a 44-foot Kadey-Krogen, designed like a houseboat, with nicely- appointed living quarters. Charlie referred to it as a "live aboard." His uncle bought it with the idea of cruising the Pacific Coast from Baja to Alaska, but soon gave up the idea when he realized how slow the damn thing was. At a maximum speed of seven knots, it took forever to get anywhere. His use of the boat dwindled and was limited to short trips to San Diego or Santa Barbara.

Innes had wondered why Charlie's uncle hadn't offered him a place to live. Caleb said the uncle didn't know his nephew was homeless.

Charlie confessed he hadn't looked in on the *Sweet Pea* for a few days. Last time he checked on it, everything was in order. He had fired up the John Deere diesel with no problems, and there was plenty of fuel in the eight-hundred-gallon tank.

The deal was, once the roads re-opened, Charlie would drive the Explorer up the coast to Alba Longa. But there was one hitch. "There's no dinghy," he said as he directed Vanessa to turn onto Tahiti Way, lined with waterfront apartment buildings. "It's in the repair shop getting patched."

"Why's that a problem?" said Tammy.

"Means I can't row you to shore. You'll have to swim," he said.

"Uh-oh," said Tammy. "How far?"

"Depends on how deep it is there," said Charlie. "We need at least a fathom, six feet of water, on the depth finder. I'll have to check the charts for Malibu. Might be twenty, thirty yards if I can find a shelf close to shore."

"Shit, shit, shit," Tammy muttered as they clambered out of the truck.

"What's wrong?" said Steven.

"I can't swim is what's wrong," she said.

"Don't worry," said Innes. "We'll get you to shore. There's life jackets onboard, right Charlie?"

"Yeah, but you can't take 'em with you," Charlie said. "You got to leave 'em on the boat."

"We'll figure something out," said Innes.

They unloaded the few items they planned to take ashore—several trash bags contained their backpacks and sleeping bags. It was raining again as they made their way to the docks. The wind picked up, and the metal halyards of the bobbing sailboats clanged against the aluminum masts like alarm bells.

Steven looked up at the darkening sky. "Are we going to have another storm? We could do this another time."

"Not to worry," said Charlie. He stopped on the dock in front of a big white trawler rolling slightly in the choppy water. "This baby's built for ocean crossing. Anyway, we'll stay close to shore."

Steven looked unconvinced. "We don't have to do this tonight, right? What's the hurry?"

Innes said, "Look Steven, the time is now. This is our only chance with the uncle's boat. Plus, the rains are coming again, we got nowhere else to go, and we're all tired of being crammed into the Explorer like sardines. No offense, Nessa."

"None taken," she said. "I'm getting sick of it, too. Let's do this."

Charlie jumped aboard and made them wait on the dock while he opened things up and turned on the lights. Vanessa noticed Caleb was shivering and wrapped her arms around him from behind, resting her cheek on his shoulder blade in the sort of parental embrace he had long ago eschewed from his father. Tammy and Steven wandered a few yards away and talked quietly.

After Charlie turned on the cabin lights, he emerged onto the aft deck and called for them to board one at a time. "Watch your footing. The boat's rockin'." He reached his hand across the watery gap to Vanessa.

Steven and Tammy returned, and Steven said: "We're not going."

"What do you mean you're not going?" Innes said.

"We worked it out. It's all good," said Steven. "Tammy can't swim, and I don't like boats. How about we take the truck back to Santa Monica and come join you when the road opens?"

"That might take days, weeks," said Innes.

"Maybe not," said Tammy.

Through the darkness Innes could detect the look of high anxiety on Tammy's face. Rain splattered the deck, punctuating the sudden tension.

"We'd rather stay in the truck until you guys get settled, if that's okay with you, Nessa," said Steven. "Charlie can stay with us if he wants."

Innes looked at Vanessa for guidance. She returned a questioning glance.

"You promise you'll come join us when you can?" he said. "We need to stick together."

"Absolutely," said Steven.

"Positively," said Tammy.

Vanessa handed over the keys, they exchanged hugs, and Steven and Tammy walked back to the truck with their backpacks and trash bags, calling to Charlie that they would wait for his return.

Charlie positioned Caleb and Innes on the fore and aft decks to untie the lines when he gave the signal. He fired up the John Deere and let it idle for a few minutes while he checked his instruments. The acrid smell of diesel exhaust rode the wind across the deck. From his spot on the bow, Innes glanced into the cabin. It was lit up like a video game arcade with glowing computer screens and illuminated readouts, switches, and dials. Vanessa called out for them to toss the ropes. They pushed away from the pylons with boathooks. Charlie threw it into reverse, backed out of the slip, and they were off.

The *Sweet Pea* was moored in Basin A, the closest one to the sea, and in minutes they were through the cut and into Santa Monica Bay, motoring north through the rising chop past Venice Beach. Charlie estimated from his charts it was about twenty miles to their destination, two-and-a-half, three hours max. The wind picked up and the rain came heavier. The *Sweet Pea* rocked and rolled but felt solid as it sliced through the whitecaps.

"Does anybody get seasick?" Charlie said. "There's Dramamine in the galley."

Caleb went below to see what else was in the tiny kitchenette.

Innes watched the green readout lights of the salt-corroded Seafarer depth finder. The numbers, toggled to show feet rather than fathoms, bounced around between twenty and thirty.

Caleb called out from the galley, "Hey, there's beer in the fridge."

"Leave it there, Cal," Innes called. "We've got some swimming to do tonight. I'm not dragging any drunks through the surf."

"You can bring me one," Charlie said.

"Great, we'll have a drunk captain," said Innes.

"Not drunk. Ima just having one. A little buzz."

"Buzzed boating is drunk boating."

"Thank you, Officer Friendly," said Charlie with a wink. Caleb handed Charlie an opened can of Coors Light. "There's food in there, too," Charlie said between swigs. "Should be reasonably fresh. Last time I looked."

Caleb and Vanessa pulled together a dinner of cheddar cheese slices, crackers, beef jerky, stuffed olives, and diet soda. Charlie invited them to take some food with them, which they gratefully stuffed into their backpacks.

After dinner, Innes and Vanessa went out to the aft deck and passed the time watching the lights of the shore drift by. The rain had eased to a soft, wind-driven mist. The Santa Monica Pier was a brilliant beacon in the foggy night, the Ferris wheel at Pacific Park lit up like a giant neon bicycle tire. The bright lights of downtown Santa Monica gave way to the softer illuminations of the hillside houses of Pacific Palisades. They watched together in silence until Vanessa cleared her throat and said, "I have something to tell you."

He turned to her and waited, not sure he was ready to hear it.

"I haven't been completely honest with you ... about Annie," she said. "We did sleep together."

He wasn't sure he heard right. Her voice barely registered above the wind and slapping waves. "Wait. What?" A surge of anger stirred within, but quickly subsided. Somehow, it made sense. "I thought you said it was sisterly love."

"It was. At first. We were soulmate girlfriends, but then we were more than that."

They stood in awkward silence as the deck swayed gently in the wind and rain. The squawking seagulls that had followed the boat sounded like they were mocking him.

"So, what happened? When?"

"It started about a year, year-and-a-half ago. You were out of town, covering a music festival in Ojai or some such place. Juan was in Mexico. I think Caleb had a sleepover somewhere. Annie came down to my place and we drank wine and watched *Project Runway*. Girls' night in. I think I said Heidi Klum looked good enough to eat, and next thing we knew, we were making out on the couch. We ended up in bed, and she spent the night. We were mortified in the morning, hung over and embarrassed. We laughed about it and swore we'd never do it again, or even speak of it. And we didn't, for a while anyway."

Innes couldn't help picturing the tryst in his mind. He was rent in two by arousal and jealousy, and torn between wanting this conversation to end, pretend it never happened, and probing for gory details, like picking a scab. "When? How?"

"Afternoon delight we called it, our little secret. Only when you were away and Cal was in school, usually. We were discreet. Everyone knew we were friends, so it didn't look weird to see Annie come by my place."

He pictured Annie furtively slipping away to Vanessa's apartment, and him completely oblivious. "How many times?"

"I don't know. Twenty, thirty, maybe more. I tried to abstain, we both did, out of respect for you, but … I was lonely and told myself I was done with men, after Juan. Maybe I felt justified, after being cheated on myself. That's no excuse, I know. Anyway, I needed someone. And Annie, she felt like you were drifting away from her, into anger and depression. So we drifted to each other. After Annie died, I figured you would never know, would never need to know. But then I thought you should know. Now that we're … friends."

Vanessa turned away and joined the boys on the bridge.

Innes stayed on deck, watching the shore lights slide by, and contemplated Vanessa's disclosure, wondering what she meant by "friends." His suspicions about Annie were true—she *was* being unfaithful. In a way that never occurred to him. What a sap. Cuckolded by a woman, by a woman he was falling in love with now, and with the woman he had been married to and still loved. How had he missed it? Had he been so tuned out to Annie and her needs? His thoughts turned to Annie's diary, packed away in the bag with his things, and he wondered what more he would learn if he read it. He wasn't sure he wanted to. He felt he should be enraged by the betrayal, at both Annie and Vanessa, but couldn't bring himself to it. His feelings of love, loss, and regret toward Annie and gratitude and affection toward Vanessa smothered any anger.

He returned to the bridge, drawn and quartered by his conflicted emotions. Charlie, tongue loosened by the can of beer, was regaling them with stories about his adventures trying to break into Holly-wood. Innes wasn't listening, still numbed by this fresh revelation. Charlie brought him out of his self-pity when he said, "We're almost there. GPS says that's it, straight ahead." The moon peeked through a gap in the clouds, illuminating a bluff against the misty night sky. "Start gathering your things."

The plan was, Caleb would swim ashore first with a rope tied around his waist in case he ran into trouble in the rough surf. After reaching the beach, he would untie the rope and Innes would pull it back onboard. Vanessa would go next, repeating the rope handoff. Innes would go last, towing the two big trash bags with their gear, knotted shut to stay dry. Once on the beach, Innes would tie their three lifejackets onto the rope so Charlie could retrieve them. All three claimed to be strong swimmers. The wind and rain were pick-ing up again, but it looked like a slam dunk.

Charlie throttled the engine back, turned parallel to the shore, and instructed Innes to drop the anchor. "This is as close as I can get," he said. The depth finder displayed ten feet. "There are some shoals around here. I don't want to get caught on one."

Charlie illuminated the beach with a searchlight. Innes clambered to the aft deck and glanced ashore. The beach looked about twen-ty-five yards away, one length of the pool where he used to swim his laps. Piece of cake. He helped Caleb tie the rope around his waist, double checked to make sure his life jacket was on tight, and hugged him. Caleb clambered down the metal ladder at the stern, lowered himself into the choppy sea, and swam for shore. Innes and Vanessa stood together on the deck and watched as Caleb neared the beach. His swim stroke was strong and sure. Innes was thankful Annie had insisted on aquatic lessons for him when he was a toddler.

Charlie, working the throttle and the gears and the wheel to keep the boat stationary against the wind, trained the searchlight on Caleb until they saw him stand up and wade ashore through the surf. He turned and waved both arms above his head and untied the rope. Innes was impressed by Charlie's multi-tasking performance. His opinion of the strange boy he'd met at the pier arcade rose by the hour.

Innes pulled the rope on board and helped Vanessa tie it on. She said, "Don't hate me. Please," and kissed him long and hard on the mouth. Before he could respond she cannonballed into the water yelling "Geronimo!" He watched as she swam the breaststroke. The back of her head bobbed up and down between the waves, her top bun surfacing like a periscope. She reached the beach as quickly as Caleb, who waded into the surf to help her ashore.

Innes hauled in the rope and took stock of the task before him. Two large trash bags, stuffed to the limit. Not heavy, but not light either. They had some air in them, so they should float.

Charlie joined him on the deck.

"Who's controlling the boat?" Innes said as he tied the rope around his waist.

"Bungee cords," said Charlie, pointing back at the bridge with a thumb. "That ought to hold things steady for a couple minutes, until you're clear. You ready?"

Innes nodded.

"Jump in. I'll hand you the bags," said Charlie.

Innes cannon-balled into the waves. The impact with the frigid water came as a shock. He surfaced coughing and gasping for air. Salt water penetrated his nostrils, creating an instant sinus headache.

"You okay?" Charlie called out, leaning over the side.

Innes coughed and spat sea water, dog paddled, and lifted a hand to signal for the bags. Charlie tossed them in and they landed with a splash a couple feet from him. He reached out and grabbed them. To his relief, they were floating. Charlie walked his end of the rope along the narrow side rail toward the fore deck. Innes turned toward the beach, hooked his arms around the bags, one on each side, like water wings, and kicked. The choppy waves slapped against his face, invading his nose and mouth with the briny sea water. This was not at all like swimming in a calm lap pool. He gasped for breath. Halfway there. Charlie pointed the searchlight at Vanessa and Caleb so Innes could see where to go. The splattering raindrops on the water beat a rhythm section to the melody of waves crashing on the shore. He tried to adjust his grip on the bag under his left arm, but lost hold of it and it squirted away. As he reached for it, a large wave crested and broke on top of him, submerging him and flipping him upside down. He lost his grip on the other bag, struggled to the surface, and popped his head out of the water coughing and spitting, the bitter taste of saltwater overwhelming his senses.

Vanessa yelled from shore, "Leave them. Let them float in."

He turned toward the beach. It was only about a dozen yards away, but he still couldn't feel the bottom. Caleb and Vanessa swam toward him.

"Don't," he called. "Stay there."

Too late. They were upon him. Caleb got to him first and grabbed hold of his life jacket. Vanessa went after the trash bags, which were floating not toward the beach but sideways in a rip current. Caleb swam to shore, pulling his father by the jacket. Innes kicked and paddled weakly, already exhausted. His wet clothes weighed on him like a lead-lined X-ray smock. By the time Caleb got him close enough to stand in the surf and wade in, he was spent. Caleb dragged him onto the beach. Vanessa was waiting there with the trash bags and helped bring him onto the sand. He collapsed there, and she untied his rope. Caleb removed their life jackets, tied them onto the end of the rope, gave it a tug and waved at the boat. The jackets disappeared into the surf, their bright orange shapes illuminated momentarily by the searchlight before they vanished into the waves. A few minutes later, as Innes lay flat on his back on the beach, still gulping for air, they heard a horn blast from the *Sweet Pea* and the sound of a surging diesel engine. The boat swung away to the east and grew smaller, its white shape fading into the rainy night.

"Fucking Charlie," said Caleb. "Dude came through."

Innes sat up, spit salty saliva, and gasped, "I must … have been out … of my fucking mind."

"It's okay, Dad, we're here," said Caleb. "It worked."

Without Charlie's searchlight, all was near black. No moonlight, only thick cloud cover. Caleb retrieved a red plastic flashlight from their things and pointed it at the bluff behind them, exposing the bottom of a steep, narrow footpath. The rain was now a downpour. The path was a straight shot angled along the cliff face, no switch-backs. Rainwater sluiced down toward them in wide rivulets. The footing looked treacherous. The bluff face was not quite dirt, not quite solid rock, but a hybrid of hard-packed fossilized mud, like brown shale. Caleb and Vanessa went first and had little trouble with the steep slippery path. Innes followed with less assurance, still exhausted from his near-disastrous swim. Trailing two younger and fitter companions, he felt old and weak, like baggage. Near the top of the thirty-foot bluff he stumbled, nearly a making fatal drop to the rock-strewn beach below. He lost his grip on his bag and it tumbled down to the sand. Caleb called through the wind-driven rain, "Leave it, Dad. I'll go back for it."

When they reached the top—a strip of grass and mud about five feet wide along the edge—they found a chain-link fence that separated them from the construction site. A sheet of black fabric blocked the view of what was on the other side. Caleb found a small cutaway in the fabric and shined his flashlight through it. They could make out a long yard leading to the dark outlines of what looked like the back of a two-story structure, clad in stucco with a terra cotta tile roof and a series of rectangular openings where windows and doors were supposed to be. While Innes examined the contours of the estate, Caleb reached into his pack, extracted a pair of wire cutters, and snipped the chain links.

"You're a regular Eagle Scout," said Innes. "Like your grampa."

Caleb cut a long vertical slice in the fence and the fabric, which they pulled open and slipped through gingerly past the sharp metal teeth. Innes recalled a similar maneuver with old man George under the freeway back in Burbank so many weeks ago, and wished his father-in-law was with them now. He thought of the ratty old tam-o-shanter stuffed into his backpack and was glad to have it.

Once inside the compound, Innes and Vanessa waited as Caleb skittered down the path to retrieve the sack. Vanessa stood behind him and wrapped her arms around him, as she had done with Caleb back at the dock. "Cold?" she said and rubbed her hands up and down his goose-bumped arms.

"Not anymore." He turned toward her and held her close. His heart was pounding from the exertion of the swim and the climb, or from something else.

They were still in the embrace when Caleb returned with the bag. "I'm back," he announced rather too loudly, and they broke the clinch.

"Let's head for that doorway," said Innes. Vanessa walked ahead of them. Caleb ambled next to his father, and when they were a safe distance behind Vanessa, he said, "Dad, are you and her ... you know?"

"The answer is no. We're just friends."

"You seem like more than friends."

"I don't know. Let's not worry about that now." He understood the unspoken subtext, that his son hadn't yet accepted his mother's death, much less the thought of another woman in his father's life.

Vanessa waited for them at the doorway. Caleb shined the flashlight inside. It appeared to be a large dining hall or ballroom, with nothing there to identify its purpose but poured concrete floors, bare plaster walls, and a vaulted ceiling. They walked through the cavernous space and approached another open doorway on the right. A faint light flickered from the next room. Innes detected the smell of smoke. In the room, three dark figures sat huddled around a small campfire burning on the bare floor.

"Hello?" said Innes.

The three turned toward them, shielding their faces from the glare of Caleb's flashlight. One of them stood. In the dim glow of the fire, he looked enormous. Well over six feet tall and three-hundred pounds, he was bald with a white goatee and dressed all in black, with dense carpets of blue tattoos covering his tanned neck and pale white upper arms.

"Who the fuck are you?" he bellowed.

"My name's Innes. This is Vanessa. And Caleb." His voice wavered.

"Where'd you come from?" the man-mountain said. "How'd you get in here?"

"We climbed up the path. From the beach," said Innes. "The road is washed out, so we came by boat."

"You gotta be kidding me."

"True story," said Innes. "So, who are you?"

"Name's Turner. These are my homies, Shithead and Dickface."

"Pleasure, I'm sure," Innes said.

Vanessa and Caleb were silent and still as statues.

"So, anyways," the tattooed giant continued, "this is our squat. Y'all are gonna have to move along."

"Seriously?" said Vanessa. She held her arms out to the sides as if to draw attention to their dripping wet miserableness.

"Yeah, pretty lady. I say who stays and who goes around here. And I say you go."

"Who died and left you in charge?" Vanessa said.

The big man raised his arm. "Here's who. Say hello to my little friend."

Innes was thinking of a retort to the stale movie cliché when a six-inch blade snapped audibly into view, pointing from Turner's hand straight up to the ceiling, gleaming in the light of the fire.

Innes remembered George's hunting knife and was grateful again for the old man's foresight. The knife was in his backpack. He made a mental note to keep it handy. "No need to threaten us," Innes said as he stared at the switchblade. "We're not looking for trouble, only a place to dry out and spend the night. This place looks plenty big. We can stay out of your way."

"Yeah, it's plenty big," said Turner. "Thing is, we start lettin' every bum what shows up here settle in, soon we're overrun. We ain't runnin' no homeless shelter here."

"What exactly *are* you running here?" Vanessa said.

"We're … ahh … lookin' after the place for the owner. Keepin' the riff-raff out."

"Like junkyard dogs," said Shitface. Or was it Dickhead? The other one let out a high-pitched bark.

"And who exactly is the owner?" Vanessa said.

"Rich folks. They payin' us to … ahh … maintain the property," said Turner.

"I'm not seeing much maintaining around here," said Vanessa. "You're squatters, homeless people like us, aren't you?"

Innes blinked at her in subtle warning not to escalate.

"None o' yer business," said Turner, holding the switchblade at his side. "Now, you gonna move along?"

"Look, Turner ... do you have a first name?" Innes said.

"Nope. Just Turner."

"We've got no place to go tonight. PCH is washed out, the boat that brought us here is gone. We only need to crash one night. Then we'll move on."

Turner considered that for a moment and squatted next to his pals. They conferred in whispers. "Okay," he announced. He stood and snapped the switchblade shut and shoved it into a pants pocket. "One night. But you gotta stay out of our way. There's a garage on the side, through the kitchen, back the way you came. You can stay there. I don't wanna see you in the morning."

The trio retreated through the great hall, exited to a muddy side yard in the rain, and made their way into a cavernous garage. Caleb extinguished the flashlight so they could peel off their wet clothes in the privacy of darkness and feel their way around in their backpacks for dry ones. Once they had changed, Caleb flicked on the light and set it on the floor on its end, pointed toward the ceiling, filling the vast space with a soft glow. Innes checked his watch, glad it was waterproof. Almost eleven. Caleb pulled out a brown plastic tarp from his backpack and spread it on the floor. They hauled out their sleeping bags and settled in for the night. The floor was cold and hard under the tarp and sleeping bags, but Innes had little doubt they would sleep well. Vanessa was already snoring. Innes kept his bag partially unzipped in case he needed to get out of it quickly.

Book X

IN THE MORNING LIGHT OF A CLEAR SKY, THE
fenced-in compound of Alba Longa emerged as a half-completed
dreamscape of multiple buildings with two porticos and floor-to-ceil-
ing openings for windows, wings of columned arcades that fanned
out across a landscape of pebble and stone walkways and several
weed-choked dirt patches likely intended for gardens. Between the
columned arcades was a half-excavated rectangular hole that looked
like it might have ambitions to be a swimming pool.

Innes found Caleb already up, smoking a cigarette by the chain-
link fence that overlooked the ocean. He had cut away a large section
of the black cloth on the fence, affording a sweeping view of the
Pacific as it absorbed the morning sun.

"I didn't know you smoked," Innes said. "Bad habit."

"I'm gonna stop someday."

"How about now?"

They didn't speak for a while, as Innes lamented how little he
knew about his only child. They watched the waves crash on the
beach below, which curved outward into a protected cove. The idea
of a nighttime amphibious assault on Malibu looked vainglorious in
the cold light of day. He easily might have drowned there. But here
they were. All they had to worry about was a three-hundred-pound
hooligan with a switchblade and two idiotic sidekicks.

"I found water," Caleb said. "There's a spigot on the side of the
main house."

"Good going," said Innes. "At least we won't die of thirst."

"What are we going to do next?" said Caleb. "What about Turner
and his buddies?"

"I don't know exactly. I have no intention of running away like
scared rabbits. I think we can persuade him to co-exist, for a while
anyway, until we get some reinforcements up here. He may be a big
mean mo-fo, but I wouldn't like his chances against Tammy. That
woman is fearless."

"I hear she kicked the crap out of a cop," Caleb said with barely
concealed admiration. "Too bad it wasn't the same cop who killed
Pops." Caleb finished his cigarette and flicked the butt through the
fence links down to the beach.

"Next time you want to litter in the ocean," Innes said, "remember your grandfather's ashes are in there, too."

"I used to mooch cigs from Pops," he said. "Only right to give him one back."

They found Vanessa setting up a clothesline with a rope she'd commandeered from the *Sweet Pea*. She'd strung it between the garage and the kitchen door to hang their wet clothes.

"Just what this place needs," said Innes. "A woman's touch."

She stuck out her tongue at him. "Help me hang these things."

Vanessa had been more distant toward Innes since they'd arrived, perhaps uncertain of her standing in his eyes after her revelation about Annie. Innes was uncertain, too, but was leaning toward forgiveness. Anyway, what was done was done.

Caleb picked up a brassiere from the pile and offered it to Vanessa. She snatched it out of his hand and draped it over the line, then smiled at him and mussed his hair.

Innes went into the garage to throw together some breakfast. Inventorying their food supply, he figured they had enough to last several days if they were frugal. Also, Caleb had liberated a six-pack of Coors Light from the *Sweet Pea's* galley.

They had just finished their beef jerky and crackers when Turner wandered out from the kitchen and stopped to admire the neatly draped clothes drying in the sun. He wore the same all-black getup from the night before, including those ridiculous Zubaz pants. All he needed was a mullet haircut, if he had any hair, to complete the '90s look that Innes had tried to forget.

"Looks like y'all are fixin' to settle in for a while," he said. He stared with great interest at Vanessa while lightly fingering the ladies' underwear on the line. "I thought we had an agreement y'all were movin' on."

"You can at least let us dry our clothes before pushing us out," said Vanessa. Her loathing hung in the air like a pestilent vapor.

Turner regarded her with a smile, or maybe it was a leer. "I reckon I can, pretty lady. Y'all can stay awhile longer. I'll let you know when time's up." He stood there for a moment, ogling Vanessa, then glared at Innes as if daring him to say something, and withdrew.

❖

For the next two days, they seldom saw Turner and his crew. At times they appeared to have left the premises, only to be heard again arguing and raising a ruckus inside the main house late at night. Vanessa stayed in contact with Steven and Tammy via her cellphone, keeping the conversations brief to conserve the battery. Steven reported the clean-up on PCH was progressing faster than expected and the road might re-open within days. Vanessa told them about their unpleasant co-squatters. Steven promised they would be on their way to join them the minute the highway opened. Vanessa also checked in with June to see if there was news from the arson investigation or the insurance companies. There wasn't. June said she would come see them as soon as the roads cleared.

On the third morning, as Innes and Vanessa returned to the garage with armloads of twigs, branches, scrap lumber, and other burnable construction debris for making fires, Innes brought up an idea that had percolated in his mind for two days. "I'm thinking about what Turner said the night we arrived. 'We ain't running no homeless shelter here.' What if this *was* a homeless shelter? Wouldn't that be awesome?"

Vanessa looked at him as if he'd suggested a bicycle trip to Venus. "Sure. And all the neighbors would throw a big party for the grand opening," she said with an eye roll. "Just like when they suggested building a new shelter in Venice. Total shit show."

"I know, it's ridiculous, a homeless shelter here makes no sense. But what if we could stay awhile? Wait for Tammy and Steven, and get our own little shelter going, the five of us?"

Vanessa snorted derisively. "How long do you think that could last? We're squatters. We could be chased out any day now."

"I know, but we can try to hold out long enough until our insurance checks come. Not have to go back to the streets or sleep in a truck. Then we could all start over somewhere, together."

"Together?" She arched one side of eyebrow at him.

"Sure, why not? Share a house. We should all stick together. We've been through a lot, right?"

Vanessa studied the taped joints of the unfinished sheetrock in the garage ceiling. After a moment, she said, "What about Turner?"

"I don't know. We'll figure something—" Their conversation was interrupted by shouts and commotion from inside the main house. "Sounds like our friends are back," said Innes.

"Where's Caleb?" said Vanessa.

"He was out looking for lumber, I think. Or sneaking a cigarette."

As they stacked pieces of wood to make a fire, Caleb ran into the garage, gasping for air, with a bloody lip and what looked like the puffy beginnings of a black eye.

"What the hell?" said Innes.

"Honey, what happened? Let me see that cut," said Vanessa.

"Those two assholes," Caleb wheezed between breaths. "Dickhead and Shitbreath. They jumped me. In the house."

"God dammit!" yelled Innes.

Vanessa examined his cut and the bruises around his eye and went to her backpack to fetch her first-aid kit.

Caleb sidled up close to Innes and whispered, "Dad. They said they were gonna rape me."

"I will fucking kill them," Innes said under his breath. "What did they do?"

"Nothing. I pushed back. They were punching and kicking me. They had me on the ground. Then the big dude came in and broke it up. He saved my ass."

Vanessa was applying disinfectant to Caleb's lip when Turner walked in. She looked at Innes. "Don't do anything stupid," she silently mouthed.

"You okay?" Turner asked Caleb.

Caleb nodded.

"I'm real sorry, man," Turner said. "Those assholes. They're dumb motherfuckers."

"They'll be dead motherfuckers they try anything like that again," said Innes, surprised by the cold fury in his voice.

"They won't. I ran their asses outta here," said Turner. "They come back, I'll kill 'em myself."

"Kind of late, isn't it? The damage is done," said Innes.

"I said sorry, man. I broke it up. I saved this boy from a beat-down. Or worse." He looked at Caleb with a creepy grin. Caleb looked away.

"Well, thanks for that," said Innes. "Right now, we'd like to be left alone."

"Later," Turner said. "Let me know I can do anything, ma'am." He bowed theatrically toward Vanessa and withdrew.

Next day, Steven reported PCH was close to reopening. He and Tammy would drive up the coast in the morning. Caleb volunteered to hitchhike back to Santa Monica and lead them to the compound. Innes was reluctant to let him go, with those two sidekicks of Turner out there somewhere. Caleb said he needed to get away, and Vanessa persuaded Innes to let him go. He asked Caleb to take the hunting knife, but he refused. Innes stuffed the knife back into his deep cargo pocket, walked with him out to the highway, gave him a hug, and sent him on his way. Legally an adult, Caleb was no longer taking orders from his dad. When Innes got back to the garage, he called Steven on Vanessa's phone and told them Caleb was on the way and to watch for him.

An hour or so after he rung off with Steven, Innes heard screams from inside the house. He recognized Vanessa's voice immediately and took off on a dead run through the kitchen door. He heard more screaming, then muffled cries, then scuffling. When he entered the living room, he came upon a scene so sickening it took him a full second or two to process it. Vanessa was face down on the bare floor, Turner on top of her, her wraparound skirt on the floor next to them. Turner had both of her arms pinned behind her back with one of his beefy arms in a wrestling hold. His other arm wrapped around her jaw, smothering her screams. In his hand, inches from her face, was the gleaming switchblade. His pants were at his knees, exposing his giant white ass, which hovered over her like an albino manatee.

Without thinking, Innes dashed across the room and aimed a flying kick directly at Turner's head. He connected and fell forward, tumbling hard onto the cold floor, banging both kneecaps. Turner let out a howl, pulled his hands to his head, and rolled off Vanessa. She struggled free. The switchblade clattered onto the floor. Innes slapped at it, sending it skittering across the room.

"Get out of here. Run!" he called to Vanessa.

She headed in the direction of the runaway switchblade. Innes and Turner scrambled up from the floor. They were no more than six feet apart. Turner pulled up his pants, sheathing his obscenely swaying erection, and grinned menacingly.

"Go out to the highway and get help," Innes yelled.

Turner charged him and doubled him over with a pile-driver to the belly. Fighting the urge to vomit, Innes lowered his guard to protect his pummeled midsection. Turner seized the opening to clamp both hands around his throat and shoved him against the wall, slamming his head against the plaster. He squeezed his powerful fingers against Innes's neck, pressing his thumbs into the windpipe. Turner's face was only inches from Innes, his expression screwed up into a mask of fiery determination. Innes could not speak or breathe. He tried to pry the fingers off his throat, but the man was too strong. The thumbs were about to push right through his windpipe and snap his neck. Innes was sure he was staring his own death in the face. He waited for the scenes from his entire life to flash by. Nothing came but pain.

A pair of tanned slender arms appeared around Turner's tattooed neck from behind. Vanessa's face loomed over his shoulder. Turner released his hands from Innes' neck and reached up to pull Vanessa's arms away. She had him in a chokehold, one wrist locked inside the opposite elbow. Her bare legs wrapped around Turner's huge waist. Turner reached back and wrapped his hands around Vanessa's neck and squeezed his thumbs against her throat. A look of panic overtook her eyes.

Innes dropped his hands to his side, gasped for air, and felt the bulge of the hunting knife in his cargo pocket. He grasped the handle with both hands and aligned the tip against the bottom of exposed rib cage. Before a thrashing struggling Turner spun away, Innes drove the blade with all his waning strength upward into the soft torso all the way to the hilt. Turner lowered his hands from

Vanessa's neck, let out a moan, and staggered backward. Vanessa dropped off him and stepped out of the way. For several seconds, the three of them stood there in the bare room illuminated by the rosy light of the setting sun. They stared at the wood handle protruding downward from Turner's bloated belly like an obscenely misplaced phallus. Innes froze in shock and disbelief. Vanessa, mouth hanging open, was silent. Turner studied the knife handle, as if unable to process what it was and how it got there. He grabbed it, pulled, and let out a howl of pain. He let go and looked up at Innes with an expression of wonder, fear, and amazement. His eyes rolled up and he fell backward, landing with a dull thud like a three-hundred-pound sack of sand, and was still.

Innes and Vanessa stood in stunned silence. Turner's body twitched for a few moments, emitted a gurgling sound, a wheezing exhale, a flatulent emission, then nothing. A foul stink hung in the air. The knife handle pointed accusingly at Innes.

"What did you do?" Vanessa said.

"What did I do? I knifed a man who was trying to rape you and kill me," gasped Innes. He massaged his crushed throat.

Vanessa wrapped her skirt around her hips, visibly shaking. "Is he dead?"

Innes knelt beside the body. "He's not breathing." Turner's eyes were open, mouth agape, face frozen in shock and awe. Innes stared at the lifeless body. It looked like a beached sea lion with its huge mound of belly. The knife handle taunted him.

"We should call the police," said Vanessa.

"I'm not so sure," said Innes. "This doesn't look good."

"It was self-defense. Attempted rape and murder. No one would blame us." Her voice betrayed fear and doubt, as if needing to convince herself.

"Maybe not. But we have no witnesses. And we're homeless people squatting here illegally. In Malibu. How's that gonna look?"

"What are you suggesting?" she said.

Innes considered their options. Get the police involved, and take their chances with the criminal justice system? Not an appealing prospect. Or cover it up, dispose of the body somehow, never mention it again, and live with the dark secret for the rest of their lives?

He already bore the guilt over Sherri. Not one of his proudest moments, but he'd worked it out in his mind and saw no alternative. He was in the same box again.

"I think we bury the body. Right here, right now, before anyone comes back. No one has to know, except you and me. Not even Cal."

"You want to cover this up? Pretend it didn't happen?" The accusatory look in her eyes shook him.

"I don't see we have a choice. Think about it. A fight between squatters, and one of them ends up dead? A murder trial? I could get convicted of manslaughter, self-defense or not." He thought about it, but his mind raced, confused, unsure he made any sense.

"It just seems wrong. Immoral." She glanced at the body again.

"I don't like it either. But we didn't ask for this. It was forced on us. Something like this could ruin our lives. My life, anyway. Now that it's worth living again."

Vanessa turned away and stared at the ceiling. Innes looked at her, the righteous moral compass, as usual. He felt like a criminal already.

"It's not our fault," he pleaded. "It's not fair we should have to face the consequences."

"Okay, okay," she said.

Innes got up off the floor. "Good. We need to stick together."

She gently touched his throat. "You're all bruised."

"You saved my life," he said.

"I tried to find his switchblade, but I couldn't. I wanted to kill the *bastardo* myself. When I turned around, I thought he was going to kill *you.*"

"You are one brave woman. Crazy, too. Amazing. Craymazing." They hugged for a moment.

"How do we do this?" she said, pulling away.

"This is a construction site," he said. His mind decelerated as he collected his thoughts. His heartbeat slowed. "There's a shed back by the fence with tools in it. Shovels and rakes and stuff. You know, by the trash pile we're using as a toilet? The ground is bare and torn up everywhere. We could dig a hole and no one would ever know, if we dig it deep enough and in the right spot. It's soft from all the rain, so digging should be easy."

"He's so huge," she said, eying the corpse. "How do we move him?"

"I'll get Cal's tarp from the garage. We'll roll him over on it and drag him out to the yard."

They decided to bury Turner and his backpack at the bottom of the huge hole in the yard that looked like it was to be a pool. That would put him many feet below ground, and many feet below the poured concrete bottom of the eventual swimming pool.

Hauling the body outside on the tarp took thirty minutes of grunting and heaving and dragging. Turner had shit himself as he expired, and they had to fight back a gag reflex from the stench. The sun had set but the moon was out, and it was bright enough to see what they were doing. Together they rolled the corpse and Turner's backpack off the tarp and into the hole, about eight feet down. A dirt mound in one corner gave Innes a path to the bottom. Vanessa tossed a shovel into the pit, and he started to dig. The ground was indeed soft, and after about two hours of taking turns digging while the other acted as lookout, they had a narrow, six-foot-deep grave. Innes pulled the knife out of the belly and pushed the corpse, backpack, and switchblade into the grave. For a moment, he considered throwing in the hunting knife as well, but decided to keep it handy in case Turner's buddies returned. He pushed the dirt in and tamped it with his feet to prevent settling. With a garden rake he smoothed over the bottom of the pit and covered his footprints as he backed out of the hole.

Innes lay the brown tarp on the garage floor to examine it with the flashlight for tell-tale blood stains or other evidence of their deed. He flipped it over to the other side, which was blue. One corner was torn, exposing the white fiberglass strands underneath. It looked familiar, and he made a mental note to ask Caleb where he'd got it.

They moved their things into the main house and slept in the great hall next to the kitchen, avoiding the living area where Turner and his cronies squatted—too much bad mojo. They stayed up for an hour drinking warm beers and replayed the terrifying events of the evening, exhausted from digging, and coming to terms with the fact they had killed a human being, vile though he was. They would bathe in the ocean in the morning, rinse off the dirt and grime, evidence of their crime.

Vanessa crushed an empty silver can and said, "Do you hate me? About Annie? You haven't said anything since I told you."

He took an uncomfortable moment before answering. "No, I don't hate you. We both loved the same woman. I can accept that. You have good taste in women. You were a good friend, too, and you obviously met her needs in a way I didn't. It's just … I've had a hard time processing it. For a long time, I've had sexual fantasies about you,"—there, he finally said it—"and felt guilty about it out of loyalty to Annie. Little did I know the woman I was fantasizing about was fucking my wife behind my back. Perverse poetic justice, I guess."

"I am so sorry. I am. I feel like such a slut. I know how it feels to be cheated on. I wouldn't blame you if you did hate me, like I hate Juan. But you're better than me. You may have fantasized about me—and don't think I wasn't aware, you're not exactly subtle, looking at my ass—but you never did anything about it. You were always a perfect gentleman. I've felt unworthy of you." She kissed him on the cheek and climbed into her sleeping bag. In minutes they were both asleep.

Her chirping cellphone woke them in the morning. Steven reported PCH was open and they were on their way. "Caleb's with them," Vanessa said. "He got a ride back to Santa Monica with a Caltrans road crew."

"That's my boy," said Innes. "Resourceful. Like his grandfather."

"What happens if Heckle and Jeckle come back?" she said.

"You mean Dickbrain and Shithead?"

"Yeah, them. What if they ask about Turner?"

"We tell them he left, went looking for them. Send them on their way."

Later, as Innes left the house to meet the others at the gate, he said to Vanessa, "Remember, we act like nothing happened. Turner and his buddies took off. That's all we know."

When the Explorer pulled up at the front door, Tammy got out and screamed with delight. "It's a damn castle," she giggled. Vanessa came out and hugged her.

"Needs work," said Steven, sizing up the place.

"What do you mean?" Innes said. "All it needs is a water and power hookup, septic, wiring, plumbing, HVAC, windows, doors, landscaping, carpeting, appliances--"

"Yeah, practically move-in ready," Steven said.

Caleb unloaded the truck, stacking boxes, crates, bags, and coolers.

"Look at you guys," Vanessa said. "What did you bring?"

"Ice. Water jugs. Beer. Food. Clothes. Towels. Toilet paper. A propane stove." Caleb recited the inventory. "And a mirror and a razor. That's for you, Dad."

"You had me at 'beer'," said Innes as he stroked his four weeks' worth of scraggly beard. He hadn't shaved since ... Sherri's. "Who won the lottery?" he said.

"My treat," said Steven. "I'm getting low on funds, though. Some of us are going to have find work, and soon."

"*¡Dios mío!* Work," said Vanessa. "I need to get back to Pasadena, and soon. I told them at the restaurant I'd only be gone a few days."

"I didn't mean just you, Nessa," said Steven. "All of us need to pitch in."

They gathered in a circle on the kitchen floor and caught up on the events of the past few days, minus a few details. Vanessa inquired about Charlie. Caleb said they meant to invite him along, but he had disappeared.

Innes cleared his throat to get everyone's attention and unveiled his scheme for the five of them to settle at Alba Longa indefinitely, or until their insurance kicked in, now that they had the place to themselves.

"He's kidding," said Vanessa. "Or deluded. This place is owned by a bank. They're not in the homeless shelter business. They're going to boot us as soon as they find out."

"*If* they find out," said Innes.

They just looked at him, shaking their heads.

❖

Next morning, the reunited Casa Grande refugees gathered around the unfinished center island of the kitchen and sliced an over-ripe honeydew for breakfast. Vanessa walked in and said, "Don't panic people, but there's a police car in the driveway."

"Oh, fuck," said Tammy.

Innes and Caleb rushed to the front of the house and peered through the window. Two deputies, a short man and a tall woman in matching olive-green pants and tan shirts, emerged from a black-and-white LA County Sheriff cruiser and converged on Vanessa's Explorer. The woman studied the license plate and wrote in a notebook.

Vanessa, Steven, and Tammy joined Innes and Caleb in the front room, the five peeking out like raccoons casing a trash can.

"What do we do now?" Vanessa whispered.

"We can't hide, they've already ID'd your truck," said Steven. "They know we're here."

Innes and Vanessa exchanged worried glances. The police were here, and there was a body buried in the back yard.

"We have to talk to them," said Innes. "Let them know we're harmless, just passing through. Only one of us, though. They might overreact to a gang of five."

"Not me," said Tammy. "They'll bust me for IMWB."

"What?" said Caleb.

"In Malibu while Black," she said.

"I'll go," said Innes.

"No, let me," said Vanessa.

The deputies turned toward Vanessa when she appeared. The woman placed her hand on her holstered sidearm, then removed it as they began to speak calmly with her. Vanessa pointed toward the window, and the watchers instinctively ducked, like toddlers playing hide and seek, a ridiculous reaction, as noted by the male deputy who called, "Come out, come out, wherever you are."

The levity of the gathering lasted only a few seconds after the five assembled around the smiling deputies. The mood shifted on a dime, and the Casa Grande crew in short order was arrayed around the hood of the LA Sheriff SUV, hands on the warm metal. The deputies frisked them for weapons. Tammy looked ready to explode, her jaw muscles flexing, as she was patted down—by a woman, true, but also a White police officer. She made eye contact with Innes, her thoughts plain on her face: If the Sheriff's department knew about LAPD's BOLO on her, she was deep in the shit. Innes hoped she wouldn't do something rash.

The deputies, convinced the squatters were harmless, took down their names. The woman went to the cruiser to check them on the computer. The man, body-builder muscles straining against his uniform, explained calmly but clearly they were trespassing on private property and would have to leave. If not, they would be arrested. Vanessa asked to speak to him. Plainly smitten, he took her to the cruiser, sat her in the back seat, and leaned into the opened door. Innes tried to keep his eyes on Vanessa, but the woman deputy stood in his way, as if deliberately blocking his view.

After several minutes, Vanessa returned. "We can stay, at least for today," she said. "But we have to be out of here soon. They're going to report in but will be back tomorrow."

"Girl, what did you say to him?" said Tammy. "You didn't do something evil, I hope."

"Tammy, please," said Vanessa. "I just explained who we are and why we're here. He's not a bad guy, just doing his job."

The deputies explained the deal, climbed into their cruiser, and left the five to ponder their future.

"I got a voicemail," Vanessa said the next morning. "From Gustavo Sanchez at the *Times*. He wants to talk to you. He's doing a follow-up column on the homeless uprising and wants to write about George."

"Seriously? That's cool," said Innes. "It would be a nice memorial for the old man, to get a write-up in the *Times*. By Gus Sanchez, no less." Innes called him and left a message with instructions to call back on Vanessa's cell.

The Sheriff's deputies did not return the next day, or the day after. It had rained again, and Vanessa reported hearing on her truck's radio about more mud slides in Malibu. The weather apparently was keeping public safety officers too busy to deal with a few squatters.

The interview took place at a decidedly un-hip 1950s-era coffee shop in Santa Monica suggested by Sanchez. Tall and tanned like an aging surfer with long white hair pulled into a ponytail, the columnist gazed down through reading glasses while writing in his spiral note-pad. The interview lasted about an hour. Innes thought it best not to disclose where he and his companions were living. He kept his focus on George and his thoughts about organizing the homeless. He ate a plain donut dunked in weak black coffee. Sanchez picked up the tab.

Two days later, Vanessa returned from a shift at La Casita and brought a copy of the *Times*. She held it up to Innes and said, "Front page, baby."

He grabbed the paper from her and stared in disbelief at the lower left corner of page one.

Lonely Death of a Faceless Man
Gustavo Sanchez

Likely you've never heard of George Aloysius Mc-Quillen. Until recently, I hadn't either, although he met his untimely end not more than 30 yards from where I stood on a chilly December afternoon in Skid Row. His death, at age 70, wasn't noted in the Times. He didn't even get an obituary.

George McQuillen was one of the roughly 47,000 people living among us in Los Angeles County who have experienced homelessness this year. Some live in their cars, some on our streets. Under our freeways. In ditches and riverbeds. They appear as anonymous, faceless, shambling figures. They clutch homemade signs on street corners. It seems like we see them everywhere. But we don't see them at all.

I never knew George McQuillen. I only learned of his death days after the fact. He was the lone fatality from the homeless uprisings last month. I was there. A police officer without malice pushed him during the melee, and he fell and hit his head. He died from the injury, but his passing didn't make it into the news reports. He died after deadline.

"Great line," said Innes. "'He died after deadline.' I want that on my tombstone."

It was a beautiful piece of writing. George would have bitched and moaned about it no end, but also would have been secretly delighted. Innes was relieved his own role in the column was small. It was all about George and the all-too-common tragedy of unrecorded, unlamented deaths in Skid Rows everywhere.

"I called him and left a voicemail thanking him," Vanessa said. "I buttered him up real good, said how wonderful it was."

Vanessa returned next day from an early shift at the restaurant and shoved another newspaper into Innes's hands. The Malibu weekly, with a front-page headline: "Police Find Homeless Camp at Abandoned Estate."

"We're fucked," was all he could think to say. The article quoted a city council member who said Malibu is a "compassionate community," but protecting residents' "property and safety" takes priority. She assured taxpayers the squatters would be gone shortly and the property secured. One homeowner quoted in the story referred to the homeless as drug addicts and criminals, although another argued no one should be forced onto the street unless adequate housing alternatives were offered.

Book XI

CALEB MET JUNE AT THE FENCE AND PULLED

the makeshift gate back to let her big black Escalade through. When she parked, her land yacht dwarfed Vanessa's Explorer.

"You still driving that gas guzzler?" were Innes' first words to June in two months, since the conversation on the payphone in Holly-wood. It felt more like two years.

"Don't I get a hug?" she said, holding her arms out like a scare-crow.

"Of course," he said, and wrapped her in his arms. Vanessa had made him promise to be nicer to June.

She kissed him on the cheek and whispered in his ear, "You had me worried."

"Worried? When you and Vanessa and Clif were monitoring me all along, like the NSA?"

"You went off the radar after I found George. I was sure you'd been murdered by some drug-crazed derelict. And it turned out George was the one who died. I'm so sorry."

"Me too." He meant it, and not only about George.

She opened the hatch of her Escalade to reveal boxes filled with groceries and household supplies from Costco. Caleb unloaded. With everything toted inside, the six former residents of the Casa Grande sat in the great hall on folding chairs June had brought and caught up on the news from Pasadena. June said there were no developments in the arson investigation; the police and fire departments viewed it as an unsolvable case. After nearly three months, the rest of the city had moved on. Soon would come the demolition of the blackened hulk that was once their home. The insurance companies would pay up eventually, she assured them, but likely would drag their feet. Clif and his family were still renting in Altadena. Terry's mother had died right before Christmas and he was living alone in her mansion in San Marino. He had lost his entire collection of vintage dresses and accessories in the fire, June reminded them, plus all his fine art.

"After I heard the explosion, I ran into the hall screaming for someone to help me with my mother," June recalled. "I couldn't car-ry her. First person I saw was Terry coming out his door in a bath-robe with a bunch of dresses under one arm and framed paintings under the other, trying to save his most precious things. He didn't hesitate. Dropped everything, picked up my mother and carried her down the stairs. By the time we got out, it was too late for him to go back. I'll never forget it."

Innes regretted every snarky thing he had ever said—or thought—about Terry Delacroix.

"I'll never forget the explosion," said Vanessa. "It's what woke me up. It shook my bed. I wear ear plugs at night to block out the noise from Old Town. I might have slept through the alarms…" Her voiced trailed off.

After a respectful pause, June looked at Innes. "Vanessa told me about your nutty scheme. To stay here, make it a temporary home of sorts. Your heart's in the right place, honey, but don't get your hopes up. You've raised quite a stir in Malibu, divided the community. And now that you're a *cause célèbre*, you got the bank's attention. They want no part of it. This place is going to be auctioned. February twelfth at the County Courthouse on La Cienega. Bids to be submitted a week beforehand. Some are already in. The sharks have been circling this boat for years."

"What will the bids be?" said Innes. "How much?"

"I don't know, but I can guess. Oceanfront estates around here can go for as much as fifty million. That's for the super-deluxe ones. This is a relatively small parcel, an awkward narrow shape, and not fully developed. Bidders might not want to keep the unfinished buildings. Could be a tear-down situation. I'd guess at least five million."

Steven whistled.

Innes was undaunted. "When did you say bids have to be in?"

The others exchanged incredulous looks. "You plan to bid, Innes?" asked Tammy with a wink and a smile.

"No, of course not, but maybe someone else will, someone who will let us stay a while longer."

"The deadline is February fifth," June said. "The winner will be announced at the courthouse a week later."

"Shit. That's only two weeks from now," said Innes. "Who's bidding?"

"Usually you'd see a lot of Chinese money come in for one of these properties, but evidently not. People think there's bad *Feng Shui* here, because of Mr. Li. Mostly it's LLCs, hard to tell who's behind them. Real estate investment trusts, land conservancies, hedge funds, billionaires, who knows."

Innes processed this new information, then changed the subject. "You sure there's nothing new in the arson case? One of these days I'd like to know who I can strangle with my bare hands."

"I know it's hard, losing Annie and everything," said June. "But I think you might have to move on. Everyone else has."

"Everyone else has *not* moved on," said Tammy, her voice shaking. "I lost my husband and my only child. Everything. If somebody set that fire, I want their ass to burn in hell."

"I know, Tammy. I'm so sorry," said June.

"Have they interviewed everyone who was at the Halloween party?" said Steven.

Innes remembered a question that had hovered in the back of his mind for months. "Did anyone ever figure out who was in that horse get-up?"

"All I remember is the bad smell, like a horse barn," said Steven. "I thought it was part of the costume."

The words "bad smell" triggered something else in Innes's memory. "Cal, that tarp of yours?" he said. "Where did you get it?"

"I found it. In the basement, at the Casa," said Caleb.

"When?"

"Halloween. I came home from our gig to get another mic stand for the after-party at Ronaldo's. You know, in our storage locker down there? Anyway, I saw the tarp and borrowed it for the party, hang it up like a curtain. I was going to bring it back."

"What time was that, exactly?" Innes probed.

"I don't know, eleven, twelve?"

"Where are you going with this, Innes? What's this about a tarp?" said Steven.

"Anyone remember the panhandler who was hanging around the front gate of the Casa the morning of Halloween?" said Innes. "Called himself Willie? Aggressive? Smelled horrible?"

"I used to see him in the park all the time," said Vanessa. "He lived out of an empty newspaper box, kept his things in it like a locker."

"He had an old blue tarp with him," said Innes. "Wore it like a shawl. I think it's the same one Cal has."

"What's your point?" said Steven.

"If it's the same tarp—and I'm almost sure it is because I remember the torn corner—that puts Willie in the basement of the Casa. What would he be doing there? Maybe the cops need to find this Willie. Cal, did you see anybody down there, or talk to anybody when you came home?"

"Nobody was in the basement. I saw Mom in the apartment. I went up there to change my shirt. She'd just got back from the movies."

"You saw Mom?" said Innes.

"I was only there for a minute. I told her I came home to change and grab another mic stand from the basement locker. She said she wanted to go to bed." A bolt of recognition lit Caleb's face. He got up and walked into the next room. Innes followed, as the others continued chatting.

"She thought I was still in there, didn't she?" Caleb said when his father caught up to him. "You were right." The look in his eyes tore a hole in Innes's heart.

"No, Cal, don't say that. I didn't know that, I made it up on the spot, like I told you. I was angry and not thinking straight."

He was not thinking straight now. Was it true? Did Annie remember Cal coming home and going to the basement? Is that why she ran back in? For so long he had desperately wanted to know. If it was from maternal instinct to find her son, that at least would lend a veneer of nobility to what had been a puzzling and senseless death. But the guilt trip such a belief would lay on Caleb would be too much to bear. He would have to dissuade his son from believing it. In truth, they would probably never know for sure.

Caleb ran out of the room. Innes followed, but he had disappeared into the yard. Innes stopped, and the bud of a slowly forming thought bloomed. The prospect of Willie as the arsonist jarred the memory of Halloween morning and how he had treated the poor man. Could he have set the fire as revenge over his mistreatment? Innes felt a familiar nausea creep in. Was the fire ultimately his fault? No, couldn't be, he told himself. He hadn't been *that* rude, he'd even given the man a beignet after their brief tussle. He pushed the thought back into the corner of his mind already crowded with guilt over the deaths of his parents and Annie and George and Sherri and Turner. Thoughts of Sherri and Turner smoked out the miasma of dread he'd managed to repress, that the police would someday knock on his door.

When he rejoined the group, Vanessa was listening to her phone. "Sanchez called back," she said. "He wants to come see our little encampment."

"Here we go," said Innes.

Vanessa said the next time she went to work in Pasadena, she would take the tarp to the police and look for Willie in the park. Innes would follow up with Sanchez and invite him out to Alba Longa.

The first thing the newspaper columnist said to Innes the next morning was, "How did you manage to camp out here for two weeks before anyone spotted you?"

"Just lucky, I guess," said Innes. "The construction fence and trees shield the view from the highway. The road closure probably helped, too."

"What about the neighbors?" said Sanchez, gazing past Innes toward the edges of the property.

"Haven't seen any. They all live behind walled compounds. Anyway, now that we've been discovered, we could get kicked out any day. That's what I want to talk to you about."

Innes gave him a tour of the buildings and grounds and explained his plan to continue their squat for as long as it took to get his little "family" back on its feet.

"You're not running some, like, crazy cult out here, are you?" Sanchez asked.

"No, we're just regular folks from Pasadena trying to survive a disaster. If we can get public opinion on our side, maybe we won't get tossed onto the street right away, and we can stay past the auction. Especially if the right person or group buys this place."

"I wouldn't rely on the kindness of strangers," said Sanchez.

"Don't be so cynical. This is the City of Angels, right?" said Innes.

"More like City of Angles, to be honest. People in LA tend to look out for their own interests first. Especially in Malibu"

"Unless you shame them with your column," said Innes.

Sanchez paused, as if considering the proposition. "You can't stay here forever, you know. Eventually, someone is going to move in and kick you out. What then?"

"I don't know. We just need more time. Until our insurance pays off. I feel responsible for these people. I brought them here. Maybe that was a mistake, but I feel like, if we're put out on the street now, I don't know if I can keep them together and safe."

Sanchez looked away and scanned the grounds. "I can't promise anything. But tell you what, I'll to talk to my editor. I like it, but as a story in its own right, a different take on the usual homeless yarn. Whether it changes anybody's minds, I wouldn't count on that."

"Of course. Thanks for coming," Innes said as Sanchez climbed into his Prius. "Do you think you can write it soon? We've only got a few weeks until the auction."

"Again, no promises. But if my editor likes the idea, I might be able to get something in Sunday's paper."

"Editors," Innes said with a knowing smirk and roll of the eyes.

Sanchez added, "You know, if I put you in the Sunday *Times*, instead of getting public opinion on your side, you might get a mob out here with torches and pitchforks."

"I'll take the chance," said Innes.

Next day, Vanessa returned from Pasadena with disappointing news. She'd found no trace of anyone named Willie, and the Pasadena police were uninterested in the tarp theory. Innes vowed to go back there himself and try again.

On Sunday, Vanessa dropped the *Times* in Innes's lap. He scanned the front page. No Sanchez. Then the front of the California section. There it was, in the upper left corner.

California Dreamers
Malibu Confronts Its Dirty Little Secret
Gustavo Sanchez

Last week I told you about George McQuillen, the homeless man in Skid Row who died quite anonymously at the hands of police during the uprising last month. That column brought in more letters and emails than any I've written in years. I wanted to put a human face on the epidemic of homelessness in our city, and apparently it worked. Hooray for me.

Then I opened a handwritten note from a nice lady named Alice in Rancho Palos Verdes. Good column, she wrote, in so many words. But what about the other 46,999 homeless people in LA County, she asked. Do they all have to die before they are acknowledged? How many more columns will you write before anything changes? I could feel her finger poking me in the chest.

I've been writing about the homeless in LA for 10 years. Their numbers keep going up. The crisis only gets worse. If Charles Dickens were alive today to write a novel about Los Angeles, our shame would be immortalized. The truth is, I've had no impact. I wonder if anyone has. It's enough to make you want to throw up your hands and say the problem is too big.

But then there are times when I meet people like Homer Innes, George McQuillen's son-in-law. Innes, himself only recently made homeless by a fire in which he lost his wife, is outraged by what he's seen in a few months on the streets. He is not willing to throw up his hands and say the problem is too big. He has tried twice to organize the homeless into an Occupy-style protest movement: once in Skid Row, which led to the accidental death of his father-in-law, and again in Santa Monica. A crazy, quixotic crusade, to say the least, but it's something. Both efforts ended in predictable failure. However, if you have been paying attention to the news, you know homelessness is getting a lot more attention these days. Homer Innes is one of the reasons. A Santa Monica proposal to ban homelessness failed, in part due to the protest he organized. Now, he and a small band of fellow homeless people, all survivors of the fatal Halloween apartment fire in Pasadena, are trying to rebuild their lives in the most unlikely of places: the shores of Malibu.

Yes, there are homeless people in Malibu.

"Did you read this?" Innes looked at Vanessa across the room.
"Of course. It's wonderful."
"I didn't know the Santa Monica thing went down."
"I know, isn't it great?" she said. Her smile warmed him.
"He called me crazy. Quixotic."
"Keep reading. It made me cry."
The rest was vintage Sanchez: lyrical, humane, and laced with barely concealed indignation. He laid out Innes's preposterous fantasy of encamping among the millionaires and billionaires of Malibu and gently mocked him for his romantic dreaminess, contrasting him with the "real heroes" of Skid Row like Jamal Muhammed. He acknowledged the concerns of neighbors about the homeless bringing crime and the effect on property values, but then his tone shifted from the gentle patronizing of an eccentric into a slowly building sense of despair, followed by frustration, followed by thundering rage. He ended with a pointed challenge to the "good people of Malibu."

America has been very good to you. You are unimaginably rich. You have taken your good fortune and ensconced yourselves behind gated walls along some of the most beautiful coastline in the world. Nobody, not I at least, begrudges you this. Meanwhile, a few miles down PCH in Santa Monica and Venice, and scattered across this vast palm-tree paradise of ours, thousands of your fellow Californians sleep in cars, under freeway bridges, in alleyways, on park benches.

We have seen you on television and social media promoting your causes: animal rights; starving children in

Africa; earthquake victims; Syrian refugees. All worthy causes. Please don't stop. But surely you have room in your hearts and your wallets for one more cause, right here in LA: Step up and make Malibu part of the solution to our homelessness epidemic, not only a gated escape from it. Don't put these good people out on the street, not until there is someplace decent for them to go. Helping one small band of squatters cannot solve homelessness by itself, of course, but it would be a start, and a powerful statement to the rest of Southern California.

This band of dreamers camped out there at Alba Longa have only a few weeks before the property is auctioned off. Surely there are some fine people in Southern California who can make things happen to let them stay awhile longer, until they get back on their feet.

Make us proud, Malibu.

On Monday, Vanessa called Pacific Rim Bank & Trust and Malibu City Hall to gauge the reaction to the Sanchez column. They assured her nothing would be done to them immediately, but they should plan to be gone by the end of the week. It seemed that the media attention and public outcry at the rough handling of the homeless by police in Skid Row and Santa Monica had persuaded Malibu to act with more caution and sensitivity.

Innes took Vanessa's Explorer in the early afternoon and set out for Pasadena with the tarp in search of Willie. His first stop was Pasadena police headquarters. He asked to see Detective Darius Jackson, who happened to be in. Jackson came out from a back office, greeted Innes warmly, and repeated his condolences over the loss of his wife. He led him into a squad room and offered him a seat in a dingy beige cubicle. The slate-gray desktop was covered with cigarette burns from another era and Venn diagrams of ancient rings left by coffee cups. Innes brought the detective up to date on his life since the fire. After a pause, he pulled the folded tarp out of his backpack.

"So that's the famous blue tarp," said Jackson. "I heard about this. Some woman came in here and said this would solve the Casa Grande case. The guys got quite a chuckle out of it."

"I'm glad they found it amusing," said Innes. "I'm the one who put two and two together and remembered seeing this tarp wrapped around a panhandler the morning before the fire. Then my son finds it in the basement right before the fire started."

"How do you know it's the same tarp?" said Jackson. His brown eyes betrayed a deep weariness. Flecks of gray infiltrated his eyebrows and neatly cropped Afro.

"I recognized the torn corner," Innes said. He unfolded the tarp and pointed to where the white fiberglass strands frayed.

"How do you know other tarps don't have the same tear?" said Jackson.

"Well, I guess I don't. But what if I'm right, and this is the same tarp?"

"Hard to prove. No way this would hold up in court. An ADA wouldn't even consider filing charges based on this."

"What if you dusted it for prints?"

"You've been watching too much television," Jackson said with an eye roll. "Look at it. It's filthy. Contaminated evidence. This material wouldn't hold a clear print anyway."

Innes refused to surrender to the logic of the criminal justice system. "What if I found this Willie character and confronted him with the tarp, and he confessed? He must know people died. He's got to be guilt-tripping."

Desk phones chirped across the squad room. Masculine laughter and profanity rang out from a nearby cubicle. Were they laughing at him?

"A confession obviously would change everything," said Jackson. "We wouldn't need the tarp."

"Will you help me find him?" said Innes. "I know he hangs out in Central Park. What if I showed him the tarp and he confessed and you witnessed it?"

Jackson considered that for a moment. "I guess I could give it a try," he said. "I know what you've lost. I owe you that much at least. We've already got a John Doe warrant for this case. Plus, if this guy's a chronic homeless, there's probably a bench warrant on him, too. But remember, if he doesn't confess, we got nothing. All we've accomplished is let him know he's a suspect. Then he can go underground. Disappear into the homeless population."

After Jackson signed out, they departed in an unmarked police car for Central Park. "Shouldn't I be wearing a wire or something?" asked Innes, glad to be in the front seat for a change.

"Too much television," Jackson said.

The charred hulk of the Casa Grande came into view. Innes was saddened and heartened by the sight. The fire- and smoke-stained façade brought back memories of that awful night. But the fact it was still there gave him hope it could somehow be saved, restored to its former glory, and—

"It's coming down next month," said Jackson.

"That is one thing I do not want to see," said Innes.

"Yeah, nobody does. But time marches on."

"What will happen to the property?"

"This is prime real estate, in the heart of Old Town. Probably be redeveloped into one of those huge condo-retail complexes," said Jackson. "Like Pasadena needs another one."

The plan was for Innes to wander through the park, look for Willie, and ask about his last known whereabouts. Jackson would observe from his car, and if Innes hit pay dirt, he'd move in to close the deal. There would be back-up if needed.

Innes entered the park at the same corner he had walked around Halloween morning when he first encountered Willie, the same corner where he had returned to the park in the wee hours, looking for Annie and her old man amid the smoke and the sirens and the crowds and the noise and the chaos, catching sight of the EMTs and the tents, feeling the crushing grief of Tammy Templeton, entering a tent to view a shrouded figure on a stretcher, descending into a bottomless spiral of despair from which he thought he would never escape.

And yet here he was. He had begun to climb out of the chasm, with a plan for the future, but felt guilty at the same time, as if he had no right to ever be happy again while Annie's ashes lay sinking into the ruined grounds of the Casa Grande.

Things continued in the park as they had before Halloween. Shrieking children played on the slides and monkey bars. Old men rolled bocce balls and tossed horseshoes. Dark shapes scattered here and there under blankets or collected in small groups, parking their shopping carts and bicycles and wagons in circles like parents with strollers. Innes wandered around the park for about twenty minutes, discouraged and ready to give it up. Then one figure in particular caught his eye as it shambled back and forth between the conclaves. A man, tall and thin, barefoot, with a faded watch cap on his scraggly bearded head. It had to be him. Innes stood behind a camphor tree and observed, rage and dread warring for his soul. The man sidled up to one group after another. Each time they kept their backs to him while he stood a few feet outside the circle, before moving on to the next group, only to receive the same reception. After a few minutes of this dreary square dance, one of the men broke away from his crowd and walked toward Innes. It was Chief Running Deer, with his loaded luggage cart and chalked sandwich board. His conspiracy theory apparently had moved past George Soros and the CIA and on to Jeff Bezos and the Russian mob.

Innes stepped out from behind the tree, keeping one eye on the lonely wanderer, and, against his better judgment, asked the Chief who it was.

"Nobody," said the Chief from under his Santa Claus beard and straw cowboy hat. "He's nobody."

"Is his name Willie?"

"Yup. That's one of his names. Nobody talks to him."

"Why's that?"

"Cuz what he done." The man nodded toward the blackened tower across the street.

"What do you mean?" said Innes. "He burned that place down?"

"I ain't sayin' he did. But *he* said it. Got all drunk at Christmas, braggin' about it. Nobody believed him. He keeps walkin' around saying he didn't mean it, or he didn't do it, then sayin' he did do it and is sorry and why won't anybody believe him? He's loco, you ask me."

This was the most coherent conversation Innes had ever had with the Chief. He pushed ahead. "Why doesn't anyone go to the police?"

The Chief looked at him for a moment, as if confronting a tourist speaking a foreign language. "You don't know much about the street, do ya?" he said. "We don't snitch on nobody. Ever. For nothing."

Innes almost replied that he knew a lot about the street, but realized he didn't. "People died in that fire, you know. If somebody set it, that's murder."

"Dontcha think he knows that? If he really did do it, that's why he don't turn himself in. It's like he's got to wander around confessing and unconfessing forever."

"Like the Ancient Mariner," said Innes.

"What?"

"Never mind. It's from Wordsworth."

"Coleridge," the Chief corrected him, and trudged away muttering and shaking his head.

Innes turned toward the unmarked police car, pointed to the center of the park where Willie sat on a park bench, and gave the thumbs-up sign. Jackson flashed his headlights in acknowledgment. Innes sneaked up on Willie from behind so as not to alarm him and sat next to him, saying nothing, looking straight ahead. Willie glanced over at Innes for a few seconds and turned away with no sign of recognition.

"This is my bench," he said in a familiar throaty croak.

"How are things in Eagle Rock?" Innes asked. He felt the urge to toy with him before putting the noose around his neck.

"Eagle Rock? Who the fuck are you? Do I know you?"

Innes decided to dispense with the chitchat and bring out the rope. He looked sideways and caught the shape of Detective Jackson out of the corner of his eye. "I got something of yours. Thought I'd bring it back." He opened his backpack and pulled out the tarp.

"What the...? Where'd you get that?" Willie said.

"This yours?"

"Hell yeah, it's mine. I thought some bum stole it offa me."

"How do you know it's yours?"

Willie pointed to a small circular hole in a corner. "That hole there. I cut out the grommet myself. Used it on a shoe I found."

"Know where I found this?" said Innes. "In the basement of that building over there, Halloween night, right before the fire. How do you suppose it got there?"

Shock and recognition lit Willie's face. He stared straight ahead, holding the tarp in his hands, and for several seconds said nothing. Innes held him in his gaze. Willie began trembling, which escalated to shaking and then came moaning, followed by sobbing and wailing, which drew glances from all over the park.

"I never ... meant ... nobody to get hurt," he said between sobs.

"Are you saying you set the fire?" Innes said.

Willie nodded, bent over, and covered his head with his arms, still shaking and moaning. Detective Jackson sat on the other side of the bench and spoke quietly to him. Innes walked a few yards away, stomach churning, torn between rage and relief. His emotional tsunami was interrupted by the sound of Willie screaming, "No I didn't!" The man stood up and ran toward the opposite end of the park, all flapping knees and elbows. Jackson stood and watched, in no hurry to pursue. A police officer emerged from a squad car on a side street and walked calmly toward Willie. He saw her and stopped, teetering precariously like a cartoon character realizing he'd run off the edge of a cliff, and turned and bounded toward the south end of the park.

"Nowhere to run, buddy!" called Jackson.

Two more officers converged on him from another direction. As Willie loped past a group of homeless men, one of them stuck out his leg and tripped him, sending him flying and landing in the grass with a thump and a loud groan. He struggled to regain his footing, but an officer was on him in seconds. She placed her knee on the small of his back and grabbed at both arms. The other officers restrained him while she cuffed his wrists behind his back. Willie howled and sobbed as Jackson and the three officers led him away. The entire homeless population of Central Park gawked in silence.

As Innes watched, his murderous rage gave way to something resembling pity. He thought about the hunting knife he had left back in Malibu and how much he wanted to bury the blade in the top of the sonofabitch's skull. He knew he was capable of such a thing, but also knew he would never again do anything of the sort. He'd had enough of hate and death. It felt good for a second to fantasize about it, but he let it go. It was like an anvil had lifted from his shoulders, one that had been there for a long time, unnoticed until it was gone.

He walked backed to the Explorer. The sun was low in the sky, painting the San Gabriel mountains the color of freshly skinned salmon. The streets of Pasadena looked less grim and depressing than they did back in November during his futile searches for Caleb. But his future lay elsewhere, to the west. He climbed into the truck and headed back to the freeway.

By Thursday, the news reached Alba Longa by way of a call from June that Willie had folded under police interrogation and confessed to everything in writing. For a few tortuous days, Innes was sure Willie had set the fire deliberately in retaliation for his rude treatment of him. The possibility ate him alive. But police said they doubted all of the man's ever-shifting explanations and concluded he'd simply set it by mistake after sneaking into the party in a stolen horse costume in search of free food, cheap booze, and a place to warm himself.

"So, what you're saying, Junie, is I was right about Willie and the tarp," he gloated into Vanessa's cellphone.

"You know what this means, don't you?" she said. "The insurance companies can close their investigations now and pay our claims."

He wanted to hope, to believe the nightmare would soon end. But something held him back. "How long will that take?"

"Not sure. Might be weeks. Months, even. These are big bureaucracies we're dealing with and they have an incentive to delay payment as long as they can. Meanwhile, what do you hear from your pal at the *Times*?"

"It's good, it's good. He got a lot of calls and emails. A few Malibu celebrities have pledged money to bid on the place, or at least offer moral support for letting us stay for a while longer. A lot of regular folks, too. Somebody started one of those internet fundraiser things, Go Jumpstart Me or something like that, to put in a bid. And the sheriff and the bank are backing off on giving us the boot until after the auction, thanks to Sanchez."

"Moral support is good," she said. "Money is better. How much has been raised for the auction so far?"

"A couple million, as of yesterday, according to Sanchez."

"They're going to need a lot more than that. Five million at least. I'd help out, but all my money's tied up in real estate."

"They've still got over a week. They'll make it."

"I hope so, baby, I hope so," she said and hung up.

A couple days before the deadline for bids, Vanessa got another call from Sanchez. The news was not good. No surprise, his column had ignited a brush fire of opposition in Malibu. Some of the celebrities who pledged had second thoughts, reluctant to put their own money into such a controversial property or allow the squatters more time to relocate, possibly for fear of lawsuits.

"We're screwed," said Innes. "We've got about a week left here, then we're out on our asses again. Back on the streets."

Book XII

FEBRUARY 5 CAME AND WENT WITH NO LAST-MINUTE
bids from angel investors. Fittingly, it appeared their last day at Alba
Longa would be Friday the thirteenth. The Casa Grande crew inventoried their things and prepared to load them into Vanessa's truck.
More than a month had passed since Innes, Vanessa, and Caleb first
arrived, cold and wet, and three weeks since Tammy and Steven
joined them. Despite no electricity and plumbing, they had made the
place almost livable with the supplies Steven and June had brought.

Tammy spent most her time on the beach at the bottom of the
bluff, staring across the ocean at the horizon. Innes sat with her some
days. They didn't need to speak.

Vanessa shuttled back and forth between Alba Longa and Pasadena, trying to keep her jobs going and income flowing, showering
and changing for work at a friend's place in Pasadena. She'd sold her
Vespa in Santa Monica when their funds had nearly run out.

Time was expiring on their squatter days. Steven was right. Soon
they would have to find jobs, no matter how menial, and legit housing, no matter how slummy, scraping by until their insurance policies
paid off.

On Thursday the twelfth, June called Vanessa shortly after noon
with the news that the winning bid was for six million.

"That's it. It's over," Vanessa said to Innes.

"How long do we have?"

"We may get kicked out as soon as today. June said we'll be hearing from the buyers' lawyers."

That afternoon Vanessa received another call, this time from a
woman who introduced herself as a lawyer representing the winning
bidders. They would arrive on Monday to walk the property; the
squatters would need to be gone by Sunday night.

On Friday morning, Innes heard a vehicle on the gravel and
stepped into the courtyard, where he was greeted by an astonishing
sight: Sliding in to park next to the Explorer was an antique limou-
sine, a Rolls Royce from the 1930s, chrome grille topped with a flying

goddess ornament, spare tire mounted on the running board. He was unable to take his eye off the apparition, intrigued and appalled by this pompous symbol of wealth and privilege. The driver's door opened and out stepped what appeared to be a short man dressed in riding clothes: a black helmet, black cropped jacket, tan jodhpurs, and black boots. In one hand he gripped a riding crop. A woman in the front passenger seat examined herself in the visor mirror. The man turned toward Innes, removed his helmet, shook bangs of black hair out of his face, and smiled.

Innes stared dumbfounded into the twinkling eyes of June Heron.

"Nice outfit, Gatsby," he said, after collecting his wits.

She walked toward him. "Don't I get a hug?" She embraced him and kissed him on the cheek. She smelled of alcohol. "We're celebrating," she said. "Now that you've solved the case, the insurance companies have terminated their investigation and approved our claims. You should have your money within a month."

Innes scooped her up in his arms, lifted her tiny body off the ground, and kissed her on the lips. He thought he might cry. "Finally," he said, "something I touched didn't turn to shit."

June laughed, slapped him on the butt with her crop, and pulled herself free. "Oh, sweetie, you have no idea how long I've waited for that. Now I can die in peace." Innes wasn't sure if she meant the kiss or the slap.

The passenger door of the limo opened, and the woman stepped out. She wore a long jade-green dress. A little green hat perched atop platinum blonde permed hair and makeup that expertly illuminated the fetching but unmistakable face of Terry Delacroix.

"Hello, dahhling," Terry said in a passable Tallulah Bankhead voice.

"Daisy Buchanan, I presume?" said Innes. Terry responded by giving him the finger.

Vanessa and Steven came out and stood next to Innes, followed by Tammy. The six of them paused for a moment, then shrieks and laughter broke the silence. Innes watched as they embraced and kissed the visitors. Vanessa, Steven, and Tammy gathered around Terry, gushing over the vintage outfit.

"I thought he—she—never went out in public in drag, outside the

Casa," Innes said, sidling up to June and speaking *sotto voce.*

"Terry's had an epiphany in the last few months, since the fire and the death of her mom. She's accepted who she is. No more part-time play acting."

Innes absorbed that news, unsure what to say. "What's with the car?" he deflected, gazing at the Rolls.

"Isn't it great? Terry and I traded my Escalade for it," said June.

"Terry and I?" Innes echoed.

"Aren't you going to ask us in?" said June, ignoring the question.

They gathered the folding chairs in a circle in the kitchen area. Caleb strolled in and sat on the floor. He exchanged conspiratorial smiles with Terry, whom he'd known as aunt/uncle T since childhood. June pulled from her shoulder bag a bottle of champagne, already opened, and they toasted the good news with red plastic Solo cups.

"I want a tour, before the Philistines ruin this glorious monstrosity," said Terry, standing up. Vanessa, Steven, and Tammy led her out of the kitchen to the side yard. Caleb followed.

Innes looked across the chair circle at June. "You and Terry?"

"Yes, we're living together. In sin, as it were. With my mother, in Terry's San Marino estate. Does that shock you?"

"Not at all. It was inevitable, actually," he said. They smiled at each other for a long moment. "I suppose I should thank you, Junie. I know I've been kind of a shit to you. But you've stuck by me—by us—always helping. Or trying to."

"You're welcome."

"Can you blame me, though? Ever since the fire, you've hovered in the background, pulling strings like a puppeteer. Trying to get me to move in with you, when Annie's ashes were still warm. You give us an apartment, then kick us out the next day, right after my car gets stolen. You follow us around like we were runaway children. You pick up the old man and dump him in Skid Row."

"I did not dump him," she said, sounding hurt. "He might have died out there on the street. I knew Vanessa and Clif would look after him. If I'd known what was going to happen..." She looked at her boots.

Innes softened his tone. "I know you only wanted to help, Junie. I should have listened to you. George might still be alive if I had taken your advice." Sherri, too, he thought but didn't say. And Turner.

June continued to stare at her boots for a few moments, then looked up at Innes. Her eyes glistened with tears. "No. You were right not to trust me," she said blubbering.

"What do you mean?" He sat next to her and put his hand on her knee.

"I have to tell you the truth now," she said. She wiped her cheek with her jacket sleeve. "You should move back to your chair over there. I want to look at you from a distance when I tell you this. And I don't want you close enough to hit me."

"What are you saying?" He respected her wishes and moved away.

"It was me who stole your car. Or had it stolen, I mean. And I didn't have any tenants coming into that unit. I lied to force you back to the street so you'd come home with me."

"Are you serious? Why?"

"Because I'm a horrible person, that's why. I thought the worse things got for you, the sooner you'd give in and come be with me." She pulled out a tissue and blew her nose. "There's more," she said. "You got a check from the insurance company. Weeks ago. Five-hundred dollars. I kept it."

"What the fuck?" His hands flexed. Her neck suddenly looked scrawny and inviting.

"I'm sorry. I was going to give it to you. Once you came to stay with me. I still have it. In my purse. You can have it now."

"It's a little late for that, don't you think?" He took a breath and unclenched his fingers. The money would come in handy until the big check comes, he had to admit. But no way would he show gratitude. "Anyway…" he started to say.

"Wait. It gets worse," she said. "I … I knew where Caleb was. All along. He called me. Twice. I met him once in Hollywood and gave him money. I made him promise not to tell."

"Jesus H. Christ, June!" Innes stood up and kicked one of the flimsy chairs across the room. It clattered loudly on the bare floor. "Are you fucking kidding me? That's my son. My whole goddamn world. And you kept him from me?" He stood over her menacingly.

"I'm sorry," she said, cowering. "I'm so sorry."

"Did Vanessa know?"

"No. Nobody knew."

"What were you thinking?" he said, glaring at her.

"He didn't want to be found. Don't you get that? He made me swear not to tell you where he was. I said I wouldn't, if he stayed in touch with me and let me help him."

Innes turned away. June's muffled sobs were the only sound.

"Anyway," she finally said, "you disappeared. No one knew where you were. Caleb had nobody. He was alone out there."

"So," said Innes quietly. "You decided to be his mother. To take Annie's place."

"No, no, that's not it. I ... I ... okay, yes. But I was worried about Caleb. I wanted to help him. Because I know how much he means to you."

Innes sat and put his head in his hands. He wanted to strangle June and hug her at the same time. She was a manipulator, a liar, an egocentric narcissist. And yet she had looked after Caleb when there was no one else. The urge to throttle her faded. Months—no, years—of stored up hostility seemed to melt away, like dissipating vapor. He stood and turned toward her, lifted her from her seat, and wrapped his arms around her. She put her head on his shoulder. They stayed in the clinch for a long while, rocking gently as if slow dancing.

Voices from the foyer signaled the others had returned. Innes and June were still embraced when they entered the room.

"Well, this is cozy," said Terry.

"Everybody friends now?" said Vanessa with a hopeful smile.

June gave a thumbs-up and a wink, which Vanessa returned.

June reported the new owners planned to keep the existing buildings and finish Mr. Li's plans for a Roman villa. That included the pool, which would seal Innes and Vanessa's terrible secret forever under tons of poured concrete. On Saturday, the contractors began to arrive, and the Alba Longa squatters had to prepare to clear out before the construction resumed. June said she could put them up temporarily in a newly vacated unit in one of her buildings in Sherman Oaks until their insurance money arrived and they could find permanent housing.

Innes began to imagine a future: a real home for him, Caleb, and maybe ... Vanessa? A fresh start as a writer, maybe a book. He thought about George and Jefferson and Jamal and Charlie and knew that, whatever else, he would join Vanessa in homelessness activism.

As the squatters began to gather their things for the move to the Valley, Caleb asked Innes to have a word with him, at the fence overlooking the ocean. They gazed at the horizon and recalled the wild night they swam to shore in a rainstorm and Caleb pulled his dad to safety from the pounding surf.

After a few moments, Innes said, "June told me everything, Cal. About you and her."

"She wasn't supposed to tell. She promised," Caleb said. He heaved a small stone into the waves below.

"I'm glad you reached out for help, even if it wasn't to me."

"I was broke and hungry and scared. I called Paco from a payphone to borrow some money. He gave me those numbers you left with his sister. I knew they weren't yours, so I called one of 'em. It was Ms. Heron. She came to see me in Hollywood, gave me some money. She's the one said I should go to Santa Monica 'cuz it was safer there. She drove me."

It dawned on Innes that June had puppet-mastered everything from afar, including, perhaps, his reunion with Caleb in Santa Monica.

"What happened to all that money?"

"It got stolen."

Innes had an alarming image of his son robbed and beaten in some filthy back alley. "When? By who?"

"A girl," said Caleb.

"Ouch."

After a lengthy silence, Caleb said, "I'm leaving, Dad. I'm not staying here."

At first, Innes pretended not to hear.

"Did you hear me, Dad?"

"What do you mean you're leaving? Where do you think you're going?"

"Charlie and me, we're going to Seattle."

"Seattle? What the hell for?"

"Charlie's uncle—his other uncle—says he can get us jobs on a fishing boat. Pays real good."

"A fishing boat? Cal, you're only eighteen. You haven't finished high school. You need to stay here and graduate."

"Finish high school where? We're not going back to Pasadena, are we? You don't even know where we're going to live."

"We'll figure something out."

"No, Dad. Me and Charlie are going to live with his uncle. Rent free, he said. I can get my GED. Or find a school in Seattle."

Innes draped an arm around Caleb's shoulder, grateful his son no longer shrank from his touch. "You're all I have left, Cal. Mom's gone. Grampa's gone. You can't leave me now."

"It's not forever. I'll be back. And you have a new life here. A new family."

Innes had no response for that.

After a moment, Caleb spoke again. "I can't stop thinking about Mom, running back into the fire to find me. I need to get away from here, as far as possible."

"Stop thinking that, Cal. That's not why she ran back in."

"How do you know?"

"Because I read her diary," he lied. "She wrote the most precious thing she owned was that little wood box full of childhood mementos and her mother's jewelry. If there was ever a fire, that was the first thing she would rescue. But she didn't. It wasn't in the sack of things she took with her. I don't know why she forgot it. It was all panic that night. I'm sure that's what she went back for."

More lies, he thought. But for a good cause, right Annie?

Caleb stared at the ocean, digesting this news. Innes hoped Caleb wouldn't ask to read the diary himself.

They argued over Caleb's plan for another half hour, but there was no swaying him. Caleb had an answer for every objection his father raised. He was an adult and had made up his mind. Innes felt his resistance fading, and wished he'd had the nerve to do something this adventurous when he was a teenager. At that stage, he couldn't even manage a trip to Venice Beach. He let go.

"So, you're going to light out for the territory," Innes said.

"What?"

"Never mind. Somebody famous once said that. Somebody like you." Innes wrapped his arms around his son and hugged him close to hide his tears.

On a cloudy, drizzly Sunday morning, Innes woke early, grabbed his backpack, and hiked down the path to the beach. Finding a relatively dry patch of sand, he sat with his legs crossed. He tried to focus on the spot where sea and sky met, but the dark gray of the waves dissolved amid the fog into the lighter gray of the sky. After a few moments of contemplation, he reached into his backpack and retrieved the thing he'd carried for weeks, the thing that had started out so light, nearly weightless, but had grown heavier with each passing day: Annie's diary. He turned it over a few times, fingering the aged leather cover, worn to suede. He pulled the hunting knife from his backpack and inserted the tip of the blade under the delicate hasp of the diary's lock. A simple twist was all it would take to pry it open and unspool years of Annie Innes's secrets. Gripping the handle, he cocked his wrist for a quick snap, then hesitated. He stared at the cover again and considered what it was he was about to do, what it was he was about to discover. The words inside were never meant for him to see. What Annie had written in her most private moments might forever change the way he thought of her, how he remembered her. What did she write about him? About Vanessa? What if he learned more about their affair than he wanted to know? What if it contained clues about why she ran back into a burning building? If it wasn't to find Caleb, what, or who, was so precious she would risk her life for it? Vanessa?

Of course. It was Vanessa.

It hadn't occurred to him, but now it was obvious. So obvious, it likely had been lodged deep in the recesses of his mind ever since

Vanessa revealed the truth about her relationship with Annie. Who was the only other person in the Casa Grande, beside her own family, whom Annie loved? Who was the only one of them they couldn't account for when gathered in safety across the street from the burning building? Innes remembered seeing Vanessa run toward a fire escape, but never mentioned it to Annie. Who was the only person who would know Vanessa slept with ear plugs? Annie had been anxiously scanning the crowd, even though she knew her family was safe, before running back into the inferno. And, finally, why had her body been found on the first floor, Vanessa's floor, and not in their second-floor apartment or in the basement where Caleb might have been?

He would never be able to mention it to Vanessa. He would never know for sure. Didn't want to know.

He withdrew the knife from the hasp and set it on the sand. A fat white seagull, perhaps seeing the knife as something to eat, landed next to Innes and stared at it. With a loud flap of wings, it flew back out to sea. Innes stood and watched the gull soar into the mist. He looked at the diary one more time, and with all his strength flung it into the path of the gone gull. It splashed into the gray waves and floated for a moment before sinking out of sight. He sent the knife on the same flight, slinging it by the blade. The diary's ink would bleed into illegible smears in the saltwater, the vast Pacific absorbing the secrets of Annie Innes.

Acknowledgements

Like it says in the disclaimer, this is a work of fiction, a product of my fevered imagination. None of this happened, although some of it is inspired by people and places I have met or seen over two decades of living in Southern California. I must also acknowledge the persistent and vivid chronicling of the homelessness crisis in Southern California by the journalists at the *Los Angeles Times*, whose work borders on the heroic. (Support your local newspaper!) Any echoes of previous works of fiction that appear in this book are entirely intentional. I stand on the shoulders of giants, including the Roman poet Virgil, whose epic *The Aeneid* provided the inspiration for a story about the dispossessed searching for a home. Writing a novel is a solitary endeavor, by and large, but publishing one takes a village. (My editor is hovering over this cliché, determined to strike it out, but I'm gonna go with it.) The village that stands behind this book is populated by citizens of unending patience and goodwill, for which I am eternally grateful. I am grateful to Naomi Rosenblatt at Heliotrope Books, who believed in my project and led me down the long road from manuscript to book, and to agent April Eberhardt, whose wise counsel guided me through the thicket of the publishing world. Special thanks to Ivy Pochoda, who provided advice and support and breathed new life into my manuscript when I was ready to give it up. I also owe thanks to Cody Sisco, Gabi Lorino, Chris Kowalchuk and all the generous writers and readers at Los Angeles Writers Critique Group who talked me through some early drafts. Kudos to Chris Daley and everyone at Writing Workshops Los Angeles who provided such a needed venue for the LA literary community. Laura Gold, Lola Ogunyemi, and Charles Webb were incredibly astute readers; a more collegial and supportive writers' group you could not find. I am grateful to the friends and family who encouraged me from the beginning and especially for their indulgence in slogging through my raw drafts. You know who you are, Sally Loving, Chris Allen, Mick Flores. Mostly, I am grateful, and oh so lucky, to be married to Rhonda Hillbery, writer, book lover, the love of my life.

—William Loving
Pasadena, California, 2020